POWER FAILURE

POWER FAILURE

BEN BOVA

A TOM DOHERTY ASSOCIATES BOOK
New York

POWER FAILURE

Copyright © 2018 by Ben Bova

A Tor Book
Published by Tom Doherty Associates
175 Fifth Avenue
New York, NY 10010

www.tor-forge.com

Tor® is a registered trademark of Macmillan Publishing Group, LLC.

The Library of Congress Cataloging-in-Publication Data is available upon request.

ISBN 978-0-7653-8803-2 (hardcover)
ISBN 978-0-7653-8805-6 (ebook)

Our books may be purchased in bulk for promotional, educational, or business use. Please contact your local bookseller or the Macmillan Corporate and Premium Sales Department at 1-800-221-7945, extension 5442, or by email at MacmillanSpecialMarkets@macmillan.com.

First Edition: October 2018

Printed in the United States of America

0 9 8 7 6 5 4 3 2 1

To Rashida, of course

It is not because things are too difficult that we do not dare, it is because we do not dare that things are too difficult.

SENECA

POWER FAILURE

Wow," whispered Tami. "Talk about old money."

Jake Ross glanced down at his wife. Tami had never seen the Tomlinson mansion before.

The black-liveried butler ushered Jake and his wife through the marble-columned entry and down the wide, thickly carpeted corridor that bisected the mansion's ground floor. Photographic portraits and oil paintings of Tomlinson family members going back to Colonial times decorated the walls.

The portrait of Alexander Tomlinson—stiffly erect, stern, almost haughty—was draped in black.

With a whispered, "In here, sir," the butler opened the double doors to what ordinarily was the formal dining room. The usual furniture had been moved out. The room now held Alexander Tomlinson's open coffin on a black-draped bier, with a small circle of stiff-backed chairs for the somberly dressed mourners.

The old man had been well past eighty, but as he lay in his coffin he looked to Jake as if he just might open his eyes, sit up, and demand to know what all the fuss was about. Tall and lean as a saber, Alexander Tomlinson had been the head of the family almost all his adult life. It was his indomitable will that had driven his son Franklin into the United States Senate.

Senator B. Franklin Tomlinson got up from his chair in the little circle of family members and greeted Jake with an extended hand and a half-whispered, "Glad you could come, Jake. And you, Tami."

Jake nodded while Tami said softly, "We're so sorry for your loss."

Tomlinson was several inches taller than Jake, slim like his father from a lifetime of tennis, handball, and sailing, his ruggedly handsome face deeply tanned. His golden blond hair was thick and wavy, with just a touch of gray that made him look distinguished. He had a smile that could light up a room, but now it was dimmed, diminished.

"Dad had a full life," he said, almost sorrowfully, "but it's not going to be the same without him."

Thinking of the old man's imperious ways, Jake sympathized, "How could it be?"

Jacob Ross had been the younger Tomlinson's science advisor since Franklin's first run for the Senate, almost six years earlier. Jake was just short of six feet tall, solidly built, with dark unruly hair and a face that he had always thought too long and horsey. Tami, standing between the two men, was like a delicate oriental doll. A Japanese-American from California, she was wearing a sleeveless knee-length black dress with a single strand of pearls.

Tomlinson's wife, Amy, got up from her chair to join them. She nodded to Jake and smiled at Tami. Amy was pretty, in a pert, perky cheerleader's way. Slim figure, sparkling eyes, lovely honey-blonde shoulder-length hair. Not even her dress of mourning black could make her look somber. She and Jake had engaged in a brief, torrid affair together, during Tomlinson's first campaign for the Senate. The affair ended when Amy told Jake she was going to marry the future senator.

Senator Tomlinson leaned closer to Tami and asked her, in a hushed voice, "Tami, do you mind if I borrow your husband for a few minutes? We've got some business to discuss."

"Of course," said Tami.

Draping an arm across Jake's shoulders, Tomlinson led him to a door on the far side of the room. Amy gestured Tami toward the semicircle of chairs and began introducing the other family members to her.

The senator opened the door and stepped into what looked to Jake like a pantry. Rows of shelves stacked with cans and jars, a few unopened cardboard cartons on the floor.

Closing the door gently, Tomlinson said, "I'm really glad you could make it here, Jake."

"I'm glad you asked us," said Jake.

None of the other Washington staffers had been invited to the funeral, Jake knew. But then, of course, Jake was the only person on the senator's staff who came from Montana; the rest of the staff were all Beltway insiders. Jake was proud that the senator thought of him almost as family.

Leaning an elbow against the shelving, Tomlinson said, "It's been a tough week."

Jake confessed, "I never gave a thought to the idea that your father would die someday. I know he was pushing ninety, but—"

"But he was larger than life, wasn't he?" Tomlinson said, with a sad smile.

"That he was."

Jake thought of the father figure in his own life, Leverett Caldwell. It was Lev who guided Jake out of the narrow gang-ridden streets of his youth and into a scholarship at the university, Lev who talked Jake into joining Tomlinson's staff for his first run at the Senate. When Tomlinson unexpectedly won his race, Jake went with him—and his bride, Amy—to Washington.

Almost wistfully, Tomlinson asked, "Do you know what his last words to me were?"

Jake shook his head.

"He was lying in the hospital bed, all sorts of tubes hooked up to him, so weak that I had to lean down and put my ear next to his mouth to hear him."

Jake studied the expression on Tomlinson's face. There was grief there, yes, but something more—something like pride, and determination.

"He said to me, 'I'm only sorry that I didn't live long enough to see you in the White House.'"

Jake tried to think of something to say.

Tomlinson went on, "He thought I could become president of the United States."

"Of course he did."

Standing up straighter, almost squaring his shoulders as if facing an approaching enemy, Tomlinson said, "Well, I'm going to make his dream come true. I'm going to run for president next year."

He wants to be president," Jake told Tami.

"That's no surprise."

Tamiko Umetzu Ross had been a news reporter before she met Jake. She ran afoul of one of the most powerful senators on the Hill though, and now she worked for EcoSanity, a public relations firm that represented mostly environmental issues and the organizations that pushed them. "We're poor but pure," Tami often joked. Ruefully.

Jake muttered, "He hasn't even finished his second term in the Senate and he wants to run for president."

Tami and Jake were sitting side by side in the minuscule first-class section of the Boeing jetliner, heading back to Reagan National Airport in Washington, DC.

Alexander Tomlinson's funeral had been small, tasteful, with only a small knot of dark-clad family members in attendance at the Unitarian Universalist Congregational Church that Senator Tomlinson's grandfather had built, almost directly across the tree-lined avenue from the Tomlinson mansion.

"Why shouldn't he run for president?" Tami asked. "He'd make a good candidate: handsome, rich—with his looks and your brains he could win."

She was grinning at her husband, but Jake was not amused.

"Yeah, he's good looking, all right," Jake admitted, "but he's almost totally unknown outside of Montana. And being so damned rich might work against him. Another playboy with delusions of grandeur."

"Don't sell him short. He's more than that," Tami said.

"You know that, and I know that, but the general public doesn't know him. He doesn't have a base of voters. The party insiders will see him as an upstart."

"Like Obama?"

Jake almost smiled. "He was a Democrat. The Republican party doesn't take to upstarts so easily."

"Like Reagan?"

"Reagan worked his way up. It wasn't all glamour. He paid his dues before running for president."

"Tomlinson got the energy plan through," Tami said. Then she added, "*Your* energy plan."

"Yeah, that seems to be working out okay. Even the Democrats voted for it, in the end."

"And it's creating jobs, bringing down people's electricity bills, isn't it? That's something he can take credit for. Thanks to you."

Jake shook his head. "I just don't think the time is right for him to throw his hat in the ring. There are plenty of other people in line ahead of him."

"But there's one other factor you're not giving enough credit to," Tami said.

"Another factor?"

"He *wants* to run. And he wants to win."

"Does he?" Jake wondered. "Or is his father still pulling his strings, from the graveyard?"

. . .

Jake and Tami lived on the top floor of a six-story-high condominium building on Connecticut Avenue, not far from Dupont Circle and the apartment Tami had shared with three other women when Jake had first met her. The two-bedroom condo was much more expensive than similar quarters in the suburbs outside DC, but Jake cherished its location, within a few minutes' drive of the Hart Senate Office Building, where Senator Tomlinson's office was.

Their flight from Helena arrived at Reagan National on time, and within little more than a half hour they were home.

Jake threw his worn old travel bag on the bed, and while Tami started to unpack her roll-on, he checked the phone's answering machine.

One call. From the executive assistant of Kevin O'Donnell, the senator's chief of staff: "A staff meeting is scheduled for tomorrow morning, Dr. Ross," came the woman's high, girlish voice. "Ten sharp."

Why didn't she call my cell phone? Jake wondered. Then he saw the time of the call on the answering machine's tiny screen. We were in the air; no cell service. Kevin set up this staff meeting while we were flying in from Helena. Wonder what it's all about.

Staff Meeting

Senator Tomlinson's suite of offices was on the second floor of the Hart building. Jake walked through the building's lobby, past the people waiting for elevators, and hustled up the marble stairs.

DC Formica, Jake called the marble that was so ubiquitous in Washington's government buildings. My tax dollars at work.

It was only a few minutes past nine when Jake pushed through the door of the suite's entry, but the lively young receptionist behind the desk there immediately told him, "There's a staff meeting at ten, Dr. Ross."

"Thanks, I know," said Jake as he breezed by, heading for his own office.

Just past the entry hall Jake saw Earl Reynolds filling a steaming mug at the coffee machine. Head of the senator's media relations team, Reynolds looked like a former college football player who was bloating into middle-aged softness. Yet his fleshy face was still handsome and his dark hair seemed to be natural.

Reynolds raised his free hand to stop Jake. "Big powwow at ten o'clock," he said, almost solemnly.

"Ugh," said Jake, as he reached for a coffee mug.

"How was the funeral?" Reynolds asked.

"Quiet. Tasteful."

"I wonder what our boy's going to do without his old man prodding him?"

"I think we're going to find out at ten o'clock."

Reynolds looked surprised, then impressed that Jake apparently knew something he didn't.

• • •

"Run for president?" Lee Di Nofrio blurted.

Kevin O'Donnell nodded, his pinched face looking more irritated than usual.

The chief of the senator's staff always gave Jake the impression that he trusted no one—which was pretty close to the truth. O'Donnell was a rake-thin bundle of nerves, with suspicious dark eyes peering out of his lean, bony face. He wore his thinning light brown hair in a ridiculous flop-over that emphasized his creeping baldness more than hid it. But he was a longtime Beltway insider, keenly aware of the ways of Washington's intricacies.

"Is this for real?" Di Nofrio asked.

"Unless we can talk him out of it," O'Donnell said.

"Isn't it too soon for him to be aiming at the White House?" asked Kathy Ellerman, the senator's aide for women's issues. She was a plumpish blonde somewhere between thirty-five and fifty, wearing a conservative dark blue skirted suit.

"Not necessarily," countered Judine Asmus. "We can position him as the party's rising star."

O'Donnell frowned sourly at her. Asmus was slim, tall, and leggy, a young black woman with chocolate brown skin and a Georgetown University degree in statistics. Nominally, she worked under Reynolds in the media relations team, but she was smart and ambitious enough to have earned the assignment of dealing with the national polling services.

Reynolds shook his head. "He'd be facing some damned strong opposition: Morgan and Sebastian here in the Senate, and Governor Hackman in Tennessee."

Asmus smiled knowingly. "He'd get plenty of women's votes."

"He'd get even more if he weren't married," Ellerman muttered.

O'Donnell growled, "Cut the crap. What's our man done that he can campaign on?"

Jake kept silent, but Di Nofrio called out, "He's chairman of the energy subcommittee."

O'Donnell shrugged. "So he inherited Santino's position when the Little Saint retired. So what?"

"The energy plan is working," Reynolds said. "Electricity prices are going down. So is our carbon footprint. And the U.S. of A. has become a major exporter of oil and natural gas."

"And the coal lobby hates his guts," O'Donnell grumbled.

"The environmentalists aren't happy with him, either," said Di Nofrio. "They want more cutbacks in greenhouse emissions."

Di Nofrio was in charge of relations with the various environmental lobbies. He was a smallish man in his thirties, smolderingly handsome, with thick, tightly curled dark hair and a swarthy complexion.

"The environmentalists are never happy," O'Donnell groused.

"So what are you going to do?" Reynolds asked. "Tell him to forget about it?"

O'Donnell hesitated. Then, "I'm going to give him my honest opinion, and tell him that the staff thinks he should wait another four years."

"At least," said Ellerman, in a stage whisper.

Jake finally spoke up. "Wait a minute. This is something pretty close to the senator's heart. Shouldn't we take a hard look at his chances, figure out a plan of campaign for him, instead of telling him we won't support him on this?"

"Who says we won't support him?" O'Donnell snapped. "We're his staff. Of course we'll support him if that's what he really wants."

"But you said—"

"I said I'll make it clear that we think it's a wrong move. We think he should wait until the next time around."

"The next time around," Di Nofrio pointed out, "there'll be an incumbent in the White House, campaigning for reelection. Not like this time around."

"Yeah," O'Donnell admitted, "there is that."

"So?" Reynolds asked.

Clearly unhappy, O'Donnell answered, "I'll have to tell him that we don't think he should get into the race this time around, but if he insists that that's what he wants to do, we'll support him like the loyal staffers that we are."

Reynolds sighed, "Heads he wins, tails we lose."

Di Nofrio added, in mock Bronx slang, "Dems de conditions dat prevail."

Senator Tomlinson's Office

It was well past the nominal quitting time. As he walked across the suite from his own office to the senator's, Jake saw that the outer workplaces were almost all deserted. Even the senator's personal executive assistant had left.

Jake had a knotty problem that the senator had to decide on. Stem cell researchers were pushing for clinical trials for using stem cell therapies to repair damaged spinal cords. More conservative medical researchers—and many top echelon bureaucrats in the National Institutes of Health—claimed that it was too soon for human trials. And there were conservative citizens' groups that were against stem cell work altogether. The issue was going to come before the Senate's committees on health and science, and Tomlinson had to decide where he stood.

Striding past the executive assistant's empty desk, Jake tapped on the senator's door.

"Come on in," came the senator's voice.

Opening the door, Jake saw that Tomlinson was at his gleaming broad desk, in his shirtsleeves and fire-engine red suspenders, a cut crystal tumbler of whiskey in one hand. Sitting in front of the desk was Kevin O'Donnell, empty-handed, looking crankier than usual.

"Jake," Tomlinson said, "Kevin tells me he thinks it's foolish of me to run for the party's nomination."

"I didn't say foolish," O'Donnell said.

Tomlinson grinned. "It sounded to me as if you did."

Jake settled himself in the handsome bottle-green leather chair next to O'Donnell. As diplomatically as he could, he said, "The staff isn't enthusiastic about the idea."

Still grinning, the senator leaned back in his padded swivel chair. "I seem to remember that when Abraham Lincoln asked his cabinet to vote on his Emancipation Proclamation they all—each and every one of them—were against it."

Jake knew what was coming, and a sidelong glance at O'Donnell told him that Kevin knew the tale too.

But Tomlinson plowed ahead. "So Lincoln says, 'Twelve against, one in favor. The ayes have it.'"

O'Donnell's expression remained stony.

Jake said, "And we won the Civil War."

His face going dead serious, Tomlinson said, "Because Lincoln transformed the war from a political battle over states' rights to a moral crusade about slavery. That's what won the war."

"That and Ulysses S. Grant," O'Donnell muttered.

"Leadership," said Tomlinson. "Leaders have got to *lead*, not just follow the safest course of action."

O'Donnell sighed and allowed himself a minimal smile. "Okay, Frank," he said as he squirmed unhappily in the chair next to Jake. "You've made your point. If you want to run for president, your staff will back you one hundred percent."

"Thank you, Kevin."

But the tension in the room was still there; Jake could feel it, like the sullen heat of an August day.

The awkward silence seemed to stretch endlessly. At last Jake said, "We've got to work out our position on the stem cell debate that's coming up."

O'Donnell seemed to stir himself. "There's still a lot of religious opposition to stem cell work."

"But they're not using fetal cells anymore," Jake pointed out. "Haven't been for years."

"But the religious right is still opposed."

Tomlinson visibly relaxed also. "The same sort of mind-set that opposed Galileo."

"The Church apologized for that," O'Donnell said.

"Four hundred years later," Tomlinson said, with a mischievous smile.

"There's still opposition out there to Darwin and evolution," Jake said. "They're still trying to rewrite the biology textbooks."

"Fanatics," said the senator.

O'Donnell countered, "You're talking about their basic beliefs, Frank. They have a right to their fundamental beliefs."

"Yes," said Jake, feeling the heat rising in him, "but they want to force their beliefs on everybody else."

"And you want to force your beliefs on them!" O'Donnell insisted.

"Whoa!" Tomlinson raised both hands in a *Halt!* gesture. "Let's keep it civil. If you two guys start yelling at each other, you can see how sensitive the subject is."

Jake realized that the senator was right. Give the other fellow the benefit of the doubt. Don't demonize the opposition, that just makes everybody dig in their heels and harden their positions.

Still smiling, Senator Tomlinson said, "You know, I had a poly sci professor back at Harvard who told us, 'Politics is the art of getting free people to work together.'"

Jake nodded and saw that O'Donnell was nodding too.

"Okay," the staff chief said. "We'll work out a position statement about stem cell research for you."

"I'll draw up the first draft," said Jake.

"Good," Tomlinson said. "Now—about my campaign for the nomination."

"You'll need a good campaign manager. A damned good one," said O'Donnell.

"The first thing I'm going to need is money," Tomlinson said, his smile dwindling. "Can't run without money."

"You need to set up a PAC," Jake realized.

"A super PAC," O'Donnell corrected. "They can raise more money without legislative restraints."

Tomlinson nodded.

"Frank," said O'Donnell, "this will be a national campaign. It's going to be a lot different from the state campaigns for the Senate, you know."

"I know. I know." Turning to Jake again, the senator said, "Jake, it was your energy plan that got me elected to the Senate. Now I need another good idea, something that will get me noticed by the national media and bring in the votes I need."

"And the money," O'Donnell added.

"And the money," Tomlinson agreed. "We're going to need a lot of money."

Inspiration

W hat's the matter?" Tami asked.

Jake looked up from his plate of pasta primavera. "Huh? Oh, nothing."

The two of them were having dinner at Ristorante Dino, two blocks down Connecticut Avenue from their condo building. It was one of their favorite hangouts: the food was reliably good, the service charming, and the wine list decently priced.

Tami said, "You've been pushing your food around your plate instead of eating it. What's bothering you?"

He looked across the table at her. Tami gave him her *tell me your troubles* expression.

"Oh, it's Frank."

"He wants to run for president."

Nodding, Jake replied, "And he wants me to come up with an issue that can get him noticed, get the media to pay attention to him, win him votes."

"Like the energy plan."

"Yeah. As if ideas sprout out of my head like popcorn popping."

With a teasing smile, Tami asked, "Well, don't they?"

"Hell no," Jake protested. Thinking back on it, he added, "Even the energy plan was really Lev's idea."

"Really?"

"Lev set it up for me, got me interested in it."

"But you did all the real work," Tami said. "You put it all together."

Jake nodded glumly and reached for his wineglass.

"So now you need to come up with an idea on your own."

"Yeah."

She took up her own glass and clinked with his. "You'll get there, Jake. You'll find it."

"Maybe."

"Of course you will."

Tami watched as he drained his glass, then refilled it. At last he returned his attention to his dinner. The restaurant was doing well, almost every table filled. Local customers, Jake thought. This is a neighborhood restaurant, not some glitzy joint that depends on tourists and visiting VIPs. Winter and summer, Dino does okay.

It was late spring. In a few weeks the summer heat and humidity would turn Washington into a steam bath. Congress would adjourn for the summer. The city would be abandoned to the tourists.

Jake remembered last summer, when Tami's family had come for a weeklong visit. One afternoon while Tami showed her parents, aunt, and uncle where she worked, Jake had volunteered to take care of her two young nephews. Tami had called it a suicide mission: keeping a pair of preteen boys occupied. But Jake had solved the problem easily by taking them to the National Air and Space Museum. The boys were fascinated with the airplanes and rockets and spacecraft on display, close enough to touch.

As he coiled a few strands of linguini around his fork, Jake recalled the boys' wide-eyed interest. The anniversary of the first Moon landing is coming up in a couple of months, he said to himself. Sometime in July. Let's see, that was in 1969—more than fifty years ago.

Tami broke into his thoughts. "So do you think that Franklin can win the Republican nomination?"

It took an effort for Jake to focus his attention on her. Is she just making conversation or is she really interested?

Jake replied, "He'd be a dark horse."

"Dark horses have won before," she countered. "Eisenhower, Carter, even Obama was just a first-term senator when he ran. And won."

Jake nodded. "It's possible, I guess."

To her surprise, Jake ordered after-dinner drinks: Sambuca, dry and anise-flavored. Tami toyed with hers while Jake knocked his back in two gulps.

He could see that the drinking bothered her. Jake paid the check, then got to his feet.

"See?" he said, holding out his hands to her. "Stone-cold sober."

Despite her concern, Tami giggled.

As they walked slowly along the traffic-clogged avenue back to their condo, Jake looked up and saw a nearly full Moon grinning lopsidedly at him.

Pointing a wavering arm at it, Jake said to Tami, "You know, there are boot prints on that sucker."

"American boot prints," she said.

"And we haven't gone back there in more than fifty years."

"The Chinese are planning to land people on the Moon, aren't they?"

Jake nodded. She knows damned well the Chinese plan a lunar program. She's a damned good newswoman, even though she's out of the news media now.

"We haven't been farther out in space than a few hundred miles since the Apollo program was stopped," he said aloud. "Up to the International Space Station. Far as we go. No farther."

"Why not?"

"Politics, mostly. There's no big voting bloc pushing for it."

"Why don't some of the private rocket companies go to the Moon?" Tami asked.

"Good question," said Jake. "Damned good question."

Then he looked up at the Moon again and muttered, "Boot prints."

The next morning Jake got to his office early, as usual. He had learned that he could get almost a full day's work done before the rest of the staff arrived and started pestering him with their questions and problems.

He booted up his desktop computer and started looking up the private companies that were ferrying cargo and people to the aged International Space Station and offering tourists rides into orbit.

Some of them professed to be working on establishing private tourist hotels in orbit, others claimed they had plans for landing people on the Moon. But the most popular goal seemed to be to send people to Mars.

All talk, Jake saw as he scanned one company's glitzy prospectus after another. They're trying to raise money. Looking at their financial pages, he saw that the only companies making steady profits were those with NASA contracts to fly resupply missions to the ISS.

By nine a.m., when one of the front office kids popped her head into his office with an offer of coffee, Jake was leaning back in his desk chair, thinking hard.

His phone buzzed. Kevin O'Donnell's executive assistant asked him to come to the staff chief's office, "as soon as you can."

Jake recognized a summons when he heard one. He shut down his computer and headed for O'Donnell's office.

Earl Reynolds intercepted him halfway there.

"Heard the news?" the media relations man asked, with a canary-fed cat's smile.

Without breaking stride, Jake asked, "About the bombing in Bogotá?"

"No." Reynolds shook his head, as if the undeclared war in Colombia was unimportant. "The Boss wants to announce his candidacy."

"Now?"

"Soon as we can get a campaign manager signed up."

Jake let out a theatrical sigh. "Fasten your seat belt."

Reynolds's fleshy face broke into a grin. "Damn the torpedoes. Full steam ahead."

Jake thought that was a great way to get sunk. But he said nothing and resolutely wound his way through the sea of desks toward O'Donnell's office.

The chief of staff was on his feet, at the window that looked out on the dome of the Capitol building.

"Good morning, Kevin," Jake said as he stepped through the open office doorway.

Turning, O'Donnell said, "Close the door."

Jake shut the door softly while O'Donnell went to his desk and sat down.

"He wants to announce that he's going to run."

Jake took one of the padded chairs in front of the desk. With a nod he replied, "Yeah. Earl told me a minute ago."

O'Donnell's face clouded over. "I told him to keep this under his hat."

"Well, you called me in here to tell me, didn't you?"

"Yeah, but if Earl's blabbing the news out in the goddamned hallways the whole goddamned world's going to know it in the next ten minutes."

Jake said nothing. He had no desire to get involved in a screaming match between O'Donnell and Reynolds. But as he sat there and studied O'Donnell's lean, tense face, Jake realized that Kevin was genuinely upset with the senator's desire to go public with his decision.

"We don't have a campaign manager, we don't have a team for him, and we don't have a penny in the bank," O'Donnell complained.

"Frank's got his own money," Jake said.

O'Donnell glared at him. "God save us from amateurs," he grumbled. Before Jake could say a word, he went on, "First, you use as little of your own money as possible. Second, the amount of money you raise is an indication of how much support you have. Try funding a campaign on your own and the pros will laugh you out of town."

"Oh? What about Trump?"

O'Donnell glared at Jake. "I want Frank to wait until we get some money in the bank and a decent campaign manager," O'Donnell went on. "But, oh no! He's hell-bent on plowing ahead."

"There's only a little more than a year between now and the nominating convention," Jake said.

As if he hadn't heard Jake, O'Donnell muttered, "If he's going to run around like a loose cannon I might as well hand in my resignation right now and be done with it."

Jake felt a pang of alarm. "But he needs you, Kevin! He depends on you."

"Then why doesn't he take my advice? Dammit, he's going to slit his own throat."

"Have you talked with him about this?"

"Last night, until two in the fucking morning. It was like talking to a stone wall."

"He's made up his mind, Kevin."

"Yes, yes, I know. But he's charging ahead blindly. He's got to listen to advice, goddammit!"

"I wish there was something I could do."

"There is."

Jake blinked.

Leaning tensely over his desk, O'Donnell said, "You've known him longer than anybody else in the office here. You were with him when he first ran for the Senate."

"He was a political unknown then," Jake said, adding to himself, An unknown from one of the wealthiest families in the state.

"Would you talk to him? Try to drum some sense into his head? He won't listen to me about this." O'Donnell was almost pleading.

"I don't know if it'll do any good."

"Will you try?"

Jake nodded. "Sure. I'll try."

Tomlinson Residence

Senator B. Franklin Tomlinson and his wife lived on a quiet, tree-shaded street in the northwest corner of the District of Columbia, in a handsome twelve-room redbrick Georgian house set well back on a perfectly clipped lawn decorated with flowering shrubbery.

When Jake had asked the senator for a private little chat, Tomlinson had suggested having cocktails together at his home, after the working day ended.

So Jake drove his new silver Dodge Dart GT from the Hart office building garage up Tomlinson's bricked driveway and parked it behind the azalea bushes that screened the parking area from the street. He still missed his battered old Mustang, but Tami had finally convinced him that a senator's science advisor shouldn't be seen in public driving such a disreputable-looking old heap.

The soft-voiced butler guided Jake to the library, where Tomlinson and Amy were sitting in comfortable armchairs by the window that looked out onto the swimming pool set into the back lawn. Tomlinson was in his shirtsleeves; Amy wore a short-sleeved, flowered knee-length dress.

The senator got to his feet, smiling. "Hi, Jake. What are you drinking?"

Glancing at the cart in the corner of the book-lined room that served as a rolling bar, Jake answered, "White wine, please."

Tomlinson already had a tumbler in his hand. Scotch, Jake guessed.

Amy stood up and headed for the bar. "I'll pour," she said. Jake wondered if Tomlinson knew about their brief affair, all those years ago. Probably not, he thought, but the possibility always made him slightly uneasy.

"So," Tomlinson said, gesturing toward the sofa near the empty fireplace, "have you come up with a surefire science policy issue for me?"

"I'm working on it," Jake said as he sat down. Amy brought a glass of wine, smiling her cheerleader's smile at him, and placed it on the glass coffee table in front of the sofa.

Easing himself onto the wingchair at one end of the coffee table, Tomlinson said, "So this is about Kevin, then, isn't it?"

Jake nodded. "He's really worried."

Sitting on the sofa beside Jake, Amy said, "Kevin's always worried," her smile vanishing.

"I think he's right," Jake heard himself say.

Tomlinson didn't look the least bit surprised. "Really?"

Hunching forward slightly, Jake said, "Look, you hired Kevin to be your chief of staff because he knows the ropes, he's a Beltway insider, he's experienced—"

"And he wants me to go slow about my nomination campaign."

Amy added, "He doesn't want you to run at all."

Jake looked from her to her husband. Amy looked grim, almost angry. Tomlinson seemed almost amused.

"I think he's right," Jake said. "I mean, you hired him for his expertise. So listen to what he's telling you."

"You think I should go slow."

"I think you should get some campaign contributions in your hands and take on a top-flight campaign manager."

"Jake, I want to get started now. I've only got a year until the party's nominating convention. I've got to make my name known. Now!"

Amy nodded vigorously.

So she's behind this, Jake thought. Amy wants Frank to be president and she wants him up and running right away.

Carefully, Jake said, "A couple of weeks won't make much difference, Frank. When you pick a campaign manager, that'll make headlines. When you get a couple of fat cats to hand you contributions, that'll make even more headlines. Just announcing you're running, with nothing in place, no staff, no money, you'll look like an amateur. The news media will laugh at you."

For the first time, Tomlinson looked concerned. "You think so?"

"You'll generate lots of media coverage when you announce that you're running—with a solid campaign manager and some money in the bank."

Tomlinson glanced at his wife. "That's what Kevin told me."

Amy accused, "So you're on Kevin's side?"

Shaking his head, Jake said, "There aren't any sides in this. We all want the same thing: Frank and you in the White House. But let's not jump the gun. Let's show that we know what we're doing."

Tomlinson said, "I suppose Reynolds could plant a few rumors. That'd get some media coverage."

"Frank, you've got to decide whether you want headlines now or the election next November."

"Both," said Amy. "Frank's got to get his name out there, he's got to be *known*."

"Then let's do our homework. Let's get a solid campaign manager and the beginnings of a staff for him."

"Or her."

Jake felt his eyebrows hike up, but he granted, "Or her."

"What you said about campaign contributions makes sense, Jake," the senator acknowledged.

"Good."

"But we've got to get moving," Tomlinson went on. "It's almost July already."

"Good," Jake repeated. "Let's get moving."

Shooting for the Moon

Tomlinson invited Jake to stay for dinner and Jake phoned Tami to join them. Once she arrived—in the middle of the evening news—Amy told the butler to serve their dinner in the formal dining room. Then she poured another round of drinks for everyone.

The formal dining room always made Jake feel a little uneasy, as if he'd pick up the wrong fork or drop a spoonful of soup on his lap. The huge chandelier dripped with crystal and Alexander Tomlinson's full-length portrait seemed to be staring at him accusingly. What's this little guttersnipe from the slums doing at my son's dining room? the elder Tomlinson seemed to be demanding.

The long table was set for just the four of them, with candles glowing, gleaming wineglasses, heavy silver cutlery, and blue-patterned dishware that the senator said went back nearly two hundred years.

Tami made her eyes go wide and joked, "Be careful, Jake. You wouldn't want to break up the set."

Halfway through the main course of roast beef, Tomlinson, sitting at the head of the table facing his father's stern portrait, asked Jake, "So what's this idea you're working on?"

Jake stopped his fork halfway between his plate and his mouth.

"The idea for a science issue," Tomlinson prompted.

"Oh! That."

Tomlinson smiled expectantly.

Sitting next to him, Tami said, "Tell him, Jake."

"It's not much more than an idea," Jake said, thinking furiously. "It's about our space program."

Amy said, "That's pretty much in the doldrums, isn't it?"

Nodding, Jake said, "Yes, that's right. What it needs is presidential leadership."

"On to Mars?" Tomlinson asked, with a grin.

"No," said Jake. "Back to the Moon."

"But we've been there."

Doing some quick arithmetic in his head, Jake replied, "Not for the past fifty-one years."

"Why go back there? What's the point?"

"The point is," said Jake, putting his fork down, "to begin to develop the space frontier. Use the Moon as a resource center. A mining and manufacturing center."

Dead silence around the table.

"Look," Jake said, warming to the subject, "the reason the program is in the doldrums is that we've been thinking of space as a series of onetime objectives, where we plant footprints and the flag and then move on. But it's not a set of tourist attractions. It's a frontier! A frontier that we can settle and use to make life better here on Earth."

"Settle?" Amy asked. "You mean with people?"

"Right. Just the way we settled the western frontier. Hell, Jefferson thought it'd take a hundred generations to settle the west. It took less than five."

"But in the west there's air to breathe and water to drink. The Moon doesn't have either."

"There's water on the Moon," Jake countered. "You just have to dig it up. And half the content of the Moon's rocks is oxygen."

"You're saying that people can live on the Moon?"

"We've got the technology to make it happen."

Tomlinson asked, "But why, Jake? What good would it be?"

"What good was Kansas, when we first got there? Zebulon Pike called the Midwestern prairie 'the great American desert,' for god's sake; not a tree in sight for hundreds of miles. Now it's the great American breadbasket. It feeds half the world."

"The Moon instead of Mars," Tomlinson mused.

"Not instead of," Jake corrected. "It's not a matter of visiting this place or that place. It's not either/or. Hell, if we had treated the western frontier that way we'd still be arguing over whether we want to build Chicago or St. Louis."

"Space is the new frontier," Amy said.

"It's a frontier waiting to be developed, and the purpose of the development is to make life better here on Earth."

"How?" Amy asked.

"For one thing, we can build solar power satellites. Take in sunlight in orbit, convert it to gigawatts of electricity, and beam that power to the ground. Bring down the cost of electricity all around the world."

"But it would be expensive building the satellites, wouldn't it?" Tami asked. "Billions of dollars."

"You could cut the expense by a factor of twenty if you took the raw materials from the Moon instead of lifting them up from Earth."

"Really?" Tomlinson asked.

Jake thought the senator was starting to look interested.

"Really," he said. "The Moon's gravity is only one-sixth of Earth's. And the Moon is airless. You wouldn't even need rockets to send the raw materials down to Earth orbit. An electric catapult could do it. Cheaply."

"So you want to go to the Moon—"

"To set up the facilities to provide raw materials for building solar power satellites," said Jake. "Show the taxpayers that space resources can lower their electricity bills. Space isn't just for astronauts and scientists. It's for everybody!"

But Tomlinson shook his head. "Giggle factor," he said.

"Huh?"

"You remember when we were putting together the energy plan?" the senator asked. "You wanted to include solar power satellites. But my father pointed out that the voters would think that's too far-out. Remember?"

"The giggle factor," Jake grumbled.

"People would think it's too fantastic," Tomlinson said. "Space cadet stuff."

"No!" Jake snapped. "We've got this enormous frontier that starts just a hundred miles away from where we're sitting. It's got resources of energy and raw materials that can make jobs here on Earth, produce whole new industries, transform the global economy—"

"But how much will it cost to get there? Can we afford the expense? Would Congress vote for hundreds of billions of dollars for some wild space adventure?"

Feeling anger simmering inside him, Jake answered, "It's not a wild adventure, no more than settling the western frontier was."

Before Tomlinson could respond, Jake went on, "Do you realize that the old Apollo program was the greatest peacetime stimulus to the American economy, ever? Sure we spent twenty billion to get to the Moon—"

"Twenty billion in the nineteen sixties. It'd be more like a hundred billion in today's dollars."

"So what? The new technologies we developed for Apollo have poured *trillions* into the economy. How much is the computer industry worth? Cell phones, the Internet. How about the ICUs in hospitals? All based on technology originally developed to keep astronauts alive in space."

"Isn't that a slight exaggeration?" Amy asked, emphasizing the *slight*.

"What about the cordless power tool industry?" Jake challenged. "That was created when NASA realized they couldn't run extension cords from Cape Canaveral to Tranquility Base."

Tomlinson broke into a hearty laugh. "All right, Jake. All right. You put together a space program, like you did the energy plan. Maybe it'll work."

Jake could feel his pulse thundering in his ears.

Then the senator added, "But it's got to make economic sense, Jake. No pouring money down a rathole. I want to see a plan that makes a net profit for the American people."

Jake nodded, thinking that Tomlinson was already talking like a political candidate.

Good.

Jake and Tami drove back to their condo in their separate cars. All the way there, Jake kept thinking, We can do it. We can go back to the Moon and start using space resources to grow the economy, make more jobs, start whole new industries.

But he knew the flaw in that thinking. An enhanced space program would have to be funded by tax dollars. NASA would have to lead the way. The benefits to the economy would come later, from private corporations. We'll have to sell the new space program as an investment in the nation's economic future.

But whoever's going to be running against Frank will paint the program as a huge new expense that the taxpayers will have to foot.

What was the term they used back in the sixties? Moon-doggle.

The giggle factor again.

That's what helped to kill the Apollo program in the first place. How do I get past that?

Tami's car was already parked in the building's underground garage, Jake saw. How'd she get here ahead of me? he wondered as he rode the elevator up to their top-floor unit.

When he opened the front door he saw Tami standing at the kitchen cabinet where they stored the liquor.

"Ready for a celebratory drink?" she called to him.

Jake went to her and gave her a swift kiss. "What are we celebrating?"

With a delighted smile she said, "Your new space program, of course."

Jake shook his head. "I'll take a drink, but we don't have a new space program, not by a long shot."

"Drambuie?" she asked, undeterred. "On the rocks?"

"Whatever."

As she poured, Tami said, "You don't seem very excited."

"I'm not. All I've done is made a lot of work for myself. Frank wants a plan that makes a net profit."

"So?" Tami asked, handing him a small snifter.

"It'd take ten years or more for the program to show any profits. Meanwhile it'd have to be funded by taxpayers' money; all expenses, no profits for at least ten years."

They walked to the sitting room sofa and sat down: Jake glumly, Tami still smiling at him.

"What about the private space companies?" she asked. "You told me they'd be interested in this."

"Most of them are barely hanging on. None of them have the equipment or the money to go to the Moon. They're mostly talk and dreams."

Tami's smile faded. "I thought they'd be eager to help."

"I doubt it."

"Maybe you should ask them?"

Jake took a long swig of the iced Drambuie. "Maybe I should," he agreed.

. . .

Isaiah Knowles, Jake remembered. He'd been a deputy administrator at NASA back when Jake was putting together the energy plan that helped get Tomlinson elected to the Senate. A former astronaut, Knowles was hot to trot about solar power satellites, but NASA's top management had scant interest in the idea. Jake had wanted to include space solar power in his energy plan, but eventually took it out because of the giggle factor.

Pie in the sky. Moondoggle. So Jake had cut out the solar power satellite from the energy plan and stuck with Earth-based ideas like new, more efficient electric power plants and methanol additives for gasoline.

And Tomlinson got elected.

Grimly, Jake told himself, That was then, almost six years ago. This is now.

It turned out that Knowles had left NASA two years earlier and was now the Washington representative for a coalition of small, struggling, private space companies that called itself the Space Futures Foundation. With an office on K Street, no less.

Knowles answered Jake's phone call warily. In the phone's small screen, Jake could see that the ex-astronaut still felt betrayed by Jake. He was an African-American, his skin the color of cocoa, the expression on his face combative.

He looked almost pained as he forced a smile and said, "Hello, Dr. Ross."

Feeling the strain, Jake forced a smile too and replied, "Jake."

"What can I do for you . . . Jake?"

"You can have lunch with me at your earliest convenience. I need to talk with you."

"The last time we talked you slit my throat."

Flinching back in his desk chair as if he'd been slapped in the face, Jake stammered, "I . . . I guess I can't blame you for feeling sore."

Knowles pulled in a deep breath. "Okay, sorry. That was uncalled for."

"I do need to talk with you," Jake said.

"Lunch, huh?"

"As soon as you can make it."

With a sardonic little smile, Knowles said, "My calendar isn't all that crowded. How about tomorrow?"

"Fine," said Jake.

. . .

They met at the Old Ebbitt Grill, within walking distance of the White House. It was a popular hangout for Washington's office workers, a place where government bureaucrats and corporate executives could meet and hammer out their differences— or at least have a few drinks together and ogle the women at the bar.

The place was jammed, as usual, but being a senator's aide carried some weight when Jake called for a reservation; when he came in he was immediately seated at a booth toward the rear. The bar was crowded four deep and the noise of dozens of conversations made the whole place quiver.

Jake sat down and ordered a club soda. No booze, he told himself. Keep your head clear.

The TV screen above the bar was muted, but Jake could see a view of the Kremlin. Russia's president, Vladimir Putin, had apparently suffered a stroke and was hospitalized. Straining to read the printout of the news commentator's words, Jake saw that Putin was hovering near death.

Jake began to fear that Knowles was going to stand him up, but at last he saw the former astronaut shouldering his way through the standees at the long bar, following the harried maître d' to the booth.

Knowles was on the small side, an ex–jet jockey, but built solidly, his midsection still flat, although his buzz-cut hair was turning salt-and-pepper.

Jake half stood up as Knowles slid into the booth opposite him. They shook hands. A waiter appeared out of the crowd and Knowles ordered a Guinness.

"Been a long time," Knowles said tightly.

"Nearly six years."

"So what'd you want to talk to me about?"

"The Moon."

Knowles stared at Jake. The waiter arrived with his glass of dark beer and departed.

Knowles took a long pull on the beer, then said, "The Moon."

"I'm putting together a program—"

"Another plan," Knowles said. "Like your energy plan."

"This one's about the space program."

"Uh-huh."

"I need to talk with the movers and shakers in the private space industry and see how interested they might be in building a permanent base on the Moon."

Knowles grunted. "Most of 'em are more interested in figuring out how they're going to survive the next fiscal quarter."

"Space tourism isn't profitable?"

"Not much. We've reduced costs, but the best ticket price we can manage is still around fifty thousand for a three-orbit ride. Fifty thou for three spins around the world, then back to New Mexico."

"Your launching center is in New Mexico?"

"Yeah, and it's running on a shoestring."

"But I thought you had big backers, Silicon Valley billionaires, that kind of money."

"Even billionaires get tired of red ink," Knowles said.

Hunching forward and leaning both forearms on the table, Jake asked, "Do any of your companies—or a combination of companies—have the hardware to reach the Moon?"

"With people?"

"Yes."

Knowles shook his head. "We've got plans. We've got rocket boosters that could be beefed up, given the financing to do the beefing. But nothing in being."

"Suppose the federal government provided the financing? Could you handle a program to build a permanent base on the Moon?"

Knowles reached for his beer, but stopped halfway there. "Why do you want to build a base on the Moon?"

Jake couldn't help grinning at him. "To manufacture solar power satellites, among other things."

Knowles blinked once, twice, then broke into an answering grin.

Money is the root of all evil, Jake said to himself. Then he added, And all good, too.

He was holed up in his office, a small but comfortable room on the far side of Senator Tomlinson's suite: solid oak desk, waist-high bookshelves filled with volumes that Jake had actually read, a window that looked out at the Supreme Court Building across Constitution Avenue.

For the past week Jake had been trying to figure out how much his proposed space program would cost. Billions, he saw. Tens of billions. Maybe a hundred billion.

Too goddamned much, he realized. Frank isn't going to stick his neck out for a program that costs a hundred billion dollars. He'd have his head cut off inside of a week.

But the facts of the matter were that space operations are expensive. The struggling private space companies had brought down costs somewhat, but launching human beings into orbit still cost at least ten million per shot. Sending people and equipment to the Moon cost still more.

Money is the root of all evil, Jake repeated to himself as he stared blearily at the numbers on his computer screen. And the federal government is the root of all money, just about. Private funding just doesn't come up with this kind of money.

It'll have to be tax dollars.

His phone jangled.

Kevin O'Donnell's narrow-eyed face took form on the phone's screen. "Meeting in the senator's office at three o'clock." Before Jake could ask, the staff chief added, "To meet the campaign manager."

The screen went blank. Jake glanced at the digital clock on his desk: 1:48. At least I'll have time to wash up and look presentable, he thought. Maybe even grab a sandwich for lunch.

At 2:57 Jake started across the suite to the senator's office. The place buzzed with expectant excitement. Even the lowliest staffers seemed to realize that something important was about to unfold.

Senator Tomlinson's new executive assistant, Francine, was sitting up straighter than normal at her desk, like a groupie expecting a celebrity to appear. She was slim and pretty enough to be a photographer's model, with curly red hair and a bouncy disposition. Smartly dressed in a tailored white blouse and light pink sweater, she smiled brightly at Jake as she said, "Go right in, Dr. Ross. They're expecting you."

The senator's inner office was already crowded with staff people sitting around the big circular conference table in the far corner, by the windows that looked out at the Capitol's dome. Jake recognized them all, of course, except for the man sitting at Tomlinson's right: fiftyish, good shoulders, wearing a dark gray suit, silvery hair long enough to tickle his collar, a smile that radiated self-assurance and calm competence.

Seeing only one chair still empty, Jake realized that he was the last one to arrive for the meeting.

Tomlinson arched a brow as Jake sat down. With a wry smile he said, "Now that everyone's here, we can begin." Turning to the stranger, he announced, "People, this is Patrick Lovett, who has agreed to manage my campaign for the presidency."

Then Tomlinson introduced the people around the table, starting with Earl Reynolds and ending with Kevin O'Donnell.

Lovett nodded at O'Donnell. "I've known Kevin for quite some years. Good to work with you at last, Kev."

O'Donnell grinned almost boyishly, and Jake realized that he must be the one who had recommended Lovett to the senator.

Looking around the table, Lovett said, "We have a lot of work ahead of us. I'll try to stay out of your way so you can do your jobs without interference, but once we've set up a campaign headquarters and hired some staff, I'm afraid we're going to have to pester you from time to time."

O'Donnell said, "That's okay, Pat. No problem."

"Good."

The meeting was brief and to the point. Lovett's job was to get the senator elected to the White House. "That's going to take lots of money, lots of elbow grease, and—"

Reynolds interrupted with a sonorous, "Blood, toil, tears, and sweat."

Lovett smiled patiently. "Not so much blood or tears, I hope. But plenty of toil and sweat."

Reynolds said, "Oh, sure. I was just—"

"I'll have to put together a media relations staff, Earl. Can I count on your help on that?"

With a glance at the senator, Reynolds said, "Sure. Of course."

"Good. Thanks."

Jake decided he liked Patrick Lovett.

As the meeting broke up and people filed toward the door, Tomlinson called, "Jake, can you stay for just a few minutes more?"

Surprised, Jake replied, "Of course."

Once everyone except the senator, Lovett, O'Donnell, and Jake had left the office, Tomlinson headed back for his desk and gestured at the comfortable deep bottle-green leather chairs arrayed in front of it.

"Jake here is working on the space issue," said the senator, as he pulled off his jacket and draped it on the back of his desk chair.

Lovett's brows rose a bare centimeter. "Space is an issue?"

"It should be," Tomlinson said.

Raising his eyebrows even a bit higher, Lovett said, "The way I see it, this campaign is going to hinge on three major issues: the economy, terrorism, and foreign relations."

O'Donnell said, "The president's getting a big break with Putin on his last legs."

"There's already talk of a summit meeting," said Tomlinson.

"She's always been lucky," Lovett agreed. "Good thing she's finishing her second term. You won't have to run against her."

"Against her legacy, though," O'Donnell said.

With a shake of his head, Tomlinson objected, "Her legacy includes a shameful neglect of the space program."

Smiling patiently, Lovett said, "Please tell me why that's important."

Tomlinson pointed a finger at Jake, like a pistol.

Trying to put his thoughts in order, Jake said, "We should be making space useful to the voter, produce jobs, new industries, make an impact on the economy."

Lovett's squarish face took on an expression of curiosity. "Tell me more."

Jake saw that Senator Tomlinson wasn't smiling. He looked interested, engaged, serious. O'Donnell seemed unreceptive, uninterested, almost bored.

Jake realized this was a test. Lovett could squash his ideas with a single frown.

Okay, Jake said to himself. Here goes. "We go back to the Moon, build a permanent base there, and begin to use the Moon as a resource center."

"Resource center?" Lovett asked. "For what? Scientific research?"

Jake replied, "Scientific research, yes. But more than that. Industrial operations. Mine the Moon's natural resources and use them to reduce the cost of space operations."

His calm gray eyes totally focused on Jake, Lovett asked, "How are you going to accomplish that?"

"For one thing, about half the Moon's surface layer—its regolith—is composed of oxygen. Most of what we launch into space, pound for pound, is oxygen. We can produce oxygen from the Moon and ship it down to Earth orbit twenty times cheaper than lifting the same tonnage of oxygen from Earth."

"Once you've got a facility in place."

"Yes, of course," Jake said.

"And what else?" Lovett probed.

"Aluminum, silicon, magnesium, titanium. If we ever get practical nuclear fusion generators, they can be fueled with helium-three from the Moon."

"That's pretty far in the future, isn't it?"

"Solar power satellites aren't," Jake said. "We could build them now, and build them twenty times cheaper by using lunar raw materials."

"Why do we need solar power satellites? People put solar panels on their roofs, don't they? My condominium building went solar a couple of years ago."

Jake answered, "Solar power satellites can deliver gigawatts of power to the ground. Base load electrical power, the kind you need to run factories and whole cities. Cleanly, with no pollution. And cheaply, once the satellites go into operation. Rooftop solar can't do that."

Lovett nodded slowly. "So I've heard. But first you have to build a considerable mining base on the Moon."

"And an electric catapult for shooting payloads back to Earth orbit," Jake added.

"That would be expensive."

He says it gently, Jake thought, but he still says it.

"Yes, it would be expensive. It would be an investment that would pay off a hundredfold, though. Or more."

Lovett glanced at Tomlinson. "What do you think of all this, Senator?"

"I think it's exciting. I think we could get the voters excited about it."

"Until they realize how much it would cost."

There it is, Jake thought. The shot through the heart.

Lovett reached into his jacket's inside pocket and pulled out a calling card. "Jake, I'm writing down the name and number of a man you should talk to."

"A psychiatrist?" Jake asked, weakly.

No one laughed.

"No," Lovett said, handing Jake the card. "He's an economist. At Princeton. If anybody can figure out a way of funding the program you're talking about, it's him."

Jake looked down at the name Lovett had scrawled on the back of the card: Zacharias Karamondis.

Zacharias Karamondis

Once he started looking up Zacharias Karamondis in the various Internet sources, Jake learned two things about the economist right away. He wasn't at Princeton University itself but at the Institute for Advanced Study, which was located a couple of miles from the school's campus. Jake goggled at the fact. Einstein took up residence there when he fled the Nazis and came to America. John von Neumann. Wolfgang Pauli. Robert Oppenheimer. The Institute at Princeton was one of the world's most prestigious intellectual centers.

The second thing Jake found was that Karamondis did not travel, not even to meet a United States senator.

"Dr. Karamondis hasn't left this neighborhood since I've been here," said the smooth-voiced executive assistant who answered Jake's phone call. "If you want to speak with him, you'll have to come here."

Jake had no objections to that. He had always wanted to see the Institute for Advanced Study. In his mind it was the ultimate temple of learning, a refuge where the best minds in the world could pursue knowledge without being bothered by the pressures of the outside world.

"It's like going on a holy pilgrimage," he said to Tami that evening, excitedly.

She grinned back at him. "Say hello to Zeus and the rest of the gang for me."

The reality was somewhat different. The Institute's buildings were practical, not monumental. The place looked more like a suburban office complex than a set of temples.

And Zacharias Karamondis didn't resemble Zeus at all.

"Call me Zach," he said affably as Jake stepped into his office. The smooth-voiced executive assistant Jake had talked with on the phone quietly closed the door behind him.

Zacharias Karamondis was nearing seventy-five years of age, Jake knew from checking his biographic sketch. His hair was still dark, though, a thinning and unruly patch that looked as if it hadn't seen a comb in at least a week. The man was fat, short, and rotund, wearing a wrinkled, rumpled pair of hideous golf slacks and an equally baggy pinkish short-sleeved shirt.

He was standing at his desk, which was cluttered with papers. A computer rested on the table behind the desk, equally strewn with journals, papers, and dog-eared books. One wall of the office was entirely bookshelves, crammed to overflowing.

Karamondis himself was fleshy-faced, his eyes barely slits set into puffy cheeks. Jake thought he looked like a good candidate for a heart attack.

Yet he was smiling warmly as he gestured to the only empty chair in front of the desk. It was a straight-backed wooden chair, though, not comfortable at all. There were two more to one side, both piled with papers.

As Jake sat down, the executive assistant reentered the office, carrying a tray bearing a teapot and a pair of cups.

"Would you prefer coffee?" she asked. Jake realized that she was quite attractive: old enough so that her hair was turning gray, but still trim of figure and bright of eye.

"A cold drink, if you have it," he replied.

"Coke? Club soda?"

"Club soda, please."

She deftly cleared a space on the desk with one hand, then gently deposited the tray there and left the office.

Karamondis sat heavily in his squeaking desk chair and reached for a half-eaten sandwich resting on a crumb-littered plate among the piles of papers on the desk. Jake noticed that the front of his hideous shirt was generously sprinkled with more crumbs.

His appearance didn't seem to bother Karamondis at all. "I know what you're thinking," he said, almost jovially. "The fat guy's eating gyros between meals."

Jake couldn't think of a reply, so he stayed silent. Karamondis's accent was decidedly not Greek. If anything, Jake thought he heard the Bronx in the man's overly loud tones.

"I've got a heart problem," he explained. "My doctor told me to eat several little meals during the day, instead of a few big ones." He bit off a chunk of the sandwich, then went on as he munched away, "So I eat six or seven times a day instead of three."

"I see," Jake said weakly.

Karamondis gulped down his mouthful, then placed the plate atop a teetering mountain of papers. He started to reach for the tea just as his executive assistant returned to hand Jake an insulated mug of club soda that bore a blue and white New York Yankees logo.

Karamondis lost interest in the tea. He leaned back in his groaning swivel chair and, clasping his hands over his ample belly, fixed Jake with a stern stare. "So . . . Patsy Lovett says you need my advice. What about?"

Somewhat haltingly, Jake started to explain his work on the space program. Karamondis nodded in all the right places.

"It makes sense. After all, we spent a hundred billion in twenty-first century dollars to get to the Moon. Why let it go to waste, if there are good economic reasons to develop an industrial base there?"

Feeling heartened, Jake said, "The problem is that the cost—"

"The problem with *everything* is the cost."

"The program could cost as much as a hundred billion over ten years."

"Pah! The petroleum industry spends that much on drilling dry holes every ten years. More!"

"But the voters, the taxpayers—"

"Why should they foot the bill?" Karamondis asked, almost belligerently.

"Who else?"

"Private capital! Why is it those dunces in Washington can't see farther than the ends of their noses? Every time they want to start a new program, they think that only tax money can finance it. Phooey!"

Jake blinked at him.

Karamondis leaned both his heavy forearms on his desk, scattering papers in every direction and threatening to topple the teapot.

"Let me ask you a question." Without waiting for a response from Jake, the economist asked, "How were the big power dams in the American West financed?"

"Power dams?"

"You know, Hoover Dam, Grand Coulee, Bonneville, the other dams that generate electricity."

Jake stared at him. What's this got to do with solar power satellites? he asked himself.

Karamondis eased back in his chair. "Since you obviously don't know, I will tell you.

"Back in the early years of the twentieth century, many people in the West—in California, Arizona, Washington State, places like that—they wanted to build dams that would control their major rivers, irrigate their dry farmlands, and generate electricity. Understand?"

"Yes, sir."

"Good. But they had problems. Building such dams was damned expensive." Karamondis chuckled delightedly at his pun. Then, serious again, "Besides, most of the projects involved more than one state. There were questions about who had the rights to the water. And profits from the dams would be a long time coming. No single state could afford to finance such a project and private investors saw all outgo and a long time before any income."

"So they went to the federal government," Jake guessed.

"Wrong. In those days the federal budget was small and tight. It would be decades before FDR came in with his tax-and-spend policies and opened up the federal treasury for everything in sight."

"Where'd the money come from, then?"

Karamondis grinned knowingly. "From a simple yet ingenious financing scheme. Simply ingenious, you might say." Again he laughed. This time Jake smiled back at him.

His grin widening, Karamondis explained, "A few pretty smart financial types figured that if the federal government offered to back long-term, low-interest loans for these projects, private investors would pony up the money for the dams."

"But I thought private investors steered clear of the projects."

"At first they did. But with Washington backing the loans, guaranteeing that the investors wouldn't lose their money no matter what, all the millions that were needed came out of the pockets of private financiers. Not a nickel of money came from the US Treasury."

It took a few moments for Jake to absorb what Karamondis was telling him. "No tax money was spent."

"Not a penny of tax money. The dams were built on private capital. All that Washington provided was the assurance that the investors would not lose the money they put up."

"And that's how the dams got built."

Karamondis nodded hard enough to make his cheeks waddle. "The loans paid out in fifty years, if I remember correctly. By then the dams had helped to power the Southwest and

Northwest. Helped to build Phoenix and Las Vegas. Tamed the Columbia River. Delivered the electricity for the Manhattan Project."

"The atomic bomb project," Jake said, feeling awed.

"So you see," Karamondis said, spreading his flabby arms, "you can build your base on the Moon and everything else you want without spending a penny of the taxpayers' money."

"No federal financing."

"Merely a federal guarantee to back long-term, low-interest loans. That will open up the spigots on Wall Street."

"Would it really work?" Jake wondered.

"It already has!" Karamondis boomed.

Senator Tomlinson's Office

But could it work?" Senator Tomlinson asked.

"It already has," Jake said, echoing Karamondis's words.

The senator's private office had changed in the nearly six years since he'd arrived in Washington. Back then the room had been decorated in soft, neutral tones of beige and soft blue, with light walnut paneling and pearl gray drapes. Over the years the décor had become bolder: the drapes were now more silvery, the carpeting royal blue, the senator's desk wider, handsomely curved, more regally imposing.

Tomlinson leaned back in his desk chair and steepled his fingers in front of his face, thinking. Sitting in front of the desk on either side of Jake were O'Donnell and Patrick Lovett.

"Zach's a clever man," Lovett said, with a satisfied smile.

"An academic," countered O'Donnell.

Senator Tomlinson said softly, "The Treasury Department guarantees the loans so that even if the whole scheme collapses the investors won't lose their money."

"That's the idea," said Jake.

"Is that legal?"

"It's been done before."

O'Donnell said, "Maybe it has, but that was before the Securities and Exchange Commission was created, I'll bet. There's probably five hundred federal regulations that'd prevent it now."

"You could look that up easily enough," said Lovett.

"Even if it's not illegal," O'Donnell insisted, "the opposition would tear the idea to shreds. The US government guaranteeing that Wall Street investors can't lose their money." O'Donnell shook his head. "You'd be crucified, Frank."

"But if we got a couple of key financial types to say they'd invest in this . . ." Lovett's voice faded away, leaving the idea dangling.

"Sure they'd invest in it! What've they got to lose?"

Jake said, "They'd be tying up their money for fifty years, maybe longer."

Tomlinson nodded warily.

Lovett countered, "It would make a hot campaign issue. It would get Frank noticed by the news media."

"Captain Moonbeam," O'Donnell groused.

Jake said, "Wait a minute. Suppose we got some of the people who've already invested in private space companies to say they'd put in seed money, with or without a federal guarantee."

"Like who?" Tomlinson asked.

"Like Harold Quinton, for example," Jake replied. "The Silicon Valley billionaire who started up Space Tours, Inc."

Lovett nodded. "I know Harry Quinton. He might go for something like this."

Jake added, "And Nicholas Piazza. He founded Astra Corporation. They're the major carrier back and forth from the International Space Station."

"You think they'd invest their own money in a lunar base project?" Tomlinson asked.

"Yes!" said Jake. "And they'd back a plan to encourage other investors to put in their money."

Lovett rubbed his square chin. "It could work. At the very least, it could start a dialogue. Give the news media something different to chew on."

O'Donnell shook his head. "Captain Moonbeam," he repeated.

Tomlinson sat up straighter. "Jake, you get this Kalamandis to check out the Treasury Department and the SEC about this."

"Karamondis," Lovett corrected. "And you don't ask him to do dog work. He'd laugh in your face."

"But I could ask him to recommend a grad student to look up the existing regulations," Jake said.

"That could work."

Tomlinson put on his million-dollar smile. "I think we're onto something. I could be the first president of the United States to fly to the Moon!"

Lovett nodded thoughtfully. O'Donnell said nothing, but the expression on his face could have curdled milk.

. . .

When they first got married, Jake and Tami alternated the chore of preparing dinner. Tami was a good and imaginative cook, although Jake teased her that a sushi dinner shouldn't count as cooking.

"You try slicing the fish and preparing the garnishes," she would counter, with faked indignation.

Jake's idea of cooking was to heat up a couple of microwave dinners. To make up for his lack of culinary capability, Jake was in charge of the cocktails and the wine cellar—a bin among the kitchen cabinets.

On special occasions they would eat out, and this night was certainly a special occasion in Jake's mind.

He got home before Tami did. Too excited even for a cocktail, Jake stewed around the living room, turned on the evening TV news, turned it off again, checked the clock on the wall, paced back and forth, debated calling Tami's cell phone—and finally heard her key turning in the front door's lock.

As she stepped into their living room Jake rushed to Tami and kissed her mightily.

She understood immediately. "He's going ahead with it?"

Nodding vigorously, Jake said, "Full speed ahead. Next stop, Moon Base One!"

"Jake, that's wonderful. But—"

"We're going to Mamie's for dinner. I've already made the reservations."

"Good!" said Tami.

Jake felt puzzled. It was his turn to cook, he knew. Usually Tami twitted him when he decided to go to a restaurant on a night he was supposed to do the cooking. Instead, she just stood there, her purse slung over her shoulder, beaming at him.

"Good?" he asked.

"I've got something to celebrate, too," Tami said. "Pat Lovett's PR man has asked me to join his staff!" Her smile could have lit up the whole District of Columbia.

"You'll be on the campaign staff?" Jake heard his own voice jump an octave.

"We'll be working together!" Tami said.

"Together again. For the first time."

Arm in arm they left their apartment and headed for Mamie's Restaurant.

Jake thought it was surprisingly cool in the New Mexico desert. Of course, the sun was barely peeking above the dunes on the horizon and a chill dry wind was blowing across the sands from the distant mountains.

Slightly more than a mile from the grandstand where Jake waited with the other bystanders, the Space Tours rocket launcher stood tall and straight, sunlight glinting off its silver skin. Six tourists were strapped into the passenger module at the top of the rocket, Jake knew. The ground crew was leaving the launchpad in minivans painted sky blue, each van kicking up a rooster tail of dust as it drove across the desert.

"FIVE MINUTES AND COUNTING," came the announcement from the loudspeakers at the rear of the grandstand. "ALL SYSTEMS ARE GO."

Jake turned his head from the rocket on its launchpad and looked at Isaiah Knowles. The former astronaut was standing rigidly at attention, his eyes riveted on the rocket launcher. It always surprised Jake that Knowles was several inches shorter than he; the man gave the impression of being bigger, more impressive. But now Jake saw that he was nervously rubbing his thumb against his forefinger. He's just as tightened up as I am, Jake realized.

"How many launches have you seen?" Jake asked.

Knowles stirred, as if coming out of a trance. "This is the

worst part," he said, his voice low. "If anything goes wrong this is where it'd most likely happen."

"FOUR MINUTES AND COUNTING. ALL SYSTEMS GO."

"Man, I'd rather be in the bird instead of out here watching," Knowles said fervently. "I'd be working, active, instead of just standing here doing nothing."

The grandstand was sparsely filled with onlookers. Families of the half dozen paying customers aboard the rocket, a few Space Tours employees, tourists with little kids, teenagers from the nearby town come to see the launch and pretend they were going into space.

"TWO MINUTES AND COUNTING," the loudspeakers blared.

Behind the grandstand rose a curved modernistic building, all deeply tinted glass and stainless steel gleaming in the rising sun: headquarters of the Space Tours Corporation that was carrying half a dozen sightseers into space for three orbits around the world.

They're going to see sights they've never seen before, Jake told himself.

Raising the binoculars that Space Tours had loaned him, Jake could see a thin whiff of white seeping from the upper level of the slim rocket. Liquid oxygen boiling away, he knew.

Then the umbilical lines carrying the LOX and electrical power dropped away from the launcher.

"THE LAUNCH VEHICLE IS NOW ON INTERNAL POWER," blared the loudspeakers. "ALL SYSTEMS ARE NOMINAL. LAUNCH IN ONE MINUTE AND COUNTING."

Jake could hear his pulse thudding in his ears. It was starting to feel warmer, with the sun climbing into the cloudless turquoise-blue sky. Everyone in the grandstand seemed to be holding their breath. Even the children fell silent.

"FIFTEEN SECONDS . . . FOURTEEN . . ."

Jake mentally counted down the seconds with the announcer. At T minus five seconds a cloud of steam billowed from underneath the rocket. Before Jake could ask Knowles if that was normal, the rocket began to rise slowly, majestically, out of the steam and up, straight, straight up into the crystal sky.

No noise. No sound at all. But then the crowd in the grandstand seemed to take in a collective breath, to stir, sighing as they watched the rocket rising higher, higher.

At last the sound reached them. A bellowing howl, like a thousand demons roaring all at once, like an overpowering ocean wave pouring over them, the rocket's thunder beat down, pulsing, shaking every nerve in Jake's body, throbbing, pounding with a power that Jake had never felt before.

Jake trembled, awestruck.

Someone behind him was chanting, "Go, go, go . . ."

The rocket was hurtling across the sky now, its pulsating roar of power dwindling. Some people cheered and waved their hands in the air. Jake saw a woman crying, tears streaming down her cheeks.

"Go! Go! Go!" Several of the teenagers took up the chant.

A bright flare from the rocket shocked Jake. An explosion?

"First stage separation," Knowles said tightly before Jake could ask. The astronaut was visibly puffing, short of breath.

The rocket dwindled until at last they could see it no longer. The sky was empty, the launchpad emptier. The crowd began to filter grudgingly out of the grandstand, but Knowles didn't move.

With a slightly bewildered shake of his head, the former astronaut told Jake, "No matter how many launches I've seen, it always gets to me."

"It certainly got to me," Jake confessed.

Knowles started to edge toward the stairs. "I think it's the subsonics in the noise from the rocket. Jangles your nervous system."

Jake thought that trying to explain the emotions he had just been put through was like trying to explain the *Mona Lisa*.

"Come on," Knowles said, with a reluctant glance at the now-empty launchpad. "Harry's waiting to see us."

Harold Quinton

The two of them followed the crowd down from the grand-stand and into the big glass-walled building. The glass was heavily tinted, Jake saw, and once they got inside, the air conditioning felt good. It might have been the emotional impact of the launch, but it was starting to feel hot outside.

Knowles led him away from the spectators streaming toward the exit doors and the parking lot outside, and headed toward a door marked MISSION CONTROL: AUTHORIZED PERSONNEL ONLY. A pert blonde teenager stood in front of the door, wearing a sky-blue Space Tours T-shirt that fit her snugly.

She raised a hand and began, "I'm afraid this area—"

"Mr. Quinton's expecting us," Knowles said.

"Oh! You must be Colonel Knowles."

Gesturing to Jake, Knowles said, "And this is Dr. Ross, from Senator Tomlinson's office."

The young woman stared at Knowles with wide china-blue eyes. After a blink, though, she dimpled into a smile and opened the door. "Mr. Quinton is right over there"—she pointed—"with the launch director."

"Thank you," Knowles said.

"Thank *you*," said the young woman. Jake saw stars in her eyes. The astronaut effect, Jake thought. A mixture of awe and admiration and romantic fantasies. Astronauts, he said to himself. Knights in shining armor.

Space Tours's mission control center was nowhere near as large as the NASA installation at Kennedy Space Center. The modest-sized room held a mere half dozen consoles. Men and women were getting up from their swivel chairs, stretching bodies that had been hunched tensely in front of their display screens only moments before. Two of the crew were still at their consoles, Jake saw. They must be monitoring the bird's flight, he thought.

As they approached him, Harold Quinton seemed to be engrossed in conversation with his launch director. It was hard to tell which one was which: both men were short, heavyset, graying. In their fifties, Jake guessed, maybe sixty. Both were gesticulating like a pair of Mediterranean fishmongers.

". . . it's only two percent below nominal," Jake heard one of them say, his voice brittle and defensive.

"I don't care if it's two-tenths of a percent," the other one answered, not as loud but equally tense. "There's six paying customers on that bird and I want everything up to snuff."

Jake realized who was who. The launch director nodded unhappily and walked away.

Knowles stepped the final few paces to where Quinton stood and stuck out his right hand. "Still giving 'em hell, Harry?"

Harold Quinton didn't look like a hard-driving taskmaster to Jake. If anything, he looked like a high school teacher or maybe an insurance broker. He was on the short side, overweight, with a round middle and a boyish, soft, apple-cheeked face. Thinning dark hair. But his dark brown trousers had a knife-edge crease to them, and his tasseled shoes glowed with polish. Four pens were clipped inside his shirt pocket.

He's a billionaire, Jake knew, who had made his fortune in Silicon Valley and was now spending a considerable fraction of it on the company he had founded: Space Tours, Inc.

A crooked smile sneaked across Quinton's youthful face as

he took Knowles's hand. "Somebody's got to put the fear of god into them. How the hell are you, Ike?"

The two men shook hands, then Knowles turned and introduced, "This is Dr. Ross, from—"

"From Senator Tomlinson's office, I know," Quinton said, extending his hand.

"Jake," said Jake.

"Good. And I'm Harry. Now what's this back-to-the-Moon talk all about?"

As Jake started to explain his ideas, Quinton led them almost at a trot back to the door and into the building's spacious main room. Jake had to hustle to keep up with him and Knowles. The launch director came running after them.

"Bird's achieved orbit and we tweaked the cabin pressure back to nominal."

"Good," said Quinton. "I knew you could do it, Sid."

Sid grinned and turned back toward the launch control center.

"Can't let things slide," Quinton said, still scurrying along. "Start down that road and the next thing you know you've got an accident. A disaster."

Jake gave up on talking. He was almost breathless trying to keep up with Quinton's pace. Outside into the bright sunshine they went, the breeze still coolish but the sunlight already feeling like a dragon's hot breath.

Quinton yanked open the door of a deep blue Bentley convertible sitting in front of the building's main entrance in a parking space marked with a sign that read NUMERO UNO—DON'T EVEN *THINK* OF PARKING HERE. He held the door open for Jake to clamber into the back seat while Knowles went around and sat on the right.

"Piazza's going to meet us in Alamogordo," Quinton said as he slid in behind the steering wheel. He revved the engine to life, let the roof slide down, then took off in a cloud of dust.

Jake found it impossible to say much as they sped down the two-lane road with the hot wind blowing in his face.

"Alamogordo's not that big a town," Quinton yelled over the buffeting wind, "but I've found a place that makes a decent steak."

And off they roared.

When you're rich you get all the breaks, Jake thought. Quinton tooled his Bentley down Alamogordo's main street and nosed into an empty parking space right in front of a restaurant marked LUCITA'S KITCHEN.

"Best place in town," Quinton said as he hauled himself out of the car.

Looks like the only place in town, Jake thought, squeezing past the folded-down front seat.

Quinton pointed to a sleek sea-green Ferrari, spattered with dust, in the next parking slot. "Nick got here ahead of us." With a shake of his head he added, "Still driving that puke-green bucket."

The three of them pushed through the double doors of the restaurant. For a moment Jake felt like a cowboy in an old western sauntering into the town's saloon.

But this was a quiet little restaurant. No bar, only a handful of tables set for four and a quartet of booths along one wall. All but two of the tables were empty.

A chubby woman came rushing up to them, smiling brightly, arms spread wide. She was wearing a frilly black dress and had a flower tucked into her luxuriant dark hair.

"Señor Quinton!" she exclaimed. "Welcome."

Quinton broke into an equally big smile as she wrapped her heavy arms around him in a motherly hug. "Lucita," he said as they disengaged, "let me introduce my friends. This is

Isaiah Knowles. He was an astronaut; he's been in space many times."

"Mucho gusto," said Lucita, with a dip of her double chin.

"And this is Dr. Ross, who works for a United States senator."

"Mucho gusto," she repeated—with considerably less ardor, Jake thought.

Lucita led them through the restaurant and into a small private room across the hallway from the kitchen. Another man was already sitting at the only table there, with a much younger fellow beside him. He got to his feet like a giraffe rising from the ground; the youngster rose more slowly, hesitantly.

"Guys," said Quinton, "this is Nick Piazza. Nick, you know Harry, of course. This is Dr. Jacob Ross, science advisor to Senator Tomlinson."

"Jake," said Jake as he extended his hand to Piazza.

Piazza's smile seemed confident, cocky. He was well over six feet tall, towering over Jake and the others. He looked quite young, slim, but when he took Jake's hand his grip was strong, almost painfully so.

Jake had looked up his biography, of course. Piazza was from Chicago and had made a name for himself as a basketball star with Notre Dame. Instead of turning pro, however, he went into the entertainment business, not as a performer but as a manager of performers. Before he was thirty he owned an Internet music company. By the time he was thirty-five he had started his own production company.

Unexpectedly, he bought out a fledgling private space company, renamed it Astra Corporation, and won NASA's contract for ferrying people and cargo to the aging International Space Station and back.

Piazza had the kind of face that would look youthful when he was eighty: bright, inquisitive pale blue eyes, strong cheekbones, snubby little nose. His hair was light, windblown, his skin a deep tan.

The younger man beside him was obviously a Native American: short, thickset, coppery complexion and midnight-dark hair tied into a queue that fell halfway down his back.

While Piazza was wearing a handsomely patterned shirt, sharply creased light gray slacks and expensive-looking tooled black boots, the youngster was in a plain blue denim shirt that hung to his hips and faded scruffy jeans.

"Good to meet you," Piazza said, with his toothy smile. Turning to the lad beside him, he introduced, "This is Billy Trueblood, my number one man and best friend."

Trueblood nodded and smiled shyly.

Jake thought, The Lone Ranger and Tonto?

Once they had seated themselves around the table, Jake asked Piazza, "How did you get interested in space?"

Piazza's face reddened slightly. "Watching people like Colonel Knowles, here, flying off to the space station. I wanted to be like you, sir."

Knowles grinned at him. "Did you ever try to get into NASA's program?"

Piazza shook his head. "Too tall."

Nobody seemed to know what to say. Then Quinton broke the silence. "You can have a free ride on one of my birds, Nick. We'll custom-tailor a space suit for you."

"Hey, I've got my own company, you know."

"So?"

His head sinking slightly, Piazza admitted, "My board of directors doesn't want me risking my butt."

Trueblood watched the exchange in silence, his head swiveling back and forth between the two men.

Grinning, Quinton proposed, "So we'll sneak you onto a Space Tours flight!"

"Tempting. But suppose it blows up?"

"Then I'll be rid of a competitor," Quinton said, grinning.

"We're not competitors, Harry, you know that. You handle the tourist trade. I'm under contract to NASA."

Jake saw his opening. "Would either one of you be interested in going to the Moon?"

"Who wouldn't be?" Piazza immediately answered.

Quinton asked, "How much would it cost us?"

"Nothing," said Jake.

"Nothing?"

"Nothing," Jake repeated.

Quinton gave Jake a hard stare. "I met a pitchman on a street corner once. I must have been about twelve, thirteen years old. By the time he was finished with me, I was cleaned out and all I had to show for it was a lousy ballpoint pen that didn't work."

Knowles put a hand on Quinton's shoulder. "Let Jake explain what he means. I think you'll find it interesting."

Before Jake could begin, Lucita came in with big bowls of guacamole, salsa, and blue corn chips.

"How do you want your steaks?" she asked.

Piazza, Trueblood, and Knowles asked for rare, Jake for medium rare, Quinton—

"I know," Lucita said, throwing a mock frown at Quinton. "Burned black."

"Right," said Quinton. "I want to make sure it's dead."

Lucita left the table muttering to herself in Spanish.

"So tell me, Jake, how are we going to get back to the Moon?" Quinton asked as he dug into the guacamole.

"And why?" Piazza added.

"To start using the Moon as a resource center, so we can build space power systems and make profits from it." Before anyone could reply, Jake went on, "And other things, as well. A new space station, where industrial labs can start developing zero-gravity manufacturing techniques—"

"Biochemical research, too?" Piazza asked. "Zero-gee might be very advantageous for biochemistry work."

Jake nodded. "If you want to go down that road."

"And it won't cost us anything?" Quinton looked and sounded suspicious. "The government's going to pay for all this?"

"Yes to the first question, no to the second."

"Ah-hah!"

Jake told them about Karamondis's scheme of long-term, low-interest loans backed by the government.

"So if it all flops, Uncle Sam gives us our money back?" Piazza asked.

"Too good to be true," said Quinton.

Lucita arrived with a huge platter of steaks, salads, and thick slabs of bread. The men stopped talking only long enough to attack the meat with forks and what to Jake looked like Bowie knives. To his delight, Jake found he could cut his steak with his fork, it was so tender.

Within seconds, though, they were deep in conversation again, probing every detail of Jake's plan.

"Let me throw something into the pot," Knowles said, stabbing at his salad. "NASA's developed a neat heavy-lift booster."

"The Space Launch System, SLS," said Piazza. "Built to launch the Orion spacecraft."

"It's built by the Marshall Space Flight Center, in Alabama," Quinton said, "but there's talk of ULA getting the contract for building follow-on versions."

Piazza explained for Jake's benefit, "United Launch Alliance is a partnership of Boeing and Lockheed Martin, two of the biggest aerospace outfits in the world. They have the inside track on heavy boosters."

Quinton clasped his hands together. "NASA and the big boys," he growled.

"It's supposed to be the primary booster for the manned Mars mission, isn't it?" Jake asked.

"Problem is," Knowles went on, "Congress hasn't authorized any manned missions to Mars."

"All dressed up and nowhere to go," Piazza muttered.

"Damned politicians," Quinton growled.

Jake understood where Knowles was heading. "A private company might buy an SLS booster. More than one."

"Might," Knowles agreed.

"I bet we could land a Phase One base on the Moon with a single SLS launch," Jake said.

Knowles nodded, but warned, "NASA would want to run the mission. You provide the payload and they launch the bird from Kennedy."

"How many do they have?" Quinton asked.

"ULA could build as many as you need," said Knowles.

"If NASA lets them."

Jake waggled a finger in the air. "No. If Congress tells NASA that's what it must do."

Quinton huffed. Then, "That'll be the day."

"Yes," said Jake. "That will be the day."

More business gets done at parties like this than on Capitol Hill," Jake said as he unconsciously tugged at the collar of his tuxedo.

"Don't be nervous," Tami said. "You'll do fine."

The two of them were standing at the doorway to the party room of Cecilia Goodlette's house, in a posh neighborhood of elegant homes, not far from the Capitol itself. The spacious room was already jammed with men in tuxedos and women in colorful gowns and glittering jewelry.

Tami's dress was pink and white, like springtime, its skirt an inch or so below her knees. Jake thought she was by far the loveliest woman in the place.

"There's Frank," Jake said, consciously preventing himself from pointing. Senator Tomlinson was deep in conversation with Senator Bradley Sebastian, chairman of the Senate's subcommittee on space, science, and competitiveness.

The two men looked enough alike to be cousins: Tomlinson tall, athletically slim, handsome, elegant in his tailor-fitted tux; Sebastian showed what Tomlinson might look like in ten years, still tall, still somewhat elegant, but heavier, grayer, bowed with years and responsibilities. And they were very different in background, outlook, and attitude. Tomlinson was from Montana, youthful, wealthy, progressive. Sebastian was from Florida, middle-aged, born to hardscrabble poverty, a neoconservative.

"They seem to be friendly," Jake said. "Maybe I shouldn't butt in."

Tami shook her head the barest centimeter. "It's your program they're talking about, I bet. Let's walk past and smile hello and see what happens."

At that moment a miniskirted waitress came out of the crowd bearing a tray of champagne flutes. Tami took one, handed it to Jake, then took another for herself.

"Now we're armed and ready," she said.

"You may be ready," said Jake. "I always feel out of place at—"

"There you are!" came the high-pitched voice of Cecilia Goodlette. "I thought you were going to snub me."

Jake forced a smile. "We wouldn't miss your party, Cecilia. You know that. I just had some work to finish up before we could come over."

Tami leaned closer to Lady Cecilia and confided, "The truth is, it takes him *forever* to get the cuff links and shirt studs in right."

Cecilia cackled happily. "Like my second husband. If he had to dress himself he'd never have gotten to his own funeral."

Tami laughed. Jake grinned weakly.

Cecilia Goodlette actually was a Lady, thanks to her titled British third husband. She had gone through four husbands altogether, divorcing two and burying two. And growing wealthier each time.

She was a short, thickset woman with a figure like a sewer pipe, an unfortunately froglike face with thick lips and a dark pageboy wig. She was wearing a stylish aqua-blue pantsuit, though, and enough jewelry to ransom a maharaja.

Cecilia was an important person in Washington's social whirl, the author of *Power Talk*, a blog unknown beyond the Beltway but followed assiduously by the movers and shakers—real and pretended—on the inside.

"And how are you, Jake," she asked, all a-smile, "now that you've got your shirt studs in?"

Jake smiled patiently. "I'm fine, Cecilia, thanks. You look very glamorous tonight."

"Flatterer." She turned to Tami. "I think you're civilizing him, my dear. When Jake first got to town I thought he was a mute!"

Jake fidgeted inwardly while Lady Cecilia prattled on, mostly to Tami. Then Cecilia abruptly excused herself to greet a newly arrived guest, an imposingly tall brown-skinned man luxuriantly bearded, wearing a knee-length golden-tan jacket and a white turban.

"Mr. Ambassador!" Cecilia fairly shrieked, loud enough for most of the people in the room to turn and look her way.

Tami clutched Jake's arm. "Now's our chance to get to work," she said.

Arm in arm, Jake led Tami across the crowded room to where Tomlinson and Sebastian were still standing, locked in earnest conversation.

Tomlinson saw them approaching and flashed his incandescent smile. "Here's Jake now, and his lovely wife."

Senator Sebastian made a fatherly smile as Tomlinson introduced Tami to him.

Then, "Jake here is working on a plan to revitalize our space program."

Putting on a mock frown, Sebastian said, "That's my turf, son."

"Yessir," said Jake. "I'd like to present the plan to you, as soon as it's in presentable shape."

"Fine. Fine." Turning back to Tomlinson, Senator Sebastian said, "The voters aren't interested in space, Frank. Astronauts aren't heroes anymore, they're just working stiffs doing strange stuff that hasn't any relationship to what the voters are really interested in."

Before Jake could contradict the senator, Tomlinson said, "But space always ranks pretty high in opinion polls."

Sebastian said, "Oh, nobody's really *against* space. But the average voter doesn't think it's as important as crime in the streets or the unemployment rate."

"Space can create new jobs," Jake blurted, "whole new industries."

"I don't see that," Sebastian said, shaking his head. "I know there are some nutcases out there who want to go to Mars." Chuckling, he added, "If they can ever raise the money. Certainly the United States government isn't going to finance them."

Smiling back at the senator, Tomlinson said, "Our plan isn't about Mars. It's about developing new industries in orbit, and on the Moon."

Sebastian's expression went from amusement to disbelief. "Industries on the Moon? What are you going to build there, blue cheese factories?"

Jake started, "We can develop—"

Tomlinson stopped him with an upraised hand. "You'll be the first to see the plan—once it's ready. You'll see that it makes a lot of financial sense. Especially for the state of Florida."

Sebastian laughed tolerantly. "Well, that's something, at least."

The Chairs

Jake gripped the steering wheel of his convertible with white-knuckled fury.

"Sebastian's so stupid he probably can't find his way to the men's room without a seeing-eye dog."

Sitting beside him as they weaved through the crowded city streets, Tami asked, "Don't you think you should slow down a bit?"

Jake shot a sidelong glance at her. "Yeah, I guess so." And he eased up on the accelerator.

"This is all new to Senator Sebastian," Tami said. "It'll take him a little while to see the importance of it."

Jake swung around a city bus as he growled, "He's a flabby-brained idiot. Chairman of the space subcommittee. It's assholes like him who've let the space program wither on the vine."

"He got interested when Frank pointed out that the plan could be good for his state of Florida."

"It's not a pork barrel project!" Jake snapped.

"I know that," said Tami. "But you've got to get people's interest; that's the way to get their support."

Jake sighed as he slowed to a stop for a traffic light. "I'll never make a politician," he said, shaking his head. "I'd rather knock heads together!"

. . .

The next morning Jake found it hard to concentrate on the reports he was sifting through on the background of the United Launch Alliance. Boeing and Lockheed were working under contract to NASA to build and launch a variety of rocket boosters. Nick Piazza's Astra Corporation had taken a slice of the business of launching cargo and personnel to the International Space Station, but ULA apparently had a hammerlock on NASA's heavy-lift launchers.

Should I try to approach NASA directly to discuss using ULA for our heavy-lift missions? Jake asked himself. Or would it be better to go through the congressional committees first, sound them out?

That would inevitably mean dealing with Senator Sebastian, Jake knew.

His phone rang. Grateful for the interruption, Jake saw that it was Tomlinson's latest executive assistant, a middle-aged woman with mousy brown hair and a downturned mouth. Jake wondered what had happened to Francine.

"Dr. Ross," she said, in a flat Midwestern twang, "the senator would like to see you at three this afternoon in his office."

Jake nodded. "Three o'clock."

Promptly at three Jake approached the senator's executive assistant. She looked up from her desk, then tapped at her phone console.

"Senator, Dr. Ross is here."

"Send him right in."

To Jake's surprise, no one else was in the office, not even Kevin O'Donnell. The senator was in his shirtsleeves, as usual, but his hands were empty and his customary bright smile was nowhere in sight.

"What's up, Frank?" Jake asked as he took a chair in front of Tomlinson's desk.

"Sebastian."

"Oh?"

"He's heard that I'm planning to run for the party's nomination and he doesn't like it one bit."

"Oh."

"He thinks I'm too young, too inexperienced—"

"He wants the nomination for himself," Jake said.

"You're damned right he does. Last night he gave me the business about serving your time, paying your dues, coming up through the chairs."

"He doesn't want you jumping in ahead of him."

Tomlinson nodded wearily. "He told me in no uncertain terms that it's his turn to lead the party. He wants to be president and he doesn't want any interference from a neophyte."

"He called you a neophyte?"

"Not in so many words, but his meaning was clear."

"What does Lovett think about this?"

Looking even more uncomfortable, Tomlinson said, "I want your opinion, Jake. You're not a politician. I can trust you."

Flattered, Jake said, "I'll tell you what I think, Frank."

"And what is that?"

"I think Sebastian is a fathead. I don't think the presidency ought to be a reward for time served. It should go to the person best qualified for the job. That's what the campaign is all about: to show the voters who you are and where you stand and let them decide."

"Pretty idealistic."

"The people haven't done such a bad job, over the years."

A faint smirk crawled across Tomlinson's face. "The people have elected some dodos, Jake. Harding. Buchanan. Not to mention the current resident of the White House."

"They also elected Lincoln, a couple of Roosevelts, Reagan—not to mention Washington and Jefferson."

Tomlinson's smirk evolved into a tentative smile.

"Look, Frank," Jake said. "You can't let Sebastian buffalo you. You can't fold up your hopes at the first sign of resistance."

"But maybe he's right. Maybe I should wait."

"For how long? Four years? You'll be facing an incumbent president then. Eight years? Who knows what the landscape will look like by then?"

"I'll be pushing sixty by then," Tomlinson mused.

"If you're elected, in eight years we'll have an operating base on the Moon and we'll be building solar power satellites in orbit. They'll name the lunar base after you."

Tomlinson shook his head. "After my father."

"Right. He wouldn't want you to turn tail at the first sign of opposition."

The senator let out a long, pained sigh. "Your space plan better be goddamned good, Jake."

"It will be."

Turning to look out his window at the Capitol dome, Senator Tomlinson said, "All right, Jake. Thanks for your confidence in me."

Delighted, Jake said, "You'll make a fine president, Frank."

"That's what Pat told me."

"Lovett? You've spoken to him about this?"

"Sure. We had lunch together."

Jake realized that Tomlinson had already made up his mind to run, despite Sebastian. *He just needed me for a little additional moral support. A cheerleader, that's what I am.*

As he got up from his chair and leaned across the desk to shake the senator's hand, Jake told himself, *Okay, I'll be a cheerleader. All the way to the White House. And the Moon.*

The Announcement

The summer grew hot. Washington turned into a muggy steambath. Congress adjourned. Like most of the politicians, Senator Tomlinson went back to his home state, to touch base with his constituents.

Jake stayed in DC, hammering together his space plan.

As expected, Senator Sebastian announced his candidacy for the Republican nomination just before Congress adjourned for the summer. Governor Davis Hackman, of Tennessee, threw his hat in the ring the following week. There were already four Democrats in the race, plus an aging billionaire businessman who was going for the White House as an independent for the third time.

Patrick Lovett suggested that Tomlinson formally announce his candidacy on July 20, the anniversary of the Apollo 11 Moon landing. At Cape Canaveral.

Kevin O'Donnell warned, "In Sebastian's backyard? That'd be like slapping him in the face!"

Tomlinson smiled patiently at his staff chief. "Pat's my campaign manager, Kevin. Let him manage my campaign."

"But—"

His smile brightening, the senator said, "You picked him for me, remember?"

O'Donnell scowled, but said nothing.

So on July 20, on a platform erected in front of the Saturn V rocket booster that had been turned into a public monument instead of the heavy-lift vehicle it had been designed to be, Senator B. Franklin Tomlinson announced, "I am a candidate for the presidency of the United States."

Jake and Tami sat on wooden folding chairs in the front row of the audience, under sunshades that protected the seated spectators. Still, the heat and steaming humidity were almost overpowering. And there were standees beyond the sunshade, nearly a thousand of them.

Lovett's done his work well, Jake thought as he sat perspiring beside Tami. The crowd might be mostly NASA workers who are afraid of the next round of layoffs, but it still looks good on TV.

Up on the platform, with half a dozen TV cameras focused on his youthful form and smiling face, Tomlinson—his shirtsleeves rolled up to his elbows—was saying, "One of humankind's greatest achievements was accomplished right here, at Kennedy Space Center. We had a president who said to the American people, 'I think we should go to the Moon.'

"And the American people responded. And the world watched in awe. We went to the Moon. We did it so well that many people to this day think it was easy. It wasn't. It took the sweat and brains and skill of nearly a million men and women. It took the lives of three astronauts. But we went to the Moon and opened the way for the human race to go to the stars."

Jake found himself on his feet applauding, pounding his hands together—as was the whole audience. The improvised tent shook with cheers.

Tomlinson waited patiently, in the heat and humidity, a pleased smile on his sweat-beaded face. Once the applause faded away, he resumed:

"I think it's time that we returned to the Moon. I think it's time that we used the initiative and energy of private enterprise, teamed with the hard-earned capability of NASA and relevant other government agencies, to go back to the Moon and use its resources to generate new jobs, whole new industries, and new goals for the American people and the people of the entire world."

The crowd surged to its feet again, clapping, whistling, cheering mightily. The TV crews swung their cameras around to show their impassioned reaction.

Tomlinson smiled brilliantly, the perspiration trickling down his handsome face now, and concluded, "Back to the Moon!"

. . .

The cocktail party in the visitors' center was jam-packed. Just about everyone from the audience outside had streamed into the building's air-conditioned gift shop, talking and accepting iced drinks amid rows of stands offering space-related souvenirs: model rockets, books, toys, memorabilia. Even with the building's cooling cranked up to full blast, Jake felt sweaty, sticky.

Tami seemed perfectly comfortable, though, as she sipped at a diet soda while the crowd surged around her.

"He's a spellbinder," she said to Jake, her voice raised over the noise of hundreds of excited conversations.

Jake was looking up at the makeshift stage at the front of the big room, where Tomlinson and Senator Sebastian were smiling side by side for the TV news teams—and the hundreds of cameras flashing among the onlookers.

"They seem happy with each other," Tami said.

"So did Caesar and Brutus," said Jake, "until the knives came out."

. . .

The whole Tomlinson staff flew back to Washington on the senator's private jet. Lovett seemed happy with the TV news coverage. Even O'Donnell admitted that the campaign had gotten off to a good start.

Once they landed at Reagan National, the senator and his

wife slipped into their waiting limousine with Lovett and O'Donnell. Everyone else went to their own cars or hailed taxicabs. Jake and Tami took a cab to their condo and collapsed into bed, exhausted by the day's heat and emotions.

"It's a good start," Jake muttered as he slipped into sleep.

Tami nodded and kissed him, but said, "Now comes the hard work."

. . .

Once he arrived at the Hart building the next morning, Jake pored over the news coverage of the senator's speech. Mostly positive, he saw, even though there was some sniping at the "space cadet" angle.

O'Donnell barged into Jake's office, his face dark as a thundercloud.

"Didn't you send Sebastian a copy of your program?" he demanded, without preamble.

"Last week," Jake said. "What's the problem?"

Plopping himself down on the chair in front of Jake's desk, the staff chief said, "I just got a call from his office, asking me where your goddamned report is. And Sebastian in on the horn with our man, complaining that Frank sprung his space program to the public without letting him see the plan first."

"But I sent it to him," Jake insisted. "It's the preliminary program, a lot of the details still have to be filled in, but I sent it to him the same day I sent it to you, Kevin."

O'Donnell glared at Jake like an interrogator trying to pry a confession from a suspect. "They claim they never got it."

Jake reached for his desk phone.

"Who're you calling?"

"The delivery service that carried the plan to Sebastian's office," Jake said. "I e-mailed the document to him and sent a hard copy through the Senate's delivery service. They'll have a record of who accepted the package."

But the delivery service had no such record. Frustrated, growing angry, Jake wound up talking with the service's supervisor, while O'Donnell sat glowering before him with his arms folded across his narrow chest.

At last Jake hung up, defeated. "They claim they have no record of picking up the package from me. Kevin, I *know* I handed it to one of their kids."

"Did you get a receipt?"

Jake shook his head. "No. He didn't ask me if I wanted one. I thought—"

Strangely, O'Donnell smiled. It was not a pleasant thing to see. "You got snookered, Jake. Sebastian must have told his people to make your report disappear."

"But the delivery service . . ."

"Senator Sebastian has a lot more clout than you do, pal."

"His people can tinker with the delivery service?"

O'Donnell pushed himself up from the chair. "He's serving notice. He's going to war against us."

The Mars Lobby

Tami was in her element, happily arranging news conferences and interviews for Senator Tomlinson, and helping to get him invited to meetings and conferences that he could use as platforms for publicity.

Just before the new school year opened, at the National Teachers Conference, Tomlinson used a line from Patrick Henry before the news media TV coverage:

"China is planning to establish a permanent base on the Moon. India has already sent robotic spacecraft to Mars. *Why stand we here idle?*"

"I told you he's a spellbinder," Tami said to her husband over dinner that night. "And he's going to get a lot of the women's vote, too."

"Because he looks like a movie star," Jake replied, between mouthfuls of roast beef.

"Because his stand on women's issues is intelligent and well thought-out," she countered, jabbing the air with her fork. "That's rare for your party."

Jake nodded, hoping his wife would let the subject drop then and there.

Kevin O'Donnell still stalked the office like a gloomy ghost, although he stopped muttering "Captain Moonbeam" in Jake's hearing.

Jake was surprised, though, that the various grassroots space organizations weren't more vociferous in their support of Tomlinson.

"Count your blessings," O'Donnell advised. "Most of those kooks would do our man more harm than good. They're the real space nuts."

Jake disagreed. "Kevin, those people have been pushing for a stronger space program all their lives. They're our natural allies."

"With friends like them, who needs enemies?" O'Donnell muttered.

Jake found out what he meant a few days later.

His name was Derek Vermeer. He was the executive director of the Mars Habitat League. He had requested a meeting with Senator Tomlinson, but O'Donnell had decided that Jake should listen to what he had to say first.

Vermeer was tall, imposing, with a gray Vandyke beard and piercing sky-blue eyes. He wore a three-piece suit of dark gray despite the August heat, with a red lapel button that bore the motto "Mars Now!"

Jake went out to the front office to meet him and shake his hand.

As he guided the visitor through the maze of desks toward his own office, Jake apologized, "I'm sorry the senator couldn't meet you in person—"

"I understand," Vermeer said, in a deep, resonant voice.

Jake showed him into his office, and before they could sit down, Jake's executive assistant asked if they'd like something to drink. Vermeer requested iced tea, Jake opted for club soda.

As he lowered himself onto his desk chair, Jake said, "I understand the Mars Habitat League wants to send a group of volunteers to Mars."

Vermeer nodded solemnly. "On a one-way trip. We plan to live on Mars."

Keeping a straight face, Jake said, "So I've heard."

The executive assistant came back into the office with their drinks. Vermeer downed half his iced tea in one long gulp, then put the beaded glass on Jake's desktop beside the coaster that waited there.

"As you no doubt know," Vermeer said, "we are crowdsourcing our funding."

Jake nodded. "How's it going?"

"Slowly, I'm afraid." The expression on his face hardening, he went on, "I am here to find out why there is no mention of Mars in your so-called space plan. No mention at all."

Jake heard the imperious tone of Vermeer's voice, saw the accusation in his piercing blue eyes.

As evenly as he could Jake replied, "Our plan is aimed at developing the resources of the Moon and cislunar space to create new industries, new jobs—"

"We've been to the Moon," Vermeer snapped. "Now it's time to go to Mars."

"You're free to go to Mars. We won't stop you."

"Oh no? Your 'Back to the Moon' nonsense will soak up funding that's vital for the Mars Habitat mission. You're preventing dedicated men and women from reaching Mars!"

"Wait a minute," Jake said, raising a hand. "Once you get to Mars, what are you going to do there?"

"Spend the rest of our lives there. Encourage more people to join us. Extend the frontier of human habitation."

"You plan to build greenhouses on Mars? Grow crops there?"

"Yes, of course."

"I don't know that we have the technology to sustain a colony on Mars for long. You might be killing yourselves."

"We're willing to sacrifice our lives to extend the human frontier. We demand that you include human missions to Mars in your so-called space plan."

Jake shook his head. "I'm sorry. Our plan is aimed at developing practical industrial development, not colonization of Mars."

"But you've got to include Mars! We demand it!"

"I'm sorry," Jake repeated. "It's going to be difficult enough to sell our plan to the voters. Adding a permanent Mars colony will only make things more difficult, impossibly difficult. It might shoot down the entire plan."

For several long moments Vermeer glowered at Jake, trying to stare him down.

At last his expression eased, softened. "You don't understand," he said, almost in a whisper. "I have a tumor. Inoperable. I only have a few years to live." He took in a deep, painful breath. "I want to die on Mars."

Sadly, Jake shook his head. "The best I can offer you is to promise that we will bury your remains on Mars as soon as it's practicable."

Vermeer said nothing. He got up from his chair, drew himself to his full height, and walked out of Jake's office without saying another word.

Despite himself, Jake felt awed, humbled, amid the treasures of the past. Over his head was the original Wright Brothers' Flyer, the first heavier-than-air machine to actually fly. A few yards away stood the Apollo 11 command module, the spacecraft that had carried Armstrong, Aldrin, and Collins to the Moon and back.

The museum was packed with flying hardware, planes, rockets, everything from Lindbergh's *Spirit of St. Louis* to the X-15 rocket plane to the complete backup hardware for the *Skylab* space station.

And the place was jammed, Jake saw. Tourists, foreign visitors, goggle-eyed kids, and grizzled veterans of the aerospace industry milled through the museum, paying homage to the history of flight, the conquest of the air, the quest to reach other worlds.

Jake wondered how he would find Roland T. Jackson in the midst of the throng that was ogling, pointing, chattering through the museum.

"Dr. Ross?"

Startled, Jake looked down on the small, slight figure of Rollie Jackson. He was a legend in the aerospace industry, a man who had designed some of the most significant flying machines the world had ever seen. And there he was, standing before Jake in a checkered sports jacket and dark slacks, tiny almost as a leprechaun, slim, his face bony, with prominent cheekbones, his eyes large and dark, his hair thinning and silver-gray. He reminded Jake of a lemur, with his big dark eyes, yet he smiled up at Jake in a warm, friendly way.

"Dr. Jackson!" Jake blurted.

"*Mr.* Jackson," he corrected. "All the degrees they've stuck onto my name are honorary. I never finished high school, had to go out and support my mother and two brothers."

Jake swallowed once before stammering, "I . . . I'm delighted to meet you, sir."

"Come on," Jackson said, "let's find someplace quiet where we can talk."

He led Jake through the crowd, up an escalator, and across the museum's upper floor, casually pointing out airplanes and spacecraft as if they were his personal heirlooms. And that's exactly what they are, Jake marveled to himself. His personal handiwork. He designed the birds he's pointed to. Designed them and a good deal of their inner systems.

At last they reached a door marked STAFF ONLY. Jackson pulled a plastic card from his jacket pocket and held it to the sensor on the door frame. The door slid open and Jackson gestured Jake through.

It was blessedly quiet here. The corridor was lined with doors marked with people's names and titles. When they reached Jackson's door, at the end of the corridor, it bore his name, without a title.

Before Jake could work up the nerve to ask, Jackson grinned crookedly and said, "They wanted to put 'Resident Genius' on my door but I couldn't let them do that. On the museum's organization chart I'm listed as a full-time consultant."

Jake's research into NASA's organizational history had led him to Jackson. He actually had been the agency's resident genius for decades before retiring from NASA to accept a sinecure at the museum, reportedly to live out his years surrounded by the air and space craft he had designed.

He led Jake into the windowless office. There was no desk, just five deeply cushioned leather chairs and, in one corner, a draftsman's tilted drawing board and a three-legged stool.

"Sit down, make yourself comfortable, and tell me about this plan of yours to get us back to the Moon."

. . .

For nearly two hours Jake explained his plan and the reasoning behind it. Jackson stayed quiet for the most part, asking a question now and then, offering a comment here and there. At one point he went to a mini fridge built into the cabinets that lined one wall and pulled out two bottles of ginger beer. Jake took the soda gratefully.

At last Jake said, "And that's about it. I've got a feeling NASA isn't enthusiastic about it, though."

Jackson pursed his lips thoughtfully and nodded.

"Why should they be?" he asked.

Surprised, Jake stuttered, "Well . . . because we . . . the plan, that is . . . will reinvigorate our efforts in space."

"Private space corporations' efforts in space," Jackson corrected. "Not NASA's."

"We won't be competing against NASA!"

"Of course you will." Jackson said it softly, almost gently. But he said it.

Jake objected, "But the money will come from private investors, not the government."

Jackson took another swig of ginger beer, then put his bottle on the carpeted floor and asked, "How much do you know about biology?"

"Biology?"

With a patient smile, Jackson explained, "If there's one thing I've learned in my years in this industry, it's that government agencies—and private corporations, too—both behave like living organisms. They struggle to survive, to grow. They eat money and excrete hardware, plus an awful lot of paperwork.

"NASA was created by the Eisenhower administration for a political purpose: to counter Soviet Russia's successes in space, to win the Space Race. Actually, to make a race of it. Then Kennedy came along and told NASA to get us to the Moon before the Russians could get there. NASA did that, and for its reward the agency was nearly destroyed by the Nixon administration."

"That's all ancient history," Jake said.

"Yes, but it's part of NASA's heritage, part of the agency's DNA. Like a biological organism that strives to live and grow, NASA is very sensitive to threats against its existence."

"But we're not a threat to NASA!" Jake insisted. "We're on their side."

"Not from the way they see it. The agency has been patiently building the Orion spacecraft and the SLS booster, aiming toward crewed missions to Mars and beyond."

"And Congress hasn't authorized the Mars missions."

"And now here you come with your 'Back to the Moon' plan. You want to set up a base on the Moon and build solar power satellites—"

"Just a demonstration satellite, to prove that space solar power can work, that we can deliver baseload electrical power from space. Once we've done that, private enterprise can build more powersats."

Jackson nodded. "I understand. But don't you see how it looks to NASA? You're invading their turf."

Jake sat there and stared at the man.

Jackson went on, "Your plan will push NASA into the background, make it easier for Congress to whittle down the agency's appropriation, push Mars further away from them. And if you move NASA away from their Mars objective, you'll be leaving Mars to the Mars Habitat League and other private organizations that haven't the funding or the technical know-how for successful Mars missions. In the end, when these private missions fail, NASA can say that your 'Back to the Moon' program killed the people who died trying to reach Mars."

Jake sagged back in his chair. "But that's not true! That's not what we're trying to do, not at all."

Jackson simply shrugged and reached for the soda bottle at his feet.

His thoughts whirling, Jake asked the older man, "What can I do to prevent such a mess?"

A smile crept across Jackson's face. Leaning toward Jake, he replied, "First, convince NASA's top brass that you're not their enemy. Make room in your plan for real NASA involvement."

"But how?"

"Get NASA involved in building your Moon base. Let the agency help with building your demonstration power satellite. God knows they've got the expertise. Don't ignore them, make them part of your plan."

Jake realized he was biting his lip. It hurt. "Involve NASA in the plan."

"Let them make a major contribution."

"A real cooperative effort between the government and the private sector."

"Cooperation, not competition," said Jackson. "That's the ticket."

I wish you'd come with me," Tami said.

Jake replied, "I wish I could." But he shook his head. "Too much to do here. I've got this meeting with NASA's top management, and a ton of work to get ready for it."

They were in their bedroom. Tami was packing her rollalong suitcase for a trip to Iowa, where Senator Tomlinson was making a dozen campaign appearances in three days.

"I don't like to leave you alone," Tami said, as she tucked a zippered bag of toiletries into the suitcase.

"I'll be okay," said Jake, standing by the bedroom doorway, watching her. "You just be careful with those news guys. Don't let them buy you drinks."

Tami stared at him.

"Well, you're a damned attractive woman, and you'll be all alone out there in the Wild West."

"While you'll be on your own in the nation's capital with a million single women."

"I'll be too busy working to notice any of them."

"Same here," she said.

Almost whispering, Jake said, "I love you, Tami."

She melted into his arms. "I'll phone you every night."

"I'll be here," he said. Then he added, "Or at the office."

.   .   .

The first evening Tami was away, Jake sat in their living room eating half a pizza and watching Tomlinson on the TV news while he waited for his wife to phone.

The senator attracted a good deal of media attention on his whirlwind tour through the state. He spoke at a county fair, a tractor factory that was about to close up, and on the campus of the university at Ames.

Outdoors under the summer sun, in his shirtsleeves, bareheaded, Tomlinson told a surprisingly large crowd of mostly students:

"Six years ago, when our energy plan went into effect, I wasn't very popular in these parts." A few scattered laughs from the audience. "The farming industry didn't like our plan's de-emphasis on ethanol additives to gasoline.

"But today, energy costs are lower, our nation's carbon footprint has been reduced by more than 10 percent, and American farmers are feeding the world once again."

Cheers from the crowd.

"Today we face a new challenge and a new opportunity," Tomlinson went on. "It's time we used our space technology to create new industries, create millions of new jobs for Americans, and lead the human race back on the path to the stars."

The predominantly young audience roared its approval.

"It's time to unleash the energy, the creativity, the skills of the American people to develop a new frontier in space.

"It's time to go back to the Moon. And this time we'll be going back to stay."

Wild cheers. Tomlinson stood on the podium, handsome, smiling, youthful, vigorous.

Jake glanced at the clock on the wall next to the TV: a little past seven thirty and Tami hasn't called yet. She must be pretty busy. Besides, it's an hour earlier out there.

The TV had switched to a pair of news analysts discussing

Tomlinson's speech: both males, both middle-aged, both wearing dark suits, plenty of makeup and—Jake guessed—beautifully coiffed toupees.

"Senator Tomlinson appeared to win over his audiences," said the first analyst.

"Especially the college students," agreed the other.

"His stand on farm subsidies went over well."

With a wry smile, "Well, he is in Iowa, after all."

"He didn't spend much time on national defense, did he?"

"No, but he worked up the crowd about his 'Back to the Moon' plan."

"You wouldn't expect that in Iowa."

"No, that was something of a surprise."

"Well, his audience was mostly college students."

"That's true enough. He'll have a tougher time selling the Moon in New Hampshire."

Jake's phone rang. He grabbed for it with one hand and muted the TV with the other.

"Hello, Jake." It wasn't Tami's voice.

"Amy?"

"Right the first time."

"Why aren't you in Iowa with Frank?"

"I'm going to have to traipse across the country for the next year and more," Amy Tomlinson replied. "I decided to stay home for this first one. You did too, huh?"

"Yeah." Jake's mind was racing. Frank's wife should be with him on the campaign trail. She shouldn't have stayed home. It looks bad.

"I thought maybe we two hermits could have dinner together. Nothing fancy, just here at the house."

Jake said, "I'm already halfway through a pizza, Amy."

"Hah. The bachelor's dinner."

"Nature's perfect food," he joked. It sounded lame.

"Want to come over for dessert?" she asked. It sounded

almost suggestive. Jake immediately tossed that idea out of his mind. Don't be an idiot! he commanded himself.

"Uh, Amy, I've got a lot of work to do . . ."

"Really?"

"And I'm expecting a call from Tami any minute."

"Oh. Of course."

"Thanks for asking, though."

Amy sounded mildly amused as she said, "Okay. But tomorrow night, eight o'clock at the house. No sense the two of us sitting around staring at four walls."

Jake didn't know what to say.

"I won't take no for an answer, Jake," she said sternly.

"Well . . . okay, I guess."

"Such enthusiasm!"

"I'm, uh, just kind of surprised, that's all."

Amy laughed lightly. "Jake, two old friends can have a dinner together without the blogs going viral over it."

"Yeah. I know. I'll see you tomorrow, eight o'clock sharp."

"Good." The line clicked dead.

Two old friends, Jake thought as he hung up the phone. We were a lot more than that. Remembering their nights in bed together, he repeated, A lot more than that.

When Tami finally called, Jake didn't say a word about Amy. He felt rotten about it, but he didn't say a word.

Dinner with Amy

At 7:58 p.m. Jake parked his silver Dart convertible well up the driveway of the Tomlinson residence, where the azalea bushes screened it from the street. Feeling slightly nervous, he went to the front door and rang the bell.

Amy herself opened the door. Surprised, Jake gaped at her. She was wearing a light blue V-necked blouse and darker mid-thigh skirt that nicely complemented her shoulder-length honey-blonde hair.

With an impish smile she said, "Butler's night off." And she gestured Jake across the threshold.

Feeling as if he were stepping into a minefield, Jake entered the house. She led him to the library, with its makeshift bar set up on the rolling cart.

"I'm drinking vodka and tonic," Amy said. "What about you?"

"Um . . . white wine, please."

Amy looked amused as she poured a Chablis and handed the long-stemmed glass to Jake.

"Cheers," he said, with a mechanical smile.

They sat side by side on the room's big sofa. Jake took a sip of the wine, then asked, "How's Frank?"

"Oh, he's busy being admired," Amy replied. "Or maybe the proper word is adored."

"Pat Lovett is with him, isn't he?"

Nodding, "Pat and a phalanx of flunkies. He's well protected, don't worry."

Jake blurted, "Are you worried?"

"About Frank?" She almost laughed. "No, Frank's a straight arrow. He's trustworthy."

Jake wanted to ask, Are you? But he kept his suspicions to himself.

As if she could read his mind, Amy said, "Oh, you're thinking about that redheaded secretary of his, Francine. I got rid of her. Purely precautionary. Frank is straight-arrow all right, but he's human. Seeing her every day . . . well, I decided to get rid of her."

"And he let you?"

"Sure. He'd do anything for me. Oh, he might look, but he wouldn't touch."

Jake didn't know what to say.

Amy did. "Not like me."

Jake felt his eyebrows climb toward his scalp.

"Come on, Jake," Amy said, "we had some good times together, didn't we?"

"Until you decided to marry Frank." Jake was surprised at the bitterness in his tone.

Amy blinked her innocent blue eyes. "I know I hurt you, Jake. I'm sorry. I'm willing to make up for it."

"I'm a married man, Amy," he heard himself say.

She shrugged. "So what? I'm a married woman. Your wife and my husband are a thousand miles away. Who knows what they're up to?"

Very carefully, Jake placed his wineglass on the coffee table and rose to his feet. "I think I'd better go home."

Amy stood up beside him, up to his shoulder. "And leave me all alone?"

He nodded, unable to trust himself to speak.

"What about dinner?"

"I'm not hungry."

"That's a shame."

He started for the library door.

Walking beside him, Amy asked, in a little-girl voice, "You're not going to mention any of this to Frank, are you?"

"Of course not."

"Of course not," she mimicked. She stopped at the door. "I'm sorry if I shocked you, Jake. But think it over. We can still take up where we left off." Then, with a sardonic grin, she added. "Well, almost."

Amy turned and headed back to the bar. Jake pushed through the library door and marched down the corridor, toward his car.

Sleepless and Alone

Jake drove home, rode the elevator from the basement garage to his top-floor unit, entered his apartment, and stood just inside his front door, trying to arrange his thoughts.

Should I tell Tami about this? he asked himself. Should I tell Frank?

He'd spoken to Tami in Iowa just before leaving for the shambles of a dinner with Amy. She was busy, happy, glad to be working on the Tomlinson campaign, fielding requests for interviews, appearances, breakfasts, lunches, and dinners.

Stepping into the sitting room, Jake saw that it was just past eight thirty. Seven thirty in Iowa, he figured. Tami's probably up to her ears in work. Or maybe dinner. He phoned her anyway, got her cheerful message: "I can't pick up the phone right now, but if you'll leave your name . . ."

Jake cut the connection.

As he rummaged through the refrigerator for something to microwave, Jake wondered anew if he should tell Tomlinson about Amy's invitation. No, he answered himself firmly. But how will I be able to work with Frank after this?

Then a new fear struck him. What if Amy tells him? What if she says I came on to her?

No, he decided. Amy's not stupid. Or vindictive.

He hoped.

Jake stretched out on the recliner in the sitting room, a thick sheaf of reports about NASA, ULA, and the fledgling private space companies spread across the coffee table, next to a half-eaten microwave dinner.

Senator B. Franklin Tomlinson was on the TV screen, smilingly fielding questions from a trio of interviewers. Jake slipped into a troubled slumber when they started asking the senator questions about his stand on income-tax reform.

The phone woke him. Muting the TV as he picked up the handset, Jake saw it was past midnight and the TV was showing some old black-and-white movie musical.

Tami's voice chirped, "You still awake?"

"Yeah, sure."

"Did you see Frank's interview? Wasn't he terrific?"

"They didn't talk much about the space plan."

"Yes, but he came through solidly on tax reform and farm subsidies, don't you think? And when they asked about foreign policy he worked in the space plan."

"I must have dozed off," Jake confessed.

"Poor baby," Tami mock-consoled him. Then, more seriously, "It must be pretty lonely for you."

"Yeah," Jake said tightly.

"I'll be home tomorrow night. We can celebrate."

"Yeah," he repeated.

. . .

Jake slept fitfully, his dreams a tangle of memories of his times with Amy and her tossing him away. He'd wake up and tell himself he didn't want her, he'd found a woman he loved who truly loved him, yet when he fell asleep again there was Amy filling his haunted dreams.

Finally, as dawn was beginning to faintly brighten his bedroom window, Jake unwound himself from his twisted sheets and stood up to face the new day.

He was the first one into the office, although Kevin O'Donnell was scant minutes behind him. Jake was filling the office coffee machine when O'Donnell came up to him, grinning.

"Finally found something useful to do, eh?"

Jake took it good-naturedly. "I've been demoted to my level of competency."

As Jake pressed the coffeemaker's red ON button, O'Donnell said, "Sebastian's scheduled a hearing on your space plan. Next Monday, bright and early."

Jake felt a pang of alarm. "But all he's got is the preliminary plan! It doesn't include the expanded role for NASA or—"

"That's good, Jake. That's good. Our man can show Sebastian that we're covering all the bases. Give him a surprise."

"You understand that what we're after is a cooperative program," Jake said. "NASA's a part of it, but they're not going to be in charge. It's not NASA handing out contracts to the private companies. It's more like using NASA as a resource they can call on for technical expertise."

O'Donnell's face darkened. "How's NASA feel about this?"

"On the technical, workaday level the staff people are fine. They're glad to be involved in getting back to the Moon."

"But NASA's management?"

Jake waggled a hand. "They're going to need more convincing."

"Could be trouble," O'Donnell said.

"We're going to need Frank's powers of persuasion."

"And then some."

. . .

Late that afternoon, Harold Quinton phoned Jake from his Space Tours, Inc., office in New Mexico. The billionaire's normally bland, unruffled expression looked strained, upset, almost angry.

Quinton came straight to the point. "My people tell me their contacts in NASA are talking about renegotiating our existing contract with the agency."

"What?" Jake sat up straighter in his swivel chair.

"Yeah. Apparently the bean counters want to amend our

contract for ferrying cargo and personnel to the ISS to include missions to the Moon. That's unacceptable!"

"I agree."

"But they tell my people it's a part of your plan," Quinton said, his face and his tone accusatory.

"No," said Jake. "We want to bring NASA into the plan as a technical resource, a partner, not the head of the whole operation."

"Well, somebody ought to tell *them* that!" And the phone screen went blank. Quinton had hung up.

Jake sat at his desk, staring off into space, wondering what to do. After a few minutes he called O'Donnell to ask his advice.

The staff chief said he was busy, but he could spare Jake a few minutes around five o'clock.

Just before five, Jake went to O'Donnell's office.

Once Jake explained his problem the staff chief broke into a rare chuckle. "The bastards can move fast when they want to," he said. "Threaten their position and they can move damned fast."

"But that isn't what we want for the program," Jake protested. "We want NASA in the program as a partner, not an overlord."

O'Donnell shook his head sadly. "They don't want to be a partner. They want to run the show."

"But that will screw up everything! It'll ruin the whole plan. Quinton and the other private firms don't want to go to the Moon under contract to the government."

With a shrug, O'Donnell said, "Then you'll have to get NASA to see things your way."

"How?"

"If I knew, Jake, I'd tell you."

Jake sat in front of O'Donnell's desk, sunk in a puddle of gloom.

"This is going to screw up everything," he muttered. "We

want private enterprise to go to the Moon, not a government program that comes out of the taxpayers' pockets. Congress would never vote the funds."

"What you want, kid," said O'Donnell, "and what you get are two different things."

. . .

Jake headed back to his own office. Most of the staff workers were closing up shop for the day, heading for the door, for a drink at a local cocktail lounge or a quiet dinner at home with the family.

Tami won't be home for another two hours, at least, Jake told himself. Maybe I should find a friendly neighborhood bar and drown my troubles.

Instead, he phoned Roland T. Jackson.

As soon as Jackson's face appeared on his phone screen Jake blurted, "I've got troubles."

The former NASA engineer listened to Jake's plaint sympathetically, his large dark eyes blinking now and then. At last he said, "That's just the kind of thing you'd expect them to do."

"I didn't expect it," Jake admitted.

Jackson's thin, almost gaunt face smiled patiently at Jake. "You've got to think of the agency as a biological organism, Jake. It feels threatened by your Moon plan, so its first reaction is to either kill it or try to take command of it."

Jake said, "Or kill it by trying to take command of it."

"Now you've got it."

"So what can I do about it?" Jake pleaded. "Senator Sebastian's scheduled a meeting of his subcommittee for Monday morning to discuss the plan."

"And NASA's top management will be there, ready and willing to testify."

Jake nodded.

Jackson pulled in a deep breath, then let it sigh out of him. "Let me make a couple of phone calls, Jake. Maybe I can get you and the agency's chief administrator together over the weekend. Maybe you can present a united front at the hearing."

Maybe, Jake thought. He doubted that anything much could be done, but it was better than nothing.

. . .

Jake parked at Reagan National Airport's special lot for congressional personnel. After a glance at his wristwatch, he hustled into the terminal building and down to the security post where passengers from Tami's flight were coming in.

And there she was, bright, perky, and smiling as she pulled her roll-on suitcase behind her. But as soon as she saw Jake, her smile disappeared.

Jake rushed to her and took her in his arms. Her lips felt warm and wonderful to him, but as they disengaged Tami asked:

"What's wrong, Jake?"

"Is it that obvious?"

"You look as if the Washington Monument fell on you."

Taking her suitcase in his hand and walking with her toward the exit, Jake said, "NASA's trying to take over the space plan."

"Well, don't let them!"

Shaking his head, Jake replied, "Easier said than done, Tami."

She listened patiently as Jake explained NASA's maneuvering while they walked out of the terminal and toward the congressional parking lot.

Jake prattled on, never once mentioning his abortive dinner with Amy.

N ow, remember what I told you, Jake," said Rollie Jackson. "NASA is not the enemy. Think of the agency as a trapped animal, fighting for its life."

Jake and the retired engineer were riding in Jake's convertible toward a meeting with Hideki Noruyaki, NASA's associate administrator for human exploration and operations. It was early Sunday morning; Washington's normally jam-packed streets were relatively free of traffic.

Without taking his eyes away from his driving, Jake replied, "Isn't that a little overly dramatic, Rollie?"

Jackson shook his head and explained, "No, not at all. For nearly a generation, now, the agency has wanted to send astronauts to Mars. Neither the White House nor Congress gives a damn about Mars. They're just willing to fund missions to the International Space Station, and every year they squeeze down a little more on that. They're starving NASA, a little more every year."

Jake glanced at Jackson, saw that he was dead serious.

"The greatest collection of intellect and talent in the world," the engineer went on, "and it's being starved to death."

"NASA's budget is damned near twenty billion this year," Jake objected.

"Yes, and it's being spent mainly on paper studies and make-work programs, without any real goals."

Before Jake could reply, he went on, "And now you come

along with the private rocket companies and a program that puts NASA on the sidelines. The agency feels endangered, and I don't blame them."

Which side is he on? Jake wondered.

His tone lightening, Jackson said, "At least our timing is just about perfect this morning. The religious folks are already in church and the heathens haven't gotten out of bed yet."

Jake couldn't help smiling as he drove his convertible, top down, through the quiet, sunny morning. He had picked up Jackson at his town house in the Capitol Hill neighborhood, not far from Lady Cecilia's home. Jackson didn't drive, Jake had learned to his surprise.

"Never found a need to get a license," he admitted cheerfully. "I've just about always lived in a city with public transportation."

"And taxicabs," Jake added.

Jackson nodded. "You know, Johnnie von Neumann, the genius of geniuses, did most of his best work in taxicabs. He'd hire a cab in the morning and have the driver tootle around town all day while he worked on his math."

"No interruptions," said Jake.

"Right."

"Expensive, though."

"Johnnie was wealthy. Hungarian nobility. Lived in hotels most of the time."

And invented game theory, Jake recalled, computer operations, helped create the first atomic bombs. Genius of geniuses, all right.

Jake turned onto E Street SW and pulled up in front of the NASA headquarters building. He even found an open parking space halfway up the block.

As he climbed out of the convertible, Jackson pointed to the curbside sign that warned that parking was prohibited—on weekdays.

"Score another point for the Lord," he said, with a grin.

Jake tapped the button that started the convertible's metal roof rising. Once he got the roof firmly attached to the windshield's frame, he slid out of the car and locked it.

"So what kind of a guy is this Noruyaki?" he asked.

Jackson shrugged. "Never met him. But my buddies who know him say he's a decent type, not an old agency paper shuffler."

"Uh-huh," said Jake.

"He's taking the time to talk with us on a Sunday morning," Jackson added. "That says something."

Jake thought it might just mean that the man had nothing better to do until the football season began.

There was only one guard in sight in the building's lobby: middle-aged, pudgy. He waved them through the X-ray scanner without getting up from his stool.

Noruyaki's office was on the top floor of the building: "officer country" in Jackson's parlance. "This is where the big brass hang out," he told Jake as they walked along the empty, silent corridors.

Up ahead, a youngish man in a Seattle Mariners T-shirt stood next to an open door. Jake had looked up Noruyaki's dossier: he was from Seattle, his degree was from Washington State University, in business administration.

"Dr. Noruyaki?" Jake called as they approached.

He grinned boyishly. "Dr. Ross, I presume."

"Jake."

Noruyaki extended his hand. "And I'm Hank. Come on into the office."

He was much younger than Jake had expected. Short, solidly built without being chubby. Dark straight hair, almond-shaped eyes of light brown.

As he led them through an outer office, Noruyaki said, "And you must be the revered Roland T. Jackson."

Jackson said lightly, "Call me Rollie."

"It's an honor to meet you, sir."

"Rollie," Jackson repeated.

Noruyaki's office looked comfortable, not stuffy. There was a desk in the corner by the windows, but he gestured Jake and Jackson to a deep leather sofa set against the far wall and pulled up a small padded chair to face them.

"So," he asked, "what's the problem?"

Jake swiftly outlined how NASA was moving to take over the space plan. "And if the agency wants to be in charge," he concluded, "the private firms will walk out on us."

Jackson added, "And the agency will need a big boost in its appropriation, which Congress won't vote for, and the plan will be dead."

Noruyaki nodded sympathetically, "Ah, the bean counters. They think they run the agency."

"So do I," Jackson said, "unless somebody has the guts to get them under control."

Noruyaki seemed to ignore that suggestion. Turning to Jake, he asked, "You think you can get your program funded from private sources? Without any tax money at all?"

"That's our aim," said Jake. "We've got to get Congress to agree to backing the long-term loans, of course."

Cocking his head slightly to one side, Noruyaki murmured, "It's an ingenious plan. But will it work?"

Jake answered, "Not if your bean counters want to turn it into another NASA operation."

"Hmm."

"Look," Jake went on, "we want NASA on the team. We need your expertise, your experience. But we need you as a partner, not a boss."

"And Sebastian's subcommittee meets tomorrow morning," Noruyaki muttered.

Jackson said, "May I remind you that the Mariners were oh-

and-two against the Yankees in the playoffs last year, and they still beat New York?"

Noruyaki broke into a huge grin. "And went on to win the World Series."

Smiling back at the younger man, Jackson said, "What was the motto of the old Seabees, back in World War II? 'The impossible we do right away; the miraculous takes a little time.'"

Jake said, "The subcommittee hearing starts at ten a.m. tomorrow."

"Just enough time to do the impossible," said Jackson.

Still grinning, Noruyaki said, "Let me make a couple of phone calls."

A couple of phone calls aren't going to do us much good," Jake grumbled as he and Jackson left Noruyaki's office.

"Not much time left to pull a rabbit out of a hat," Jackson agreed.

The corridors were empty and silent. As far as Jake could tell, Noruyaki and the two of them were the only people in the building.

Plus the security guard in the lobby, who had his phone to his ear as Jake and Jackson stepped out of the elevator.

"Here they are now," said the guard. Still clutching the phone, he asked, "Which one of you is Dr. Ross?"

"That's me."

Wordlessly, the guard handed the phone to Jake.

"Dr. Ross?" Noruyaki's voice.

"Yes."

"Are you free for lunch this afternoon? William Farthington would like to talk with you. And Mr. Jackson, of course."

"Farthington? The head of NASA?"

"Yes."

"When and where?"

. . .

Where was Farthington's home in Alexandria. When was noon.

As Jake followed his GPS's calm female voice over the

Arlington Memorial Bridge into Virginia, Jackson said lightly, "High noon. Hope this isn't going to be a shoot-out."

"From the little I know about Farthington," Jake said, "he's a career bureaucrat, a born paper pusher."

Jackson nodded. "Yes. There were a lot of very disgruntled people in the agency when the president nominated him to head up NASA. But he sailed through the congressional confirmation hearing like a breeze."

"They say he's a caretaker, not a space advocate."

Jackson's tone turned darker. "Everybody thinks he's there to preside over NASA's shrinkage."

Jake mulled that over as he drove slowly along a tree-lined street in an upscale residential neighborhood. Shrinkage, he thought. Maybe Farthington could see the space plan as an advantage to him.

Then Jackson added, "But he's a wily old coot. After you shake hands with him, count your fingers."

• • •

William Farthington reminded Jake of a caricature of a high school math teacher: short, a little paunchy, with gunmetal blue-gray eyes and a deceptive smile. Almost entirely bald, he had the straight-backed, square-shouldered posture of a soldier—which he had been most of his life, according to the Web sources Jake had tapped on their way to this noontime meeting. Farthington had been a major general in the United States Army Quartermaster Corps, a logistics genius, not a battlefield leader.

NASA's chief administrator met them at the door to his substantial redbrick home wearing a shapeless sky-blue bathrobe over swimming trunks. He smiled politely as he shook hands with Jake, then turned to Jackson.

"Hello, Rollie," he said, his grin widening. "How's the museum business?"

Jackson grinned back at him. "I'm just trying to avoid being turned into an exhibit myself."

Leading them into the handsomely furnished house, Farthington said, "I thought we'd have lunch by the pool, out back."

"It's a nice sunny day," Jackson agreed.

As they stepped out into the sunshine by the kidney-shaped swimming pool, Farthington said to Jake, "Hank Noruyaki tells me you've got a problem with the agency?"

"Yessir," Jake replied.

"Welcome to the club," Farthington said, morosely.

They sat on beach chairs under gaudily striped umbrellas while a dark-skinned butler in tan slacks and a short-sleeved white shirt brought them a tray of beers, ice cold.

Jake briefly outlined his space plan, and the NASA bureaucracy's move to co-opt it.

"Senator Tomlinson, eh?" Farthington murmured. "Bright young fellow. He'll go far."

"Not if NASA scuttles his space plan."

"Well, you *are* stepping on the agency's toes, you know. You've got some of the old-timers scared shitless."

Jake nearly choked on his mouthful of beer. Jackson seemed to be suppressing a guffaw.

Completely serious, though, Farthington said, "Listen, I know what they think of me up on the Hill. And in the White House, too. Harmless old Farthington. Retired Army fart. Bloviating Billy, the old windbag: just the man to preside over NASA's downsizing."

"Bloviating?" Jake asked.

Farthington explained, "Bloviate. According to *Webster's* it means to speak or write verbosely, windily."

"Oh."

With a bitter smile, Jackson said, "Maybe they think you can join me over at the museum."

"Like hell I will. They think NASA's an expensive toy for

the scientists and a handful of retired astronauts. They're waiting for the ISS to fall apart; then they'll close up shop."

Jake stared at him. "Is it that bad?"

"It's worse," said Farthington. "Our enlightened Congress has imposed a hiring freeze on NASA. People—good, smart people—reach retirement age and they're out the door, with no replacement. Our talent pool is evaporating."

"But the science work," Jackson objected. "NASA's sent probes out to Pluto, for god's sake. Europa, the Mars rovers. NASA's led the greatest wave of exploration since Columbus and Magellan."

"Unmanned missions. Robots, not people. They don't generate public support. The taxpayers want to see astronauts—what did that old TV show say? 'To boldly go where no one has gone before.'"

"Manned Mars missions," said Jackson.

"Which the White House won't ask for and Congress wouldn't appropriate the money for even if she did."

"Back to the Moon," said Jake. "And this time we stay. This time we build bases and open the frontier to private industry."

"Congress won't vote funds for that, either," said Farthington.

"They won't have to," Jake said. "We'll fund it privately."

"With the government backing the loans," Farthington added.

Jake realized that the NASA administrator was fully aware of his program.

Jackson pointed out, "In the meantime, your contracts people are trying to take over any efforts to send Space Tours or other private firms to the Moon."

Farthington nodded unhappily. "Sometimes those bean counters go off on their own. They figure the agency's upper management shouldn't get in their way."

Jackson let a small smile creep across his lips. "NASA's never been a single, unified organization. It's a collection of fiefdoms, each guarding its own territory."

"Tell me about it," Farthington replied. "Sometimes I feel like King John facing his barons as they wave the Magna Carta in his face."

Unhappily, Jake asked, "So what can we do about it?"

Farthington focused his gunmetal eyes on Jake. "I've been asked to appear at Senator Sebastian's hearing tomorrow morning."

"And?" Jackson prompted.

"I imagine that Sebastian and his friends expect me to blow some hot air about how NASA has led the nation's space program since 1958 and should continue to do so."

Jake held his breath.

"Bloviating Billy," Farthington said, with some bitterness. "Sometimes they pronounce my name without the *h*."

Jake glanced at Jackson, who was leaning toward the NASA administrator, eager to hear his next words.

"You realize I'll be stepping into a minefield here," Farthington said. "My own people expect me to say that NASA should be in charge of any program to return to the Moon. Hell, half of them will want me to say that we should forget about the Moon and aim for Mars." With a bitter little smile, "A Mars effort will keep most of 'em employed until they reach retirement age."

"So what are you going to say?" Jake prodded.

Farthington's smile brightened. "I'm going to bloviate, just as they expect. But my hot air will blow your way, Dr. Ross. Underneath my torrent of words, I'll say that NASA is ready and willing to support your plan for returning to the Moon. But it'll take 'em a week or more to figure out that that's what I've said."

Jackson broke into a laugh. "Don't make any enemies," he said.

"Don't let them know you're their enemy," Farthington countered, "until it's too late for them to do anything about it."

Subcommittee Hearing

Jake felt nervous. The subcommittee's hearing room was hardly half-filled and the bank of seats up front for the senators themselves was still empty, five minutes before the hearing was scheduled to begin. Not even Senator Sebastian had shown up yet. And Frank Tomlinson was nowhere in sight.

He's got to be here, Jake told himself. He's the main witness. Turning to survey the rococo-decorated chamber, Jake saw Rollie Jackson sitting a couple of rows behind him. With William Farthington at his side. Isaiah Knowles was striding down the central aisle; he smiled tightly at Jake as he slid into a pew a few rows back.

Oh god, Jake thought as he recognized Derek Vermeer entering the chamber. Mr. Mars. Perfectly dressed in a dark three-piece suit with his MARS NOW lapel pin.

The chamber itself was smallish, with a double bank of seats in the front of the room for the subcommittee members, an open space before them with a desk where witnesses would testify, and benches for the audience. Long windows along one wall, with a table for news media reporters and photographers nearly empty. One TV camera, from C-Span, with a pair of operators standing idly beside it.

Tami came in through the doors from the corridor outside and hurried to the news media table. She smiled at Jake as she took a chair there.

At two minutes before ten, Senator Sebastian came through

the door behind the double row of senators' seats and took his place front and center, followed by several aides and other subcommittee members and their aides. Jake thought they all looked bored: none of them was talking with any of the others.

They've probably hashed out their strategy for this hearing. Now they're going through the motions of listening to the witnesses.

Senator Tomlinson slipped onto the bench beside Jake precisely at ten o'clock.

"Good morning, Jake," said the senator, with a bright grin.

Jake had to swallow twice before he could squeak out, "Morning."

Sebastian was wearing a white summer-weight suit that looked to Jake a trifle large on him, as if he had lost several pounds after he'd bought it. He put on a smile and tapped the desktop with his knuckles.

"This hearing will come to order."

The few murmured conversations in the chamber went silent. Sebastian nodded. "We are here to examine a proposal for the future of this nation's efforts in space," he said, "a proposal sponsored by our esteemed colleague, Senator B. Franklin Tomlinson, of Montana. Senator Tomlinson, please take the witness chair."

Tomlinson got up and strode to the witness desk, his hands empty, no notes at all. Hope he remembers it all, Jake thought. A lone news photographer scurried from the reporters' table to snap his picture.

As he sat at the desk, Tomlinson said, "I want to thank you, Senator Sebastian, and all the members of the subcommittee, for extending me the courtesy of listening to what I consider to be a bold, innovative plan for developing the resources of space for the benefit of the people of America and the entire Earth."

And for the next half hour Jake listened as Tomlinson ran

flawlessly through the space plan. The senators had already read the preliminary plan that Jake had sent them, or at least their aides had. Now they were free to ask questions, make suggestions.

It wasn't until Tomlinson was almost finished with his presentation that the senator from New Jersey, a thin, waspish-looking woman with shoulder-length ash-blonde hair, raised her hand.

"Senator Ianetta?" Sebastian asked. "You have a question?"

"Yes," she replied in a low, smoky voice. Turning to Tomlinson, she asked, "Senator, do you expect the United States government to take all the risk of this very expensive program?"

Tomlinson smiled his warmest at her. "I expect the federal government to guarantee the loans that will finance the program, yes. The loans themselves will be raised in the private financial market. Not a penny of taxpayer money will be involved."

"But if the program fails, if it collapses, the US Treasury will have to pay back the investors."

Still smiling, Tomlinson replied, "The program will not fail."

"How can you be certain of that?"

"Because I have faith in the capabilities of our private space industry. Several companies are already operating in space. All they need is the capital backing to open up the space frontier and return us to the Moon."

"With loans that the federal government guarantees."

"Exactly," said Tomlinson. "It's been done before, and it's worked. What was the Homestead Act, if not a federal guarantee to the people who settled the western frontier? We're not asking for a handout, we're offering a new frontier that can create whole new industries and produce millions of new jobs."

"On the Moon?"

"Right here on Earth, mostly. Right in your own state of New Jersey."

Ianetta pressed, "But you expect to send people to work on the Moon."

"Indeed I do," Tomlinson replied. "I expect us to return to the Moon, and this time we'll stay. This time we'll start developing our new frontier."

Dead silence in the hearing room. Jake wanted to applaud, but he froze in place.

"Thank you, Senator Tomlinson," said Sebastian. "Now we'll hear from Colonel Isaiah Knowles, of the Space Futures Foundation."

And so it went, through the long morning, one witness after another giving his opinion on the space plan. Knowles in favor, Vermeer complaining it would interfere with his hopes for reaching Mars. Not one woman among the witnesses, Jake realized. Maybe we should have recruited a female astronaut.

Then Sebastian called out, "Our final witness this morning is General William T. Farthington, chief administrator of the National Air and Space Agency—NASA."

Wearing a light gray jacket and darker slacks, Farthington walked leisurely to the witness desk and sat down. He smiled pleasantly at the senators arrayed before him.

"Senator Sebastian, it's a distinct pleasure to appear before your distinguished subcommittee. This plan proposed by Senator Tomlinson is of vital interest to NASA. It involves nothing less than the future direction of our efforts in space."

For more than a quarter of an hour Farthington spoke glowingly of NASA's existing programs, and of the agency's hopes and plans for the future. Jake thought it was like reading a slick, colorful real estate salesman's brochure. The senators seemed to be nodding off as Bloviating Billy droned on.

At last Farthington summarized, "In short, gentlemen—and lady"—nodding at Ianetta—"NASA has the tools and the trained experts to help implement programs that can return us to the Moon, or reach farther and put human explorers on Mars. NASA stands ready to help open the space frontier."

A few people sitting behind Jake actually broke into applause. Did Farthington bring his own flunkies to the meeting? Jake wondered.

Senator Sebastian smiled beatifically down on the NASA administrator and said, "Thank you, General Farthington. Are there any questions from my distinguished colleagues?"

Jake thought that the panel of senators sitting before him looked more dazed by Farthington's rambling testimony than anything else. The man didn't say anything, really; he just summarized what the agency had been doing for the past few years and mentioned plans—hopes, really—for future operations. More robotic missions to Mars and Jupit'r's moons; continued flights to and from the International Space Station; he even mentioned aerodynamics research that NASA was conducting for new hypersonic airliners.

"I'd like to ask General Farthington," said the senator from Texas, who looked more like an investment broker than a cowboy, "specifically what he thinks of Senator Tomlinson's plan to return to the Moon."

With a genial smile, Farthington replied, "Technically, it appears to be feasible. We'll have to study it in more detail, of course."

"Of course," said the Texan, frowning slightly. "And this idea of having the federal government guarantee private loans to finance the program?"

Farthington hesitated. Then, "Senator, my background is in logistics, not high finance. It will be up to you to decide if that's a viable way of funding Senator Tomlinson's proposed program."

"How risky do you think the program is?"

"Technologically? I think it can be doable, but of course

we'll need to study the fine details." Smiling again, Farthington added, "The devil is in the details, as you know."

Senator Ianetta interrupted with, "Would you fly to the Moon on a private spacecraft, sir?"

Farthington's moon-shaped face contracted into a thoughtful frown. At last he replied, "I suppose that, sooner or later, private spacecraft will be the major means of reaching the Moon."

"But what about Mars?" asked the Texan, throwing a glare in Ianetta's direction.

"NASA has devoted considerable resources to studying human missions to Mars. As you know, we have developed the Orion spacecraft and the SLS booster that can carry a team of five astronauts to the Red Planet."

Sebastian seized the floor. "But the program under discussion today doesn't include any missions to Mars."

"Not at present," Farthington answered. "But when the time is right, I'm sure that we'll be able to reach Mars."

"And when will the time be right?" the Texan asked.

"When the White House and Congress decide it is," Farthington replied. "NASA stands ready. To paraphrase Winston Churchill's famous words, give us the go-ahead and we will finish the job."

Oh great, Jake thought. I can see the headlines: NASA ready to go to Mars.

. . .

Jake rode back to the Hart building with Tomlinson in the senator's limousine.

"It could have been worse," Tomlinson said, his face grim. "Farthington could have shot us down."

"Maybe he did," Jake said gloomily. "On to Mars," he muttered.

"He didn't quite say that," the senator countered.

But, as Jake feared, Mars was the headline of the blogs, the afternoon newspapers, the TV news shows that evening. The space plan was hardly mentioned. That evening Derek Vermeer was interviewed by CNN:

"Mars is the logical objective of our space efforts," he said, looking straight into the camera, stern and knowledgeable with his goatee and MARS NOW button.

Sitting at his kitchen table with Tami, Jake felt like throwing up.

Tami hiked her eyebrows and pointed out, "It's not over, Jake. The subcommittee will study your plan and make its report in a few weeks."

"They don't like the idea of having the government guarantee the loans," Jake muttered. "That's the stumbling block."

"Then you should be pushing the idea," said Tami. "Get some media coverage for it. After all, getting back to the Moon without taking a penny out of the taxpayers' pockets is newsworthy."

"Maybe."

"Of course it is! Have Frank do a speech about it. Get some of the Wall Street reporters involved."

Jake mused, "Going back to the Moon on private funding. That's what the plan is all about."

The microwave pinged. Tami got up from the table and pulled out Jake's chicken parmigiana. She placed it on the table in front of him, then slid her own beef teriyaki dinner into the microwave oven.

Jake picked up his fork and pushed the food around his plate.

"Don't wait for me," Tami urged. "It'll get cold."

But Jake replied, "Rollie Jackson told me I shouldn't make enemies. Make alliances with those who oppose you."

"Good advice," said Tami. "If you can do it."

Jake looked into her dark eyes. "Suppose we set up part of our base on the Moon as a training center for Mars explorers."

Tami blinked at him. "Oh?"

"Learn how to work and survive on Mars by training on the Moon. Low gravity, airless, high radiation environment. Test the equipment and techniques you'll need on Mars."

"Couldn't you do that on the space station?"

Jake shook his head. "The ISS is too confined. And it's in zero-gee. The Moon's surface is better."

The microwave pinged again. They both ignored it.

"Use the Moon to train Mars explorers," Tami mused.

"To study and perfect the tools and techniques they'll need on Mars," said Jake.

"Make the Mars people your allies, instead of your enemies!"

"It could work," Jake said, brightening. "It just might work!"

His smartphone broke into "Stars and Stripes Forever."

Jake fumbled the phone out of his pants pocket. "Hello."

"Jake, it's Harry Quinton."

Uh-oh, Jake thought, his momentary excitement vanishing like a popped balloon. More trouble.

Before he could ask, Quinton said, "Just got a call from my Washington rep. He says his pigeon in NASA's contracts department told him to forget about their previous call to tack on Moon missions to our existing contract. Says they got the word straight from the head honcho, Farthington himself. Leave our existing contract alone."

"They're not going to try to muscle in on lunar missions?" Jake asked, incredulous.

"Apparently not. Nice going, pal."

Shakily, Jake replied, "Glad to hear it, Harry. Glad to hear it."

"On to the Moon, baby!" Quinton's voice brimmed with enthusiasm.

"On to the Moon," Jake repeated. Then he added, "What do you think about putting a training facility on the Moon?"

"Training facility? Training for what?"

"For manned Mars missions. Test out the equipment and

procedures they'll need in the Moon's low-gee, high-radiation environment."

For several moments Quinton did not reply. At last he said, "You ought to talk with Nick Piazza about that. He's more interested in going to Mars than I am."

"He is?"

"Yep. Nick's a real daredevil underneath that cool exterior of his."

Jake thanked Quinton and made a mental note to contact Piazza in the morning.

Campaign Headquarters

The place looked like an abandoned supermarket. Which is exactly what it was.

"Welcome to the Tomlinson campaign headquarters," said Patrick Lovett, spreading his arms wide. Instead of his usual carefully tailored suit, the campaign manager was in baggy jeans and a T-shirt that proclaimed PEWAUKEE LAKE, PLAYGROUND OF WISCONSIN. Jake saw a claw hammer hanging from his belt.

The interior space was cavernous. The former supermarket had been totally gutted, nothing but a few desks huddled in one corner. The ceiling was lined with bright fluorescent lamps, the floor cleared of display cases, although Jake saw electrical outlets lining the walls and what looked suspiciously like a wilted cabbage leaf flattened in a corner.

As he ushered Jake and Tami into the empty, echoing space, Lovett said, "In a week you won't recognize this place; it'll look like the command center of a national political campaign." Pointing here and there, he went on, "Desks, computers, communications consoles—the works."

"In a week?" Tami asked.

Waggling a hand in the air, Lovett amended, "Ten days, at the most. And it's only a ten-minute taxi ride from the Hill!"

Jake asked, "How much is this going to cost us?"

"Donated," Lovett replied, with a satisfied grin. "The head of the supermarket chain is one of our supporters."

"Shipping green vegetables to the Moon?" Tami asked, with a giggle.

"Could be," said Lovett. "Could be."

. . .

True to his word, Lovett transformed the onetime supermarket into a working campaign headquarters: desks, computers, communications consoles, volunteers busily chattering into phones, aides scurrying along the long rows of buzzing workstations. And looming above them all, a gigantic poster of the candidate himself, striding energetically, smiling, youthful, confident.

The first Republican Party debate was coming up in less than three weeks. Tomlinson would share the platform with Senator Sebastian, Governor Davis H. Hackman of Tennessee, Senator Edwin G. Morgan of California, and a grassroots candidate from Minnesota, a dentist who had polled surprisingly large numbers with a campaign based on ultraconservative values.

Lovett was determined to get Senator Tomlinson prepared for every contingency. "You can't simply talk about the space plan," he told the senator. "You don't want to be seen as a Johnny-One-Note."

"Or Captain Moonbeam," Kevin O'Donnell added.

Jake was sitting with the three of them in Tomlinson's private office in the campaign headquarters. Unlike most of the "private" spaces in the building, Tomlinson's office had walls that actually extended all the way up to the ceiling. And Lovett had the room swept for electronic bugs several times each week.

The senator was in his shirtsleeves, leaning back in his desk chair. Lovett and O'Donnell had both peeled off their suit jackets. Jake was still wearing his sports coat, sweating in the room's feeble air-conditioning.

"It's the financial aspect that's going to attract the greatest criticism," Tomlinson said. "We need a lot of support there."

"True enough," said Lovett, nodding. Turning to Jake, he asked, "What have you got on that, Jake?"

"Not a helluva lot," Jake admitted. "Haven't been able to find a major Wall Street type who's willing to stick his neck out at this stage of the game."

Waving a hand in the air, Lovett said, "We don't want a Wall Street man. We need somebody from the Senate. A senior figure, a respected senator who's willing to say that the federal government should back these loans."

O'Donnell asked, "You mean somebody like Zucco?"

"The chairman of the Senate finance committee?" Tomlinson asked, clearly incredulous.

"He's from New Mexico, isn't he?" Lovett asked. "You'll be launching a lot of rockets from New Mexico."

O'Donnell said, "Or from Texas, if he won't play ball with us."

Jake objected, "Maybe he doesn't agree with our plan. Maybe he really thinks Washington shouldn't guarantee the loans."

Lovett answered, "It doesn't matter what he thinks. What matters is, does he want his state to benefit from the program?"

"He's known as a man of principles," O'Donnell pointed out. "Solid reputation."

Lovett shrugged. "Can't hurt to talk to him." Jabbing a finger at Tomlinson, he asked, "You willing to buttonhole him?"

The senator's usual smile was nowhere in sight. "I can give it a try."

"Try hard, Frank," Lovett said. "It's important. If the highly respected chairman of the finance committee says he's in favor of backing the loans, it could be the difference between getting the plan approved or seeing it all go down the toilet."

"I'll try," Tomlinson repeated.

. . .

There was a second Tomlinson campaign headquarters in Montana, of course. Not as large or as busy as the nerve center in

Washington, still Tomlinson made trips there nearly weekly, usually with his wife.

Outwardly, Amy made an ideal candidate's wife. Pretty, pert, her cheerleader's smile and bright personality charmed almost everyone she met. She traveled with her husband almost everywhere he went. Almost. Only rarely did she stay home while the senator went on the road.

It was a week before the first debate was scheduled. Senator Tomlinson was in New Mexico, ostensibly to tour the rocket launching facility at White Sands: Spaceport America. His host for this visit was Harold Quinton, head of Space Tours, Inc. Accompanying Senator Tomlinson was Senator Oscar Zucco (R-NM), chairman of the Senate finance committee.

Jake sat alone in his condo, watching Tomlinson on the local evening TV news. Senator Zucco was at Tomlinson's side. Both men were smiling for the cameras: Tomlinson tall, handsome, vigorous; Zucco a smallish wisp of a man, white-haired, frail-looking.

Answering a reporter's question, Tomlinson smiled as he said, "We're hoping to make Spaceport America here a key part of our new space program." Nodding toward Quinton, standing on his other side, the senator went on, "We'd like to see rockets from this private launch facility taking Americans back to the Moon."

Jake knew that Tami was among Tomlinson's entourage. And he heard the results of her work when the sleek-looking female reporter asked, "And you plan to do this without spending a penny of taxpayer money?"

Tomlinson's smile turned boyish. "I think Senator Zucco can answer that better than I can."

Zucco took half a step forward, enough to upstage Tomlinson ever so slightly. "It should be possible to finance this new space effort entirely from private sources—with backing from the federal government."

Suddenly Jake's TV screen showed the local news anchor pair. "And now here's Peter Panetta with tomorrow's weather forecast."

"Shit!" Jake snapped, and reached for the remote. He tried several more channels but none of them were showing Tomlinson.

Glancing at the wall clock, he punched the speed dial for Lovett's private number. Busy.

As he tried to decide whether or not to phone Tami, the phone on the end table jingled.

He reached over and picked it up. "Hello."

"Jake, are you busy?" Amy's voice. "Can you come over to the house?"

Amy sounded different: tense, strained. Before he could reply to her, she added, "Please, Jake. I need your help."

Help

Despite warning bells ringing in his head, Jake drove to the Tomlinson home and parked his convertible well up on the driveway, behind the screening azalea bushes.

To his relief, the butler opened the front door.

"You are expected, Dr. Ross," he murmured, then turned and led Jake down the hall to the library.

Amy was standing in the far corner of the book-lined room, by the wheeled cart that held a small forest of bottles, wearing a soft blue sweater over a white pleated skirt. Cheerleader's outfit, Jake thought. She clutched a stemmed martini glass in one hand. As soon as the butler closed the door she rushed across the carpeting to Jake.

"Jake, I'm in trouble."

"What? What's wrong?"

She made a tight little smile. "I had dinner with the wrong man."

Jake felt his face pull itself into a puzzled frown.

Almost automatically, Amy asked, "What are you drinking? Scotch?"

"Club soda," said Jake, thinking, Keep your head clear.

Amy went back to the improvised bar. "I know Frank keeps club soda here someplace."

Stepping up beside her, Jake said, "Never mind. What's the problem?"

She turned to face him, her usually sparkling blue eyes downcast, her golden hair tumbling to her shoulders.

She raised her eyes squarely to meet Jake's. "Last week, when Frank went to Helena, I invited a friend over here to dinner."

Oh, Christ, Jake moaned inwardly. "A friend?"

"An acquaintance. I'd met him a couple of months ago at one of Lady Cecilia's parties."

"Who is he?"

"Herb Manstein. He's a public relations guy for some major corporation. Nice guy, I thought."

"I don't know him," said Jake.

"Well, anyway, we had dinner here—"

"Butler's night off?"

Amy winced visibly. "Yes, Ian had the night off. Like when I asked you over for dinner."

Jake said nothing.

"I was lonesome," Amy said, almost whimpering. "I invited Herb over, we had a quiet dinner together, and then he went home."

"That's all that happened?"

"That's all." Amy stood before Jake like a witness trying to face down an accusing district attorney. Then her bravado seemed to crumble. "He phoned me this evening and said he was going to tell Lady Cecilia about it."

Jake felt the breath gush out of him. "Cecilia? So she can splash it all over her *Power Talk* blog?"

"Nothing happened!" Amy insisted. "We had a nice dinner and he went home. Period. End of story."

Jake walked across the library and sank down onto the big sofa beneath the portrait in oils of a Tomlinson ancestor.

"It's not the end of the story, Amy. You know that."

"But nothing happened!" she repeated, still standing by the bar. "Nothing!"

"Doesn't matter," said Jake. "Cecilia puts the story on her blog and in a flash it'll look like you're screwing this guy while Frank's off in Montana. Great."

Crossing to the sofa and sitting beside Jake, Amy pleaded, "Can you stop him? Get a lawyer to put an injunction on him or something?"

Jake shook his head. "All he has to do is tell what actually happened. You invited him into your home while your husband was out of town. People will draw their own inferences."

"But I didn't do anything!" Amy insisted, sounding desperate.

Jake grabbed her wrists. "Listen to me. It doesn't matter. People love scandals, and they don't have to strain their imaginations to turn your dinner into a sexual liaison."

"Oh, god!" Amy broke into tears.

"This could ruin Frank's chances, destroy him completely."

Amy leaned her head on his shoulder, sobbing uncontrollably. Jake slid his arm around her.

"How could I have been so stupid?" she choked out.

"You weren't stupid," Jake said gently. "You were innocent. Naïve. You thought this Manstein, whoever he is, was a decent guy."

"What are we going to do?"

Jake flinched inwardly at the "we," but he lifted Amy's tear-streaked face with a hand under her chin and said, "I presume Frank doesn't know anything about this."

"Nothing. He's in New Mexico today, giving speeches and all."

Jake thought, Tami's out there with him. To Amy he said, "Let me talk to Cecilia. She can be pretty decent when she wants to be."

"You think so?" Amy asked, in a little-girl voice.

Nodding, Jake answered, "I'll try."

Lady Cecilia

Jake pulled his phone from his pocket and punched Lady Cecilia's number. She answered on the third ring.

"Jake." Her voice sounded amused. "How nice to hear from you."

Trying not to sound anxious, Jake asked, "Cecilia, how are you?"

"I'm fine. And you?"

"Plenty busy with Frank's campaign."

"Yes, I can imagine."

With a glance at Amy's tear-streaked face, he asked, "Do you have a few minutes free? There's something I'd like to talk with you about."

Archly, Cecilia replied, "Jake, darling, isn't that ending a sentence with a preposition?"

He forced a laugh. "I suppose it is."

"Can you come over now? I'm not doing anything special."

"Now?" Don't appear too eager, Jake told himself. "Yes, I'm not doing much of anything tonight, either."

"Good. Come right over." And she hung up.

As he clicked his phone off, Jake said to Amy, "She sounds as if she was expecting me to call."

Biting her lip, Amy nodded wordlessly.

Jake got up from the sofa. "I'd better get over to Cecilia's place."

Amy remained seated on the sofa. "Jake . . . please. Do whatever you need to do. But get her to drop the story."

"I'll try my best."

. . .

It started to rain as Jake drove through the night and the wet streets, squinting through his flapping windshield wipers. He wondered what he could say to Cecilia, how he could convince her to ignore what she undoubtedly considered a choice morsel of insider gossip.

He hadn't come up with any ideas as he drove up the driveway and parked in the back of Cecilia's house. A rear door opened, revealing a butler—or somebody—standing there, opening a big golf umbrella. Jake waited for him to sprint to his car, then got out and together they hurried into the house.

Cecilia was waiting for Jake in the small room she used as a studio to send out her blog, *Power Talk*. Short and curveless, she was wearing a hip-length pumpkin-orange tunic over a pair of charcoal slacks. To Jake she looked like a fireplug with legs.

Without preamble, she said, "This is about Amy Tomlinson, isn't it?"

Jake nodded. "Yes, it is."

Gesturing to the padded leather chairs in front of her desk, Cecilia glanced at the rain-spattered window and said, "Nasty weather out there. Do you want a drink?"

"Uh, no thanks."

Cecilia smiled, her thick lips peeling over her teeth. "Well, sit down and tell me her side of the story."

Jake perched tensely on the chair; Cecilia arranged herself on the identical chair next to it. Still smiling, she said, "Relax, Jake. This isn't the Spanish Inquisition, you know."

For lack of any better ideas, Jake came straight to the point. "What did Manstein tell you?"

Her brows rising slightly, Cecilia replied, "He said Amy invited him to her home for a quiet dinner for two. Nobody else there but the cook, who served the food. Her husband was in Montana and she said she was lonesome."

"And that's it."

Cecilia's smile turned sly. "Is it? Just the two of them in that big old house? Manstein's a handsome guy, you know. Amy's . . . well, she can be flirtatious."

"That's not true."

"Isn't it? She invited you over for dinner, didn't she?"

She knows about that! Jake tried to hide his surprise, but knew he didn't succeed.

"We're . . . old friends."

"Yes, I know. From back in Montana. You two had quite a thing going during Tomlinson's first campaign."

"For god's sake, that was six years ago. She married Frank."

"Uh-huh."

"Look, Cecilia, nothing happened between Amy and Manstein. Just dinner. That's all."

"How do you know that's all?"

"She told me."

"And you believe her?"

"She's never lied to me."

"Really?"

Jake started to answer, but held himself back. Cecilia was grinning at him, like a fat cat confronting a juicy canary.

Pulling in a deep breath, Jake said, "You know this could hurt Frank terribly. It could ruin his chances—"

"Oh, Jake. He's running a distant third in the polling. He's barely ahead of that dentist from Minnesota."

"It'll hurt his marriage, too."

Cecilia's grin widened. "You mean he doesn't know she invites men to dinner while he's away?"

"Cecilia, don't run it. Please."

She shook her head. "If I don't, Herb will simply go to some other outlet. Then where would *I* be?"

"Who is this guy, anyway?"

"Herb Manstein? He works for Rockledge Industries, in their advertising department. Kind of a dashing figure. Handsome, knows how to spend money."

Jake asked, "Married?"

"Divorced, I believe. Unattached, at any rate."

"I'll have to talk with him."

"That seems like a good idea," Cecilia said, still grinning.

"Look . . . can you sit on the story until I've had a chance to talk to Manstein?"

Cecilia's face went serious. For a long moment she said nothing. Then she reached to her desk and pulled the telephone receiver from its base.

"His number's on the speed list. Under Manstein."

Herbert Manstein

Manstein did not answer Jake's call, so Jake left a terse message for him. Then he left Lady Cecilia's home, splashing across the parking area to his convertible and driving homeward.

As he edged the car through the rain-spattered night he wondered if he should tell anyone in the office about this mess. O'Donnell? He's Frank's chief of staff; Kevin might know what would be best to do.

But then he thought, Frank doesn't know anything about this! If I tell Kevin I'll have to tell Frank, too. And I can't do that. I can't mention this to anyone in the office. Pat Lovett? No, not him either. Best not to say a word to anyone, at least until I've talked with Manstein.

Jake remembered Benjamin Franklin's dictum: Three people can keep a secret—if two of them are dead.

And he remembered Mr. Jacobi, Senator Santino's muscle guy from Rhode Island. Jacobi would take care of Manstein, all right. He damned near killed me. That's why he's in a federal penitentiary.

Jake almost laughed when he realized how desperate his thoughts were. Jacobi. The beast from the east.

His smartphone buzzed in his pocket. Tami, he told himself. Startled out of his thoughts, Jake put the incoming call on the car's Bluetooth receiver.

"Dr. Ross?" A man's voice, with just a trace of a European accent. "You called me?"

Jake's mind clicked. "Mr. Manstein."

"Yes."

"I'm Senator Tomlinson's science advisor. I'd like to meet with you, if I can."

A moment of hesitation. Then, "The senator's science advisor, you say."

"And a friend of his wife's."

Another hesitation, longer. Jake saw the fountain of Dupont Circle illuminated against the steady rain. Almost home.

"You want to meet with me?"

"Yes, the sooner the better."

"I agree. How about breakfast tomorrow?"

"That would be fine."

"Capitol Grill? That's near K Street and—"

"I know where it is," Jake said. "What time?"

"Oh, say nine thirty."

"Nine thirty, Capitol Grill. See you then."

"Very good."

Jake held back the instinct to thank Manstein. He heard a click and his dashboard panel flashed CALL TERMINATED. Feeling as if he needed to wash his hands, Jake swerved around a limousine and pulled across the avenue, onto his building's driveway.

. . .

The first thing Jake did upon entering his apartment was go to the bathroom. After washing up, he phoned Tami in New Mexico. Two-hour time difference, he thought as he heard her phone ring. She's probably having dinner.

"Jake!" Tami sang out cheerfully. "Did you get my message?"

"I just got in," he replied, dropping onto his desk chair. "Haven't checked the messages yet."

"Oh?"

"I got an emergency call from Amy."

"Oh?" Tami's voice changed register.

Jake spilled the whole story to his wife, hardly taking a breath between sentences. She listened in silence.

At last Tami said, "So you're meeting with this Manstein character?"

"Breakfast meeting. Tomorrow morning, nine thirty."

"Kind of late for breakfast."

"He picked the time and place."

Tami was silent for several heartbeats. Then she asked, "What are you going to say to him?"

"I'm going to tell him that it would be better for all concerned if he kept his damned mouth shut." And Jake felt surprised at the anger in his tone.

Patiently, Tami replied, "And what are you prepared to offer him to keep his damned mouth shut?"

"Offer him?"

"The man's after something. Money probably. You said that Cecilia told you he knows how to spend money, didn't she?"

"You mean he's trying to blackmail Amy?"

"Sounds that way to me," said Tami.

"I hadn't thought of that."

"Find out what he wants, Jake. Don't make any commitments, but find out what he's after."

．．．

Jake slept fitfully that night, his dreams vaguely menacing. He awoke at sunrise and was in his office at the Hart building just after seven a.m. When his executive assistant showed up about an hour later, he told her to cancel his morning appointments.

"I've got to attend a meeting, out of the office," he said.

She nodded, but pointed out, "The senator is due to land at Reagan at 10:10. He'll be coming directly to the office from the airport."

He'll be groggy from the red-eye flight, Jake thought.

His assistant wasn't finished. "Mr. O'Donnell has scheduled

a luncheon meeting in the senator's office. Himself, Mr. Lovett, a couple of campaign aides. And you."

"Luncheon meeting?" Jake asked.

"Twelve noon."

"I'll be back in time."

. . .

Capitol Grill was a long-standing favorite of the K Street crowd, where corporate reps and congressmen could hash out their problems and opportunities, their goals and obstacles, over the best hamburgers in town.

The place was half empty at nine thirty: just a few guys in their gray suits at the bar, and a half-dozen tables filled. Jake asked the maître d' for Mr. Manstein's table and got a blank look.

"There's no reservation for Mr. Manstein," said the slick-haired maître d'.

"Dr. Ross?"

Jake turned to see a man his own height, well built, handsome in a polished, continental way: pinstriped dark blue suit with a white flower in the lapel, no less. He was smiling, but it looked faintly condescending to Jake. Dark hair, combed straight back.

Almost hesitantly, Jake extended his hand. "Mr. Manstein."

"Herb."

"And I'm Jake."

"Very good." With a nod to the maître d' Manstein started confidently toward the tables. "There's no need for a reservation at this hour, Jake," he said. "Is there, Mickey?"

"Not usually," said the maître d', pushing to get ahead of Manstein.

Once they were seated in a booth at the rear of the restaurant and a waiter took their drink orders—cabernet sauvignon for Manstein, iced tea for Jake—Manstein asked, "To what do I owe this meeting, Jake?"

"Your conversation with Lady Cecilia." What else? Jake added silently.

"Oh. That."

Jake said, "That."

Manstein smiled across the table, but Jake thought it was cold, calculating. The man's handsome face looked as if it had been carved out of ice.

Waving one hand in the air, Manstein said, "I thought Cecilia might be interested in the dinner Amy and I had. A little social note for her blog."

"It puts Amy in an awkward position."

The waiter arrived with their drinks. Once he left Manstein said, "I suppose it does look a little . . . awkward, as you say. She invites me to her home while her husband's away and the servants are out."

"People might draw the wrong conclusion," Jake said.

Folding his hands prayerfully beneath his chin, Manstein replied, "My dear Dr. Ross, I have no control over what conclusions people might draw."

"Yes, you do."

"Do I?"

"You can call Cecilia and tell her not to run the story. Tell her you've changed your mind."

Again that cold smile. "But I haven't changed my mind."

"You should."

"Why?"

"The story will hurt Mrs. Tomlinson terribly. It will hurt her husband—"

"The senator from Montana," Manstein said. "The senator with the plan for a new space program. *Your* plan, actually, isn't it, Dr. Ross?"

He's done his homework, Jake realized. Aloud, he asked, "Do you think it's fair to have that plan destroyed by gossip and innuendo? To have the senator's career destroyed?"

This time Manstein raised both his hands, palms up. "What can I say? She invited me to dinner. I arrived on time to find her husband was out of town and all the servants, except for the cook, were not in the house. We had a pleasant dinner together."

"But if Cecilia puts that on her blog her audience will leap to the conclusion that you two went to bed afterward."

"As I said, I'm not responsible for what people imagine."

"But you are!" Jake countered.

"That's your opinion." Manstein pulled one of the menus from the clip in the middle of the table. "Do you want to order something to eat?"

"No."

"I thought not. Cecilia tells me you and Mrs. Tomlinson had quite an affair a few years ago."

"That was before she married the senator."

"And she invited you to a quiet little dinner a few weeks ago. Just the two of you."

Jake fought down the surge of fury that boiled up inside him. He stared at Manstein's smug, grinning face.

"All right," he said, almost snarling. "What do you want?"

Manstein sighed a great melodramatic sigh. "I would like," he said, "someday to retire to my ancestral home in Austria."

"Austria."

"Yes. Not far from the old von Trapp estate. You know, 'The hills are alive with the sound of music.'"

"I saw the movie."

"Yes. It's very expensive real estate. I could never afford it on my Rockledge salary."

His damned smug smile was rubbing Jake raw. Not trusting himself to hold his temper much longer, Jake started to slide out of the booth.

Manstein looked surprised. Alarmed. "You're leaving?"

"I don't think we have much more to talk about."

"But we haven't settled anything."

"I'll call you," Jake said. "As soon as I've had a chance to talk to Senator Tomlinson."

His expression hardening, Manstein said, "It will have to be today. I won't wait longer."

Jake nodded once, got up, and left the Capitol Grill.

As Jake entered the lobby of the Hart S.O.B. he saw B. Franklin Tomlinson heading for the marble stairs that led to the second floor, with half a dozen campaign aides around him.

"Frank," he called, shouldering through the people waiting for the elevator.

The senator turned, his eyes pouchy, his usual smile wilted. "Jake. Waiting for me?"

"Sort of. We've got to talk."

Tomlinson started up the stairs, Jake beside him.

"Yes. Amy phoned me when I got off the plane."

"Oh."

"She told me all about this Manstein character."

Jake glanced at the aides climbing the stairs with them, then said in a near whisper, "He wants money."

The senator shook his head. Keeping his voice low, too, he grumbled, "How could she be so stupid? I mean, inviting a single guy to the house. With all the servants out."

"Except the cook," Jake pointed out.

They pushed through the double doors of the senator's suite, into the outer office. The receptionist smiled out, "Welcome back, Senator."

Tomlinson flashed a quick smile at her and breezed past, with Jake right beside him, step for step. The campaign aides peeled away, heading for their own desks.

The senator's executive assistant was standing at the door

to his private office with a coffee mug in one hand. "Noon meeting is all set, Senator. Tuna salad, plus liverwurst and cheese sandwiches."

"Fine," Tomlinson said. "Hold all my calls, will you?"

"Senator Zucco wants to talk with you."

"Not now."

Tomlinson ducked into his inner office, Jake at his heels. As the senator pulled off his suit jacket and tossed it onto a chair, Jake stood tensely in front of the desk.

"Sit down, Jake," the senator said. He looked and sounded tired.

Jake plopped onto one of the padded chairs in front of the desk. "This could be real trouble, Frank."

"You talked with Cecilia?" Tomlinson asked.

"Yeah. She says if she doesn't run the story somebody else will."

Shaking his head, Tomlinson said, "Amy swears nothing happened. It was all very innocent."

"But it won't look that way once it's out in the blogosphere."

"This isn't the first time she's done this, is it? I know she invited you over a couple of weeks ago. At least you had the good sense to leave."

"She told you about that?"

"Yep. She was amused about it. Said you bolted like a scared rabbit."

Very funny, Jake thought. The two of them must have had a good laugh about me.

Then the senator muttered, "I wonder who else she's invited."

Oh god, Jake groaned inwardly. Are there more, waiting to be interviewed by the news media?

Trying to make a smile, Tomlinson said, "Well, from now on Amy travels with me wherever I go."

Locking the barn door after the horse has been stolen, Jake said to himself.

"What do you want to do?" he asked the senator.

"Do? I'd like to blow this fucker Manstein's brains out!"

"Something more practical," Jake said.

The intercom buzzed. "Mr. Lovett is here."

Tomlinson tapped the button and replied, "Get O'Donnell. Tell him to drop whatever he's doing and come in here. With Lovett."

He added, "Then call my wife and tell her I'm in the office, safe and sound. I'll call her in an hour or so."

. . .

Lovett and O'Donnell sat in stunned silence as the senator told them about Amy, Manstein, and Lady Cecilia.

"And that's it," Tomlinson concluded.

Looking uncomfortable, Lovett asked quietly, "All of it?"

"All of it."

O'Donnell, his lean face looking even more pinched and scowling than usual, asked, "You're sure that's all?"

"My wife says nothing happened. I believe her. That's all."

"It won't look that way once the news media gets hold of the story."

"There isn't any damned story!" Tomlinson snapped. "They had dinner together. Nothing more."

Looking at Jake, Lovett asked, "You met with this Manstein character?"

"A couple of hours ago."

"What's he want?"

Jake huffed. "He wants to retire to his native Austria and live like a movie star."

"We're not going to pay for *that*."

"We're not going to pay for anything," Tomlinson said through gritted teeth.

"Now wait—"

The senator waved his campaign manager to silence. "If we

give the son of a bitch anything—a penny or a million dollars—he'll come back for more. He'll have us by the balls."

"So what do we do?" Jake asked.

"We tell him what J. P. Morgan said: 'Publish and be damned.'"

"That was the Duke of Wellington," Lovett corrected. "Somebody tried to blackmail him."

"I'm in good company," the senator grumbled.

"Wait a minute," O'Donnell said. "Jake, you said this Manstein guy works for Rockledge Industries?"

"Yeah."

O'Donnell shifted his focus to the senator. "Rockledge does a good deal of aerospace work, don't they?"

Jake answered, "They're a major prime contractor."

Raising his fingers as he made his points, O'Donnell said, "One: Rockledge stands to gain if our space plan goes through, right?"

Nods of assent.

"Two: If Manstein's story gets out, Frank's campaign for the nomination goes down the drain."

"Very likely," Lovett replied, in an unhappy whisper.

"Three: If Frank's campaign goes down the drain, the space plan goes down with him."

Senator Tomlinson muttered, "Right."

O'Donnell continued, "Four: If somebody informs Rockledge about this, the corporation suits might tell Manstein to keep his big mouth shut."

The senator sat up straighter. "You think so?"

Smiling like a magician who had just pulled a rabbit out of a hat, O'Donnell said, "I know Rockledge's top Washington rep. We play golf together now and then."

"Do you think . . . ?" Tomlinson asked.

"Let me talk to him," O'Donnell said, pushing himself up

from his chair. "He's a reasonable guy. He'll put two and two together."

"Go talk to him," Tomlinson said, really smiling for the first time.

As O'Donnell hurried out of the office, Jake said, "It might work."

But Lovett shrugged his shoulders. "Even if it does, it's just a finger in the dike."

Tomlinson grinned at his campaign manager. "A finger in the dike is better than being ass-deep in a flood, Pat."

Job Opportunity

By the time Jake got home that evening he felt completely wiped out, physically and emotionally drained.

O'Donnell had talked with Rockledge's senior Washington representative and reported that Manstein would be told to stay quiet. Senator Tomlinson promised that from now on his wife would travel with him wherever he went.

"Even to the bathroom," he said, with some fervor.

Lovett insisted that the senator concentrate on preparing for the first debate, which would take place in two weeks.

"This will be your first real opportunity to let the voters see you on national TV, and hear what you've got to say, Frank," the campaign manager stressed. "First impressions are the most important."

Tomlinson nodded agreement, a little grimly, Jake thought.

Late that afternoon, as he was getting ready to leave the office, Jake received a call from Lady Cecilia.

"I ought to be very irate with you, Jake," she said. In his desktop phone's tiny screen, Cecilia looked as if she was trying to appear irked, but not quite making it.

"Me?" Jake replied, trying to sound innocent.

"Yes, you. You got Herb Manstein to back off on his story."

"Cecilia, I just had a brief meeting with him. We didn't come to any conclusions."

"Somebody got him to clam up."

"Maybe he got an attack of conscience."

Cecilia barked out a single, "Hah!"

Trying to think like a politician, Jake said, "Listen, Cecilia, suppose I get Frank to sit for an interview with you. Would that please you?"

Her expression turned crafty. "Before the debate or afterward?"

"Take your pick."

"Before the debate." Then she added, "And if he does well, another one, afterward."

Jake swallowed visibly, then replied, "I'll see what I can do."

So as he closed the front door of his condo Jake slumped tiredly and let out a long, sighing breath. Safe at home, he thought.

"Is that you, Jake?" Tami called from the bedroom.

"No," he hollered back. "It's the iceman."

She stepped into the sitting room, looking warm and lovely in a checkered red and black tunic over a black miniskirt. But puzzled.

"Iceman?" she asked.

"It's an old line, from back in the neighborhood where I grew up."

Tami nodded, satisfied. Then she asked, "You never did play the phone message I left for you last night, did you?"

Suddenly feeling embarrassed, Jake said, "No, I guess I didn't. What with this business with Amy and—"

Smiling, Tami came up to him and placed both her hands on his shoulders. "That's okay. Now I can tell you face-to-face."

"Tell me what?"

"I got a job offer! Anchoring the evening news on TV!"

"Really?" Jake felt a thrill of excitement for his wife. He knew that Tami was a newswoman at heart. "Anchoring the evening news? Which station?"

"KSEE-TV. It's one of—"

"KSEE?" Jake asked. "Where the hell is that?"

"Fresno!" Tami exclaimed. "My hometown!" Her smile was utterly happy.

"Fresno," Jake echoed. "In California."

"It's a very progressive station," Tami bubbled on excitedly. "Two of their anchors have gone on to national TV shows."

"But we live here in Washington."

"For now. I explained to the guy who recruited me that I couldn't go until after the elections. He's willing to wait until the Republican convention, next summer."

Going to the sofa and dropping wearily onto it, Jake said, "Tami, I can't go to California. For god's sake, by next November I might be science advisor to the president of the United States."

Her happy smile fell apart. Sitting down next to him, she said softly, "Oh Jake, you know Frank's not going to make it. He's way behind Sebastian and even Governor Hackman. Not to mention the Democrats."

"I can't walk out on him. I'd feel like a Judas."

Almost pleading, Tami said, "Jake, this is a wonderful opportunity for me."

"But not for me."

Tami stared at him for a long, silent moment. Jake could feel his pulse thumping in his ears.

"I was afraid of this," Tami said at last. "I knew there'd be a problem but I was too excited to think about it."

"I can't go to California," Jake repeated.

Then he saw the disappointment in her eyes, and realized he was crushing her hopes.

"Honey," he said, trying to explain, "a lot of Frank's campaign is tied up with the space plan. *My* plan, *my* ideas. I can't walk out on him."

Tami hesitated, then said, "I could go to Fresno after the Republican convention. If Frank gets the nomination you could stay with him until the election in November."

"And what if he wins?"

"He won't."

"He might. He could. I'm doing everything I can to help him win. You're on his payroll, too, you know."

"I'm just one of dozens of PR flunkies. His campaign doesn't depend on me."

"But it does depend on me," Jake said. "At least a little."

"A lot," Tami corrected.

Jake spread his hands in a gesture of futility. "So you can see why I can't go to California, can't you?"

Tami nodded, but said, "Can you see why I've got to go to Fresno?"

He nodded back at her, but said, "Honey, maybe, if Frank gets elected, you can get a position here in Washington."

"Jake, I can't turn down this offer. They don't grow on trees, you know. Anchor on the evening news! I can't turn it down."

"I know," he said. "I understand. But . . ."

"But this could break up our marriage, couldn't it?"

"No!" he snapped. "I won't let that happen."

But inside, Jake wondered what he could do to keep Tami with him.

Billy Trueblood

The next morning when Jake got to his office he saw that a message from Nicholas Piazza was waiting for him.

Too early to call California, he thought. But I can at least let him know I got his call.

To his surprise, instead of a machine's message, Piazza himself answered.

In Jake's office wall screen, Piazza was smiling widely, looking pleased with himself, wearing an Astra Corporation T-shirt. It must be just past five a.m. out there, Jake thought, taken aback that Piazza was awake, let alone at his desk.

"You're up early," Jake blurted.

Piazza's smile turned smug. "I'm always up early, Jake. That's how I stay ahead of the competition."

Somehow Jake felt subtly put down.

"Jake, Harry tells me you want to add a Mars training facility to the lunar base."

Hiding his surprise, Jake said, "It could swing Vermeer and the Mars lobby to support the space plan."

"Ah, you're thinking like a politician."

That *is* a put-down, Jake thought. But he ignored it and asked, "Do you think it's doable? Can we set up a facility without screwing up the rest of the lunar base?"

"You ought to come out here and talk with my tech guys about that."

"I don't have time for that, Nick. What with the debate coming up and everything—"

Piazza countered, "I'll send a plane out for you, fly you here and back the same day, just about. But you really ought to talk with my geeks face-to-face."

Jake closed his eyes briefly, then agreed reluctantly. "Okay. I'll make room. But will your technical staff have enough time to make a decent assessment of the problem?"

His grin widening to show lots of teeth, Piazza said, "Hell, Jake, I've had 'em working on this possibility for the past couple of months."

"You have?"

Breaking into a chuckle, Piazza revealed, "I saw this coming long before you did."

"I guess you did," Jake replied weakly.

· · ·

The very next day Jake was awakened at five thirty by a call from California.

"Sorry to call so early, Dr. Ross," said a sharply nasal woman's voice, "but Mr. Piazza wants you to know his personal jet will be landing at Reagan National at 8:19, your time."

Groggily, Jake muttered, "It's already on the way here?"

"Yes indeed," said the woman.

Jake hung up, blinking sleep from his eyes, then turned to explain what was happening to Tami, who was barely conscious. "Go back to sleep," he told her. "I'll phone you when I'm heading back home, probably late tonight." Or more likely early tomorrow morning, he added silently.

He took a taxi to the airport and got to the private plane terminal exactly ten minutes before Piazza's Cessna Citation touched down. The newly risen sun cast long shadows across the airport gateways. He watched through the terminal's freshly washed window as the twin-engined plane rolled to a stop outside. By the time Jake had made it down the stairs and out onto the rampway, he saw that Billy Trueblood was clambering down the plane's aluminum ladder, his dark plaited queue bouncing on his back.

"C'mon, Dr. Ross," Trueblood called urgently. "We don't want to miss our takeoff slot."

"Nick sent you out to get me?"

"He sure did. Told me to take good care of you."

With only his slim briefcase, Jake hustled up the ladder. Trueblood closed the hatch and the Citation surged forward.

Gesturing to the empty cabin, Trueblood said, "Take any seat you like."

The seats were all luxurious: wide and deeply cushioned. A private flight, just for me, Jake thought as he slid into the second one. He found that it pivoted almost a full three hundred and sixty degrees.

The pilot's voice sounded over the speakers built into the cabin's overhead. "Fasten seat belts for takeoff."

As Jake clicked his seat belt, Trueblood said, "I'll have some breakfast for you once we reach cruising altitude."

Jake said, "Wonderful. Thanks." Trueblood nodded wordlessly and headed toward the rear of the cabin.

Once they leveled off, Trueblood brought a tray of eggs, juice, and muffins. "Coffee's on the way," he said as he handed the tray to Jake.

"How about you?" Jake asked. "Aren't you having breakfast?"

With a shy smile, Trueblood answered, "Already had mine, before we landed."

The Native American started to head toward the rear of the cabin again, but Jake stopped him with, "Why don't you sit here beside me, Billy? Keep me company."

"Okay, if that's what you want."

As they winged westward, Jake asked, "How'd you meet Nick?"

"Oh, he was visiting the orphanage up by Shiprock, and he sort of adopted me."

"You're a Navajo?"

Shaking his head, "No, sir. Zuni."

Once he got Trueblood talking, the whole story came out. Piazza spent a lot of his time—and money—doing good, Billy explained. "Hardly anybody knows about it. He keeps it kind of secret. Billionaire helps little folks. Says if the news media ever got wind of it he'd be buried alive in people asking him for money."

"He adopted you, though."

"Sort of. I was eleven. Mr. Piazza took me into his home and put me to work. He wanted me to get an education and make something of myself, not grow up to be a welfare case. I've learned a lot from him. I can even fly this plane, just about!"

"You have a pilot's license?"

"I'm working on it."

"That's terrific."

"Mr. Piazza's been like a father to me." Then, his expression tightening, Trueblood added, "More than a father."

For the rest of the flight Trueblood talked about all that Piazza had done for him. But Jake thought he heard a note of dissatisfaction in the young man's words. Abandoned child becomes ward of charitable billionaire, Jake thought. What's he got to be dissatisfied about?

"This space thing you and Mr. Piazza are working on," Trueblood asked, "are you really going to set up a base on the Moon?"

"We sure are," Jake replied. "We're going to expand the space frontier: the Moon, the asteroids—the whole solar system. It's full of energy and natural resources that we can develop and use."

Strangely, Trueblood frowned at the thought. "Like you whites expanded through our lands."

Surprised, Jake put on a smile. "Hey, Billy, there's no natives out there. We're not going to war with anybody."

"Yeah, I know. But . . ." He lapsed into silence.

"But what?" Jake probed.

His dark face clearly troubled, Trueblood stammered, "Well . . . there's so much that needs to be done here on Earth . . . so many people need help . . . all the money you'll be spending on space isn't going to help the people who need it most."

"But it will!" Jake insisted. "We won't be spending the money on the Moon! We'll spend it right here on Earth. Developing space will mean more jobs here, Billy: new industries, new opportunities—"

"For the rich."

"For everybody!"

"Not for my people. Not for the ones who need the help the most."

Nick Piazza was at the Spaceport America airstrip to greet Jake when the swept-wing Cessna landed. Jake came down the ladder and shook hands absently with the billionaire, still troubled that Billy Trueblood couldn't see the grand vision for the space plan that he himself envisioned.

If we can't get Billy with us, Jake was wondering, what about the rest of the country? I don't want the plan to be seen as a rich-versus-poor confrontation.

Piazza apparently had no inkling of Trueblood's doubts. As soon as Jake set foot on the tarmac Piazza grabbed him by the arm and practically dragged him to a waiting baby-blue SUV.

"We've got a lot of ground to cover," Piazza said, bending his tall, lanky frame to squeeze into the SUV.

The rest of the day was a whirl of meetings and presentations by the half dozen "geek guys" that Piazza had assigned to making a first pass at designing a Mars training facility for the Moon.

Piazza introduced the seven-person team. Only one of them was a woman. The conference room they sat in was small and windowless, with a rectangular table facing a floor-to-ceiling wall screen. Piazza sat up front, Jake at the end, directly facing the screen.

"As you can see," said the team's leader, pointing to a schematic drawing of the proposed facility's layout, "we've kept the floor footage to an absolute minimum—"

Jake studied the proposed layout while Piazza leaned back in his chair, beaming like a proud paterfamilias.

"—but all the essentials are in place," the lead engineer continued. Pointing with a handheld laser, he explained, "Space suit testing center—"

"Pressure suit," one of the engineers corrected. "You shouldn't call it a space suit."

Glowering at the younger man, the team leader conceded, "All right, pressure suit." Moving the red spot of his laser pointer, he continued, "And here is the medical exam center, the long-duration testing facility . . ."

The presentations droned on until Jake felt he was drowning in technical details. But then he realized, These guys are proud of what they're doing. They're designing a facility that's going to be built on the Moon!

". . . and as for a vacuum chamber to test the suits and other equipment," the team leader said, with a big grin, "all we have to do is step outside. The vacuum at the Moon's surface is more than ten times better than the best vacuum chambers we can build on Earth. It's considerably lower than the vacuum of low Earth orbit."

Lunch was brought into the conference room while one engineer after another made their presentations. The lone woman in the group was a medical specialist; she explained the medical section of the facility.

Jake sneaked a glance at his wristwatch as the final presentation was winding up. Nearly four o'clock, Pacific time. Seven p.m. in Washington. Figuring five hours for the flight back to DC—

Piazza got to his feet, reminding Jake of a carpenter's ruler unfolding. "That's about it, Jake," he said, beaming happily. "What do you think?"

"Very impressive," said Jake.

"Think it'll impress Vermeer and his Mars gang?"

Jake made a smile. "Hell yes."

"We're halfway to Mars already!" Piazza crowed.

The engineers around the table grinned and nodded at their boss's approval.

. . .

Most of the flight back to Washington Jake spent discussing—arguing, politely—with Billy Trueblood the issue of space development versus welfare operations.

"It's the same old story," Trueblood complained. "The rich get richer and the poor get poorer."

Getting exasperated with the kid's stubbornness, Jake snapped, "Then get yourself rich."

"How? How's a Native American going to do it? You think they'd take me at Harvard? Or MIT?"

"Of course they would! With Nicholas Piazza recommending you, they'd be glad to—"

"I don't want to ride on Mr. Piazza's coattails," Trueblood objected. "I want to make it on my own."

Jake saw anger in the Zuni's dark eyes. And something else. Something very much like fear.

Softening his voice, Jake said, "Billy, you've done well in school, haven't you?"

An almost sullen nod.

"You're getting yourself a pilot's license. Nick didn't do that for you, you did it for yourself."

"I guess I did."

"You could get yourself into a first-rate college. MIT would be happy to take you."

"Yeah," Trueblood answered sullenly. "Big-time university accepts a Native American. They'll sell the story to all the news blogs."

In the end, all Jake could do was shake his head. Until he hit on, "Come on to Washington. You can work on Senator Tomlinson's staff. You can help me with the space plan."

Trueblood stared at Jake. "Don't you understand? I don't want to be window dressing! I don't want to be your token redskin! I want to be me, I want to do things that nobody else can do!"

Feeling defeated, Jake said, "Well, good luck, Billy. If you ever need help, just let me know."

"Yeah. Thanks."

By the time Jake got back to his condo he felt totally drained, his head stuffed with technical details by Piazza's engineers, his mind stymied by Billy Trueblood's adolescent angst.

Tami was waiting up for him. One look at Jake's weary face, though, and she said, "Pretty pooped, huh?"

Jake nodded. Then he remembered that his wife was going to California, whether he went with her or not.

The end of a perfect day, Jake thought.

How do I look?" Senator Tomlinson asked.

He was standing in a corner of the overcrowded dressing room, in front of a full-length mirror leaning against the concrete wall, dressed in a perfectly fitted light gray suit, a hairdresser and makeup woman fussing on either side of him.

"Like a movie star," said Amy, standing behind the senator on tiptoes to look at her husband's mirror image.

"Like the next president of the United States," Pat Lovett prompted.

They were in Chicago for the first Republican Party debate. Jake could see why it was called the city of the big shoulders. He sat wedged into a corner of the little room, which was jammed with campaign workers and several hangers-on, including at least two brazenly dressed women who looked like call girls to Jake.

The room seemed to vibrate with expectation. A big crowd was clumping into the auditorium outside, together with the cream of the nation's news media. In the other dressing rooms along the concrete passageway were Senators Sebastian and Morgan, plus Tennessee's Governor Hackman and the upstart dentist from Minnesota, Yeardley Norton.

A guy with an earphone clamped across his thickly curled blond hair popped his head through the dressing room's door and yelled, "Two minutes!"

Senator Tomlinson turned from the mirror, smiling brightly, and said, "It's showtime!"

Cool, Jake thought. Very cool. I just hope he remembers everything we've been drilling into him and doesn't freeze on camera.

Tami wasn't in the dressing room, but out in the special rows of seats reserved for the news media. For the past two weeks she and Jake had been behaving like shipwrecked survivors living on a desert island, hoping for rescue, staring disaster in the face.

The marriage is already breaking up, Jake thought. There's a wall between us now. We're just going through the motions. Yet despite his morose thoughts, he grinned inwardly at the memory of their lovemaking. The motions we're going through are pretty damned good. Hotter than ever, as if each time might be our last. Shipwrecked castaways, he told himself.

Pat Lovett opened the door to the corridor and crooked a finger at the senator. "Time to face the voters," he said to Tomlinson. The senator nodded, put on his brightest smile, and went through the open doorway with his campaign manager. The crowded room emptied quickly.

· · ·

Jake hurried to his seat between Lovett and O'Donnell as the five candidates strode onto the stage to thunderous applause from the standing-room-only audience. The auditorium felt hot, airless. Jake could sense his heart thumping beneath his ribs. How can Frank look so relaxed and smiling up there? he wondered. A lot of politics is show business.

Three national news media stars sat facing the five candidates, who stood on a raised platform, each of them behind a lectern. The auditorium was filled to the rafters with people who had come to see fireworks.

The order of their appearances had been settled by lot, with

Senator Sebastian first, Yeardley Norton second, and Tomlinson third, followed by Governor Hackman and finally Senator Morton.

Sebastian offered no fireworks. Instead he radiated calm, experienced competence: a smiling, knowledgeable grandfather in a dark blue suit.

"I'm glad you asked that, Phil," he said, in answer to the first question posed to him. "The biggest issue before us is the economy. The present administration has stumbled there quite badly, with inflation on the rise and real wages stagnating. We'll have to work very hard to bring prosperity back to the middle class, but we can do it and we *will* do it."

A wave of applause filled the auditorium.

Dr. Norton was a waspish, peppery little man: lean, sharp-featured, with a voice like a dentist's drill. Somehow he reminded Jake of Harry Truman.

"You want to get the economy moving again?" he challenged. "I'll tell you how to do it. Get rid of the dad-blasted tax code, all two thousand pages of it! Institute a flat tax: ten percent of your income. No deductions, no exceptions." He paused for a heartbeat, then fairly shouted, *"And shut down the Infernal Revenue Service!"*

The auditorium erupted with thunderous applause, whistles, cheers. A lot of Norton backers here, Jake realized. But this is the Midwest; mavericks always thrive here.

The third news media representative, a sleek, chic-looking woman with long blonde hair and a mid-thigh skirt, waited patiently until the tumult died down. Then she asked:

"Senator Tomlinson, what do you feel are the major issues of this campaign?"

Tomlinson smiled at her and replied, "I agree that getting the economy moving forward again is very important. In fact, it's central to everything we want to accomplish.

"The continuing war against terrorism is important, too.

Vital. We've got to back our troops fighting in Colombia and Venezuela with everything we've got. And we've got to improve our relations both with our key allies and with nations such as Russia and Iran that have opposed us in the Middle East."

"But you've been concentrating on your 'Back to the Moon' space program," the blonde said, almost accusingly. "How is that going to help the economy, or the war on terrorism, or our foreign relations?"

Tomlinson's smile widened. "That's a very good question, Gloria. You know, America has always been a frontier nation. And we have a frontier now, today, just a hundred miles from where we're standing."

Pointing straight up, Tomlinson went on, "The space frontier is sort of like the frontier of the old west. It offers us tremendous riches, waiting to be developed, more wealth in energy and natural resources than the entire Earth can provide. It's there, we've seen it, we've measured a tiny bit of it. Nobody owns it. There are no natives to drive away. It's waiting for us to go out there and develop it and *use* that wealth to create new industries and millions of new jobs. To make life better for every human being on Earth. To make America stronger than it's ever been."

Looking across the other candidates standing behind their lecterns, he added, "And we can accomplish all this without spending a penny of taxpayers' money—if Senator Sebastian would stop his opposition to the loan guarantee bill that's currently bottled up in the Senate."

Before any of the newspeople could react to that thrust, Tomlinson went on, "There are untold riches in space, waiting for us to develop. New wealth means new jobs—jobs right here on Earth. If we share this new wealth from space fairly, equitably, with all the peoples of Earth, we can cut out the roots of terrorism. We can bring new hope to the poorest people of

Earth. And we can certainly improve our relations with the other nations, whether they're allies of ours or not."

Tomlinson stopped and looked out over the audience. Not a sound. No applause, no cheers, nothing but silence.

Absolutely struck dumb, Jake thought. With a sigh, he remembered that the audience at Gettysburg didn't applaud Lincoln's little speech, either.

Like a lead balloon," Tomlinson groused as he sat, shoulders slumped and head bowed, back in the dressing room. It wasn't crowded now: only Jake, O'Donnell, and Lovett were there with the senator.

Sitting next to Jake on the room's tatty sofa, O'Donnell murmured, "Like a turd in the punch bowl."

"It wasn't a barn burner, that's for sure," Lovett admitted, standing at Senator Tomlinson's side. "But the point is, Frank, that you got your point across. Space can help grow the economy and make this country a world leader again."

Tomlinson looked up at his campaign manager. "The reaction was awfully quiet."

"You've given them a lot to think about."

The door opened and Amy entered the dressing room, with Tami right behind her.

Jake shot to his feet. "Tami, how'd the newspeople feel about the senator's ideas?"

She glanced at Tomlinson's downcast face, then replied, "They're skeptical, mostly. Some of them call the space plan pie in the sky."

"So you're going to have to convince them, Frank," said Lovett.

"We've got plenty of evidence on our side," Jake said.

"Do you?" O'Donnell asked.

Jake snapped, "Yes. We can prove that the technology developed for the Apollo lunar program led to home computers, the Internet, cell phones, GPS—trillions of dollars added to the economy. And millions of jobs."

"That was then," O'Donnell said, sourly. "This is now."

Amy piped up with, "Well, Frank's got his work cut out for him, doesn't he?" Turning to beam her cheerleader's smile at her husband, she added, "And you're just the man to do it, dear."

O'Donnell shook his head. "It's a long road, a really long road."

Tomlinson smiled wryly at his chief of staff. "Even the longest journey begins with a single step, Kevin." Rising to his feet, he said, "Let's get started."

Lovett broke into a grin. "Let's see what the polls say before we throw in the towel."

Squaring his shoulders, Senator Tomlinson said with some heat, "We're not throwing in any towels, Pat. I'm in this race to stay. And to win."

Suddenly Amy quoted Churchill. "We shall fight them on the beaches and the landing fields, we shall fight them in the cities and the streets . . . we shall never surrender."

She almost got it right, Jake thought, surprised.

Then he heard O'Donnell mutter, "Churchill also said that they'll have to fight with beer bottles, because that's all they had left."

Lovett kept his grin in place as he said, "Don't be such a sourpuss, Kev. The campaign's just getting started. If we're going to quote Winnie, remember this one: 'Let us so conduct ourselves so that a thousand years from now men will still say, "This was their finest hour." '"

That's not exactly correct either, Jake knew. But he kept his mouth shut.

. . .

"What do you think?" Jake asked Tami as they rode a taxi to their hotel.

"He's in a hole, and it's going to be tough to dig out of it."

"Lady Cecilia wants to do a sit-down interview with him."

"Another one?" Tami asked. "Frank did a sit-down with her last week."

Feeling uncomfortable, Jake confessed, "I . . . uh, I sort of promised her. Payback for dropping the Manstein story."

Tami fell silent for several moments. Jake watched the lights from the street reflect off her pretty face as the taxi weaved through the downtown Chicago traffic.

"Well, if you promised her I guess we'll have to go through with it." Then she added, "If Cecilia is still interested."

"There is that," Jake admitted.

. . .

The next morning, Jake was surprised to see that Tomlinson had actually risen in the nationwide polls. Not by much, less than three percentage points. The pundits' analyses of the slight bump almost all agreed that most of the people polled hadn't heard about Tomlinson's space plan, and were curious to know what it was all about.

Tomlinson was still in fourth place, barely ahead of the feisty Dr. Norton. But at least he hadn't lost any ground.

Be grateful for small miracles, Jake thought.

As he sat in his office scanning through the polls and analyses, Jake thought, It's not much, but it's better than we expected.

Jake accompanied Senator Tomlinson to Lady Cecilia's house for his post-debate interview. It was well past ten p.m., the tag end of a long day of news media appearances and re-hearsals for new television ads.

"It's been a week since I've been in the Senate," Tomlinson muttered as the limousine drove slowly through the narrow streets of Cecilia's Capitol Hill neighborhood.

"Kevin's keeping you apprised of the Senate's business, isn't he?" Jake asked. "You haven't missed any important votes."

"The vote on raising the debt ceiling comes up next week," the senator said. "Kevin thinks it's just as well that I miss it."

Nodding, Jake said, "You can't be blamed either way if you don't vote on it."

Tomlinson made a sound that might have been a resigned groan. In the darkness of the limo's rear seat, Jake couldn't make out the senator's facial expression.

But he said, "I ought to take a stand on the issue."

Jake countered, "Listen to Kevin. Either way you vote, the other side will use it against you."

"I know, but . . . I don't like weaseling out on it."

"When you're president you can take a stand."

Tomlinson went, "Hmmf."

The limo stopped in front of Lady Cecilia's three-story house. Every window was ablaze with light. Tomlinson opened his own door and ducked out of the limo before the chauffeur could get to him. Jake slid across the rear bench while the driver held the door open for him.

"Beat you again, Danny," Tomlinson said to the chauffeur, grinning.

"You're just too fast for me, sir."

Lady Cecilia was standing in the front doorway as Jake and the senator came up the bricked walkway.

"Right on time," she called to them.

Tomlinson replied, "For you, Cecilia, we skipped two cocktail parties and an ambassadorial dinner."

He bussed her on the cheek. Cecilia's froggish face beamed happily, but she said, "You're a charming liar."

Feigning innocence, Tomlinson protested, "It's true! Ask Jake."

Jake said not a word as Cecilia showed them into her home.

. . .

Senator Tomlinson sat, seemingly at ease, to one side of the small desk in the room Cecilia used to record her interviews for her *Power Talk* blog. Sitting at the desk, Cecilia wore a maroon blouse with gold piping. Tomlinson was in a dark blue suit: his Washington uniform, Jake thought.

The senator looked tired. Jake saw lines around his eyes that he'd never noticed before. Why shouldn't he be tired? We've been running him around like a racehorse for weeks now. And there's months more to come.

Cecilia wasted no time with preliminary chitchat. After introducing the senator, she opened the interview with:

"You said in last night's debate that your space program could help to invigorate the economy. How?"

Tomlinson launched into his standard patter about new industries and new jobs. Jake, sitting to one side of the bearded, overweight techie who was handling the camera, nodded in rhythm to the well-rehearsed lines.

But Cecilia interrupted the senator's spiel with, "Well, maybe your program could generate jobs for engineers and astronauts. But what about the millions of ordinary folks who are unemployed or underemployed? What about them?"

Smiling tiredly, the senator answered, "Engineers and astronauts need plumbers and carpenters, secretaries and truck drivers, babysitters, grocery clerks, bank tellers . . ."

"Isn't that the trickle-down economics theory?"

Tomlinson hesitated, then replied, "Cecilia, the unemployment situation is basically a problem of education. Our schools are not turning out graduates who are prepared for high-tech industries. They're failing our kids in that area."

Putting on a surprised expression, Cecilia asked, "You mean our public schools aren't doing their job?"

Very seriously, the senator answered, "I'm afraid they're not. Most youngsters graduating high school aren't prepared for high-tech jobs. Or even low-tech jobs, for that matter. That's why I hope that a vigorous space program can get our schoolchildren interested in science and technology again."

"The STEM subjects," Cecilia said. "Science, technology, engineering, and math."

Nodding to Cecilia, Tomlinson said, "I'm hoping that our return to the Moon can stimulate kids to tackle those subjects. And motivate our educators to emphasize them. That could be a powerful boost for our educational systems. And for our economy as a whole."

Looking delighted, Cecilia said, "Thank you, Senator Tomlinson, for your very insightful views."

Firestorm

"Well, Frank, you've just thrown away the teachers' vote."

Patrick Lovett was perfectly serious as he faced Senator Tomlinson. Not angry, but deadly troubled.

Then he turned to Jake, "And you let him do it. You just sat there and let him make an enemy of the National Education Association. Three million votes down the drain. More."

The three men were at the campaign headquarters, holed up in Tomlinson's makeshift office. Outside, aides and volunteers were answering phone calls and handling their routine chores. Tami was out there, Jake knew, fielding inquiries from the news media about the senator's "attack" on the nation's public schools. Inside the office, the normally unflappable Lovett was standing in front of Tomlinson's desk like an accusing prosecutor.

"I didn't say anything that isn't true," Tomlinson replied stubbornly.

"What's truth got to do with it?" Lovett snapped. "The NEA is *powerful*, Frank. It's resisted every attempt to reform the schools since god knows when. Remember Bush's No Child Left Behind program? Where is it now? In the garbage can, that's where it is. And that's where we're going to be if we can't patch things up with the teachers' union."

Jake thought, At least Pat said "we" and not "you."

His jaw set, Tomlinson said, "I'm not going to back down from what I said."

Lovett plunked himself down on one of the rickety chairs in front of the desk. "There's a firestorm blazing out there, Frank. Cecilia's blog has been picked up all through the Internet. Major news media outlets want to interview you—not about your space plan but about your attack on the teachers."

"I can't back down."

"Nobody expects you to back down, but you've got to soften the message. Don't be so confrontational."

"Jesus Christ, Pat, it's the truth!"

Lovett sucked in a deep breath. Then he said, slowly, patiently, "You assume that the National Education Association is involved in education. It's not. It's a union, like the United Auto Workers or the Teamsters. It's the biggest goddamned union in the country!"

"But—"

Lovett steamrollered on. "Its main goal, its purpose, is to protect its members. Not education. Not teaching kids. It exists to protect its members and get them the best employment conditions it possibly can. Remember that, Frank."

Tomlinson muttered, "Okay, I'll remember it."

"And remember this, too," Lovett said, leveling a finger at the senator. "Fighting with the NEA takes away from your real, central point, your space plan. And you've got no choice but to put this firestorm out, one way or the other. Otherwise your real message gets lost."

Jake heard himself offer, "Maybe we could use this to get Frank more media time, get him noticed more."

"Making lemonade out of the lemon?" Lovett responded. "Nice trick, if you can do it."

"Could we arrange a meeting with the head of the NEA? A sort of peace conference?"

Lovett stared at Jake for a long, silent moment. Then he suggested, "Yeah. Maybe with a couple of astronauts included."

"We'd be trying to work out ways where public schools could start to put more emphasis on STEM subjects."

"Who do we know in the NEA organization?" Lovett asked.

Senator Tomlinson's dark expression eased into a small grin. "There's my cousin, Connie Zeeman."

Jolted with surprise, Jake blurted, "Connie's with the NEA?"

Tomlinson nodded. "One of their fundraisers. Didn't you know, Jake?"

Before he'd met Tami, Jake and Connie had been involved in a brief but intense affair. The senator had introduced the two of them to each other, and seemed to know every move they made together. Jake had often suspected that Connie provided detailed accounts of their tumultuous sex games to her cousin.

"No, she never mentioned that," Jake choked out.

"Let's see if Connie can help us meet with NEA's upper management," Tomlinson said, grinning knowingly.

Lovett, apparently oblivious to the byplay between Jake and the senator, said, "That's a beginning. Meantime, I'll tweak some of my contacts, see what we can accomplish."

"Good," said the senator.

Lovett got to his feet, but before he turned to leave the office, he leveled a warning finger at Tomlinson. "Make no mistake, Frank. This is a fire that's got to be put out quickly. Every minute you spend appeasing the NEA is a minute taken away from the story you're trying to tell the voters."

"I understand," Tomlinson said, looking solemn once more.

But as soon as Lovett left the office the senator said to Jake, "I'm not going to appease them or anyone else."

Jake tried to soothe the senator. "Appease isn't the right word."

"Then what is?"

Thinking of his times in bed with Connie, Jake replied, "Seduction."

．．．

As he drove home that evening, Jake debated telling Tami about Tomlinson contacting his cousin. He had told his wife about his affair with Connie, and Tami had taken the news with good grace. But now, with the tensions straining their marriage, he wondered how Tami would feel about Connie's reappearance on the scene. He wondered how he felt about it.

He got home before Tami, but as soon as she stepped through the front door Jake pecked her on the lips, then said, "Frank's calling his cousin, Connie, to help him with this NEA mess."

"Connie?" Tami asked, her brows knitting slightly. "She's back in town?"

"No, she's still home in California." Then he added, "So far."

Tami let her tote bag slip off her shoulder and thump onto the table by the front entrance. With a smile to show she wasn't accusing, she asked, "Is Frank pimping for you now?"

Jake felt his cheeks burn. "Tami!"

She patted his cheek. "I'm sorry. That wasn't fair. It was supposed to be funny."

As they went to the kitchen and the wine closet by the fridge, Jake explained the problem with the NEA.

Tami nodded. "I've been fielding requests for interviews with Frank all day long. Cecilia's blog has gone viral."

"We're trying to set up a sort of peace conference with NEA's top people."

"Good idea. Like Obama and Putin, back then."

"We'll try to do better than that!" Jake said fervently as he reached for a wine bottle.

Damage Control

Jake spent most of the next morning trying to reach William Farthington, NASA's chief administrator. All he got for his efforts was a succession of aides and assistants who assured him that Farthington would return his call as soon as he possibly could.

While stewing in anticipation, Jake called Isaiah Knowles, at the Space Futures Foundation.

"You free for lunch?" he asked the former astronaut.

Knowles's usual truculent expression morphed into a guarded smile. "Running out of friends?"

Jake smiled ruefully. "Just about. This NEA thing has me running around in circles."

With a single curt nod, Knowles said, "I figured. Okay, how about Ebbitt's Grill, 'round one o'clock?"

"I'll see you there."

Shortly before noon, Senator Tomlinson's executive assistant called Jake. "Can you drop in to the office for a few minutes, Dr. Ross?"

"Sure," Jake answered, thinking, When the senator rubs his magic lamp, the genie appears. Every time.

Senator Tomlinson was in his shirtsleeves, leaning back in his desk chair. The video screen that dominated one wall of his office showed Connie Zeeman, looking as fresh and energetic as Jake remembered her.

"Hi, Jake!" she called as soon as he came within range of the desk phone's camera.

"Hello, Connie," he said as he sat in one of the bottle-green leather chairs in front of the desk.

She looked just the way Jake remembered her: bright, sparkling eyes, sensuous full lips, sandy hair cropped short, like an athlete's, V-necked sweater showing an enticing bit of cleavage.

Senator Tomlinson seemed at ease as he said, "So we're trying to do some damage control. Can you get me an appointment to meet with the NEA's top man?"

"Top woman," Connie corrected.

"Whoever. I've got to patch up this unfortunate misunder-standing—"

Connie's cheerful expression hardened. "It's not a misunder-standing, Frank. You said the schools aren't doing their job."

"Well, they're not."

"Dora Engels doesn't see that as a misunderstanding. It's a slap in the face, as far as she's concerned."

"You've spoken to her about this?"

"She's spoken to me," said Connie. "She's pissed as hell."

"Great," Tomlinson moaned.

Jake said, "We'd like to set up a meeting with her, sort of a peace conference."

"Lots of luck."

"No, this is serious," Tomlinson said. "We need to smooth this over. And quickly."

"Dora won't have a one-on-one with you, I'm pretty certain," Connie said.

"How about a conference involving the head of NASA and a few astronauts?" Jake suggested. "Plus Frank, of course."

"And the purpose of this conference would be?"

"To see how NASA and the space community can help teachers to get their pupils interested in the STEM subjects."

Connie shook her head negatively. "That's like the old Young

Astronauts program. It didn't work then and it won't work now."

"Why not?"

"Because most teachers won't participate. How're they going to squeeze in time for special sessions on space travel when their school hours are already crammed full?"

"That's what the conference would be about," Tomlinson said. "Finding the answer to that problem."

Connie's expression turned thoughtful. "In other words, you want a conference that's aimed at helping teachers."

"And their pupils," Jake added.

"Maybe that could work."

"I'm not going to go in sackcloth and ashes," Tomlinson warned. "I don't want this to look like I'm begging them for forgiveness."

Her normal grin returning, Connie said, "But that's what you'll be doing, isn't it?"

"No," Jake snapped. "We're trying to help the teachers to get their pupils interested in the STEM subjects by using space as an incentive."

"Sure you are."

Tomlinson said, "The main thing is to get the NEA to support me, not work against me."

"As I said before, fellas, lots of luck."

. . .

The Old Ebbitt Grill was crowded, as usual, but Jake immediately spotted Isaiah Knowles sitting in a booth next to the window looking out onto the street. He brushed past the harried maître d' and slid into the booth across the table from the former astronaut.

"Hi, Ike, how are you?"

Knowles's dark-skinned face broke into a guarded smile. "I'm keepin' my head above water. How about you?"

Ruefully, Jake answered, "Trying to keep from drowning."

"This NEA thing?"

"Yeah."

A rail-thin waiter took their drink orders—ginger beer for Knowles, club soda for Jake—then quickly disappeared into the throng crowding the bar.

"Two big-time boozers we are," Knowles said.

"Yeah."

"So what're you doing to smooth the NEA's feathers?"

"Trying to arrange a conference with their top people," Jake replied. "We want to convince them that they can use the kids' interest in space to get them to study the STEM subjects."

Knowles shook his head. "But the teachers don't know the STEM subjects, most of 'em. And they don't want to take the time to learn them. I know! We tried to convince them when I was in the agency. Hit a stone wall."

The waiter reappeared with their drinks. "You ready to order lunch?" he asked as he put the glasses on the table.

Both Knowles and Jake ordered hamburgers: medium rare for Jake, medium well for Knowles. The waiter scratched on his order pad and disappeared again.

Hunching over the table slightly, Jake said, "Look, Ike, this meeting doesn't have to accomplish anything except getting the NEA on Frank's side. We can't afford to have them working against us."

"Guess not."

"I'm trying to get Farthington to come along with us."

"Bloviating Billy? Yeah. He could talk 'em deaf, dumb, and blind."

Jake grinned. Then he said, "Hey, maybe we can get some people from the private space firms: you know, like Harry Quinton and maybe Nick Piazza."

"Good idea," said Knowles. "Let the kids see real billionaires."

"And a few astronauts."

Knowles's brows rose a few millimeters. "Lots of retired astronauts out there. You could maybe put together a regular corps of 'em."

"That's an idea."

"I'm one of 'em."

"I know."

"I've done more space missions than any of 'em, did you know that?"

"Really?"

"And I'm good-looking. And black. I think I ought to head up your astronaut corps."

"Would you?"

With the brightest smile Jake had ever seen on his usually dour face, Knowles said, "Why not? You don't need to bother Farthington. There's enough retired astronauts to do the job."

"But we can't just ignore NASA. The agency's got to be a part of this."

Knowles acknowledged, "Yeah, I suppose so."

"This could be terrific," Jake enthused. "Real astronauts visiting the schools, talking to the kids."

Knowles raised a cautionary finger. "If the NEA goes for it."

Nodding vigorously, Jake responded, "Oh, they'll go for it. How could they refuse?"

"You'd be surprised," said Isaiah Knowles.

"Trick or treat?" Jake muttered tiredly to Kevin O'Donnell, who had tapped just once on his office door and then stepped in.

"What tricks do you know?" O'Donnell said as he closed the door behind him.

"I don't know any tricks."

O'Donnell smiled crookedly. "Then you don't get any treats."

Jake studied O'Donnell's face as the staff chief sat down in front of his desk. Kevin smiled rarely.

It was past six p.m. Most of the senator's staff people had left the office long ago. Jake had spent most of his day trying to put together a team of former astronauts to form a coherent group that was willing to speak to schoolchildren and use the kids' natural interest in space to encourage them to study the STEM subjects. Farthington had promised to bring NASA into the program, but so far the agency had offered no help to back up that promise. Harry Quinton had quickly agreed to help as much as he could; Nicholas Piazza seemed eager to face schoolchildren.

"I've got an eight-year-old grandson who tears my head off every time I see him," Piazza said. In Jake's phone screen, the man looked actually pleased.

"Eight years old?" Jake asked.

"Going on a hundred and two," Piazza said, laughing. "The kid's a real terror."

Tomlinson was slipping in the national polls, although he

seemed to be holding his own in Iowa and even New Hampshire. But for how long? Jake constantly asked himself. We've been working so hard on assuaging the NEA that the senator's space plan has hardly been mentioned in the news media for the past several weeks.

Looking across the desk at O'Donnell's nearly smirking face, Jake said, "I've been working since seven thirty this morning on this damned NEA problem, Kevin. I'm in no mood for kids' games."

O'Donnell cocked his head slightly to one side, as if to determine the truth of Jake's statement. Then his smile went from teasing to pleased.

"Got the NEA's acceptance of our request for a meeting. Thought you'd want to know."

Jake felt his eyes widen. "They'll meet with us?"

"Yep. Dora Engels herself, and five key members of her inner circle. They just e-mailed a formal acceptance, with a hard copy heading our way through snail mail."

"Great!" Jake enthused. "That's just great!"

"They want to keep the meeting small, quiet. The senator, Farthington, a couple of ex-astronauts."

"Ike Knowles," said Jake.

Nodding, O'Donnell went on, "They're happy about Harold Quinton. NEA people don't get to see billionaires face-to-face very often."

"Guess not."

Then O'Donnell added, "And you."

"Me?"

"You're the head man on the space plan, aren't you?"

"Yeah." Jake's voice trembled slightly with excitement.

"You're going."

"When? Where?"

"Next Monday morning, at their headquarters on Sixteenth Street."

"After Halloween," Jake said, immediately feeling stupid about it.

"That's right. No tricks and no treats."

Jake thought, I don't care if there's no treats. I just hope they don't pull any tricks.

As he got up from the chair, O'Donnell said, "By the way, Derek Vermeer phoned the senator, said he's very pleased that we're including a Mars training facility in the plans for the Moon base."

"That means the Mars lobby's swung around to our side!"

"No," O'Donnell corrected. "But it means they won't actively oppose your space plan. Frank's very pleased."

Nodding, Jake said, "So am I."

. . .

As soon as O'Donnell left, Jake phoned Farthington's office at NASA headquarters and once again got an assistant. He left a message, then tried Isaiah Knowles's cell phone. A message machine.

Feeling frustrated, Jake left for home.

The lobby of the condo building was aglow with plastic jack-o'-lanterns and various witches, black cats, and assorted hob-goblins. As he rode the elevator to his unit, Jake felt almost sorrowful that no children were allowed to go door-to-door begging for candy. Against the condo association's rules. Not that there were so many kids living in the building, he reminded himself. He didn't really know his neighbors well, but he hardly ever saw any children in the elevators.

Tami wasn't home yet. Jake knew she was working just as hard as he was, trying to keep the NEA flap from becoming a media sensation. Senator Moonbeam versus the National Education Association. That'd be a great way to destroy Frank's campaign.

Jake poured himself a glass of wine, turned on CNN, and settled himself on the sofa to wait for Tami. It's her turn to cook, he remembered. We'll go out to Mamie's. She'll be tired after putting in another long day.

The big news story on both CNN and Fox News was the funeral arrangements being made for Vladimir Putin. The Russians were going all-out, turning their president's death into an international showcase. Heads of state from all over the world had been invited to Moscow. The president of the United States had already agreed to attend. Her last chance at being in the international spotlight, Jake thought.

The front door opened and Tami came in, looking bone weary. Jake jumped up from the sofa and reached for her as she let her tote bag slump from her shoulder to the table by the door.

"Dinner at Mamie's," he announced, after pecking her on the lips.

She smiled tiredly. "No, let's eat here. I don't feel up to going out."

"But—"

"The fridge is full of leftovers. I'll heat up something."

"You sure?"

"Sure." Tami headed for the bathroom.

"Got some good news," Jake said. "We're set for a meeting with Engels and her people next Monday."

Tami brightened a bit. Then she said, "I heard something today."

"More good news?"

She shook her head. "Herbert Manstein has quit Rockledge Industries."

"Quit? Where's he going?"

"He's joined Senator Sebastian's campaign staff."

Suddenly Jake felt just as weary as Tami.

She was actually good-looking, Jake realized. Much better looking in person than the photos on the NEA's website. Dora Engels stood about five six, Jake judged, on the slim side, with shoulder-length chestnut-brown hair and penetrating dark brown eyes that looked like they could nail a student to his chair. Strong cheekbones and a firm chin that could be stubborn.

But she smiled graciously as she welcomed Senator Tomlinson, William Farthington, Isaiah Knowles, and Jake to the conference room next to her office. It was on the small side, windowless, paneled in light wood, with chairs along the two side walls and a table that could accommodate twelve.

"It's a pleasure to meet you," she said to the senator as she shook his hand.

Turning his smile to full wattage, Tomlinson replied, "The pleasure is all mine."

Jake had ridden to the NEA headquarters with the senator in a chauffeured black sedan. Farthington and Knowles had been waiting for them in the lobby.

"Quinton hasn't shown up yet?" Jake had asked.

As if in answer, Jake's smartphone had buzzed.

Harold Quinton looked annoyed, harried, in the phone's minuscule screen. "Just touched down at Reagan," he said. "We ran into some weather over Kansas."

Jake got a mental picture of a tornado blowing Quinton's plane all the way to Oz.

"You okay?" he asked.

"Yeah, yeah. But I'm going to be late for your meeting."

"That's all right."

"I hate being late. Bought the fastest executive jet on the market and I'm still late."

"I'll make your apologies."

And that's what Jake did as Dora Engels gestured to the empty chairs along the conference table.

Her brows knitting ever so slightly, she asked, "Will Mr. Quinton be attending our meeting?"

"He'll be here shortly," Jake said as he sat down near the foot of the table. "He flew in from California, had some rough weather on the way."

"I see," said Engels. "Well, shall we start without him?"

"By all means," Senator Tomlinson said. He was sitting at Engels's right.

After introductions up and down the table, Engels said, "We're here today to clear up this unfortunate misunderstanding that Senator Tomlinson caused recently."

His face going serious, Tomlinson said, "I'm very sorry if my words hurt anyone's feelings. I was trying to point out a problem that needs to be addressed."

"STEM teaching," said the gray-haired woman on Engels's left. Jake noticed that all the NEA people were sitting on one side of the table, the senator, Farthington, Knowles, and Jake himself on the other.

Not good, Jake thought. Not good at all.

Four of the five NEA people were women, ranging from middle-aged to white-haired. The fifth was a lanky youngish man with a military-style buzz cut, wearing a sports jacket and a polka-dotted bow tie.

Tomlinson nodded at the woman who had spoken. "STEM subjects are important, vital to the nation's future."

The young man across the table said, in a twangy nasal voice, "We're all agreed on that, but how can you expect overworked and underpaid schoolteachers to add more time, more effort in an already overcrowded school day?"

"That's what we're here to ascertain," said Farthington. "I'm sure the senator, here, is eager to help all he can. And certainly NASA stands shoulder to shoulder with the NEA in its efforts to help our hardworking teachers in every way possible."

Jake suppressed an urge to gag.

A timid knock on the conference room door, and an assistant poked her head in. "Mr. Harold Quinton is here, Mrs. Engels."

"Show him right in!"

As Quinton came in, everybody around the table got to their feet.

"Sorry I'm late," he said.

By god, Jake thought, Harry looks like he belongs on their side of the table. The billionaire was wearing a rumpled tweed suit. Short, roundish, balding, he reminded Jake of a mathematics teacher he had suffered through in high school.

Jake moved down one seat lower so Quinton could sit next to Isaiah Knowles.

"Now that we're all here," said Dora Engels, "let's get down to business."

. . .

Two hours later, Engels summarized, "So you're willing to put together a group of current and former astronauts who will tour the nation's schools giving presentations aimed at stimulating the students' interest in STEM subjects."

"That's right," Tomlinson said.

Directing her stern gaze to Farthington, she asked, "And NASA will participate in this program?"

"Certainly," Farthington replied. "NASA will be glad to

participate. We've been doing something like this on an informal, one-at-a-time basis, but I believe that organizing the effort is a grand idea, an idea whose time has come."

Engels dipped her chin in what might have been a nod. Then, "That's all well and good, but who's going to pay for this program? You can't expect school districts that are already strapped for funds to support this new program."

Very straight-faced, Senator Tomlinson said, "I'll pay for it. Out of my own pocket."

Before anyone around the table could react, Quinton smiled gently and said, "I'll split the costs with you, Frank."

Engels seemed surprised, and genuinely impressed. "That . . . that's very generous of you both."

Jake thought, Rich or poor, it pays to have money.

"There's one thing we haven't considered," said the bow-tied young man on the other side of the table. "How are the teachers going to fit these shows into their already crowded schedules?"

By dropping their feel-good sessions, Jake thought. Instead of trying to teach the kids self-esteem, they could try giving them something that actually gives them a sense of accomplishment.

But Jake kept his mouth shut.

Farthington put on his ingratiating smile and answered, "Why, I picture having our astronauts talk to the children after regular school hours. No need to interfere with their usual classes."

All five of the NEA members shook their heads in metronome synchrony.

The young man said, "You mean you expect the teachers to put in more hours, after the regular school day? And it would complicate the school bus schedules."

Jake got a vision of a tall, beautiful tree being nibbled to death by maggots.

But surprisingly, Engels said, "Those are details that can be worked out at the local level. We can offer the program to the local school districts and let them decide how to fit it into their schedules."

"Or if," said the young man.

"Or if," Engels conceded.

. . .

It took another hour before the meeting finally broke up.

As they stood in the sunshine outside the NEA headquarters building, Senator Tomlinson said, "I wonder if we accomplished anything in there."

"You did, Senator," Jake replied. "You got the NEA off your back. You turned a potential enemy into a partner."

"More than that," said Farthington. "Engels and her people can announce that they've revived the Young Astronauts program, aimed at the noble cause of getting kids to tackle the STEM subjects. Schools have gotten a lot of complaints about sidestepping STEM, ducking the tough subjects. Now Engels can say they're doing something about it."

Quinton shook his head. "There's a better than even chance that nothing will come of this."

Farthington waved an index finger in a *No, no, no* gesture. "As far as the education bureaucracy is concerned, starting a new program to address a perceived problem is more important than solving the problem." Then he added, "Come to think of it, that's the way any bureaucracy behaves."

"The Young Astronauts program," Jake said. "Well, it's better than nothing."

"This time we'll make it work," Quinton muttered. "This time we'll get results."

Jake thought that that remained to be seen, but Farthington was right: the important thing is that they'd turned the NEA from an enemy into a partner.

Tomlinson shrugged, then glanced at his wristwatch. Searching for his own chauffeured sedan among the cars and taxis cruising along the crowded street, he asked Quinton, "I'm ready to drink some lunch; how about you, Harry?"

"Sounds good."

At last the sedan wove through the traffic and pulled up at the curb.

Tomlinson asked Farthington and Knowles, "You want to join us for lunch?"

Farthington shook his head. "I've got to get back to the office."

Knowles said, "A wet lunch sounds good. Thanks."

The four of them left the NASA administrator standing at the curb, waiting for his car.

As they pulled away, Jake remembered that Herbert Manstein now worked for Senator Sebastian. He hadn't had a chance to tell Senator Tomlinson about that.

I'll wait until after lunch, Jake told himself. No sense ruining his lunch.

Jake felt as if he were waiting for the headsman's ax to fall on his neck. Manstein was now on Senator Sebastian's payroll, ready to reveal his juicy piece of gossip whenever the senator told him to.

Outwardly, everything seemed normal. Tomlinson campaigned in Iowa and New Hampshire, with occasional trips to other early primary states in the South. So did Sebastian. The two candidates crossed paths several times over the next few weeks, but never appeared at the same place at the same time.

But the national popularity polls were taking their toll on the candidates. Yeardley Norton was the first to drop out of the race. The feisty Minnesota dentist's poll numbers never climbed above 10 percent, except in a few Midwestern states, and funding donations to his campaign shriveled. He promised to "keep on fighting for the little folks" when he announced he was quitting the race.

"Sounds like he's working for the leprechauns," Kevin O'Donnell quipped.

Two weeks before the second debate was scheduled, California's Senator Morgan threw in the towel, urging his followers to give their support to "the man who will win for us next November, Senator Bradley Sebastian, of the so-called Sunshine State of Florida."

Patrick Lovett studied the polls and trends and told Tomlinson and his campaign workers, "It's boiling down to a two-horse race, our man against Sebastian."

Amy went with her husband wherever he went, always standing beside him, smiling prettily and waving to the growing crowds. In New Orleans, Tomlinson gave a speech about international trade that was well-received in the news media—and on Wall Street. In Denver, his speech on the war against terrorism won praise from the conservative wing of the party.

But it was Tomlinson's concept of a renewed space program that got him the most attention.

"A couple of centuries ago, American pioneers headed west, saying to themselves, 'There's gold in them thar hills.' Well, now it's time to head into space, to return to the Moon, because there's gold out there: new industries, plentiful natural resources, new breakthroughs in energy and low-gravity manufacturing, new jobs for our next generation of bright youngsters, a new frontier to be developed."

Jake watched the news reports assiduously. The snide references to "Senator Moonbeam" grew less and less. Articles about potential space industries and developing lunar resources started to appear in local newspapers and TV broadcasts.

But despite all that, the bill introduced by Tomlinson to allow the Treasury Department to guarantee low-interest, long-term loans for private investors in space development remained locked in the finance committee, with no vote scheduled and none expected as long as Sebastian remained opposed.

The loan guarantee bill languished in the Senate's limbo. Even though Senator Zucco chaired the finance committee, he hadn't the stomach to challenge Sebastian on the matter. All the talk in the world isn't going to get the bill out of committee, Jake realized. It's the key to the space plan, and as long as it stays bottled up like this, the plan is little more than talk.

Still, Tomlinson's poll numbers inched higher every week. Sebastian was still well ahead, but Tomlinson was gaining on him.

Yet Jake couldn't shake his feeling of impending doom.

"It's like having the Sword of Damocles hanging over your head," he said to Tami as they were dressing for the big Thanksgiving dinner Tomlinson was hosting at the new Grand Hyatt hotel. "Sebastian's got Manstein in his pocket, ready to spring on Frank whenever he needs to."

Searching through a bureau drawer for the proper earrings, Tami wondered, "What's he waiting for?"

"The right moment," Jake answered morosely. "The exact moment when it will hurt Frank the most."

She found the earrings she wanted, started to attach them. "And the senator is just plowing ahead as if there's no problem. Why doesn't he try to sit down with Sebastian and come to an understanding with him?"

Standing before the bedroom's full-length mirror as he laboriously knotted his tuxedo's black bow tie, Jake shook his head. "What kind of an understanding could they come to? They both want the party's nomination. Only one of them can have it."

"And neither one will back off."

"We're heading for a train wreck," Jake said. "Two locomotives on the same track, rushing at each other."

With a cheerless smile, Tami murmured, "Where is Casey Jones when you really need him?"

. . .

If Tomlinson was worried about the Manstein problem, he certainly didn't show it at his Thanksgiving dinner. The Grand Hyatt's main ballroom was swarming with guests: campaign workers, political allies, what looked to Jake like half the US Senate, plenty of news reporters, and camera crews.

The senator—with his glitteringly gowned wife at his side—worked his way through the crowd, smiling and shaking hands.

When they came up to Jake, Tomlinson said, "Do you see that Mars guy anywhere?"

"Derek Vermeer?" Jake shook his head. "Nope, haven't run across him."

"He was invited. And he accepted."

Jake shrugged. "He's sort of an odd duck, you know."

Tomlinson grinned. "Maybe he is, but he's happy with us now that we've included a Mars training facility in our Moon base plans—I think."

Before Jake could reply, the senator said, "That was your idea, Jake. Good going. Turn an enemy into an ally. We'll make a politician out of you yet."

Jake forced a smile as he said, "I'll look through the crowd for him, tell him you want to say hello."

"Good."

With Tami trailing along at his side, Jake worked his way through the crowd.

Grinning as she sipped champagne, Tami said, "Frank should have given this bash on Halloween. It would have been more fun to see these folks in costumes."

Jake countered, "The gowns are pretty impressive. And the jewelry."

"But the men all look alike in their tuxedos." She giggled. "A ballroom full of penguins."

Jake had barely sipped from the champagne flute he held in his hand. "Halloween would've been too early. Frank wouldn't have gotten such a big crowd a month ago."

After several more fruitless minutes of searching Jake conceded, "I guess he's not here."

"He should have sent his regrets," Tami said. "It's rude to just not show up."

Jake led her through the throng of partygoers and out into the hotel's lobby. It was considerably quieter there.

Pulling his smartphone from his jacket pocket, Jake tapped Vermeer's number. It rang once, twice . . .

"Hello?" A woman's voice, tight with anxiety.

"Derek Vermeer, please," said Jake.

"Who's this?"

"Dr. Jacob Ross, from Senator Tomlinson's office."

"Oh! He was supposed to attend the party tonight, wasn't he?"

"Yes. Can I speak to him, please?"

The woman's voice edged up a notch. "We're in the hospital. He's dying!"

"What?"

"He collapsed earlier this evening. We're in Howard University Hospital." Her voice broke, then she sobbed, "They don't expect him to make it through the night."

Jake felt the breath gush out of him. "Howard University Hospital?"

"Yes."

"We'll be there in a few minutes!"

. . .

There's a special air about a hospital, Jake thought as he and Tami hurried down a long corridor toward the room where Derek Vermeer lay dying. Is it the smell of antiseptic, the tension, the pain? All of that, he decided, and more. The fear, Jake realized. The fear of death hung over every corridor, every room, every part of the hospital.

Jake had pushed through the crowded hotel ballroom to tell Senator Tomlinson that Vermeer was dying. The senator shook his head. "Too bad."

"I'm going to see him," Jake said, surprising himself.

Tomlinson nodded. "Give him my sympathies."

Now Jake dashed down the pastel-painted corridor, practically towing Tami in one hand. Abruptly, he stopped.

"Four twenty-two," he said, puffing. "This is it."

Tami was panting, too. She mumbled something about high heels as Jake tapped on the door.

A tall, rake-thin woman opened the door. Her bony face was runneled with tears.

"I'm Jake Ross—"

"You're too late, Dr. Ross," the woman whispered. "My brother died a few minutes ago."

She opened the door wider, and Jake and Tami stepped into the room. It held two beds, one of them empty, the other surrounded by an emergency team with a crash cart, methodically disconnecting the tubes and wires from Vermeer's body. The monitor consoles along the wall were all turned off, silent. Vermeer lay in the bed, his eyes staring sightlessly at the ceiling.

No, Jake thought. He's staring at Mars.

A nurse gently closed Vermeer's eyes, then pulled the bedsheet over his face.

His sister broke into open sobs. Tami wrapped her arms around the woman, making consoling noises. The medical team pushed their cart out into the corridor and left the room, shutting the door quietly behind them.

Jake stood there, feeling utterly helpless, even stupid in his tuxedo.

Then he realized that the two women made an incongruous pair: Tami barely came to the sister's shoulders, even in her heels.

"He so wanted to reach Mars," the sister was whimpering.

"He will," Jake heard himself say.

Both women stared at him.

"I promised him that his remains would be buried on Mars. I'll see to it that they are."

The beginning of a smile worked its way across Vermeer's sister's face. "That's very kind of you."

"And we'll name the Mars training facility at the lunar base after him," Jake added.

"He would have liked that."

Jake recalled reading somewhere, long ago, a line that a famous general once uttered: "We bury our dead and we keep moving forward."

Reaching out to Tami, Jake said, "Come on, honey. It's time to move forward."

The Second Debate

New York, New York," Jake muttered to himself. "The town so big they named it twice."

Madison Square Garden was filled to capacity for the second Republican Party debate. Outside on the windy Manhattan streets it was a cold and dark early December night. Here in the auditorium the atmosphere was heated by the press of bodies, the air of expectation.

From his seat in the VIP section, within spitting distance of the stage in the center of the auditorium, Jake waited tensely for the debate to begin. Tami was across the way, with the news media corps, as usual.

Patrick Lovett made his way along the crowded aisle to the chair next to Jake's, looking cool and unruffled. "Good crowd," he said. "Plenty of our people here."

Jake nodded, too nervous to speak. Frank's got to do well tonight, he knew. There's only one more debate before the Iowa caucus. He's got to gain more ground on Sebastian.

The crowd buzzed with expectation as the panel of four news media stars took their places. Then the huge auditorium rocked with applause as the three candidates strode in, smiling and shaking hands with one another, and took up their positions at their lecterns.

As the newsman selected to be moderator introduced the candidates (needlessly, Jake thought), Amy came scampering down the aisle and slipped into the chair on Jake's other side.

"He looks wonderful," she said, glowing. But the way she clutched at Jake's arm told him she was wound tight.

Sebastian, Tomlinson, and Governor Hackman would make their opening statements in that order, the moderator explained, based on their current standings in the popularity polls.

Senator Sebastian gave a solid little speech, emphasizing his experience, pointing out that in addition to his "long years" in the Senate he had served two terms as governor of Florida. "So I have executive experience, too," he concluded, casting a sly glance at Tomlinson, standing next to him.

With a handsome grin, Tomlinson began, "I'm too young to have served as long as Brad has. But I've managed to accomplish a few things since I've come to the Senate.

"For one, the energy plan that I presented to the Senate nearly six years ago has produced new jobs across these United States, reduced our nation's carbon footprint considerably, and lowered the costs of electricity and gasoline."

A smattering of applause broke out.

Yesterday's news, Jake thought. What have you done for me lately?

Tomlinson went on, "You're paying less for fueling your car, and your electricity bills are lower because we are using new technology to develop our natural resources. And those natural resources include the brains and toil of American workers."

More applause, louder.

"Now it's time to use our brains and skills to open the space frontier. Time to use the resources in space and on the Moon to create new industries, new jobs, new wealth, and opportunities for America and the whole world. It's time to return to the Moon!"

The crowd applauded again, but Jake thought it was noticeably less than before. He hasn't sold the idea, Jake realized. Not yet.

Governor Hackman's opening statement was blandly forget-table, Jake thought: especially coming after Tomlinson's ex-pansive vision.

Then the news people started grilling the candidates. The first question to Tomlinson was, "Won't it be prohibitively ex-pensive to get back to the Moon and build a permanent base there?"

Tomlinson smiled his best high-wattage smile and replied, "We plan to return to the Moon and build permanent facili-ties there without spending a penny of taxpayer money. It will be financed by private investors."

Glancing at Sebastian, he went on, "The bill for creating that system of private investment is bottled up in the Senate at the moment. We're hoping that Senator Sebastian will use his considerable influence to help get the bill to the floor of the Senate for a vote."

Before the next question could be asked, Tomlinson added, "Incidentally, Tom, you'll be able to invest in the program, too. Individual private citizens will be able to invest in developing the space frontier. As I've said before, there's gold in them thar lunar hills—and you can share in it."

Laughter and a smattering of applause.

Lovett nodded happily. "He's hitting the right note."

The next questioner asked, "How will your space plan help us in the war against terrorism?"

"By making us wealthier," Tomlinson immediately replied. "By making the whole world wealthier. By showing the world that we have better things to do than suicide bombings. By showing people everywhere that developing the space frontier can make them richer."

"Really?"

"Look," Tomlinson said, leaning forward slightly on his lec-tern, "one of the things we hope to do is build solar power satellites—power stations in orbit that can beam gigawatts of energy down to receiving stations on the ground. And where would be the best places for those receiving stations? The clear desert areas of the American southwest. And the deserts of the Middle East, too. The vast Sahara Desert could become the energy source for all of Europe!"

Only a few hands clapping.

The moderator said, "That's a lot to think about."

"Start thinking, then," Tomlinson said. With a grin.

"Okay." The moderator took a breath, then turned to Hackman. "Governor, what do you see as the most important issues in this campaign?"

And so it went. Until one of the news media panelists asked Tomlinson, "Your 'Back to the Moon' plan sounds so . . . so futuristic, so far-fetched. Do you really expect the American voters to go for what sounds, frankly, like a wild-eyed fantasy?"

Tomlinson's smile faltered, but only for an instant. "Carrie," he replied, "automobiles were once a wild-eyed fantasy. So was stem-cell therapy and the global extermination of polio. Space flight itself was considered a fantasy—until we started orbiting satellites and eventually landed American astronauts on the Moon."

Looking beyond the seated panelists, toward the rows and rows of the audience, Tomlinson continued, "But I'll tell you what, Connie. We have a good cross-section of American voters here in the hall." Raising his voice louder, he called out, "How many of you believe that we can return to the Moon and begin to develop the space frontier? Come on, raise your hands."

For a long moment, the auditorium was absolutely still. Then a few hands went up. Abruptly, the lights set high in the ceiling came on, showing the packed rows of seats. Tomlinson stood at his lectern, smiling expectantly.

Lovett muttered, "This is a mistake."

Jake raised his right hand and twisted around to look at

the rest of the vast auditorium. People were raising their hands, getting to their feet and waving both arms in the air. Within moments there was a sea of raised hands and a growing murmur that rose to a rumble, a cheer, a rising tide of clapping and whistles and joyful laughter.

Stretching his right arm toward the audience, Tomlinson bellowed over the crowd's roar, "There's your answer! Americans are a pioneering people, and they're ready to move out to the space frontier!"

Lovett pulled a handkerchief from his jacket pocket and mopped his brow.

. . .

It was nearly midnight. Tomlinson's suite at the Waldorf Astoria was still packed with campaign workers and well-wishers. Lovett sat in an armchair, his third whiskey in his hand, still shaking his head.

"He reminds me of what the flyboys used to say about test pilots," he was saying to Jake, sitting beside him in an identical chair. "More guts than brains."

Jake waved a clutch of messages torn from the computer in the adjoining room. "The blogs are going wild. It was a masterstroke."

"Another masterstroke like that and I'll have a heart attack," Lovett moaned. "Do you realize what could have happened if his little ploy fell flat?"

"It didn't," Jake said happily.

The wall-screen TV was tuned to a news broadcast; it showed the sea of hands in Madison Square Garden, then cut to Tomlinson's happy, grinning face. Jake didn't know if the sound was muted or not, there was too much noise from the well-wishers to tell.

Tami came through the crowd, smiling happily. "The morning newspapers are all carrying the story on their front pages."

"Why not?" Jake said carelessly.

Lovett kept shaking his head. "He's got the guts of a burglar. The guts of a burglar."

"It worked," Jake told him.

"This time," said Lovett. "He'd better not try something like this again."

Jake glanced at his wristwatch, then pushed himself up from the chair. To Tami he said, "We'd better get some sleep. Big day tomorrow."

"The finance committee hearing," she said.

"Right."

They said good night to Lovett, then made their way to Senator Tomlinson, who was deep in conversation with a couple of older men: Wall Street types, Jake thought. Amy was standing beside her husband, smiling brightly and nodding.

Jake waved at the senator, then he and Tami worked their way through the crowded room, out into the blessedly quiet hallway, and down the elevator to their own floor.

As he closed the door to their room, Jake saw that the red message light on the bedside phone was blinking.

Jake picked up the receiver and tapped the message button.

Herbert Manstein's clipped, cultured voice said, "Dr. Ross, I am in New York and would like to see you. Are you free for lunch tomorrow?"

Welcome Home

In the bathroom of his hotel mini suite brushing his teeth, Jake heard the TV soundtrack: together with the British prime minister and the leaders of Germany and China, the president of the United States was having an "informal chat" with the five men who were apparently running the Russian government—for the time being.

Politics, Jake thought. Putin's not even cold yet in his grave and they're talking about what comes next. I guess it's important, though. Maybe they can work out a way to deal with the Middle East.

Once he turned off his electric toothbrush Jake could hear the TV announcer intoning, "While economic issues will probably predominate this impromptu discussion, the leaders will undoubtedly talk about the stability of the new government of Syria, and Russia's efforts to conclude a new trade treaty with western Europe."

Yeah, Jake said to himself. And the war against the Latin American terrorists. And maybe even the future of the Russian space program. I bet our "Back to the Moon" plan has them jittery.

As he stepped back into the bedroom he saw Tami sitting tensely on the front edge of the little sofa.

Pointing to the TV screen's image of the American president in Moscow chatting smilingly with the British prime minister, Tami said, "That woman leads a charmed life. Here she is, a lame duck on the last months of her presidency, and she gets to have the international spotlight on her again."

With a laugh, Jake asked, "You think she poisoned Putin?"

"I wouldn't put it past her."

The phone rang. Jake went to the bed in two swift strides and lifted the receiver.

Patrick Lovett's voice said, "It's all set. Paolino's, down on Eighteenth and Irving Place."

Jake nodded. "I'll tell Manstein. Cab drivers can find it?"

"No sweat."

"Okay." Jake cut the connection, then punched out the number Manstein had left the night before. No answer, so Jake left a message, including the fact that Senator Tomlinson's campaign manager would be coming along with him.

Tami saw the worried look on his face. "Do you think he'll be spooked and not show up?"

"I don't know," Jake answered. "Might spoil the cloak-and-dagger atmosphere. On the other hand, the bastard might feel puffed up to have Frank's campaign manager at the table."

The two of them went down to the lobby coffee shop for breakfast, then returned to their suite. No phone messages.

Jake turned on C-Span, hoping they were covering the Senate finance committee's hearing. They weren't. Senator Zucco did not want TV cameras poking into his committee's hearing. Not that the committee was going to take up the loan guarantee bill, Jake knew. Sebastian wanted it kept from a hearing and Zucco bowed to Sebastian's pressure. Power politics at its finest, he thought sourly.

So Jake paced the small room, feeling caged in but unwilling to leave the hotel room. Manstein might call, he kept telling himself.

Tami was stuffing her tote bag with a mini computer and batches of papers: she was responsible for arranging the news media's representatives at Senator Tomlinson's speech that afternoon at the Museum of Natural History's Hayden Planetarium.

"It's like trying to herd cats," she complained just before she left. "A bunch of prima donnas."

"Not like Walter Cronkite, huh?"

She cocked a brow at her husband. "Oh, old Walt had his moments, from what I hear."

Jake chuckled. "Goes with the job, I guess."

"Takes a big ego to get ahead in the news business," Tami said. Then she pecked Jake on the cheek and left him wondering if she had an ego big enough to get ahead in the news business—an ego big enough to break up their marriage.

• • •

Jake's bearded, turbaned cabdriver used his GPS to locate Paolino's restaurant. Pat Lovett was already sitting at a table in the rear of the place when Jake walked in.

Paolino's was in the basement of a brick apartment building. The place looked like a hallway to Jake, long and narrow. But more than half of the tables were already filled, even though it was only a few minutes past noon.

"This is one of the undiscovered gems of Manhattan," Lovett said, once Jake sat down. "A quiet neighborhood restaurant with great food, a fine wine list, and wonderful service."

"How did you find it?" Jake asked absently. He glanced at his wristwatch. Manstein was already several minutes late.

"I used to live in this neighborhood, years ago. The Gramercy Park area is a fine place to live. None of the hustle and bustle of farther uptown, yet you're in the heart of the city."

Jake understood that when Pat said "the city," he meant Manhattan. The other boroughs of New York were *not* "the city" as far as Manhattanites were concerned.

"We used to worry every year when the newspapers brought out their 'best restaurants' list," Lovett went on, cheerfully. "If they mentioned one of your neighborhood joints, the prices would double, the waiters would start wearing tuxedos, and the chef would quit. The place would close down in less than a year."

It was hard for Jake to tell if Lovett was serious or not. Exaggerating, at least, he figured.

"Mr. Lovett!" A short, chunky, gray-haired man in a light gray suit and loosely knotted paisley tie came striding up to their table, arms spread wide.

Lovett jumped to his feet. "Paulie! How the hell are you, pal?"

"I was in the kitchen when you came in," said Paulie. "Welcome back!"

The two men embraced, their faces glowing with comradeship.

Jake got up from his chair and Lovett introduced him. Paulie seemed unimpressed with a mere science advisor to a US senator. It turned out that Paulie was the owner of the restaurant.

"I started as an assistant to the chef, when I was a kid." Paulie held a hand waist high to show how little he was then. "My grandfather taught me the business."

They chatted amiably for a few moments more, then Paulie excused himself and went up front to the bar to greet a pair of new arrivals.

Lovett said, "Paulie's the third generation to own this place."

A waiter came up with a bottle of red wine. "Compliments of Paulie," he said, in a decidedly Manhattan accent. "He says *benvenuto*, welcome home."

Lovett laughed softly. "I haven't been here in more than five years. Still, it feels like home."

Jake had never seen the man look so relaxed, so content.

Then he spotted Manstein entering the restaurant. Paulie spoke to him briefly, then began to lead him down to their table.

"That's him?" Lovett asked.

"That's him."

Lovett's tranquil smile disappeared.

Manstein...and Sebastian

Manstein was wearing an elegant off-white suit: Italian silk, Jake guessed. His precisely knotted tie was royal blue. He smiled handsomely as he followed Paulie to their table at the rear of the restaurant.

Jake and Lovett got to their feet as Manstein approached, looking perfectly relaxed. Jake was wound tight, and a glance at Lovett's face showed he was in dead-serious mode.

"Mr. Manstein," Jake said, "this is Patrick Lovett, Senator Tomlinson's campaign director."

Manstein extended his hand. "Delighted," he murmured.

Lovett said nothing.

As they sat down, a waiter came to the table and poured a glass of wine for Manstein.

He sipped at it, then nodded. "An Italian wine. Valpolicella, I believe."

Jake looked at the bottle's label. "Right."

"A decent wine," Manstein allowed.

Opening the menu before him, Jake asked, "What brings you to New York?"

"I am here to extend an invitation to you—or, rather, to Senator Tomlinson."

"An invitation?" Lovett asked.

"Yes. But perhaps we should order our food first."

He's enjoying this, Jake thought. Keeping us dangling. He's having fun.

Paulie himself came to the table, made a few suggestions, and took their orders: veal piccata for Lovett, a green salad for Manstein, and an antipasto plate for Jake.

As Paulie left, Lovett asked, "What about this invitation?"

Manstein leaned forward slightly and replied in a low voice, "Senator Sebastian would like to meet with your Senator Tomlinson. Privately, away from the news media and all that."

"He can do that in Washington, just about any day of the week," Lovett said.

"Oh come now, sir," Manstein replied. "They are two very busy and popular men. More than half the time they are out of Washington, campaigning. And when they are in the capital they are surrounded with news reporters and others."

Lovett nodded. "True enough. Still—"

"Still," Manstein interrupted, "Senator Sebastian feels it would be advantageous to have a quiet, face-to-face meeting. Without news reporters and cameramen, without hordes of underlings hovering around."

"He wants to talk to our man with no one listening in," Lovett said.

"Precisely. Oh, I suppose he could be accompanied by one or two of his staff. But no more. The meeting should be quiet, unnoticed—"

"Secret," Jake said.

Manstein almost smiled. "A rather melodramatic way of putting it. Let us say, private, confidential."

Secret, Jake repeated to himself. He glanced at Lovett, whose facial expression was halfway between intrigued and dubious.

"And what would be the subject of this quiet little meeting?" Lovett asked.

With a shrug, Manstein answered, "What else? The campaign. The race for the party's nomination. Perhaps even the campaign afterward, for the presidency."

Jake asked, "Will you be at this meeting?"

"I presume so."

Lovett started to ask another question, but a waiter came up to the table, pushing a cart that held their lunches.

Once the dishes were served and the waiter wheeled the cart away, Lovett said, "I'll have to speak to the senator about this, find out what he wants to do."

Manstein speared a lettuce leaf with a fork, then looked up. "I would advise you to have him make up his mind as quickly as he can. Senator Sebastian is a very busy man."

"He's not the only one," Jake snapped.

Manstein smiled. Like a snake.

As they flew back to Washington on Tomlinson's executive jet, Jake realized that a few days in New York had changed his view of the nation's capital. Looking down on the Washington Monument, the Mall with its row of museums, the Ellipse, and the White House, Jake recognized the city as a smaller, quieter town than he'd regarded it before. New York blared, it buzzed, it zoomed faster than any place he'd seen before.

Lovett was holed up with the senator in the private compartment in the plane's rear discussing their luncheon with Manstein while Amy and Tami were sitting together, up in the front row of the passenger compartment, heads together as they chatted like schoolgirls. Wonder what they're talking about, Jake asked himself. From the smiles on their faces it can't be anything very serious. Christ, Amy looks as if she hasn't a care in the world.

Jake pulled out his smartphone and called his office to find out how the finance committee's hearing had gone. After several rings, his administrative assistant finally picked up the phone.

"I'm sorry, Dr. Ross, I had to go down to Mr. Reynolds's office to get the results of the finance committee's hearing."

"And?" Jake prompted.

"Senator Zucco has scheduled a vote on the loan guarantee question for next Monday."

Astounded, Jake spluttered, "He did? Next Monday? Were there any objections to the issue? Any discussion?"

In the miniature screen of Jake's smartphone, the young woman's face looked perplexed. "I don't think so. Mr. Reynolds seemed pleased with the results of the hearing. He said the session was strictly routine, pretty dull."

"Okay," said Jake. "Thanks."

Pretty dull, he thought. Strictly routine. That means there wasn't any controversy. Zucco's set a vote for Monday. That means he expects it to sail through the committee in good shape. Or maybe he expects it to get shot down, once and for all.

Jake felt like gnawing his fingernails. The loan guarantee measure was the key to the entire space plan. If it didn't pass, the idea of having private investors finance the plan would go down the drain.

Monday, Jake told himself. Maybe I should try to wangle a visitor's seat for the session.

．．．

Once they got back to their condo unit and started to unpack, Jake asked Tami, "What were you and Amy talking about? You looked like a pair of sorority sisters dishing the dirt."

Tami pulled a wrinkled skirt from her travel bag, held it up and shook it. With a shake of her head she said, "I'll have to iron this one."

"Send it to the cleaners. Let them do it."

"Why spend the money when I can—"

"I can cover it in my travel allowance," Jake said.

She shot him a disapproving look. "My tax dollars at work? I can iron a skirt, for goodness' sake."

"Your time is worth money," he argued.

"And you're turning into a Washington insider."

Jake was surprised at the accusation. "Me?"

"You."

With a shrug, he said, "Okay, iron the skirt. I've got a couple of pairs of slacks that need ironing too."

Tami waggled a finger at him. "Oh no you don't. Iron your own slacks."

Jake suddenly realized that she was grinning at him. And she had very effectively avoided answering his question.

Pulling his rumpled slacks out of his roll-along suitcase, he asked again, "So what were you and Amy talking about?"

"Nothing important."

"You were doing a lot of giggling."

"It was nothing important," Tami repeated.

"Such as?"

She glared at him. "Hey, I'm supposed to be the interviewer, remember? I'm not used to being cross-examined."

"Cross-examined? I'm not grilling you. I merely asked you—"

"It was nothing," Tami said. "Just two women chatting. Nothing earth-shattering."

"Nothing about this Manstein thing?"

"Would we giggle about that?"

"I guess not," Jake admitted. He returned to emptying his suitcase.

"She was telling me how she has to be Frank's bodyguard when they're on the road. Lots of young chicks after his body."

Before he could think, Jake shot back, "And who's her body-guard?"

"That's not fair!"

"She's put Frank in a spot. He's going to be blackmailed. He could be ruined." Jake was surprised at the anger in his tone.

Tami stared at him, openmouthed. "It's that bad?"

"Sebastian wants to have a meeting with Frank. Very private. With Manstein."

"Oh," said Tami.

"Oh," Jake echoed.

"Will you be there?"

"I think so. I haven't talked about that yet with Frank and Lovett."

"Where and when?"

"Not settled yet." Suddenly Jake realized Tami was pumping him, as if he were a news source. "Hey, this is all hush-hush. Not for publication."

"Of course," she said. But Tami's expression reminded Jake of a sleek cheetah on the prowl. For the first time he wondered how far he could trust his wife.

Finance Committee

Senator Zucco had his finance committee purring along like a well-oiled machine. From his visitor's chair by the door of the room Jake watched Zucco greeting the arriving senators as they took their places in the double bank of seats in the front of the hearing chamber.

Oscar Zucco was small, and he seemed old, bent, frail, with wispy white hair and a prominent hooked nose. His smile looked genuine enough, Jake thought: like a kindly old grandfather beaming genially at his offspring.

Once he called the meeting to order he said, in a soft tenor voice, "Our first order of business this morning is to vote on the bill to have the Treasury Department guarantee long-term, low-interest loans for private firms to invest in new space development programs."

"Point of order, Senator."

Jake felt his brows knitting. He didn't recognize the woman who spoke. She was fiftyish, chunky, dark hair streaked with gray.

"Senator Fitzgerald, of Massachusetts," said Zucco, with a little nod in her direction.

Her heavy-featured face serious, almost grim, Senator Fitzgerald said, "This is a momentous bill. Giving the Treasury Department the power to guarantee loans is a serious step in a direction that is fraught with pitfalls. I believe we should discuss the matter further."

Zucco stared at her for a hard moment. Then, "We have discussed the ramifications of this bill, discussed them very seriously. You were unfortunately absent from several of our sessions."

"I had other obligations . . ."

Zucco blinked his eyes and nodded. "Yes, I understand. But the committee has decided—in your absence—to vote on the matter this morning. Further discussion would merely go over ground we have already considered."

Suppressing a grin, Jake thought that Zucco might look frail, but he knew how to cut the legs out from under an opponent.

"I still think we should give this momentous bill more serious, deeper consideration."

"Are you making a motion to that effect?" Zucco asked. His tone was still mild, but Jake thought he heard iron underneath it.

"I so move," Fitzgerald said.

"Second?"

Three other hands went up around the table. All Democrats, Jake realized.

Zucco took it all in stride. He called for a vote on Senator Fitzgerald's motion, and it was voted down, along party lines.

"Very well," said Senator Zucco. "Now let us proceed to vote on the bill."

It passed. Even a handful of the senators who voted with Fitzgerald backed away from her and helped pass the bill. Jake breathed a sigh of relief.

Zucco's screwed Sebastian, he thought. In public. Tomlinson's stock will go up and Sebastian's down.

Suddenly Jake realized, We've won! Zucco's made his calculations and he's jumped to our side!

Jake felt like leaping up from his visitor's chair and baying at the Moon.

. . .

"Don't start counting your chickens just yet," warned Kevin O'Donnell, once Jake bounced into the office wearing a triumphant smile. "Sebastian could still scuttle the bill when it comes up for the full Senate's vote."

Jake's cheerful mood slipped a notch. "What do you mean?" he asked the staff chief. "The bill should win a yes-or-no vote in the full Senate. And it'll pass in the House easily."

As O'Donnell led Jake past the desks and cubicles in the front of Senator Tomlinson's suite back toward his own office, he explained, "Yeah, so it passes in the Senate and the House. Then it goes to the president for her signature."

"You think she'd veto it?"

O'Donnell stopped at the door to his private office. "In a New York second. Lots of people are against your idea of having the government guarantee loans to private investors. I'm not sure I go for the idea, myself."

Suddenly feeling deflated, Jake muttered, "And we won't have the votes to override a veto."

O'Donnell patted Jake's shoulder. "If our man wins the presidential election next November, you can get the bill reconsidered."

"But if Sebastian wins. Or the Democrats."

O'Donnell made an elaborate shrug. "That's politics, Jake. The best-laid plans can get kicked into the trash bin of history."

"Thanks for the good news, Kevin," Jake growled. And he headed off toward his own office, on the other end of the suite.

National Defense

Patrick Lovett leaned back in his desk chair, a satisfied smile on his face.

"That was the key to your whole space plan, Jake," he said. "Now it goes to the president for her signature."

"If she decides to sign it," Jake said. He was sitting on a molded plastic chair in front of Lovett's desk.

They were in the Tomlinson campaign headquarters; Jake could hear the buzz and swirl of activity out on the floor of the former supermarket beyond the flimsy six-foot-high partitions of Lovett's office.

Lovett's smile turned crafty. "Doesn't really matter if she signs it or not," he said. "If she vetoes the bill it gives us a solid issue for next fall's campaign. If she signs it, we can push the space plan as Frank's program, play up the job creation and economic impact of it all."

"Heads we win, tails she loses."

Lovett nodded. "We're in a good position."

"What about Sebastian, though? He's still ahead of Frank by more than ten percentage points."

"Frank's poll numbers are creeping up on Sebastian. We've got one more debate coming up, then the party caucuses in Iowa."

"And the New Hampshire primary, right afterward."

Lovett said, "The more people see and hear Frank, the

higher his poll numbers. I think Sebastian's scared. That's why he wants this meeting with our man."

"Have you settled on a time and place?" Jake asked.

"They're both going to be campaigning in New Hampshire next week. Sebastian's people have arranged for a quiet meeting in the home of an old friend of his. A week from Sunday."

Jake nodded.

"Better pack your woolies," Lovett said. "It gets cold up there in the hills."

"I'm going?"

"You, me, and Frank. Sebastian's bringing two of his people."

"Manstein'll be one of them."

"More than likely," Lovett agreed.

"Nobody else."

"Nobody. I'd appreciate it if you didn't mention this to your wife."

"Tami can keep her mouth shut."

"Maybe. But she's a newswoman and I don't want to take any chances."

Jake said, "I understand." But he saw another wedge being driven between himself and Tami.

. . .

When Jake got back to his office in the Hart S.O.B. he had a phone message from William Farthington waiting for him. He immediately called through the open office door to his executive assistant and told her to answer the NASA administrator's message.

I wonder what Bloviating Billy wants, he asked himself.

Farthington smiled his usual disarming grin in the phone screen.

"Good of you to return my call, Jake. I know you must be awfully busy."

Jake smiled back and returned the BS. "Always happy to talk with you, sir. What's up?"

His expression turning more serious, Farthington said, "I want you to meet an old friend of mine: General Harold Harmon. He's the chief of the Air Force's Space Command."

Jake's heart sank. Another expert who wants to stick his two cents' worth into the space plan, he thought.

But he said to Farthington, "Sure. Where and when?"

"At your convenience, Jake. But the sooner the better."

Jake tapped his computer keyboard to call up his appointments schedule.

"How about Friday?"

"Fine!" said Farthington. "We can have lunch with Hal in his office in the Pentagon."

Feeling certain that this would be a waste of time, but unwilling to risk offending Farthington, Jake replied, "Okay. Have one of your people send me the details, would you please?"

"No need. I'll meet you in the visitors' entrance at noon, precisely."

. . .

The Pentagon reminded Jake of an ants' nest: people scurrying along everywhere, intent, busy, purposeful. Most of them were in uniform, but even the civilians seemed to be focused, hurried. Out around the parking lots men and women in gym gear were jogging determinedly, as if they were in training for the Olympics.

Farthington met Jake at the visitors' entrance and guided him through the business of getting through the security check. At last, with a badge clipped to his jacket lapel, Jake followed Farthington through a maze of hectic corridors to a bank of elevators.

"This place can be kind of confusing to newcomers," Farthington said genially as the elevator doors closed. "Lots of lieutenant colonels scrambling to earn their eagles."

Jake wasn't sure what that meant, but he nodded anyway.

"I first met Hal Harmon when we were both in West Point. He went into the Air Force, did all right for himself."

"Head of the Space Command," Jake agreed.

"They call him 'Hardass Harmon,' you know," Farthington said, with a grin. "But not to his face."

The elevator doors slid open. The corridors weren't quite as frantic at this level, but still there were plenty of men and women in uniform pacing purposefully along. Jake felt out of place in his sports coat and slacks, but then he realized that Farthington was wearing civvies too.

They entered an office suite and were immediately ushered by an airman to General Harmon's private office.

Harold Harmon was a four-star general, and he wore those stars on his shoulders as if they defined who and what he was. His hair was silver-gray, chopped down to a military buzz cut. His face was not hard, exactly, but certainly firm, chiseled. Steel-gray eyes. Strong, almost painful grip when he took Jake's hand.

The general led his visitors to the round conference table in one corner of his spacious office. Through its windows Jake could see the rows upon rows of white crosses of Arlington National Cemetery.

"Take a seat," General Harmon said, in a deep voice. Three trays covered by silvered domes rested on the table. Our lunches, Jake guessed.

As Jake reached for the domed cover nearest him, General Harmon said, "They knocked out another one of our birds yesterday."

Jake blinked at the general. "Huh?"

Ignoring the tray in front of him, General Harmon leaned forward slightly in his chair and said, "What I'm about to tell you is top secret."

Jake started to say, "I'm afraid I don't have—"

"I know you don't have a formal clearance, but I figure the

science advisor of a US senator knows when to keep his mouth shut." He glanced at Farthington. "Besides, Billy vouched for you."

Jake put the lid back on his lunch.

"In the past six months," Harmon said, his face grim, "three of our recce birds have gone dark."

"Reconnaissance satellites," Farthington said, by way of explanation. "Incapacitated."

"Their sensors just shut down, *poof*!" The general snapped his fingers. "Like that."

Jake didn't know what to say, so he said nothing.

"My bright guys tell me it's probably a high-power laser overloading the birds' sensors. Blinding 'em."

"A laser?" Jake asked.

With a single curt nod, Harmon said, "We have international agreements not to place weapons of mass destruction in space. But lasers are weapons of *pinpoint* destruction."

"And they shut down the reconnaissance satellites' sensors."

"On three of our birds."

Farthington said, "It's not an accident. Somebody's shooting at us."

"But who?"

"We suspect the Russians. Maybe the Chinese, but it's more likely to be the Russians."

"But why?" Jake asked. "What's going on?"

With a grim smile, General Harmon answered, "It's a test. They're testing their laser system. And they're testing our ability to respond to the threat."

"It's a sort of undeclared war," Farthington said.

Jake said, "Can't the UN do something?"

Harmon made a sour face. "That debating society? Hah. Besides, we want to keep this as quiet as possible. No fuss. No publicity. We've triangulated the most likely location of the laser. It's in one of the Russians' milsats, we're pretty sure."

"Military satellites," Farthington translated.

"So we're going to take care of that bird. It's going to get hit by a piece of space junk. *Bang*. Off the air. Out of commission. Too bad."

"But that's . . ." Jake hesitated, then finished his thought, "that's an act of war, isn't it?"

Harmon answered with a tight grin and, "No. It's just a little game we're playing. The Russians are trying to see how far they can go. If we ever get into a real shooting way, they'll want to knock out as many of our milsats as they can. This is just a test to see if we can figure out what they're doing, and respond to it."

"But why are you telling me about it?"

"You're pushing this new space plan."

"But it's entirely peaceful!"

"Sure it is," said the general. "But you'll be putting a lot of assets on the Moon and in cislunar space. Tempting targets, possibly."

"You think the Russians would try to damage peaceful civilian space facilities?"

"The Russians, maybe. Or the Chinese. Or the Iranians, or some bunch of terrorist wackos. Lots of possibilities."

"Holy god," Jake muttered.

"Sooner or later you're going to need protection," General Harmon said. "I thought you ought to know that, understand the situation. The more assets you put in space, the more tempting targets you're setting up for a potential enemy."

"Sooner or later," Farthington agreed.

"Okay," said the general. "Message sent and received. Let's eat lunch."

Jake had no appetite at all.

It looks like a Currier and Ives Christmas card," said Tami.

She and Jake were riding in a chauffeured black sedan through the snowy hills west of Nashua, toward a rustic hotel next to the campus of Daniel Webster College, near the state's capital.

It was late afternoon, but cloudy, dark, ominous. By five p.m. it would be black as night, Jake knew. The land was blanketed with snow, although the road had been plowed down to the bare paving, and it was warm enough inside the sedan so that both Jake and Tami had unbuttoned their heavy winter overcoats.

Senator Tomlinson was giving a televised speech in Nashua. He and Patrick Lovett would rendezvous with Jake at the hotel at six p.m., then the three of them would be driven to the home of Senator Sebastian's friend, farther out in the hills.

"Hope it doesn't snow again," Jake said, peering up at the cloudy sky.

"Weather forecast doesn't call for snow," said Tami.

Jake nodded absently. He was still thinking about General Harmon's revelation. They're fighting a battle in orbital space. A silent, undeclared, contest. But it's real. We've got to be prepared to protect ourselves in space. Damn!

"When is Senator Sebastian showing up?" Tami asked.

"Six thirty or so," Jake replied. "He's flying in from a rally in Boston. The house where they're meeting has an airstrip."

Tami's brows rose. "Convenient."

With a tight grin, Jake started, "Rich or poor . . ."

". . . it pays to have money," Tami finished. They both laughed.

Jake and Tami took a light dinner at the hotel, then Lovett showed up at the entrance to the dining room, looking almost like a local in a heavy British thorn-proof coat and a ridiculous-looking fur hat with earflaps jammed down over his head.

Jake dabbed at his chin with his napkin, got up from his chair, and leaned over to kiss Tami. "Remember," he whispered, "this is all not for publication."

With a bit of a grimace, Tami whispered back, "I know. Deep cover."

"Loose lips sink ships," Jake quoted inanely, then he hurried toward the waiting Lovett.

The ride out to the designated country estate was quiet, tense with expectation. Tomlinson, Lovett, and Jake sat squeezed into the rear seat of the sedan. Jake recognized the driver as one of the Tomlinsons' servants, from the senator's house in DC.

"Hope it doesn't snow again," Lovett said.

Favorite topic of conversation in New Hampshire, Jake thought.

The house was a rambling old wooden structure, only one story high except for a sort of turret poking up near the front entrance. The owner himself—a lanky, balding New Hampshireman—led them through the front entrance, past several closed doors, and finally into a spacious recreation room in the back of the house. Pool table, ping-pong table, bookshelves along one wall that held mostly magazines, a cold and dark fireplace, and a single wide window that looked out onto the snowy woods.

"I've known Brad Sebastian since we were in the infantry together, back in Afghanistan," their host said, in a twangy New Hampshire drawl. "Good man. He'll make a fine president."

"He's not here yet?" Lovett asked.

As if in answer, the drone of an airplane's engines came throbbing through the dark sky.

Their host smiled cannily. "Right on time." And he hurried across the room to turn on the gas-fed fireplace. Suddenly the room seemed cheerier.

About fifteen minutes later Senator Bradley Sebastian entered the room, with Manstein and another youngish man flanking him.

The host left the room, almost tiptoeing, and closed the door firmly behind him. Jake, Tomlinson, and Lovett stood facing Sebastian and his two aides. Jake got an impression of the Earps and the Clantons at the O.K. Corral.

Senator Sebastian broke the silence. "I'm glad you could come."

Tomlinson gave him a guarded smile. "Good of you to invite us, Brad."

Sebastian gestured to the big leather sofa and scattering of chairs on the other side of the pool table. "Let's be comfortable. Do you want anything to eat? Drink?"

"We've had dinner," Lovett said as he started toward the chairs.

As they sat—Tomlinson's trio on the sofa, Sebastian's on the armchairs facing them—Lovett asked, "So we're all in our places. What do you want to talk about?"

"The campaign, what else?" Sebastian said.

Jake saw that Manstein seemed a bit uptight; his usual knowing smirk was nowhere in sight.

"It's getting interesting, isn't it?" Tomlinson said. He seemed relaxed, at ease. "I had a good audience this afternoon in Nashua."

Sebastian looked tired, Jake thought, like a grandfather who'd been working too hard. He was actually perspiring. Can't be the fireplace, Jake told himself. It's all the way over on the other side of the room.

"I want to bring the party together," he said, his voice calm, reasonable. "It's a fatal mistake for the two of us to be competing against each other. We'll be handing the White House to the Democrats if we can't find a way to work together."

"I'm not so sure of that," said Tomlinson. "After all, the primaries exist so that the voters can see the candidates, listen to their ideas, make up their minds about who they want to represent them."

"We should be looking at the November election, not trying to slit each other's throats."

Before Tomlinson could reply, Lovett put a hand on the senator's arm and asked Sebastian, "What do you have in mind?"

Sebastian blinked once, twice, then licked his lips. "You withdraw your candidacy and I'll support you for president eight years from now."

With a crooked grin, Tomlinson said, "You're assuming you'll be reelected next time around."

"If you win this time in November," Lovett added.

"That's right," Sebastian replied. "If the party's united we can beat whoever the Democrats run next year."

Breaking into a knowing grin, Lovett said, "Our incumbent president isn't doing very well, is she?"

"She's not running."

"Good thing, too. She's made a mess of everything she's touched."

"We can beat whoever the Democrats put up," Sebastian insisted. "*If* our party is united. We can't afford to be fighting each other."

Tomlinson shook his head. "Seems to me that the polls show both you and I are comfortably ahead of whoever the Democrats choose."

"That doesn't mean much," said Sebastian's aide.

"I want a united party," Sebastian repeated. "That's the way to win next November."

"A united party," said Tomlinson. "With you at its head."

"Yes! I've earned the right! I've put in my years. I *deserve* the nomination."

Tomlinson leaned back in the softly yielding sofa. "That's for the voters to decide, isn't it?"

For a long moment Sebastian remained silent, staring hard at Tomlinson. Jake could hear the soft whooshing of the gas-fed fireplace all the way across the big room.

Very softly, reluctantly, Sebastian said, "I could knock you out of the race, you know. I could ruin your career entirely."

Tomlinson's chin went up a notch. Turning his eyes toward Manstein, he replied tightly, "Maybe."

"Why can't you be reasonable?" Sebastian asked, almost pleading.

"I made my father a promise, on his deathbed," Tomlinson answered. "I can't go back on that."

And Jake thought, Even from the grave, Frank's father is manipulating him.

Manstein spoke up. "Death cancels all debts, you know."

"No, it doesn't." Tomlinson looked as if he wanted to get up and slug Manstein.

Jake broke in. "If you go public with your little story, we'll demand that you take a lie detector test. In public. Whose reputation will be ruined by that?"

Manstein waved a hand in the air. "I will simply refuse to answer any questions about what took place after my private little dinner with your charming wife. After all, a gentleman does not kiss and tell."

Lovett actually grabbed Tomlinson's arm, holding him down on the sofa.

"Nothing happened and you know it!" the senator snapped.

"I know it," said Manstein, with his irritating smirk. "You know it. But will the public accept that idea?"

"They will if you tell the truth."

With a sad shake of his head Manstein retorted, "Ahh, you Americans with your touching faith in the will of the people. Don't you understand that the more I deny anything happened the more your precious public will believe the worst?"

Tomlinson yanked his arm free of Lovett's grasp and jumped to his feet. "Go ahead and shoot your mouth off! Say what the fuck ever you want. You tell your story and Amy and I will tell ours and to hell with you!"

Senator Sebastian raised both his hands in a placating gesture. "Frank, Frank, be reasonable. There's no need for getting angry."

"The hell there isn't," Tomlinson barked. "This slimy son of a bitch is trying to ruin my wife and you're helping him to do it!"

Lovett stood up beside Senator Tomlinson. "Cool it, Frank. Don't let your temper get the better of you."

Sebastian, almost pleading, said, "Frank, don't you realize I've been keeping this whole matter quiet? I've kept everything under wraps."

"For now," Tomlinson said.

"For as long as I need to," Sebastian replied. "All I'm asking from you is to step aside gracefully—and I'll find a place for you in my cabinet. Maybe secretary of the interior. Or commerce, if you prefer that."

Tomlinson shook his head. "I appreciate it, Brad. But no thanks. I'm in this campaign until the bitter end."

Manstein's smirk turned into a pitying smile. But he kept his mouth shut. Good thing, Jake thought as he got to his feet. For two cents I'd punch out the bastard myself.

Tomlinson turned to Lovett. "Come on, Pat. This has been a waste of time."

And he stalked past Sebastian, who remained in his chair, looking like a grandfather who was bewildered by his grandson's impolite behavior.

Riding with Jake and Senator Tomlinson through the dark, moonless night back to the hotel where Tami waited, Patrick Lovett shook his head disapprovingly.

"You broke one of the basic rules of the game, Frank."

Sitting in the middle of the sedan's rear seat, Tomlinson grunted, "Did I?"

"Ever hear of Ev Dirksen's three rules of politics?"

Jake, on Tomlinson's other side, remembered that the old senator's first two rules were, "One: get elected. Two: get re-elected."

"Yeah." Lovett explained, "And the third rule is, don't get mad, get even."

"Big deal," Tomlinson muttered.

"You lost your temper, Frank. Not smart. Didn't you see that Sebastian was trying to placate you? He doesn't like this Manstein business any more than you. He's keeping Manstein quiet, for god's sake!"

"Is he?"

"Yes, he is. But you're pushing him into letting Manstein blab the story to the media."

"Let him."

"Are you crazy?"

Tapping Lovett's leg with a stiff finger, Tomlinson said, "Pat, as long as Manstein is around he'll hold that story over us. He can go public with it tomorrow, or a month from now.

He can spring it at the opening of the party convention next summer. I say we should let him tell his story now, while we've got time to let it play out in the media. By next summer it'll be old news."

Jake sat there on the senator's other side, feeling stunned at this revelation of political strategy. Let them fire their best shot; we'll weather the storm. Maybe Frank's right. Maybe that's the best course of action. Get past Manstein once and for all.

But Lovett said, "That'll be awful rough on your wife, you know. They'll be after her like a pack of wolves."

"Amy can handle it. We've talked it over. She's ready to face them down."

For long moments Lovett said nothing. The car was silent except for the purr of the motor and the drone of the tires on the roadway. The snowy landscape slid by, silent and cold. In the distance Jake could see the lights of a lone farmhouse breaking the darkness.

At last Lovett said, in a near whisper, "That's a tough path you've picked out."

"Do you see any easier ones?" Tomlinson demanded.

Lovett puffed out a long sigh. Then, "No. I wish I did, but I don't."

"Then let's face this head-on."

"Damn the torpedoes, eh?"

"Right," said the senator.

Jake thought of Custer charging into the whole Sioux nation at the Little Bighorn.

. . .

Earl Reynolds looked stunned. "Go public?" he gasped.

Jake was sitting in Senator Tomlinson's office with Pat Lovett, Kevin O'Donnell, and the media relations director, the four of them in the deep leather chairs arrayed in front of the senator's desk.

"Go public," said Tomlinson. "The sooner the better."

Reynolds's beefy face morphed slowly from astonishment to careful calculation.

"Break the story now, get it out in the open," he mused.

"Get it behind us," said Lovett.

O'Donnell shook his head. "It'd be better to keep it covered up."

"No," said Lovett. "That puts the ball in Sebastian's court. He can spring it whenever and wherever he chooses. Where it'll do the most harm to us."

Jake thought that O'Donnell looked even more disconsolate than usual. "You can't tell the media that Frank's wife might have been fooling around behind his back. That's suicide!"

Reynolds turned slightly in his chair to look squarely at the senator's office chief. "Maybe not, Kev. If we break the story in the right way, at the right time—"

"The time is now," Tomlinson said firmly. "Before Manstein can give his version of the story."

"Amy actually had the guy over for dinner while you were out of town?" Reynolds asked, in a *tell me it's not so* tone.

"Yes," the senator replied, tightly.

"And the servants were out of the house?"

"All except the cook," Tomlinson said, his face growing grimmer.

"Jeez."

Lovett said, "But if we break it the right way—"

"Get the fuss and fury behind us, now, before the Iowa caucuses," Tomlinson said.

"It'll kill Iowa for us," O'Donnell muttered.

"Better than losing Carolina," said Lovett. "Or Pennsylvania."

"Or California," Jake piped up.

Lovett almost smiled. "Hell, it might even help us in California."

Nobody laughed.

A week later, Jake had just returned from a quick trip to Los Angeles, where he had met with engineers and executives from United Launch Alliance to nail down the details of buying six launches of their heavy boosters as part of the first phase of building a permanent base on the Moon.

To Jake's shock, Senator Tomlinson was waiting for him in the back seat of the limousine he had sent to meet Jake on his arrival at Reagan Airport, smiling at him when the chauffeur opened the stretch limo's rear door.

As Jake climbed into the capacious rear seat, the senator said, "Jake, I need you to do me a favor."

Putting his briefcase down beside him, Jake asked, "A favor? Sure. What is it?"

As the chauffeur chucked Jake's well-worn travel bag into the limo's trunk and slammed the lid shut, the senator replied, his smile dimming noticeably, "You know Amy's giving the speech tomorrow at the Career Women's luncheon."

Jake hadn't known, but he nodded anyway.

"I want you to go with her. Give her some moral support."

Another shock. For several moments Jake sat in silence as the chauffeur slid in behind the wheel and pulled the limo away from the curb.

At last Jake squeaked, "Me?"

"You."

"Frank, I don't think I'm the best man for the job. After all, I—"

Tomlinson interrupted, "You, Jake. She's known you since back before we came to Washington. She trusts you."

Jake's memory flashed back to the nights he and Amy had spent in bed together, before she decided to marry Tomlinson.

Trying to keep the reluctance out of his voice, Jake said, "Sure. Okay. I'll do it for you, Frank."

"Thanks, Jake. I owe you one."

. . .

Amy sent the family car—a maroon BMW sedan—to pick up Jake at the Hart building. She was sitting in the back seat, wearing a knee-length skirted suit of sky blue that complemented her honey-blonde hair.

"Hi, Jake," she said, smiling brightly, as he ducked in beside her.

Jake studied her face. No tension, no worries, just her big cheerleader's smile and sparkling blue eyes.

"Big speech," he muttered.

"I guess," Amy said. Before Jake could think of anything more to say, she added, "It's sweet of you to come with me. I feel really protected."

Jake thought, You don't need any protection. You've got ice water in your veins. But then he saw that Amy's hands were clenched into fists on her lap. Is this bold front all camouflage? he asked himself. Is she really scared?

"Is there anything I can do?" he asked. "Anything you need—"

"Just sit out there and smile at me, Jake. Show me I have a friend in the audience."

Friend, Jake repeated to himself. Yeah, friend.

"Okay," he agreed. "Sure."

Amy chatted away blithely about the campaign and how well her husband was doing in the polls as they rode toward the newly renovated Westin Georgetown hotel, where the luncheon was being held. Jake said nothing, even though he knew that Tomlinson's poll numbers weren't gaining much on Sebastian's. And her speech today could sink them altogether.

As they approached the hotel Jake asked, "Do you have your speech?"

Amy tapped her temple. "In here. I've got it all memorized."

Jake nodded. "I guess that's better than reading it."

"Of course."

He wanted to ask her if she had gone to bed with Manstein that night, but found that he couldn't. He couldn't mention even the first word of the question. And, in truth, Jake was afraid of the answer Amy might give him.

Instead he told her, "You know that Earl Reynolds has tipped off a couple of his news contacts about this."

Nodding, Amy replied, "Frank told me. Don't worry, I'll smile for the cameras, in all the right places."

"Don't be nervous." It was a stupid thing to say and Jake knew it.

With a little laugh, she said, "I'm not as nervous as you are."

Jake realized that she was right.

. . .

As soon as they entered the hotel, Amy was immediately surrounded by the Career Women's executive committee. Nearly a dozen women, ranging in age from their thirties (Jake guessed) to white-haired maturity. All smartly dressed, all smiling and clustered around Amy. Jake tagged along as they escorted Amy to the hotel's ballroom, chatting and laughing, totally ignoring him.

The ballroom was only about half full, almost entirely with women. Jake was surprised to see Tami across the crowd, standing at the improvised bar with a couple of guys. Must be newspeople, Jake thought.

Amy was completely occupied with the fawning executive committee, so Jake made his way to the bar.

He gave Tami a peck on the cheek. "You didn't tell me you'd be here," Jake said to her.

"I didn't know until an hour or so ago. Earl Reynolds asked me to mother-hen the news folks."

Jake nodded and ordered a club soda from the skinny Hispanic kid tending the bar. Only two news reporters. And one cameraman. They don't expect anything worth headlines from this little soirée. With an inner sigh Jake told himself, Well, we'll see.

"Ladies," came an amplified woman's voice from the dais up at the front of the room. "Luncheon is served!"

Jake had to leave Tami and go sit beside Amy for the lunch. The food wasn't bad, he thought: thin slices of roast beef with some tastily done vegetables. Nobody'll get fat on this, he realized.

Then the organization's chairwoman went up on the dais and introduced Amy, telling the assembled membership, "She's going to reveal some of the joys and problems of being a prominent senator's wife during a hectic national political campaign."

Amy rose to polite applause and stood behind the microphones. Jake glanced across the room at Tami; her eyes were on him, not the speaker. Jake smiled at her and she grinned back.

Amy started talking about the hectic details of a political campaign. "Your life's not your own anymore. And you're traveling so much that some days you wake up wondering what city you're in."

A few polite chuckles.

"Laundry becomes a major problem," Amy went on, with a rueful look. "When you're down to your last clean pair of . . ." she hesitated just a moment, then went on, ". . . pantyhose, with three more speeches that afternoon, you're facing a real crisis!"

Considerable laughter.

Slowly, Amy's speech became more serious. She spoke about helping her husband to stay healthy despite all the demands on his time and energy, and her own encounters with the news media.

"They want to know how I *feel* about women's issues. I wish they'd ask about what I *know* about the problems women face in the workplace."

Hearty applause.

Amy went on, "You're under a microscope all the time. You can't have a private life, can't have a relaxed quiet evening at home, even."

Here it comes, Jake thought.

"Why, one evening when I was at home while my husband was on a campaign trip, I invited a friend—a male friend—to have dinner with me at my home. Just a quiet dinner between two friends."

Jake looked over the audience. The women were totally focused on Amy. "The very next day the man told one of my husband's aides that he was going to the media and tell them that I had invited him to my house while my husband's back was turned."

Absolute silence from the audience.

"He was going to suggest to the news media . . ." Amy's voice broke a little. ". . . suggest that we'd had sex together. Some friend!"

Jake heard hisses from the audience.

Dabbing at her eyes, Amy continued, "He wanted money to keep his mouth shut. He wanted to blackmail me, blackmail my husband. Over an innocent little dinner!"

Boos broke out across the ballroom.

Putting on a rueful little smile, Amy said, "So one thing I've learned is that a woman has to be extra careful in everything she does. There's no such thing as a quiet little dinner between friends. Not for a woman. People are always ready to believe the worst about you. Some people will try to exploit you, to *use* you—one way or the other."

She lowered her head demurely. Applause rose from the women in the audience, scattered at first, but quickly they rose to their feet, clapping vigorously, even calling out Amy's name.

Jake got to his feet too, thinking, Amy's a cheerleader, all right. She's got these women totally on her side.

The committee's chairwoman climbed up onto the dais again and put an arm around Amy's shoulders. Leaning into the microphone, she said, "Thank you, Mrs. Tomlinson, for your forthright and informative speech." Gesturing to the standing audience, she added, "We all appreciate your honesty very much."

Amy smiled bravely at the audience.

The chairwoman continued, "We usually have a brief question-and-answer period now, but if you'd prefer to skip it . . ."

"Oh no," Amy said, in her little-girl voice. "I'll try to answer a few questions."

The newsman standing beside Tami at the bar called out in a foghorn voice, "Are you telling us that you never realized how . . . uh, improper it would look for you to have dinner alone with a male friend while your husband was out of town?"

Her face a picture of innocence, Amy replied, "I never even thought about that. I mean, if a woman can't have a dinner with a friend what are we supposed to do? Do you want to lock us in a tower whenever our husbands go out of town?"

The newswoman asked, "The two of you weren't alone, were you?"

"The cook was in the house."

"Just the cook?"

"The rest of the staff had the night off."

"Really?"

Amy said, "My cook is very protective. I never for a moment felt uncomfortable or threatened."

One of the women in the audience raised her hand. Amy nodded at her.

"And after dinner, he just went home?"

"Yes."

"You didn't even have an after-dinner drink?"

Amy blinked at her. "No, we didn't. We both had lots to do the next morning. I saw him to the door, he said good night, and that was it."

Jake looked around at the women seated at the luncheon tables. They want to believe her, he saw on their faces. Poor little rich girl, being threatened with blackmail by a big bad man.

The news reporters seemed more skeptical, but they knew better than to try to badger Amy. Not here. Not now. Not in front of this audience of believers.

The chairwoman stepped up to Amy's side again. "Thank you so much, Mrs. Tomlinson. I think this has been the most interesting luncheon we've ever had."

They got to their feet again, applauding lustily. Amy dipped her chin in acknowledgement.

Jake looked across the room toward Tami. The grin on her face said, *She's pulled it off.*

. . .

It took fully half an hour for Amy to work her way from the dais to the ballroom's door. Every woman in the audience, it seemed, wanted to speak to her, shake her hand, be near her.

She should be the one running for president, Jake thought. She'd take a hundred percent of the women's vote.

Tami worked her way through the crowd, to Jake's side.

"Quite a performance," she said into Jake's ear.

Jake nodded.

Amy reached for Tami's hand. "I'm so glad you're here, Tami. Why don't you and Jake come over to the house this evening and have dinner with us?"

Tami looked up at Jake, who shrugged, then nodded. "We'd be happy to," he said.

. . .

Jake got home early, and as he waited for Tami to arrive he scrolled through the TV news broadcasts. Nothing on the national networks, but all of the local stations carried brief reports on Amy's luncheon talk.

Just a snippet, but there was Amy standing at the lectern, looking somehow hurt and aggravated at the same time as she said, ". . . if a woman can't have a dinner with a friend what are we supposed to do? Do you want to lock us in a tower whenever our husbands go out of town?"

Then the screen showed the station's anchorwoman shaking her head and saying, "There certainly *is* a different standard of expectation for a woman than for a man."

. . .

As he tooled his Dart GT up the driveway of the Tomlinson residence, Jake saw several other cars already parked there.

"This isn't going to be a quiet family dinner," Tami said.

"No," Jake said. "Looks like we're in for an after-battle analysis session."

Sure enough, Lovett, O'Donnell, and Reynolds were already in the library with Senator Tomlinson and Amy. One of the butler's assistants was handling the bar.

Tomlinson, a heavy scotch already in his hand, greeted, "Jake! Tami! Come on in! What're you drinking?"

The senator wasn't drunk, Jake thought. But he was certainly letting off steam that had been bottled inside him ever since their meeting in New Hampshire with Sebastian and Manstein.

Reynolds was standing in front of the big wall-screen TV,

clicking away on the remote control. Jake saw he was sampling various website blogs.

The senator walked them to the bar, set up on a folding table. "What do you think of my wife's performance?" he asked Tami. "Doesn't she deserve an Emmy? Or an Oscar, even."

Tami smiled graciously. "She certainly won over her audience."

Jake nodded and asked the young liveried man behind the bar for a Jack Daniel's. Tami ordered a white wine.

Reynolds trundled over to the bar, a happy grin on his beefy face. "Even Lady Cecilia is congratulating her," he crowed. "Amy's the top story on tonight's *Power Talk*."

The butler announced that dinner was served. Jake held his drink in one hand and Tami's hand in the other as the whole group headed for the dining room.

"It's a triumph," Reynolds kept repeating. "A triumph."

Jake saw relief and satisfaction on Tomlinson's smiling face. Amy seemed pleased with herself.

But he worried about what Sebastian's reaction would be. There's going to be a counterattack, he told himself. There's got to be.

But for this night, for this group, there was nothing but good cheer.

Then Tami whispered in Jake's ear, "The proof of the pudding will be in the poll results."

T he eve of St. Agnes," Jake quoted to himself as he stared out the window of the Embassy Suites hotel at the snow sifting down from the darkened sky. "'Ah, bitter chill it was . . .'"

He frowned, trying to remember the rest of Keats's poem. Something about a hare limping trembling through the frozen grass.

From across the bedroom Tami asked, "What are you mumbling about?"

Turning toward her, Jake said, "An old poem, about the coldest night of the year."

It was February first, in Des Moines, and it had been snowing most of the day and into the night.

"It's not that cold," Tami said. "Not for Iowans. They're used to this kind of weather."

"It'll keep the turnout low," Jake groused. "We need a big turnout to win."

Pointing to the muted television set against the wall, Tami said, "Projections call for Frank to come in second."

"To Sebastian."

"With Hackman a distant third."

Focusing on the screen, Jake saw a pair of news commentators jawing away in muted silence, but no numbers posted.

"Too early for any returns," he mumbled.

The phone rang. Tami picked it up, then handed it to Jake. "Pat Lovett," she said.

Lovett sounded upbeat. "It's going to be a long night. Why don't you two come on up to the senator's suite? We've got some decent desserts and drinkables. Homemade pies!"

Jake glanced at Tami before answering. "Okay. Thanks. We'll be there in a little bit."

Tami insisted on changing into "something more dressy" and started rummaging through the clothes hanging in the closet. Jake figured his slacks and sports coat would be adequate until Tami pointed out that there would probably be newspeople—and cameramen—in the senator's suite. Reluctantly, Jake pulled on the one necktie he had brought along.

Senator Tomlinson's suite was already noisy and crowded with campaign workers and aides when Jake and Tami got there. And, just as Tami had warned, a trio of news reporters had ensconced themselves at the bar.

As Jake ordered a cabernet for Tami and a Jack Daniel's on the rocks for himself he heard one of the aides telling another:

". . . they waited until yesterday to have Manstein tell his story."

"The day before the voting here in Iowa," said his companion, a tall slinky-looking young woman with glitter in her long dark hair.

Earl Reynolds pushed into their conversation. "Manstein looks like a low-life bastard. People will figure, if he's telling the truth, it means he set Amy up. If he isn't telling the truth, then he's a lying son of a bitch."

"It doesn't help that he's on Sebastian's payroll, either," the male aide added.

Nodding sagaciously, Reynolds concluded, "Well, if Sebastian expects that jerk's story to sink Frank's chances he's dead wrong."

"We'll see soon enough."

"When the hell are the returns coming in?"

"Pretty soon, should be."

Jake led Tami from the bar to the opposite corner of the jam-packed room, past the muted wall-screen TV, to where Senator Tomlinson—with Amy at his side—was shaking hands with a lineup of well-wishers. The senator spotted Jake in the crowd and grinned at him and Tami.

"He doesn't look worried," Tami said, practically shouting to be heard over the noise.

Frank's still in campaign mode, Jake thought. Smile at everybody and press the flesh.

He towed Tami past the Tomlinsons, toward a sofa where Pat Lovett and a pair of his aides were bent over some sort of graph. Lovett had a Bluetooth clipped to his ear.

Tami said, "That looks like the kind of chart they use to bet on football games."

Jake shook his head. "That's a county-by-county grid of the state of Iowa. Pat's ready to fill in the numbers."

Lovett looked up as Jake and Tami approached. "Glad you could make it." Gesturing with a nod of his head, "They've got some pretty good food in the next room."

Jake sipped at his Jack Daniel's before replying, "Thanks. Can we get you anything?"

"A million votes or two."

Jake grinned derisively and headed through the mob toward the next room, with Tami alongside him.

• • •

It was almost three a.m. Tami was sitting bleary-eyed on the end of the sofa where Lovett was still fiddling with his graph. Jake, too nervous to sit, had been pacing across the big room for nearly half an hour. The big TV screen showed the gross voting numbers, but now the script scrolling along the bottom of the muted screen showed that the network commentators were discussing the breakdown of the voting patterns.

The final tally showed Sebastian had won, but not easily. He polled 43 percent of the Iowa vote, with Franklin Tomlinson at 38 percent, significantly more than had been expected. Governor Hackman had earned merely 19 percent of the vote, about half of what the "experts" had predicted.

The hotel room had emptied out considerably. The noise level had dropped to a few quiet conversations. There was ample room for Jake's pacing now. He saw Earl Reynolds quietly leaving, with the slinky brunette on his arm.

Senator Tomlinson came in from the bedroom, in his shirt-sleeves, without Amy. As he headed for the bar, he passed Jake and said, "I've done interviews with CNN and Fox News. I'm ready for some scotch."

The hotel-provided bartender had long since gone home, so Tomlinson stepped behind the bar and yanked out the nearly empty bottle of Chivas Regal.

Jake, who hadn't had a drink since his first Jack Daniel's, grinned wearily. "I'll join you, Frank."

He looked across the room to Tami, slumped tiredly on the sofa, who shook her head negatively.

Lovett looked up from his graph.

"We did all right," he said, to no one in particular.

But Tomlinson said, "Better than we expected."

"I think the Manstein problem is finished," Lovett said, with a tight smile. "We should thank Amy—"

"Amy's asleep," said the senator. "She was exhausted."

Lovett nodded, then tapped his graph with the pencil in his hand. "Frank, you scored big with the young voters, ages eighteen to thirty. They were the margin of your bump over the predictions."

"They're the ones who want to see us reinvigorate our space efforts," Tomlinson said.

Jake piped up, "They want to go to the Moon."

"I think we ought to lean on the space button a little harder in New Hampshire," Lovett said. "Capture the youth vote with it."

Tomlinson broke into a tired grin. "The children's crusade."

Jake countered, "The wave of the future."

The Wave of the Future

Compared to Iowa, Washington felt balmy, even though the DC area had been hit by a snowfall the night after the Tomlinson entourage landed at Reagan National.

Jake and Tami had awakened to their radio announcing, "... more than two inches of snow have blanketed the metropolitan area, with accumulations of up to four inches in the Maryland suburbs."

Two inches of snow in the city. Laughable in Iowa. Back in Montana, two inches would barely count as a snowstorm. But here in the nation's capital, a two-inch sprinkling was enough to snarl traffic and close schools, Jake knew.

He kissed Tami on the cheek and got out of bed. Peering through the window, he saw that Connecticut Avenue was already clogged with cars and buses. Nobody was shoveling off the sidewalks, though. The sky was clear, and an afternoon's sunshine would melt most of the snow away.

It was well past ten a.m. by the time Jake at last parked his convertible in the Hart building's underground garage. Traffic had been a mess, as he'd expected. The senator's office was barely half-occupied. As he made his way past the mostly empty desks, Jake thought that a good many of the office staff wouldn't even bother trying to get to work today.

But Kevin O'Donnell was there. He'd left a terse phone message for Jake: "Come to my office as soon as you get in." Brusque. Like a commanding general giving orders to one of the rank and file. Kevin wasted neither words nor time. Then Jake grinned inwardly. Kevin had to leave the message himself; his administrative assistant was probably still at home, taking a snow day off.

Jake quickly scrolled through his other messages. None of them were urgent, so he got up from his desk and headed for O'Donnell's office. The place was starting to wake up. Still fewer than half the staff had come in, but at least Jake smelled coffee brewing.

He tapped once on O'Donnell's door, then stuck his head in. "You rubbed the lamp, O master?"

Sitting behind his desk looking crankier than usual, O'Donnell blinked at Jake's little joke, then said, "Come on in. Close the door."

"What's up?" Jake asked as he sat in one of the padded chairs in front of the desk.

"Hackman wants to talk."

"Governor Hackman?"

O'Donnell nodded. The expression on his lean, narrow face was equal parts irritation and suspicion.

But Jake felt suddenly buoyed, excited. "You think he's going to throw in the towel?"

"No. At least, not yet."

"Then why—"

"He's sniffing around for a deal. I'll bet he's already set up a meeting with Sebastian."

"Does Pat Lovett know about this?"

"I talked with him half an hour ago. He's stuck in a traffic jam on the other side of the Teddy Roosevelt bridge."

"So why'd you call me?" Jake asked.

His sour expression easing not by a millimeter, O'Donnell said, "We want you to meet with Hackman's people."

"We? You mean you and Pat?"

"And the senator. I talked with him at some length this

morning. He's staying home today, doing a couple of media interviews on Skype."

"But why me? Why not Pat? Or you?"

Shaking his head, O'Donnell answered, "We're too visible. Hackman wants everything kept ultra-quiet. You can sneak out to South Carolina and nobody would notice you."

Thanks a lot, Jake groused silently. Aloud, he asked, "And what am I supposed to do?"

"Listen to what Hackman's people have to say. He won't meet with you himself, but a couple of his top aides will."

"And?"

"Find out what the hell they want," O'Donnell snapped, irritated. "If the governor is willing to drop out of the race, he's probably thinking of throwing his support to either Sebastian or us. Find out what he wants in return."

Jake got a mental impression of a Renaissance-era schemer, complete with long black cloak and a hidden dagger. Machiavelli, he thought. Is that what Kevin thinks of me?

"Kev, I'm just the senator's science advisor. I don't think—"

"It doesn't matter what you think! You don't even have to think! Just listen to what they have to say, don't make any commitments, and bring the information back to us."

Jake groused, "You could get a Western Union delivery boy to do that."

O'Donnell raised his eyes to the ceiling and muttered something too low for Jake to hear.

Running a hand through his thinning hair, he focused his dark eyes on Jake. "Listen to me. We need somebody we can trust for this meeting. Somebody who's got a couple of ounces of brains. Hackman's people will expect to see somebody who's pretty damned close to the senator. You're the guy Frank named for the job. Capisce?"

Despite his exasperation, Jake grinned at the harried staff chief. "I understand."

"You'll do it?"

"Sure. Where and when?"

"Hackman'll be campaigning in South Carolina next week. We'll set up the meeting for Charleston or maybe Myrtle Beach. Someplace where the governor isn't, so there's less chance of some media snoop seeing you."

With a wry grin, Jake confessed, "Kevin, I'm not well-enough known for the media snoops to recognize me."

"Exactly why we picked you for this assignment." And for the first time O'Donnell broke into a tight smile.

. . .

Jake left O'Donnell's office and made his way back to his own. To his pleased surprise, his administrative assistant had arrived at her desk, smiling up at him. Her fur-trimmed coat was thrown over one of the visitors' chairs and her boots looked wet, sloshy.

"Mr. Piazza called to remind you of the launch at eleven thirty, our time."

"Thanks, Nancy," Jake said as he pushed through the door to his private office. Glancing at his wristwatch, he saw that it was a few minutes past eleven.

"Nancy," he called through the half-open door, "remind me a couple of minutes before eleven thirty, will you, please?"

"Certainly, Dr. Ross."

Jake remembered that this was the first mission of Astra Corporation's new upgraded rocket booster, Astra Super. The bird had performed flawlessly through three test flights and today was carrying four astronauts—one of them a Russian—to the International Space Station.

Still thinking of the meeting in South Carolina that O'Donnell was setting up, Jake dug into his morning schedule. The Senate's subcommittee on science was due to hold another hearing on climate change, and Jake had to get the senator prepped for it.

At precisely 11:28 Nancy buzzed to remind Jake of the launch.

He thanked her and flicked on the big wall-screen TV, already tuned to the space news channel.

Standing in the brilliant New Mexico sunshine, the Astra Corporation launching rocket stood straight and tall, with four solid rocket boosters strapped to its base and a swept-winged crew module at its tip. Jake turned his attention back to the coming subcommittee hearing until he heard:

". . . five . . . four . . . three . . ."

As he looked up at the TV screen the umbilical cord feeding liquid oxygen into the launcher's first-stage tankage dropped away. Billows of steam rose all around the launch stand, obscuring the rocket vehicle's lower section.

The announcer said, ". . . two . . . one . . . liftoff! We have liftoff!"

The rocket rose straight and true into the turquoise New Mexico sky.

And blew up.

Accident?

Jake felt it like a blow to his solar plexus.

A fiery ball of red and orange blossomed around the launch stand, streaked with oily black swirls. A flash of something too swift to follow zoomed up and out of the TV picture. Jake could see the launcher's slim body toppling into the fireball, secondary explosions bursting like deadly fireworks.

"It blew up!" shouted the stunned announcer.

Four people, Jake thought. A Russian and three Americans. One of the Americans was a woman.

"Astra Super has exploded," the announcer was recovering his wits, "at T plus six seconds. The crew module's escape system apparently worked . . ."

The screen switched to a slow-motion view of the explosion. Jake saw the swept-winged crew module streak off into the air, away from the explosion, hurtling high and away with the four astronauts inside it.

A new voice came through, deeper, calmer, tense but unruffled. "The crew module's emergency escape system has apparently functioned as designed."

A different camera view showed the crew module's blunt cylinder of dull metal separating from the swept-winged upper stage of the launcher. It arced higher into the clear blue sky, propelled by a pair of blazing jets at its rear.

"Escape module separation on schedule," the voice stated,

cool and composed. "Parachute deployment should take place . . . *now*."

Four little parachutes popped out of the escape pod's nose. Jake knew they were drogue chutes, not big enough to bring the module down safely. They yanked out a quartet of huge chutes, striped in gaudy red, white, and blue, which unfolded and blossomed out like protecting angels. The escape pod swung back and forth beneath them like a dark little pendulum.

"Main chutes deployed," said the flat, calm voice. Jake presumed it was the launch director speaking. "No word from the crew."

The crew members had been slammed with eight gees when the escape pod blasted free of the doomed rocket launcher, Jake knew. They were probably unconscious from the tremendous acceleration. Or dead.

"We're okay!" a different voice shouted. "Banged up a bit from the gee force. Bet we all have black eyes tomorrow."

The launch director's voice suddenly became animated. "You had us worried down here, pal."

"Escape system works as designed. No troubles."

"Thank god."

Thank the engineers who designed the escape system, Jake added silently. And thank Nick Piazza for insisting that the pod be built into the crew module.

The TV cameras followed the escape pod's graceful descent to the desert floor. It hit the dusty ground, bounced once, then came down for good, leaning over on one side. The huge parachutes spread over it like brightly colored protective draperies.

A small armada of vans and ambulances were rushing toward it, throwing up billows of dust across the desert.

Jake sat riveted in his desk chair as the emergency crew got to the escape pod, pried open its hatch, and carefully, tenderly, lovingly helped the four battered astronauts into the waiting ambulances.

They're all able to walk, Jake saw. The emergency team was helping them, holding their arms, boosting them into the ambulances. But they were all alive, even if battered.

More than three miles away the wreckage of the Astra Super's lower stages still burned at the launchpad.

· · ·

As the ambulances hurried toward the small hospital built into the Spaceport America facility, Jake broke free of the spell that had kept him watching the TV scene and grabbed his desktop telephone to call Senator Tomlinson.

The senator himself answered on the second ring.

"Did you see it?" Jake asked Tomlinson's image in his phone screen.

"I sure did," the senator replied. "Nearly had a goddamn heart attack when the bird blew up."

"You've got to get to the Senate and call for an investigation."

Tomlinson shook his head. "Jake, the Senate's closed today. The snow."

"Then get Reynolds to set up media interviews for you. This accident has to be investigated and you've got to lead the call for it. Don't make it look like it's being forced on us."

"Have you checked this out with Pat? Or Kevin?"

"Not yet. Time is of the essence. You want to lead this parade, not follow it. Call Reynolds. Now! I'll talk it over with Kevin—and Pat, when he shows up."

Looking thoughtful, Tomlinson replied, "Maybe you're right. I'll tell Earl to set up some interviews."

"I'll ask Kevin to get a police escort for you, so you can get to the office right away."

Ruefully, the senator said, "Guess I'd better get dressed."

Only then did Jake realize that Senator Tomlinson was still in his pajamas. Deep blue with sprinkles of stars.

. . .

Nicholas Piazza was grim-faced.

In the image on Jake's office wall-screen TV, the head of Astra Corporation no longer looked like a cheerful teenager. His lean, bony face was set in a belligerent scowl. Jake thought he looked like a kid who was itching for an opportunity to punch someone. Hard.

"We can't rule out sabotage," he said to Jake.

Christ, Jake thought. The metal of his rocket's wreckage hasn't even cooled yet and he wants to hang the explosion on a saboteur.

"Nick," he said to the wall screen, "isn't it too early to tell if somebody deliberately—"

Piazza tapped his chest. "I *know* it was sabotage. In here. I know it. That bird was inspected time and again. We had four people on board! Do you think we'd just let the damned launch go off without checking and rechecking everything?"

"No, I guess not," Jake backpedaled. "But sabotage? Who in hell would want to blow up your rocket?"

"Terrorists, that's who! The bastards who dragged us into this damned war in Latin America!"

Oh my god, Jake said to himself. Nick's gone off the deep end. Then he thought, It's just the shock of the explosion. He'll calm down in a little while.

But Piazza growled, "I've called the FBI. They're sending a team here to investigate."

Charleston, South Carolina

Jake stood on the windswept balcony of his hotel room and stared across the water of the bay toward Fort Sumter. At this distance there wasn't much to see, the fort was all the way out at the entrance to the bay, while this rundown hotel was on the city's waterfront, miles distant.

Wishing he had a pair of binoculars, Jake muttered to himself, "That's where the Civil War began. That's where they started killing each other."

It was a chilly day, even though the sky was clear and sunshine made the waters of the bay sparkle. Nowhere near as cold as New Hampshire, Jake told himself. Or Iowa. But he shivered in his suede sports jacket nonetheless.

He heard the phone ring inside his room. Hackman's people, Jake thought. They had picked this hotel; it was out-of-the-way enough so that the chance of Jake being spotted by a news reporter was minimal. As if a reporter would recognize me, he grumbled to himself as he ducked back into the room and slid the balcony door shut.

He picked up the phone on its third ring.

"Dr. Ross?" A woman's voice.

"Yes," Jake replied, unconsciously nodding. With all the secrecy about this meeting, Jake was surprised that Hackman's people hadn't insisted on code names.

"We're about five minutes away from your hotel. Could you please wait for us down in the lobby?"

"Sure. See you in five."

The line clicked dead.

The hotel lobby looked seedy. You'd think they'd keep a hotel right on the waterfront in better shape, Jake said to himself. Then he realized that this was an independent operation: no Marriott or Hyatt or other national chain with deep pockets. This was a mom-and-pop establishment, a family business struggling to stay alive.

A dark sedan pulled up at the entrance and Jake started for the door. Then he saw that a short, squat, red-haired woman got out of the car. She didn't look like a political operative in Jake's eyes, more like a chambermaid coming in to start her working shift.

But she pushed through the lobby's glass door, spotted Jake, and walked straight to him.

"Dr. Ross? This way, please."

Jake followed her outside and ducked into the car's rear seat. The woman sat up front, beside the driver.

As the car pulled out onto the street Jake asked, "Where are we going?"

"Downtown Marriott," the woman replied.

Jake grunted. They stay at the Marriott. Me they put in a dump, like a witness against the Mafia.

Within a few minutes they swung into the Marriott's parking lot and pulled up in front of a big black Cadillac. The woman pointed. "They're waiting for you in the Caddy."

Jake got out of the sedan. Somebody in the Cadillac opened its rear door. Jake climbed into the capacious car, sat down, and pulled the door shut.

The man sitting beside him on the rear bench was big, like a retired football player, with thick wavy gray hair, heavyset, wearing an expensive-looking suit of dark blue. On the jump seat facing Jake was a young woman, sharp-faced, peroxide blonde, in a tailored white blouse and forest-green jacket with short sleeves.

"Hello, Dr. Ross," said the big gray-haired man, smiling

broadly as he extended a meaty hand toward Jake. "I'm Bernie Untermeyer, Governor Hackman's chief of protocol."

Untermeyer's voice was heavy, gravelly, with more than a hint of a Dixie accent.

Jabbing a thumb toward the woman, he went on, "This here is Louise Anderson, my assistant."

Nodding, Jake said, "Pleased to meet you."

"We're happy y'all could come down and meet with us," said Untermeyer.

"Senator Tomlinson was very pleased that you suggested this meeting," Jake replied.

"Good. Good." Untermeyer patted Jake's knee, making him flinch with surprise.

Louise Anderson said, "Your Senator Tomlinson is doing quite well in this campaign." Her voice was sharp, like a dentist's drill, making Jake feel still more uncomfortable.

"Which our governor is not," said Untermeyer, with a sad wag of his head.

"What are the governor's plans?" Jake asked.

Untermeyer glanced at Anderson, then replied, "He's pretty disappointed in the Iowa results. And the New Hampshire situation doesn't look all that cheerful, either."

"Of course," Anderson cut in, "he expects to do better on Super Tuesday. All those southern states are much more inclined toward him."

"I suppose so," Jake noncommittalled.

Untermeyer retook command of the conversation with, "But the governor's a realist. He's wonderin' if he shouldn't cut 'is losses, withdraw from the race, and urge 'is followers to vote for somebody else."

"Somebody else," Jake echoed.

"Could be your Senator Tomlinson," said Untermeyer, with a toothy grin spreading across his heavy-jowled face.

Jake said, "That would be fine with us, I'm sure."

"Point is, what would the governor gain from throwin' his support to your man?"

Jake held his tongue for a moment, then asked, "What does the governor want?"

Again Untermeyer looked over to Anderson. Jake got the impression that she was actually running the show, and this bulky gray man was merely a stalking horse.

"Governor Hackman's made a strong issue out of immigration policy," Untermeyer said at last. "Whoever he backs has got to come down against lettin' all these Latinos and A-rabs enterin' this country."

Jake got a mental image of the Statue of Liberty lifting her torch beside the Golden Door. But he said, "Stronger immigration policy."

"And more jobs for the state of Tennessee," Untermeyer added.

Anderson leaned toward Jake and said sharply, "This space program of yours. You're talking about a million new jobs. We need some of those jobs in our state."

"I see," said Jake.

"And more federal assistance for welfare," Untermeyer resumed. "Our state's being spent into bankruptcy by fed'ral welfare mandates that we're forced to pay for!"

Jake said, "And if Senator Tomlinson backs these issues . . . ?"

Bringing out his toothy smile again, Untermeyer replied, "Why, if your senator promises to back those issues, I'm sure the governor will urge his backers to vote for your man."

"Super Tuesday is less than a month away," Anderson reminded.

Jake nodded. "I understand."

"Good. Good." Untermeyer patted Jake's knee again. This time Jake managed to resist the urge to recoil.

"I'll explain your position to Senator Tomlinson and we'll see what his reaction will be."

"There is one more thing," Anderson said.

"Oh?"

"The governor would like to be invited to be in the new president's cabinet," she said, slowly, carefully. "Maybe secretary of energy?"

Jake heard himself reply, "That's an area that's very close to Senator Tomlinson's heart."

"And your own," Untermeyer jumped in. "You drafted the senator's energy plan, didn't you?"

"That was six years ago . . ."

"But it was a good plan. It's workin'."

"Governor Hackman will make a fine secretary of energy," Anderson said.

Jake spread his hands and replied, "I'll see what the senator thinks about all this."

Untermeyer made a soft little chuckle. "Good. You do that. Personally, I'd hate to see th' governor's votes go to Sebastian."

"So would I," said Jake—the first unreservedly genuine statement he'd made since climbing into the Cadillac.

Tighter immigration control," said Senator Tomlinson, "space jobs for Tennessee, more federal assistance for welfare programs—"

Kevin O'Donnell added sourly, "And the secretary of energy's job for him."

"That's what he's after," Jake said. "I got the impression we could finesse the first three if we promised him the energy job."

The three men were sitting in Senator Tomlinson's office in the Hart building, reviewing Jake's visit to South Carolina.

O'Donnell muttered, "Oak Ridge is in Tennessee. Nuclear power."

"And TVA," the senator added.

"Huntsville, Alabama's just across the border," O'Donnell added.

"The Marshall Space Flight Center."

"It's a lot to think about," O'Donnell muttered.

"I'll talk to Pat about it," Tomlinson said. "Getting Hackman's support could be a real boost to us."

O'Donnell shook his head. "It's not so much getting his support, Frank. It's keeping his support out of Sebastian's hands."

Suddenly Jake felt like one of the politicians who hammered together the Treaty of Versailles in 1919, redrawing the map of Europe, creating new nations. They ended World War I— and sowed the seeds of World War II.

Jake left the impromptu conference and made his way back to his own office.

His administrative assistant looked up from her computer screen. "Mr. Piazza called again. Twice."

Jake sighed. Nick Piazza was getting paranoid over the accident to the Astra Super, insisting that it had to be the result of sabotage. In the ten days since the accident he had phoned Jake every day, often more than once a day.

Wearily, Jake plopped down on his desk chair and called through the open office door. "I guess we'd better talk to him, Nancy."

. . .

Piazza looked calmer, but his boyish face still had a hard edge to it.

"Jake, could you talk to the guys running the FBI?" Before Jake could reply, he went on, "I mean, their guys from the local office here in New Mexico did a perfunctory examination of the wreckage—"

"I thought they called in their experts from Washington," Jake interrupted.

"Yeah, they did. And the NTSB people looked over the wreckage too."

"And they found no evidence of sabotage?"

"Not yet. They're still working on it."

Jake tried to keep the exasperation out of his voice as he asked, "So what do you want the FBI to do now?"

"Trace the people in the launch crew," Piazza replied without an instant of hesitation. "One or more of them fucked up my rocket!"

"Nick, rockets do blow up sometimes."

"Not mine!" Piazza snapped. "We haven't had a failure in years. This accident is going to raise my insurance rates through the roof, unless we can show that it was sabotage."

"And how can you show it was sabotage?" Jake asked.

"Get the FBI's top people down here! Get NASA's accident investigation people down here. For god's sake, how can we operate when there's a saboteur on our team? Maybe a whole squad of terrorists?"

"A terrorist group would've taken credit for the explosion. Nobody's said a word."

"Not yet." The expression on Piazza's face was strained, angry, frustrated. But Jake realized the man was right. How can he launch his rockets if there really is a terrorist on the launch crew? Or more than one terrorist? Nobody's going to invest billions of dollars just to finance disasters.

"Nick," Jake heard himself say, "I'll get the senator to call the FBI's director. We'll see what we can do."

Piazza looked as if he was going to break into tears. "Thanks, Jake. Thanks so much. The future of all our hopes depends on this."

Nodding, Jake agreed, "I suppose it does."

. . .

That evening, as Tami was chopping raw fish for their dinner, Jake told her about Piazza's fears.

Without lifting her eyes from the chopping board, Tami said, "We've been getting plenty of calls about the accident."

"Still?"

"Yes. I thought they'd die away by now, it's been more than a week. But the calls keep coming in: What progress has the investigation made? Will Astra try to launch another one of their Super birds? Is it safe for people to go up in Astra's rocket?"

"What do you tell them?"

Tami put down the thick-bladed knife on the wooden work surface next to the kitchen sink and turned to Jake with a shrug. "What can we tell them? The investigation is in progress. Plans for another crewed launch are on hold until the investigation is concluded."

Jake went to the cabinet where they stored the liquor, muttering, "It's enough to drive a man to drink."

"It's worse than that," Tami said. "They want the senator to make a statement. They're starting to interview kooks who claim that space flight is too dangerous for human missions. They're saying the whole space plan ought to be scrapped."

"I haven't heard anything like that!" Jake snapped.

"Not yet," Tami said. "But it's coming. I've been trying to convince Earl that he ought to be preparing the senator for a grilling at Thursday's debate, but he's been shoving the matter under the rug."

"Holy Christ," Jake muttered. "This could be real trouble. With the New Hampshire primary next week."

"And the third debate in two days."

"We've been hoping to get Governor Hackman to throw his support to us," Jake said. "But this could blow everything clean to hell."

Tami said, "Earl would rather look the other way. He says we should be positive, not get defensive about the accident."

Jake reached into the liquor cabinet and pulled out a half-empty bottle of Chardonnay. With a shake of his head he said to Tami, "This isn't going to be enough."

The Third Debate

The auditorium was packed. Even though the temperature outside in the dark New Hampshire night was close to zero, the site of the Republican Party's third presidential debate was warm, even steamy, from the press of bodies.

Jake sat just behind the trio of news media stars who would moderate the proceedings, his winter overcoat folded on his lap. Up on the stage, hot with spotlights, were three lecterns for the three candidates.

All of Senator Tomlinson's people had been disappointed that Governor Hackman had not yet thrown in the towel. No decision had come from the governor's campaign headquarters about whether he would quit and, if he did, who he would give his support to: Tomlinson or Sebastian.

Jake had personally vetted Hackman's qualifications to be secretary of energy. The governor had visited the Oak Ridge National Laboratory back when he'd campaigned for reelection, more than three years earlier. He'd given a speech at one of the TVA power dams a year before that. That was it. Hackman had never made a public pronouncement about energy policy, as far as Jake could find. Of course, energy was largely a federal issue, although the energy industry provided plenty of jobs in Tennessee.

"Tell him you'll name him," Pat Lovett had urged Senator Tomlinson. "We need his votes."

Tomlinson hesitated. Perhaps fatally, Jake thought. Kevin

O'Donnell quite openly resisted the idea of handing the Energy portfolio to Hackman. "The man's a lightweight," O'Donnell insisted. "Frank's supposed to be strong on energy policy. Putting Hackman in the energy seat will detract from Frank's reputation."

Jake found himself agreeing with both men: Hackman was a lightweight, but he had a block of votes that could help get Tomlinson the nomination.

A roll of applause rose from one end of the auditorium to the other as the three candidates strode onto the stage, each of them smiling at the audience and the moderators, then shaking hands with one another as if they were truly friends.

The questions from the three moderators started with softballs, Jake thought. Balancing the federal budget, a favorite piece of campaign mythology. National defense: none of the candidates was in favor of cutting down the defense budget, as the Democrats had been talking about.

"As long as we have terrorists and guerrillas on our southern doorstep," intoned Senator Sebastian, "we must keep our soldiers and sailors and airmen at the peak of their efficiency."

Tomlinson and Hackman said much the same, in slightly different words.

Then came the shot Jake had been worrying about.

The female moderator—well groomed, perfectly coiffed, keeping her sculpted face unsmilingly serious—asked Senator Tomlinson:

"Senator, in light of the recent disaster at Astra Corporation's last launching attempt, there have been some experts who have done mathematical analyses that show that rockets are inherently unsafe, especially too risky to carry human crews. Do you agree?"

Tomlinson put on the smile he used to gain himself a moment to think.

"Dorothy," he replied, still smiling, "there have been mathematical analyses that show that bumblebees can't fly. Yet somehow the little creatures buzz around beautifully."

"Come on, now, Senator—"

His expression growing serious, Tomlinson said, "The point is, Dorothy, that we can launch a hundred rockets without a hitch, but one failure starts the boobirds yowling.

"Planes crash," the senator went on. "Thousands of people are killed every year in car accidents. People fall down stairs and break their bones, for god's sake!"

"But rocket explosions are dangerous," the newswoman insisted.

Raising a finger, Tomlinson said, "May I point out that the rocket launcher had a crew escape system built into it and that its escape system performed as designed. Nobody was hurt, except for a couple of black eyes and a chipped fingernail."

"And the loss of a multimillion-dollar rocket launcher."

With a sad shake of his head, Tomlinson said, "You've often heard me compare our drive to open up the space frontier to the nineteenth-century expansion of our nation across the frontier of the old west. Did those pioneers turn back when they were hit by a dust storm? Or attacked by Indians? Or when a wheel fell off one of their wagons? No! They overcame those adversities and pushed on. That's what we're doing in space."

Jake jumped to his feet, clapping his hands as hard as he could. Slowly at first, but then like a growing avalanche, the entire audience rose to their feet and applauded.

And Tomlinson hollered into his microphone, "We're not turning back! We're going to open up the space frontier!"

. . .

"A damned good performance," Patrick Lovett was saying, a tumbler of whiskey in one hand and a confident smile on his face.

Senator Tomlinson's hotel suite was jammed with campaign

workers, aides, visitors, hangers-on, all of them talking, gesticulating, jabbering at once. Jake was standing in front of the theater-sized TV screen, watching a cable news channel. It was muted, and he probably couldn't have heard the commentators' chatter anyway, there was so much noise in the suite, but their words were scrolling along the bottom of the big screen.

Preliminary polls of people who had attended the debate and others who had watched on television were similar: Tomlinson had pretty much squelched the rocket-safety issue. But Sebastian still held a six-point lead over him.

And Hackman was a distant third, further behind than he had ever been.

"When's the sumbitch going to make up his mind?"

Jake turned his head to see Kevin O'Donnell standing beside him, in his shirtsleeves and conservative black suspenders, his eyes focused on the TV screen.

"Hackman's done for," O'Donnell went on, pointing at the poll numbers on the screen. "When's he going to throw in the towel?"

Jake said, "As soon as somebody gives him the secretary of energy job, I guess."

O'Donnell snorted contemptuously. "Big pain in the ass."

Suddenly the scene on the TV switched to a crowded hotel suite festooned with Hackman banners and balloons.

"Oh-oh," O'Donnell said. "This could be it."

The room fell silent as Jake turned on the TV set's sound. Everyone focused on the screen. Senator Tomlinson and his wife came up silently between Jake and O'Donnell. Lovett, Earl Reynolds, everybody stood waiting, hoping.

Governor Hackman strode into view, still in the suit he'd worn for the debate, with his wife and two of his grown children alongside him.

"This is it," O'Donnell whispered.

"Folks, I have an announcement to make," Hackman said,

with a brave smile. He was a good-looking man, tall, trim, his hair thick and silvery, his red and black striped tie pulled slightly loose from his collar.

"Although we've fought as hard as we could to win our party's nomination," he said, in a clear rich tenor voice, "the poll numbers have been disappointing."

His smile dimming, the governor went on, "I frankly don't see any point in continuing this struggle. It's taken a toll on my family, and it's taken a toll on my responsibilities as governor of the great state of Tennessee."

One of the women grouped behind him, wearing a loud green HACKMAN! sash, broke into quiet sobs.

"Therefore I am withdrawing my candidacy for the party's nomination. I will continue to work for the causes that we all believe in—more and better jobs for our people, a stronger immigration policy, better protection for our nation's borders."

A spatter of half-hearted clapping.

"And I urge all of you who have supported me to give your hearts and your votes to the next president of the United States—Senator Bradley Sebastian!"

"Shit!" snapped O'Donnell and Lovett simultaneously.

Tomlinson said nothing. But the expression on his face was the same Jake had seen at the funeral of the senator's father.

. . .

The gathering in Senator Tomlinson's suite broke up quickly after that. O'Donnell and Lovett huddled in a corner, heads together, talking like a pair of football coaches who had just seen the other side score a touchdown.

Jake went through the departing crowd to Tami, who looked sad, disappointed.

"I'm sorry, Jake," she said quietly.

He grasped her arm and said, "Let's go to our room."

"Don't you want—"

"I'm in no mood to listen to Pat and Kevin doing a post-mortem." And he led her to the door.

Tomlinson stood in the middle of the emptying room, his expression serious, but not defeated. Jake heard him saying to one of the guests, "This isn't the end of the road. Far from it."

But he didn't sound very confident.

. . .

Once in their own suite, Jake wormed out of his jacket and tossed it on the bed. Tami pulled off the high-heeled shoes she'd been wearing.

"That's a relief," she said.

"The shoes, or Hackman's decision?"

Standing in her bare feet, Tami barely reached Jake's shoulder. "Oh, Jake, I'm not happy about his decision. I know you had your heart set on getting Frank into the White House."

"It doesn't look very likely now," he admitted.

"No, it doesn't."

Afraid of the answer, Jake still asked, "So where does this leave us?"

Tami sat on the edge of the bed. "I guess this simplifies the situation. I'll go to Fresno after the Republican convention. Or maybe before. You can stay with Frank until he concedes the nomination to Sebastian."

Dropping down onto the bed beside her, Jake said, "And then I'll come out to Fresno, huh?"

She nodded.

With a wry grin, Jake said, "I'll be out of a job."

Placing her hands in his, Tami said, "Not for long. You can go back to astronomy, if you like. Or give lectures about politics." She brightened. "I'll bet I could get you a slot as the station's expert on politics! You could become a TV personality!"

"Tami Umetzu's husband," Jake said bleakly.

She stared at him.

Feeling miserable, Jake said, "Tami, honey, I don't want to

go to Fresno. I want to stay in Washington. I want to stay with Frank."

And he remembered from the time he first arrived in DC, an old Beltway insider warning him of Potomac Fever. "Once they get here, they never leave. They only leave this town feet first."

Tami's cheerful expression crumbling, she asked, "And you don't want to stay with me?"

"Of course I want to stay with you! In DC."

"But I can't! Don't you understand, Jake, this job in Fresno is my big chance. I can't turn it down."

"I understand," he said. "I just don't like it. Not one little bit."

"What are we going to do?" Tami asked.

Jake realized he had no answer.

Unexpectedly, Tomlinson gained more from Hackman's quitting the race than Sebastian did. He came within two percentage points of tying Sebastian in the South Carolina primary and actually won the Nevada caucus by a hair-thin margin.

Lovett was jubilant after the Nevada win. At the analysis session the day after, in Tomlinson's campaign headquarters, he tapped a sheaf of printouts and concluded, "Frank's message is getting through to the voters. He's offering them a new vision, a new hope."

O'Donnell, though, said dourly, "Nevada. Six electoral votes."

"It's a trend," Lovett insisted. But then he added, "Maybe."

"We'll see in a week," O'Donnell said.

Super Tuesday. Twelve state primaries or caucuses on the same early March date, including Massachusetts, Texas, Georgia, and Virginia.

Jake had never been so busy in his life. He jetted from one rally or speech to another. He coached Senator Tomlinson on the finer points of the space plan, the budgets for research organizations such as the National Institutes of Health, and the ever-present controversies over stem-cell studies, abortion, and women's health. Meanwhile Tami coached Jake himself when he did TV interviews about the space plan.

How much will it cost?

Billions, but the money is being raised from the private investment market. Not a penny of taxpayers' dollars is going into the space plan.

But isn't the federal government backing those investments?

They're long-term, low-interest loans. Any American can invest in our future in space. You can own part of our expansion into the space frontier!

Isn't space flight dangerous?

Actually, it's safer than commercial air travel. And far safer than driving a car.

How are these private firms going to make profits in space?

By building solar power satellites that can deliver gigawatts of electrical power to the ground cleanly, without pollution. Their power source is the Sun, ninety-three million miles away! One such space power satellite could replace all the fossil-fueled and nuclear power plants in a whole state the size of Florida.

Anything else?

There sure is. Factories in orbit and on the Moon's surface will be able to produce new metal alloys that are lighter yet stronger than anything made on Earth. New chemical products, including new medicines, are possible. We'll get the raw materials from the Moon's surface and, sooner or later, from mining asteroids.

What about tourist facilities in space?

Would you like to have a zero-gravity honeymoon in orbit? If you like waterbeds, you're going to love zero-gee. And how about planting your bootprints on the Moon, where no one has ever stepped before? On the Moon you can fly on your own muscle power, like a bird. Or visit Apollo 11's Tranquility Base. Or . . .

By the time Super Tuesday finally arrived, Jake was physically and emotionally exhausted. As he lay sprawled across the bed in their Connecticut Avenue condo, he asked Tami:

"How does Frank do it? He's been on the go nonstop since before Christmas. What's holding him up?"

Tami flopped onto the bed beside him, just as frazzled as Jake was.

"Frank has a powerful force driving him," she said. "The image of himself in the Oval Office."

Jake nodded. "Yeah. And his father pushing him. That's a powerful driver, all right."

"All-consuming," said Tami.

Jake couldn't help wondering about Tami's all-consuming drive to become a news media star. Was it going to consume their marriage?

When all the votes were counted, Super Tuesday turned out to be nearly a tie. Tomlinson won in Texas and Massachusetts—a feat that dumbfounded most of the news media's analysts—and came to within a hair of taking Georgia and Virginia. Sebastian won all the other states, but none by a margin of more than a few percentage points.

"It's all going to come down to New York, New Jersey, and, finally, California," said Pat Lovett.

He, Jake, O'Donnell, and Earl Reynolds were having lunch with the senator in Tomlinson's home, the afternoon after Super Tuesday, seated at one end of the long table in the formal dining room, dominated by the imperious portrait of Senator Tomlinson's late father.

With a mischievous grin, the senator said, "Once this campaign is over, win or lose, I'm taking Amy on our sailboat out across the Caribbean. And we won't bring a telephone with us!"

Lovett grinned back at him. "By that time, Frank, you'll have a team of Secret Service people guarding you. You'll be the president-elect."

Tomlinson muttered, "No plan is perfect." And he turned his attention back to the hamburger he'd been munching on.

Jake noted, "The pundits claim that the space plan's attracting the younger voters."

"And some older ones, too," Lovett added. "People who're worried about the economy, about their jobs."

"Do you think we can take New York?" Tomlinson asked eagerly. Before anyone could reply he added, "And New Jersey?"

"Stranger things have happened," said Lovett.

O'Donnell cautioned, "Those are going to be two tough hurdles. Lots of union votes there. Lots of entrenched power."

"What about California?" Jake asked.

"From what I've seen," Lovett replied, "we've got a good chance at California. Lots of aerospace industry votes."

With a pleased grin, Tomlinson said, "We've really got a chance to beat Sebastian."

Lovett nodded. "And whoever the Democrats finally decide to nominate."

Jake hoped they were right. But he heard himself ask them, "Do you think this fight between you and Sebastian is hurting the party?"

O'Donnell glared at him.

"I've heard some analysts saying that we're splitting the party, which could be good for the Democrats," Jake explained. It sounded lame, even to his own ears.

"That's bullshit," O'Donnell growled.

Lovett shook his head. "There's a certain amount of truth to it, Kev. If the battle between Frank and Sebastian gets especially bitter, if the loser's people stay home in November instead of voting for the winner—that could hand the election to the Democrats."

"So what are we supposed to do," O'Donnell wondered, "play nice-nice with Sebastian? We're in this to win, dammit!"

Tomlinson dabbed at his lips with his napkin, then carefully put it back onto the table. "Vince Lombardi said, 'Winning isn't the most important thing. It's the only thing!'"

Jake had heard a different version of that line, but neither he nor the others around the table contradicted the senator.

• • •

The month of March turned into a slugging match. After Super Tuesday, Sebastian and Tomlinson traded primary victories almost evenly. Almost.

Sebastian took Kansas, Kentucky, and Louisiana but Tomlinson pulled an upset victory in Michigan, by just two percentage points. Sebastian won in Florida and Illinois but Tomlinson managed to squeak through to a narrow victory in the pivotal Ohio primary.

As April approached, with voters due at the polls in New York, Pennsylvania, Connecticut, Wisconsin, and elsewhere, the hectic pace of the contest grew even hotter.

"We can do it!" Lovett kept encouraging everyone he talked to. "We can overtake Sebastian and win the nomination!"

"Yeah," O'Donnell warned. "And maybe split the party so badly that the Democrats take the White House in November."

Jake's world became a blur of meetings, interviews, preparing position statements for Senator Tomlinson, talking, handshaking, wheedling, urging. He hardly saw Tami during those frenzied weeks, barely had time to wonder what would happen to them when the campaign was finally over.

The buzz of his desktop intercom snapped Jake awake.

He was in his office in the Hart building. The digital clock readout on his computer screen blinked 3:28 p.m.

He sat up straight in his desk chair. I must've fallen asleep, Jake told himself as he reached for the intercom switch.

"Yes?"

His administrative assistant's voice said, "Mr. Knowles is calling, Dr. Ross."

"Ike?" Jake hadn't heard from Isaiah Knowles in months. Blinking the sleep out of his eyes, he said, "Put him on, Nancy."

Isaiah Knowles's cocoa-colored face somehow always looked pugnacious, even when he was smiling. The former astronaut seemed to be ready to challenge anyone, anywhere, anytime. On the big wall screen of Jake's office, Knowles's image was slightly larger than life, more than a little intimidating.

"Hello, Jake," he said, with a tight smile.

Jake nodded. "How are you, Ike?"

"Been working with Nick Piazza the past couple months," Knowles said. "You got some spare time to talk things over?"

Spare time was what Jake had least of, but he realized that if Knowles was working with Piazza it had to be about the launch accident of the Astra Super.

So he said, "How about getting together for a drink, around six o'clock?"

"Can you come over to my office?" Knowles replied. "I want Rollie Jackson to join us."

Jake wondered what Jackson had to do with anything, but he answered, "Okay. Six o'clock. Your office."

"See you then," said Knowles.

. . .

Jake took a taxi to the Space Futures Foundation offices on K Street. Easier than trying to find a parking spot.

Knowles was waiting for him in the suite's reception area. The offices were almost entirely empty; most of the staff had already left for home, or their favorite watering hole.

"You're working for Nick Piazza now?" Jake asked as he shook hands with Knowles. It always surprised him that the ex-astronaut was a couple of inches shorter than he. The man gave the impression of being bigger, burlier, than he actually was.

"Moonlightin'," Knowles said grimly. "Got to make ends meet, you know."

"Your foundation isn't doing well?"

With a somber expression that somehow looked almost menacing, Knowles said, "Your fancy-dancy space plan's soaked up most of our support. Our backers are all on your band-wagon now."

The law of unanticipated results, Jake thought. But he said only, "I didn't realize it would work out that way."

Knowles shrugged. "You're helping my foundation to accomplish its goals. Your space plan is going to get us back to the Moon. That's the important thing."

Jake nodded. "I'm glad you see it that way, Ike."

A timid tap on the corridor door made them turn in time to see Roland T. Jackson standing in the open doorway. The retired engineer was wearing a dark suit with a patriotic red, white, and blue star-spangled tie.

"Rollie!" said Knowles, rushing to him. "Come on in."

Jackson was almost Knowles's height, but he gave the appearance of being much smaller, frailer, almost childlike compared to the sturdy former astronaut.

"Hello, Ike," said Jackson, quickly adding, "Jake. What's this all about? Why did you ask me here?"

"Not for drinks," Jake guessed.

"Not drinks," Knowles acknowledged as he led the two of them back into the depths of the foundation's suite.

Knowles's private office was spare, utilitarian. A desk, a couple of unmatched upholstered chairs, a small round table by the only window, with four cheap contoured plastic chairs around it. The window looked out onto another high-rise office building.

"The Astra Super accident," Jake guessed as they sat themselves down around the circular table. The plastic chairs squeaked under their weight.

"Maybe it wasn't an accident," Knowles said, his face bleak, almost angry.

Jackson arched a brow. "What makes you say that?"

An hour later, the little table was covered with graphs, computer readouts, and hand-scribbled notes. The wall screen showed an enlarged schematic of the rocket's first-stage propulsion system. And Jake understood why Knowles had invited Jackson to the discussion. The older man was a sounding board, a backup expert, checking out Knowles's ideas about the cause of the accident, offering insights of his own to Knowles's opinions.

Jake had phoned Tami half an hour earlier to tell her he'd be late for dinner. She wasn't home yet herself, so he left a message.

Jackson was saying, "But the NTSB, the FAA, the NASA team, all the investigators have gone over all this material, Ike. They haven't found anything incriminating."

Knowles had tossed his jacket onto his desk and pulled off his necktie. He countered, "They haven't found anything because they've been looking in the wrong direction."

Jake grunted, "Huh?"

Tapping his tablet computer, Knowles looked up at the wall screen. The schematic drawing focused on some piping. Jake saw the legend "LOX main feed" neatly printed atop the drawing.

"Liquid oxygen is tricky stuff," Knowles said.

Jackson grinned. "Any stuff that's cooled down to minus a couple of hundred degrees is tricky."

"Right," Knowles agreed. "Now what happens if you weaken the piping that's got the LOX running through it?"

"Weaken it how?" Jake asked.

"Scratch it with a knife point. Or maybe the blade of a screwdriver. Just score it a little. An inch or so. Just enough to make the pipe burst when the LOX comes roaring through at full pressure."

"Make the pipe burst?"

Bobbing his head up and down, Knowles said, "Yeah. The piping's made of plastic, you know."

Jackson objected, "High-strength reinforced plastic that's capable of handling cryogenic temperatures."

"Not if it's been weakened," Knowles argued. "Look. At T minus three seconds the LOX line starts feeding liquid oxygen into the main engines. The main engines fire at T-zero. The liquid oxygen line gives way. LOX sprays all over the hot rocket nozzles. Boom!"

Jackson stared at the schematic on the wall screen for a few silent moments. Then, "That could cause the explosion, all right."

With a harsh smile, Knowles said, "Damned right."

"You wouldn't even have to scratch the line, just smear a little solvent on the pipe and let it eat the plastic away."

"I hadn't thought of that," Knowles said.

"Only one problem with your theory," Jackson said, his voice gentle, almost fatherly. "There's absolutely no evidence that it's right."

Knowles leaned back in his complaining plastic chair.

"No evidence," he echoed.

His tone still mild, Jackson said, "If somebody deliberately weakened the oxy line, all the evidence of his tampering was blown to hell and gone by the explosion."

"Yeah, I guess so."

"It's a reasonable idea, Ike, but without evidence it's just an idea. A hypothesis. A hypothesis that you can't prove."

"Whoever did it was damned clever," Knowles acknowledged.

"The explosion he caused destroyed the evidence that he caused it," Jackson mused. With a brief nod, he agreed, "Damned clever."

"How do we find out if the idea is right?" Jake asked.

Jackson said, "As I understand it, the FBI has looked into the personnel files of everybody on the launch team."

"Everybody who came within a hundred yards of the bird," Knowles said.

"And they found nothing suspicious?"

"A couple of the technicians admitted to smoking weed in their spare time." Knowles looked and sounded disgusted.

"That's it?"

Nodding, the former astronaut said, "Far as the FBI could find, nobody on the launch crew got a sudden influx of cash. Nobody bought a new house or ran off to Cuba."

"Nobody was bribed," Jake said.

Jackson sighed wearily. "And any evidence of tampering was blown to hell by the explosion."

"Pretty much," said Knowles.

Slowly, Jackson pushed his chair back from the table and got to his feet. "Then I'd say we're wasting our time here. We ought to be man enough to admit we're up against a blank wall."

Knowles exploded, "Dammit, somebody deliberately blew up that rocket! He's still on the launch crew! He can blow up the next launch! Maybe kill people!"

Another launch failure could cripple Nick Piazza's operation, Jake knew. It could throw the entire space plan into the garbage heap.

"We've got to find out who did this," Jake said.

With a wry smile, Jackson said, "I know. But until you show me how, we're wasting our time here."

Jake looked across the office, to the clock on the wall. It read 8:45.

"I guess you're right," he admitted. "Time to go home." He too rose to his feet.

Knowles glared up at the two of them. "I *know* I'm right. Some little bastard fucked up the launch."

"Knowing is one thing, Ike," Jackson said, softly, kindly. "Proving it is something else."

. . .

Jake phoned Tami as he walked out onto K Street and tried to hail a cab.

"You're all right?" she asked, her voice high with apprehension.

"Yeah, sure," Jake answered. "I'll tell you about it when I get home."

"But you're all right."

"I'm fine, hon. See you in a few minutes." And he felt a warm, elated glow. She cares, he told himself. She really loves me.

Jake explained his impromptu meeting with Knowles and

Jackson to Tami over dinner: leftover lamb chops from the night before.

"Knowles is right," Tami concluded. "Whoever did it will strike again."

"Maybe," Jake said. "Nick ought to beef up security for his next launch."

"And strengthen that liquid oxygen piping."

Shaking his head, Jake said, "That would add weight to the launcher. You want to keep a rocket's weight down as much as you can."

"But—"

Jake's cell phone broke into "Stars and Stripes Forever." He yanked it out of his pocket. Nick Piazza's somber, determined face filled the tiny screen.

Without preamble, Piazza said, "Ike just told me about your meeting."

"We didn't accomplish much, I'm afraid," said Jake.

"More than you think," Piazza said grimly. "I'm replacing the whole launch crew for our next shot."

"The whole crew?" Jake blurted.

"Damned right. If one of my people caused the explosion, he won't be around to screw up the next one."

Jake mentally added "or she." But to Piazza he said, "Nick, won't it take time to train a new crew?"

"I don't care how long it takes, I'm not going to give that motherfucking saboteur another chance to screw me."

"When are you scheduled to launch again?" Jake asked.

"Not until the end of May. That's enough time to train a new crew, more or less."

Jake thought, The end of May. The California primary's the first Tuesday of June. If there's another explosion it'll ruin our chances of taking California.

My god! Jake realized with a shock. I'm thinking like a politician!

The whirlwind of Tomlinson's campaign rushed on: speeches, interviews, another debate—this time with Sebastian and Tomlinson alone on the stage, facing each other.

Sebastian kept hammering on the federal loan guarantee question. "It's a giveaway, nothing less," he insisted. "A welfare giveaway for billionaires. It means that you, the taxpayer, will be held responsible for the billions of dollars that this pie-in-the-sky space program is going to cost."

Tomlinson countered, "The loan guarantee program will allow our new efforts in space to be financed by private investors, not by your tax dollars. It's an idea that's worked before, and it can and will work again."

Sebastian took the New York primary. And Connecticut, Pennsylvania, and Maryland. Tomlinson won Delaware and Rhode Island.

O'Donnell sneered, "With those two and a couple of bucks you just might be able to buy a coffee at Starbucks."

But a week later Tomlinson scored a solid victory in Indiana, and the following week took both Nebraska and Oregon.

At campaign headquarters, Pat Lovett stared thoughtfully at the big wall screen showing the various states in red and blue.

Shaking his head, the campaign manager muttered, "It's not following the usual pattern. Frank's winning in the Midwest and far west. He's getting the farmers and the high-tech geeks."

Standing beside him, Jake suggested, "Maybe it's a new co-alition forming. Like FDR, when he put together the Old South and the northern big city machines."

Lovett stared at Jake. "You've been reading political history."

"A little," Jake admitted.

Quite seriously, Lovett said, "If you've got time for that, we haven't been working you hard enough."

And he walked away, leaving Jake standing there in front of the map, feeling somewhere between dumbfounded and annoyed.

. . .

June began with a heat wave in Washington, daily high temperatures inching up into the low nineties, humidity high enough to curl women's hair and take the crease out of men's trousers. The California primary was less than a week away. And two days before that, Nick Piazza was scheduled to launch another Astra Super at Spaceport America, in the White Sands desert of New Mexico.

Jake felt torn between his desire to see the launch and his superstitious fear that if he was there, in person, he'd witness another disaster.

Nick Piazza had no such worries. "I'll send a plane to pick you up in Washington, fly you out there, and get you back home before the California primary."

On the wall screen of Jake's office, Piazza looked relaxed, totally at ease, as if this next launch was guaranteed to succeed. Jake felt decidedly otherwise.

"Your new launch crew is ready to go?" he asked.

"Ready, willing, and eager," Piazza replied, almost jovially. "They're gung ho."

Feeling reluctant, Jake heard himself say, "Okay, I'll fly out the day before the launch and return right after it."

"You won't stay for the after-launch party?" Piazza asked.

Shaking his head, Jake said, "Don't have the time to spare, Nick."

Grinning broadly, Piazza said, "Work is the curse of the drinking man, Jake."

Jake smiled back weakly at him. *Just get the damned rocket off the ground successfully,* he pleaded silently. *The partying doesn't mean a damned thing. Getting the bird into orbit is what's important.*

. . .

Tami insisted on going, too.

"One way or another, this is going to be a huge story," she said. Then imitating a previous presidential contender, she stressed, "*Huuuge.*"

Jake laughed and cleared it with Piazza.

Senator Tomlinson was campaigning in California, drawing big crowds in the high-tech Silicon Valley area and the Southern California aerospace industry region. But the turnout for him in Los Angeles itself was disappointingly small; Lovett's people had to work hard to make the crowd look big enough for the TV news cameras.

The afternoon of their flight to New Mexico, Jake and Tami rode in one of Senator Tomlinson's limousines to Reagan National Airport. It was early afternoon, and traffic through Washington's sweltering streets wasn't as bad as it would become in a couple of hours.

"We'll be there in good time," Jake muttered as he sat beside Tami in the air-conditioned limo.

"And we gain two hours from the time difference," she added.

Jake nodded. "Nick Piazza told me a while ago that he likes to spend New Year's Eve in New Mexico. He said he can watch the ball go down in Times Square and it's only ten o'clock in Albuquerque."

"You mean he goes to sleep then?" Tami asked. "That's sacrilegious!"

"That's Nick," Jake said, with a chuckle.

. . .

When they got out of the limousine, at the hangar where Piazza's sleek, swept-wing Cessna Citation was waiting, Jake was surprised to see Billy Trueblood standing by the twin-jet plane.

As they shook hands, the Native American grinned happily and told Jake, "Nick needed somebody to sit in as copilot on this flight."

Surprised, Jake asked, "You're qualified for a Citation?"

"Got my license and nearly fifty hours in the air."

"I didn't know that."

Trueblood's grin faded. "There's a lot of things about me that you don't know."

Jake and Tami followed Trueblood up the aluminum ladder and into the plane's posh interior.

"Take any seat you like," Billy said. "It's all yours, this flight." And he headed up into the cockpit, closing the windowless door behind him.

Jake and Tami sat side by side in a pair of the commodious swiveling chairs that lined the passenger compartment. The plane's aisle separated their seats, but they were close enough to reach out and hold hands.

A tractor towed them out of the hangar and the twin-jet engines spooled up. Jake felt the plane tremble like a retriever dog catching the scent of a bird, heard the muted roar of the engines. Then they taxied out to the end of the runway, raced forward until the runway markers were a blur, and lifted up into the sky.

Trueblood's voice came through the cabin speakers, sounding calm, professional. "We'll be flying at forty-eight thousand feet, well above the weather. Average speed will be five hundred miles per hour. Next stop, Spaceport America."

Jake unconsciously frowned.

"Something wrong?" Tami asked. The plane's acoustical insulation was so good that she could speak in a normal conversational tone.

"We're supposed to be going to Albuquerque," Jake said. "We're staying at the DoubleTree overnight."

Tami shrugged. "I suppose that's what Billy meant."

"I guess," Jake said, uncertainly.

They climbed through a layer of clouds, bouncing slightly in the mild turbulence, then smoothed out into a clear blue sky. Beneath them a sea of clouds undulated gracefully, above them was nothing but sunshine.

"If you go high enough," Jake said, smiling, "you can find the sunshine."

"Philosophy? From you?" Tami teased.

"I'm a man of hidden talents," Jake replied.

Jake had just cranked his seat back for a nap when his cell phone started playing Sousa. Fumbling it out of his pocket, Jake saw that the caller was Nick Piazza.

"Hello, Nick," he said to the image on the little screen. "We're on our way—"

"Is Billy with you?" Piazza asked urgently.

"Yeah, he's copiloting the plane."

"No, he's not. He's flying it by himself and he doesn't know how to land it."

Suicide Flight

What?" Jake tried to jump to his feet but his seat belt restrained him.

"The airport people found the regular pilot unconscious in the hangar's locker room," Piazza was saying, his words spilling out fast, in a torrent.

"Billy's flying the plane by himself?"

"He doesn't know how to land it!" Piazza repeated.

"Jesus!"

"He hasn't answered my calls and he won't reply to the traffic controllers. Let me talk to him!"

Glancing at Tami, who looked stricken, Jake unclicked his seat belt and hurried up the aisle to the cockpit door. It was locked.

Pounding on the door, Jake yelled, "Billy! It's Nick! He wants to talk to you!"

"No deal," came Trueblood's muffled voice from the other side of the door. "Tell him I said good-bye."

"What the hell are you doing?" Jake yelled.

Down the aisle, Tami's face looked ashen. She sat in her seat as if petrified.

"What do you think I'm doing?" Trueblood replied. "I'm gonna crash this bird into the Spaceport America building, wipe out Astra Corporation's control center. Put an end to this rocket launching business."

"But you'll kill us!" Jake hollered. "You'll kill yourself!"

"That's right. More publicity. Author of the space plan dies in Spaceport America crash. We'll get plenty of publicity."

"Why?" Jake shrieked. "Why the hell do you want to do this?"

"To get back at Nick. Get back at all you palefaces. First you took our land. Then you took us, took me. Now you're going out to take everything in the solar system. The Moon. Mars. It's got to stop, man. I'm stopping it. Now."

"That's crazy!"

"So I'm crazy. So was Sitting Bull, and Red Cloud, and Geronimo. And Crazy Horse, he was the craziest of them all, I guess."

Jake glanced at the window. The plane was flying straight and level, okay so far, but Trueblood was rushing toward death and he was going to take Jake and Tami with him.

"You said you wanted to get back at Nick. Why? He's been like a father to you."

"More than that, man. A lot more than that."

"He took you in when you were an orphan, for god's sake. He's made a good life for you."

"Yeah, sure. He loves me to death."

Even through the locked cockpit door, Jake heard the bitterness in Trueblood's voice.

"Loves you to death?"

"Yeah. Whenever he wants to. Whenever he gets the urge. Only now I'm too old for him. Now he wants a younger kid."

Tami came up beside Jake, wide-eyed with fear and sudden understanding. "Nick's molested you?"

Trueblood laughed shakily. "That's the polite way of saying it. He's been fucking me since I was eight years old."

"Oh my god," Jake gasped.

"And now he wants to dump me. I don't know if I should be glad or sad."

"Nick is a pedophile?" Tami asked.

"Does a camel have humps?" Trueblood countered.

Desperate for anything that might change Trueblood's attitude, Jake asked, "But why should you kill yourself?"

"Why not? Sorry to take you with me, Jake, but it'll make an even bigger story."

"Nick's the one you're mad at," said Tami.

"Yeah. And the one I love. Crazy world, isn't it?"

"Don't do it, Billy," Jake pleaded. "You've got your whole life ahead of you."

"That's not a helluva lot to look forward to."

Jake and Tami argued with Trueblood through the locked cockpit door as the plane flew smoothly toward New Mexico. The clouds that had blanketed the eastern states petered out and they could see the great Midwestern farmlands, green and fertile, stretching from horizon to horizon. Then the mountains started to rise, with pockets of snow still visible here and there. Rivers flowed, glistening in the sun, until the land turned dry and brown.

Jake's throat felt raw from shouting at Trueblood. Tami looked truly frightened, her eyes darting here and there, seeking a way out, an escape.

Trueblood refused to talk to Piazza, or anyone. "I'm finished talking. I've made up my mind," he said.

Even in the cell phone's minuscule screen Piazza looked frantic. "I never intended to hurt him! I didn't think it would come to this!"

But it has come to this, Jake replied silently. This kid's going to kill himself and Tami and me with him. A new thought popped into his mind: Has Nick told the launch crew to get the hell out of the launch center? And the other people in the building?

"Better get back to your seats," Trueblood's voice commanded over the plane's intercom speakers. "Strap in."

What the hell for? Jake asked himself. But he took Tami by the hand and led her back to their seats.

"He's going to kill us," Tami half whispered, her voice trembling.

Jake nodded. Then, instead of getting into the seat, he marched back to the cockpit door.

"So you're going to let Nick win," he said.

"What?"

"You're going to let Nick win. You're going to show the world that the Zunis are just another bunch of dumbbell terrorists with nothing better to do than slaughter innocent men and women."

Silence from the cockpit for a few heartbeats. Then, "We're not terrorists."

"That's not what the news media will say. I can see the headline, 'Native American Terrorist Kills Himself and a Few Dozen Others.'"

Trueblood did not reply.

"And Nick Piazza finds himself another playmate," Jake continued. "Crashing into the spaceport's control center won't stop Nick from going ahead with his life. All you'll be doing is removing a problem that neither one of you knows how to resolve."

"I know how to resolve it," Trueblood shouted. "Now get back in your seat and strap in."

"Did you write Nick a farewell letter? Disappointed lovers are supposed to write farewell letters before they commit suicide. And murder."

"Shut up and get back in your seat!"

"Why should I? I'll be just as dead standing up."

"Just get back in your seat." Trueblood's voice was almost beseeching.

Jake looked through the plane's nearest window. Spaceport America's scattering of buildings and launchpads was coming into view, off on the horizon. He could see the Astra Super standing on its platform, waiting for tomorrow's launch. A cluster of technicians was swarming around its base.

Jake shook his head and headed back toward Tami. He sat down, dutifully clicked on his safety belt, then reached out and took her hand in his.

She was trembling, her eyes wide with fear. But dry. She wasn't shedding any tears.

Jake squeezed her hand. "Together," he whispered.

Tami had to swallow before she could reply, "Together."

The Plunge

We're circling," Jake realized.

Outside the plane, the Spaceport America buildings slid by again. The Astra Super rocket stood straight and tall at its launchpad two miles away.

"Circling?" Tami asked.

Jake's phone blared again. Piazza. "Let me talk to him," Nick pleaded.

"He doesn't want to talk to anybody," Jake said.

"Jesus Christ, he can't do this! He mustn't!"

"He's doing it."

Tami pointed at the window beside her. "We're circling again."

He's working up the nerve for the final plunge, Jake thought.

Sure enough, the plane started climbing. Then it turned and began a thundering dive toward the Spaceport building, gleaming in the desert sun.

Jake reached for Tami's hand again and squeezed it hard. She squeezed back, her eyes shut tight, her mouth open in a silent scream.

This is it! Jake knew.

Suddenly the plane angled upward. Jake's stomach dropped out of his body and he saw the Spaceport building flash by as the Citation climbed into the clean blue sky.

"He didn't do it!" Jake exulted.

Tami opened her eyes. "He didn't do it!" she echoed.

Trueblood's voice came over the cabin intercom, low, subdued. "I couldn't do it," he confirmed, almost sobbing. "I couldn't do it."

Jake unclicked his seat belt and staggered to the cockpit door. "Thanks, Billy. You did the right thing."

"Yeah." Trueblood's voice sounded shaky.

"You chose life over death," Jake continued. "It's a hard choice. But it's the right one."

"You don't know how hard it was."

"Thank you, Billy. Thanks for our lives. And your own."

A few heartbeats of silence. Then, "We're not out of the woods yet. I've never landed a Citation before."

"You can do it."

"Maybe. You guys strapped in?"

"Tami is. I'm going back to my seat now."

"Okay. I'm gonna try to put this bird down at the Spaceport strip. No traffic to worry about, like Albuquerque."

Jake nodded as he got into his seat, fastened the safety belt, and yanked it tight enough across his lap to cut off the circulation in his legs. Despite everything, Tami made a pathetic little smile for him, her eyes teary.

Now she lets the tears out, Jake noted. He reached out to her again and they clasped hands once more.

The Spaceport's ground controller's voice came snarling through the intercom speakers. "What the hell d'you think you're doin'? Buzzin' the building like it's a fuckin' air show? You're gonna have your license revoked, mister."

Trueblood merely replied, in a strictly professional tone, "Request landing instructions, please."

It was a tense five minutes. Jake saw the desert scrubland coming up fast, heard the roar of the landing gear's hatches opening, watched the ground coming closer, closer, flashing past.

Then the plane hit the ground with a brutal thump, waddled

back into the air, finally banged down again hard enough to send a flash of pain shooting up Jake's spine.

But they were on the ground, rolling along the runway, engines roaring in reverse to kill their speed. Through the closed cockpit door Jake heard Trueblood give off a heartfelt yowl of victory. Or maybe anguish.

Aftermath

The doctor scribbled on his prescription pad. "Take two of these as necessary," he said, tearing off the prescription and holding it out across his desk to Jake.

Tami sat at Jake's side. Her examination had shown everything was all right.

"It's just a slight sprain," the doctor said, sounding bored. "Tension. It'll go away in a couple of days."

Jake got to his feet shakily and took the prescription in one hand. "Thank you, doctor," he said.

Nick Piazza appeared at the doorway. Looking at Jake and Tami, he asked, "You're both okay?"

"Nothing but shattered constitutions," Jake said. Gripping Tami's hand as she stood up, he added, "I never want to go through anything like that again."

Piazza nodded.

"Where's Billy?" asked Tami.

Pointing along the corridor outside the physician's office, Piazza said, "Down there."

"How is he?"

"He seems okay. Quiet. I think it's just starting to hit him, what he tried to do," Piazza said, leading them to the door. He pushed it open and the three of them stepped into the small-ish room. Jake closed the door firmly behind them.

Before anyone could say anything, Piazza looked at True-blood and said mournfully, "This is all my fault."

Trueblood got up from the chair he'd been sitting in and said, "It sure is."

Billy stood facing Piazza, but didn't move an inch toward him. Jake saw that Nick towered over the younger man, as he did with almost everybody.

With a pitiful little shrug, Piazza admitted, "I treated you like shit, Billy. What can I do to make up for it?"

"Make sure they don't lift my license," Trueblood said.

"Yeah, sure. But there's got to be more."

Nodding, Trueblood said, "I guess we should both get some counseling."

"I've been thinking," Piazza said. "NASA runs the astronaut training center. How'd you like to become an astronaut?"

"A gay astronaut?" Trueblood almost laughed. "I don't think so."

"There's got to be something!"

"I'll think about it. I'll let you know."

"But where will you go? What will you do?"

Trueblood stared down at his shoes for a moment, then brought his eyes up to stare into Piazza's. "I'm going back to the reservation. Talk to the medicine men there. See what they have to say."

"Anything, Billy. I'll do anything."

"To keep this all a secret? Yeah, I know."

"To help you find your way!"

With a curt nod, Trueblood said, "That's what the medicine men are for. They help a man find his way." Then he added, "Sometimes."

The four of them agreed that what had happened between Trueblood and Piazza would remain their business, no one else's. Tami promised that she wouldn't tell a soul. "This is between the two of you," she said, then added, "But don't go buzzing into buildings again, Billy. Not ever!"

He actually managed a smile. Raising his right hand in a three-fingered Boy Scout salute, he swore, "Not ever."

Piazza instructed his personal driver to ferry Tami and Jake to the DoubleTree hotel in Albuquerque.

"What about you?" Jake asked Piazza as they approached the black sedan.

"I've got to talk with my people here, make sure this story doesn't get spread to the media. A lot of fences to mend. Jerome will take you to the DoubleTree and then come back here for me."

As he followed Tami into the car, Jake realized that Jerome's name in Spanish was Geronimo.

. . .

Jake found it hard to sleep. He kept seeing the Spaceport buildings flashing past, hearing the roar of the Citation's engines as they dove toward the ground. Time and again he sat up in bed, soaked in cold sweat.

Next to him, Tami's sleep was troubled too; she tossed and moaned but she didn't wake up. It's going to take a lot more than a few pills to get us over this, Jake told himself.

As dawn began to ease the darkness outside their hotel window, Jake finally gave up all pretense of sleeping and went to the bathroom. By the time he came out Tami was standing at the window looking out at the slowly brightening sky.

"A new day," she said, turning toward Jake.

He folded her into his arms. "The nightmare's over. Time to get back to work."

They grabbed a quick breakfast down in the hotel's lobby, then drove out to the Spaceport. It felt eerie: almost every one of the Astra employees knew that the building had been buzzed by the boss's Citation, although only a few knew who was flying the plane and what his original intention was. Piazza had called the whole team together and told a half-truthful story about Billy's "escapade." He never mentioned attempted suicide or the reasons for it.

At last Jake and Tami went out into the chilly early morning to watch the launch. The sun was just over the horizon, already starting to warm the desert. Waiting out in the grandstand as the countdown ticked away, Jake felt his pulse quickening, as it always did at a launch. I wonder how many of these things I'll have to watch before they become humdrum? he asked himself.

And the answer came to him. It'll never happen. Every launch is a drama, a contest between human willpower and the forces of nature.

The thought calmed him. Standing there in the open grandstand with a few dozen other onlookers, Jake felt not calm, far from calm, but ready to face whatever came, willing and even anxious to see this latest step in the settlement of the new frontier.

Turning toward Tami, he slid an arm around her waist and pulled her close. Inanely, he said, "We're on our way."

She smiled up at him. "I just wish they wouldn't schedule these launches at the crack of dawn."

Jake laughed. Tami's sense of humor had returned.

The countdown proceeded smoothly. As the loudspeakers counted, "... THREE ... TWO ... ONE—" Jake suddenly wished he was in the spaceship perched up on the rocket's nose. He wanted to be going into space himself. He remembered an old line that somebody had written long ago:

"When once you have tasted flight, you will forever walk the earth with your eyes turned skyward, for there you have been, and there you will always long to return."

Smoke billowed, the rocket engines lit off, their hot flame burning through the steam, and the Astra Super began to climb into the bright morning sky.

"There they go!" somebody hollered.

The meager crowd cheered, and the rocket rose smoothly across the heavens. The sound from the launchpad finally reached the spectators, wave after wave of thunder rattling every nerve in the body.

"ASTRA SUPER IS ON ITS WAY TO THE INTER-NATIONAL SPACE STATION," the launch announcer said. Jake let go of a sigh of relief. And he saw that Tami did, too.

Pat Lovett had chosen the Stanford Court hotel as Tomlinson's local campaign headquarters.

"It's pricey but it's impressive," he had justified the choice to anyone who questioned it.

Kevin O'Donnell, who had remained in DC for the California balloting, smirked, "Pat knows how to spend the boss's money."

The Stanford Court's ballroom was packed with people. Jake actually staggered backward a step or two when he opened a side door and got hit with the noise. It seemed that half the city was jammed in there, everyone talking, yammering, bellowing at the same time. A band was blaring somewhere in the confusion, but it was impossible to tell what it was supposed to be playing. Red, white, and blue bunting festooned the ballroom, thousands of red, white, and blue balloons were hovering up along the ceiling, campaign workers and call girls and well-wishers and news media people were gesticulating, hollering into each other's ears, laughing and shouting with earnest abandon.

Huge television screens had been set up in the ballroom's corners, each of them flicking from one newscast to another. Each of them showed the same thing: the race between Tomlinson and Sebastian was too close to call. The two men were running literally neck and neck.

Jake forced himself into the waving, weaving, hollering crowd, standing on tiptoes to catch a glimpse of Senator Tomlinson.

He was up on the makeshift platform that the hotel's people had erected—and decorated in red, white, and blue—with Amy standing at his side as they nodded and smiled and shook hands with a weaving parade of men and women. Tomlinson was clutching Amy as if he was afraid that she'd disappear if he let go of her.

Tami had gone to Fresno, partly to be interviewed as "a knowledgeable insider" about the Tomlinson campaign, partly to renew her acquaintance with the people who expected her to join their news staff in a few weeks. Then she was to meet Jake at her parents' home in the suburbs.

Alone, feeling disgruntled and afraid for his marriage, Jake wormed his way past several jam-packed bars, heading for Tomlinson.

Looking around at the raucous crowd, Jake recalled a line from *Faustus*: "Why this is hell, nor am I out of it."

Why does Frank put up with all this? he asked himself. Looking at the candidate and his wife, Jake saw that Tomlinson was beaming that gigawatt smile of his at the people swarming up to shake his hand, to press the flesh so that they could go back home and tell anyone who'd listen to them that they'd actually met Senator B. Franklin Tomlinson and shook the man's hand.

The noise was overwhelming Jake, making his head throb. But he was getting closer to the senator, actually forcing his way up the steps to the top of the rickety stage, a few feet away from the glad-handing politician.

Tomlinson's smile broadened even wider as he spotted Jake approaching. "Jake!" he yelled, dropping the hand he'd been shaking. "Come on up. What's the latest?"

Glancing at the nearest TV screen, Jake hollered, "Still too close to call."

Then Jake realized, it was well past midnight and the race was still too close to call. That's good! Tomlinson was running even with Sebastian. He might even win the California primary!

But then he remembered that the outlying districts would be the last to show their results. The districts where the farmers, the winegrowers, the small-town residents voted. Sebastian country, he knew.

"It's been a good fight," he yelled into Tomlinson's ear.

"Hasn't it?" the senator replied, absently reaching for the next hand to shake.

Wearing a chic royal-blue cocktail dress, Amy was smiling fixedly as she shook hands, too. She looks wilted, Jake thought. This sure takes a lot out of you.

But the senator didn't seem tired at all. He was pumping away, smiling brightly, apparently as overjoyed as he could be to meet each and every voter who approached him.

This is meat and potatoes for Frank, Jake saw. He loves this. The attention. The adulation. I'm so happy that you could come here and meet me. Together we can accomplish great things. That's the message that Frank was sending out almost telepathically to the voters.

Jake shook his head in admiration. Frank's got the touch. He loves this. He's not going through this for his father. He's doing it for himself. He *wants* to be president of the United States.

Suddenly Pat Lovett appeared at the senator's side, pointing excitedly at the nearest TV screen.

All the screens flicked to the same picture. The crowd's babble hushed. A serious-faced commentator, glancing at the TV monitor on his desk before looking back into the camera, announced:

"The latest polling returns, which include all but three percent of the state's districts, show that Senator Franklin Tomlinson has won the California primary by a margin of fifty-two percent of the vote, against forty-five percent for—"

The rest of the newsman's words were drowned in a mammoth roar of exhilaration. The ballroom exploded with jubilation.

Fresno

Jake skipped the victory party. He checked out of the Stanford Court and drove his rented Mercedes down toward Fresno. It was nearly two a.m. but he didn't feel the least bit drowsy. Too wired.

Frank's won the California primary! he kept repeating to himself. He's actually got a real chance to get the party's nomination this summer.

Clicking on the car's radio as he raced eastward on Interstate 205, Jake listened to Senator Sebastian's concession speech: short, dignified, ending with a pledge to "carry this fight right into the convention, if we have to."

"You won't be the only one, pal," Jake said aloud to the senator from the solitude of the rented car.

He made the turn at the intersection of Interstate 99 and headed south toward Fresno. Won't be there until damned near dawn, he realized. So what? Tami's there, visiting her folks. That's where I want to be, too.

The car's GPS guided him to the Umetzu residence with softly spoken instructions. Jake made one wrong turn, and the woman's "Recalculating" sounded mildly reproving to him.

At last he glided to a stop next to the three-story clapboard house. A street lamp on the curb about twenty yards away brightened the area enough for Jake to read the house's number, and his faithful GPS guide announced, "You have arrived at your destination."

The place looked quiet, closed up for the night. Not a light showing. Suddenly the long night caught up with Jake: he felt dead tired. Yawning as he shut down the car's engine, he cranked his seat back, closed his eyes, and fell asleep almost instantly.

. . .

"Jake! Are you all right?"

His eyes flashed open and Jake saw Tami—with two of her younger brothers beside her—peering anxiously through his driver's-side window.

Breaking into a sheepish grin, he saw that it was full daylight on the suburban street, and Tami's father was coming down the porch steps toward his car.

"Hi," he said, as he opened the door. Stepping outside the car, he wrapped an arm around Tami and bussed her, then explained, "I figured you'd all be asleep so I came without calling."

Tami broke into a delighted laugh. "You could have called! We didn't go to bed until we heard Sebastian's concession speech."

Mr. Umetzu extended his hand to Jake. "It's good to see you again. Your man did all right for himself last night."

With a laugh, Jake agreed, "He sure did."

Pointing to the crowded driveway running alongside the house, Mr. Umetzu said to the elder of his two sons, "Move a couple of the cars so Jake can park on the driveway."

"Okay, Dad."

Within a few minutes Jake's Mercedes was on the driveway and the five of them were climbing the porch stairs, heading for the front door, where Mrs. Umetzu stood waiting with a beaming smile. She was a formidable-looking woman: white hair pulled back in a bun, thick body, heavy arms and legs. Twice the size of her slimly elegant husband.

"You're just in time for breakfast," she said cheerily. "How do you like your eggs?"

"Any old way," Jake said, one arm still around Tami's waist.

. . .

Breakfast was cheery, with Tami's brothers asking Jake about the Tomlinson campaign, her father sitting at the head of the table smiling approvingly, and her mother shuttling back and forth between the kitchen and the dining room table, carrying trays of steaming food.

Only one of Tami's sisters was at home, the other lived in San Francisco with her husband, an advisor with a major wealth management firm.

The talk around the table was all about the election and Senator Tomlinson's chances to capture the Republican nomination. Tami said, "If Tomlinson does win, it'll be Jake's space plan that wins it for him."

Jake put down the coffee cup that he'd been sipping from. "And Frank's foreign policy ideas, and his economic program, and his stand on terrorism . . ."

Tami's eyes widened slightly at that last statement. She's thinking of Billy Trueblood, Jake realized, counting himself an insensitive fool for mentioning the subject.

Recovering before anyone else around the table could notice, Tami shook her head stubbornly. "It's your space plan, Jake. It gives the people hope for the future. It gives us something to work toward, to aim for."

"Developing the new frontier," said the younger of her brothers. "That's something to shoot for."

Mr. Umetzu smiled at his son. "So are you going to become an astronaut?"

"I might," the lad said. "I'm taking a special course on lunar construction techniques next fall."

"You're gonna be a lunatic?" his older brother teased.

Mr. Umetzu glanced at his wristwatch. "The two of you will be late for school if you don't get moving."

Both boys scrambled out of their chairs and pounded up the staircase to their room.

Tami's sister and mother began clearing the table. As Tami got up to help them, her father said, "Let's go into the living room and let the ladies take care of the dishes."

Surprised, Tami started to object. "I can help . . ."

Crooking a finger at his daughter, Umetzu said, "I want to talk to the two of you."

Jake followed his wife and father-in-law into the spacious, meticulously decorated living room. Umetzu gestured to the sofa beneath a breathtaking photograph of the Grand Canyon he himself had taken years earlier, then pulled up one of the armchairs to face Jake and Tami.

Without preamble, the older man said, "It seems to me that you two have a big decision to make."

Jake glanced at Tami, who looked suddenly concerned, as if she expected her father to lecture them both severely. She looked like a sheepish little kid who'd been caught sneaking cookies.

Trying to keep his voice even, nonconfrontational, Jake replied merely, "Yes, we do."

"I know you may think your decision is none of my business," Umetzu said softly, "but as head of the family I feel I have some responsibility here."

"I understand," Jake said.

"My children are very dear to me."

"Your daughter is very dear to me."

Umetzu smiled gently and nodded his approval. But then he continued, "My daughter has been offered a very good position here in Fresno," Umetzu said, his face a noncommittal mask.

"And I'm an advisor to a man who might become president of the United States."

"Which means you would be separated by nearly three thousand miles. That's not good for your marriage."

"No, it wouldn't be," Jake agreed.

In a very small voice Tami said, "Unless you decide to stay in Fresno." Then she added, hopefully, "Or maybe in San Francisco, Silicon Valley, someplace nearby."

Jake wanted to counter, Or you could stay with me in DC while I help the new president start up our space plan.

But he remained silent, frozen, staring not at Tami but at her father.

Umetzu sighed. "Where is Scotty with his transporter beam when you really need him?"

No one laughed.

Tami said, "This anchor position is the chance of a lifetime for me."

"Maybe Frank or Kevin or *somebody* could get you a slot in the DC area," Jake said. It sounded pretty desperate, even to himself.

"Too much competition there," Tami replied. "Everybody wants to be on Washington TV. I need to prove myself, work my way up. Fresno is where I can get a start."

Umetzu raised both his hands. "In my day, a wife followed her husband's career, wherever it led."

Tami started to object, "But—"

"But it's no longer my day, I know that," Umetzu went on. "You have your career to think about."

Tami's eyes started to fill with tears. "I had a good career in DC until Senator Santino wrecked it."

Jake remembered. The Little Saint had gotten Tami fired from her position as a reporter on the local Reuters news bureau because of an environmental story she had broken, and effectively blackballed her in the entire region. Santino had been a ruthlessly powerful figure in the US Senate in those days. Now he was in a nursing home but Tami was still persona non grata in Washington.

"So what are you planning to do?" Umetzu asked. "Both of you."

Jake heard himself reply, "If Senator Tomlinson doesn't win the Republican nomination, I'll quit his staff and come out here."

"You will?" Tami blurted.

Nodding solemnly, Jake said, "I will."

She threw her arms around him and they kissed.

Umetzu waited until they broke up their embrace, then asked, "And what if your senator wins the nomination?"

Shrugging, Jake admitted, "I don't know. That would change things, wouldn't it?"

"Considerably. And what if he is elected president? Could you leave then?"

Jake was silent for several long moments. Then, staring at Tami, he said, "That would change things even more. That would change things a lot."

Winging high above the craggy peaks of the Rocky Mountains, practically bare of snow, Jake leaned toward Tami and said, "He might make it, you know."

She turned from the window she'd been staring through. "You mean Tomlinson?"

"Who else?"

"And then what?"

Jake shook his head. "I don't know. I don't think it would be fair for me to leave him at that point."

Looking as if she'd just watched a puppy die, Tami said, "Jake, I've got to take the KSEE job. It's the break I've been searching for."

"Your father's right, we can't have a marriage with three thousand miles between us."

"No, I guess not."

"When do you have to give your answer to KSEE?" he asked.

"I should have told them while I was in Fresno. I asked them to give me another week."

"Another week," Jake echoed.

"Jake, I've got to say yes to them! I can't turn them down!"

"I know," he said, hating the necessity, the *finality* of his wife's decision.

Tami forced a grin. "Maybe Frank will lose to Sebastian, after all. That would mean we'd only be separated for a couple of months."

Jake nodded and tried to smile back at her. He failed.

Maybe Frank will win, he thought, and I'll stay in DC while Tami goes to Fresno. Shit!

. . .

For a week the two of them lived like strangers in their condo, neither of them daring to bring up the subject of Tami's parting. Jake fumed to himself. We ought to be shouting at each other, he told himself, yelling and throwing things. I ought to *demand* that she stay with me. I can get her a job somewhere in DC. It might not be what she wants, not be as good as the Fresno offer, but at least she'd be with me, we'd be together.

And she'd hate me. I'd have ruined her career. That's not fair. It wouldn't be right.

Jake realized he didn't care what was right and wrong. He loved Tami and he wanted her to stay with him. He talked with Earl Reynolds about finding Tami a job in the DC area.

"Not easy, Jake," Reynolds said, his handsome face pulling into a frown. "She's overqualified for most of the available spots, underqualified for the big ones. She doesn't have the chops to knock off one of the local anchors."

Jake nodded; Reynolds's assessment had been just about what he'd expected.

"I could keep her on here, on my staff," the PR man suggested.

Jake forced a smile. "That's not what she wants, Earl. This job out in Fresno is what she's looking for."

Reynolds grimaced. "The Walter Cronkite syndrome."

"Yeah. Guess so."

. . .

Jake drove Tami to Reagan National, pulling up in the special lot reserved for congressmen and their aides.

"You could've dropped me off at the curb," Tami said as Jake tugged her oversized roll-along bag out of the convertible's trunk.

"No," he said, slamming the trunk lid with unnecessary violence. "I'll go to the ticket counter with you."

"They have curbside check-in," Tami pointed out.

"Big deal."

They checked Tami's bag at the curb and Jake walked into the terminal building with her. At the entrance to the security check area, they stopped, both of them suddenly feeling awkward.

"Uh . . . call me when you arrive," Jake said.

"Sure."

"Have a good flight."

"Sure," she repeated.

Jake fidgeted for a miserable moment, then grabbed her in both his arms. "Tami, don't go! Please don't go!"

Looking up into his eyes, she said, "If you don't want me to, I won't go."

There it was. The moment of truth. She's willing to throw away her chance of a lifetime—for me. If I'm a big-enough scumbag to tell her I want her to stay here with me, she'll do it. And end up hating me for it.

Jake had to swallow hard before he could say, "Go on. Call me when you land."

Without another word Tami turned and started up the aisle toward the TSA officers, the roll-along behind her. Jake stood rooted to the spot, watching her leave him.

Suddenly Tami turned back toward him and shouted, "I hope he loses big! I hope he gets trounced!"

Then she turned again and hurried along her way.

Back-Channel

The campaign roared on, with Sebastian and Tomlinson neck and neck as they raced across the country giving speeches, interviews, meeting with local leaders, wooing votes. Jake stayed in Washington for the most part, but even when he had to travel he phoned Tami every evening.

She seemed happy enough, caught up in the excitement of the campaign and a plethora of local happenings, ranging from a suspicious warehouse fire to a heroic dog that saved a ten-year-old boy from drowning by rousing a pair of firefighters to rescue the lad when he got swept away in a flooded river.

Tami sent Jake DVDs of her appearances on the evening news. She seemed bright, knowledgeable, cheerfully smiling. She even interviewed Senator Tomlinson briefly when he swung through Fresno on his way to a major party rally in San Francisco.

Bright, Jake thought, watching her on the TV in their empty condo. Knowledgeable. Cheerful. But he thought he caught an edge of sadness in Tami's smiling face, an undertone of misery. Jake shook his head, frowning. That's projection, he told himself. You're miserable so you think she ought to be miserable, too.

She's not, he saw.

. . .

As if Jake wasn't already up to his earlobes in work, William Farthington called him, exactly one week before the GOP nominating convention was scheduled to begin in Philadelphia.

"Hello, Bill," Jake said tightly to the image of NASA's chief administrator on his wall screen. "How are you?"

For once, Bloviating Billy didn't waste time on niceties. "Hal Harmon wants to talk to you."

Surprised, Jake asked, "General Harmon?"

"Right away," Farthington said, his face dead serious. "Tonight, if you can."

Jake didn't have to check his calendar. He had nothing on tap for the evening.

"Okay. Where and when?"

"My house. Nine thirty."

No dinner this trip, Jake said to himself. The expression on Farthington's face, though, told him something serious was percolating. The head of the US Air Force's Space Command doesn't call for a private meeting to talk about trivia.

So he downed a TV dinner that purported to be manicotti, tossed the emptied container into the trash, then went downstairs for his car.

Fortunately, Jake had programmed the location of Farthington's suburban Alexandria home into his convertible's GPS. Traffic was on the light side, and he pulled up onto the NASA administrator's driveway a few minutes early. Two other cars were already there: a sleek gray hatchback and a dead black Mercedes. A shadowy figure was sitting behind the steering wheel of the Mercedes, smoking a cigarette. He looked lean, youngish.

William Farthington himself opened the front door for Jake. No servants? Jake asked himself.

Farthington led him to a small book-lined study toward the rear of the big house. Two men got to their feet as Jake stepped in: General Harmon and a stranger. Harmon was in civilian clothes: his tweed sports coat looked like it hadn't been pressed for ages, but his slacks were razor-creased. Jake imagined he could see the general's four stars still on his shoulders, perfectly in place.

Farthington said, "You already know General Harmon, Jake." Gesturing toward the other man, he introduced, "This is Grigor Medvedev, of the Russian foreign secretary's office."

The word for Medvedev was *compact*, Jake decided. He was the shortest man in the room, but his physique was burly, like a middle-aged weightlifter. Jake thought he must spend a lot of his time in a gym. His face was squarish, with a lump of a nose and a strong, stubborn chin. His eyes were small, squinty; his hair dark but thinning, brushed straight back from his advancing forehead.

"Mr. Medvedev," Jake said as he shook hands with the Russian.

"Dr. Ross," said Medvedev. "Author of the so-called Tomlinson space plan."

Jake smiled. "Success has a thousand fathers."

Each of the other three men already had drinks in their hands. Farthington said apologetically, "I'm afraid the servants have the night off." Pointing to the bar built into the bookcase near the room's only window, he asked, "Can I get something for you, Jake?"

"A club soda will be fine."

As Farthington went to the bar, General Harmon explained, "Grigor and I have known each other since we sorted out the mess in Syria."

Medvedev nodded solemnly. "Without coming to blows."

Jake recalled Bashar al-Assad's final, desperate attempt to get Russia and Iran to prop up his tottering regime. The world had come closer to a nuclear confrontation than most people realized. If Medvedev helped get past that hurdle he must be an important man in the Russian foreign ministry.

At last Farthington handed Jake his club soda and all four

men seated themselves in separate armchairs around a bare coffee table.

"So what's this all about?" Jake asked. "Why have you asked me here?"

Medvedev broke into a guarded smile. "Typical American: straight to the point."

General Harmon also came close to smiling. "Jake, this is what is called a back-channel meeting."

"Back-channel?"

"Mr. Medvedev wants to discuss this undeclared war we've been having in Earth orbit."

"Before something serious happens," Farthington added.

Medvedev leaned back in his armchair, a glass of what must have been vodka in one hand, studying Jake as if trying to decide how far he could trust him.

"You are advisor to Senator Tomlinson, are you not?" he asked.

With a nod, Jake agreed, "I'm the senator's science advisor, yes."

"Good," Medvedev said, with a humorless smile. "Perhaps we can achieve something here."

Achieve what?" Jake asked.

Gesturing with his free hand, Medvedev replied, "An end to this nonsense of attacking each other's satellites."

All Jake could reply was, "Oh?"

Looking squarely at the Russian, General Harmon said, "You can incapacitate our satellites and we can knock out yours. We've proven that. So where do we go from here?"

"I am here to determine if we can arrange a truce, a gentleman's agreement to stop this nonsense. It is doing more harm than good."

Farthington ran a hand across his nearly bald scalp. "I think we're agreed on that point."

Medvedev hunched closer to Jake. "Once these things are set into motion, they can be very difficult to stop." Glancing at Harmon, he went on, "Military operations can take on a life of their own, you know."

"Are you saying," Harmon asked, "that the Russian government would be willing to stop attacking our satellites?"

"It is possible. Not easy, but possible. Of course, you would have to agree to stop attacking our satellites."

"Our countermeasures are strictly defensive," Harmon objected. "Your people started this shoot-out."

Medvedev smiled his somber little smile again. "We are not here to argue about who started the struggle. We are here to see if the struggle can be stopped."

"Certainly it can," the general snapped. "Just stop shooting at us."

Medvedev shook his head. "That's not an agreement; it's a surrender. Our military leaders would never accept it."

"Then what would they accept?" Jake asked.

"An assurance on your part that you will not attack our satellites."

"And your government would offer a similar assurance to us?"

"Yes. Of course."

Harmon shook his head. "Reminds me of something the head of the Warner Bros. movie studio once said: 'An oral agreement isn't worth the paper it's written on.'"

Jake broke into a chuckle, then realized that no one else was laughing. He stifled the laugh.

"Let me try to explain," Medvedev said. "This conflict in orbit is taking place in the deepest secrecy. You have not told your news media about it, not even your Congress. Neither have we, of course. Officially, the conflict does not exist."

"But satellites are being knocked out of commission," said Farthington.

"Exactly so," Medvedev agreed. "The question is, how do we put an end to a conflict that neither side admits to exist? Before it escalates into something more serious."

Silence descended on the book-lined study.

Until Jake said, "By trusting each other."

General Harmon shook his head. "That's a hard one. Trust doesn't come easily."

"But it must come," Medvedev insisted. "If we cannot agree to trust each other, the militarists will take control of the Kremlin. Sooner or later, you will face a growing military confrontation and I will have a bullet in my brain."

Farthington realized, "You're taking a considerable risk, talking to us like this."

"More than you know," said Medvedev. "That young fellow waiting for me in the car outside might very well be an intelligence agent. Ever since Vladimir Putin died, the Kremlin has been in an uproar. Who will take up the reins of government? Who will be Russia's new leader?"

Jake realized, "Then this issue of attacking each other's satellites is only the tip of the iceberg, isn't it? We're really talking about establishing trust between our two nations, moving to a healthier relationship."

Medvedev didn't reply. But he nodded.

"We were allies once," General Harmon murmured. "Against the Nazis."

"That was a long time ago," said Medvedev.

"It's what Obama wanted to accomplish," Jake realized. "A reset of the relationship between us."

Farthington half whispered, "If we could accomplish that . . ." His voice faded into silence.

"If we could accomplish that," Medvedev took up, "we could make the world a safer place. We could confront the terrorists wherever they exist. We could build new trade agreements." Looking straight at Jake, he added, "We could join you in your movement to develop the frontier of space."

"If we can trust each other," Harmon added, almost gruffly.

"If we can trust each other," Medvedev repeated. "You Americans have a tradition of keeping your military out of politics. Unfortunately, we in Russia must always look over our shoulders to see if our military is dogging our tracks."

"Wellll," Harmon said, stretching out the word. "We're willing to stop if you are."

"On nothing but our unsecured word?"

The general smiled. "We can do better than that, I think." And he reached out his hand toward Medvedev.

The Russian stared at General Harmon's hand for a moment, then grasped it in his own.

"A gentleman's agreement," Harmon said.

Medvedev pumped the general's hand vigorously. "Gentleman's agreement," he said, looking genuinely pleased for the first time since Jake entered the room.

Farthington said, "I think it would be a good thing for us to keep this back-channel open. We can meet here whenever you want to."

"Easier than meeting in Moscow," Medvedev agreed.

"I'll bet," said Harmon.

Getting to his feet, Farthington announced, "This calls for another round of drinks. Grigor, another vodka?"

"Da."

"Hal, you sticking with Bushmills?"

The general glanced at Medvedev, then said, "Da."

As he headed toward the bar Farthington asked, "Jake, another club soda for you?"

"I think I'll switch to Jack Daniel's."

"Good!"

Once they were all settled with their fresh drinks, Jake heard himself ask, "Can one of you tell me why you wanted me in on this meeting? I mean, I'm flattered, but international agreements aren't really in my job description."

Medvedev actually laughed. "The author of the space plan is so modest?"

Jake felt puzzled. "I don't understand."

"Your space plan is the key to the future," the Russian explained. "It offers us a way to cooperate instead of competing. It gives us the opportunity to move out to the stars."

"That's a big step," Jake objected.

Farthington stepped in with, "Even the longest journey begins with a single step."

Medvedev hoisted his glass. "To the author of the space plan, the creator of a better future for all of us."

Jake felt his mouth drop open. And he loved it.

Philadelphia

Jake wanted to tell the world that it was *his* space plan that gave Medvedev and his cohorts in the Kremlin the courage to try to stop the undeclared war in space.

But he knew he couldn't say a word about it to anyone, of course. Not even Tami.

She was excited, too, when she phoned Jake the next night. "They're sending me to Philly! I'm going to cover the convention!"

"We'll be together!" Jake crowed.

"Yes!"

Excited as a schoolboy, Jake immediately phoned the Downtown Courtyard hotel in Philadelphia and upgraded his room to a studio suite with a king-sized bed. Kevin will growl at the added expense, he thought, but I'll pay the difference out of my own pocket if I have to.

O'Donnell, Pat Lovett, and just about the entire campaign staff poured into Philadelphia a couple of days before the convention's official opening. Senator Tomlinson stayed home in DC with Amy, getting some well-earned rest before the mammoth meeting was gaveled to order—and prepping for a speech he was scheduled to deliver at the Brandeis University commencement ceremonies in suburban Boston.

Jake arrived at the hotel early in the afternoon before the convention was to open. As he unpacked he noted the view of the Philadelphia city hall through the suite's lone window.

Jake straightened up and stared at the dreary, overly ornate edifice. At its center rose a tall elaborately decorated spire, topped by a statue of William Penn, all in drab, depressing gray.

That's got to be the ugliest building I've ever seen, Jake said to himself, shaking his head at the thought that somebody actually *designed* the building to look that way.

It was grotesque. Yet it was almost hypnotic. Jake tore his gaze away from the city hall and forced himself to finish unpacking. Tami was arriving later in the afternoon and he wanted to be waiting in the terminal for her, with a bunch of flowers to offer her.

The hotel seemed filled with Tomlinson campaign workers. Jake bumped into people he knew—or at least recognized—in the hallway, in the elevator, cramming the hotel lobby down on the main floor.

He mumbled brief hellos as he made his way toward the front entrance and the line of taxicabs waiting there.

He was ten minutes early for Tami's flight, which gave him just enough time to select a bouquet of roses from the flower shop in the terminal, and then hurry to the area where Tami's flight was discharging its passengers.

And there she was! A tiny figure, almost hidden by a gangling family wearing sashes and buttons, all proclaiming SEBASTIAN! Slim, dressed in a no-nonsense checkered hip-length blouse over tan jeans, Tami was towing her roll-along suitcase and had a sizeable tote bag slung over one shoulder. She was deep in conversation with a much bigger guy dressed in a Tomlinson T-shirt and baggy blue jeans.

And then she saw Jake. Tami raced toward him, the roll-along bouncing behind her. She dropped the suitcase and flung both her arms around his neck. They kissed mightily as the other passengers streamed around them, grinning appreciatively.

Once they disengaged Jake handed her the roses and breathed, "Hello, honey."

He saw tears in her eyes. "Hello, Jake," Tami said.

She introduced the guy she'd been talking to, her cameraman, while Jake picked up the roll-along she'd dropped. By the time they reached the terminal's entrance Jake had forgotten the fellow's name. There was a long line waiting for cabs but Jake and Tami weren't bothered, they talked nonstop until at last the taxi supervisor yelled at them, "Here's your cab, lovebirds!"

Jake and the cameraman stowed the luggage in the trunk while the taxi driver sat behind his wheel with his meter already chugging away. The cameraman got into the front seat, Jake and Tami sat together in the rear and off they went to the Downtown Courtyard hotel.

. . .

"A suite!" Tami gushed as Jake led her through the front door. He was so excited that he thought about lifting her off her feet and carrying her in, but decided that might be too much.

Tami took in the suite's appointments with a swift glance, dropped her shoulder bag on a chair, and placed the bouquet of roses tenderly on the table next to it. She moved into the bedroom and immediately spotted the city hall standing grimly outside the window.

"Wow," she said. "That's—"

Jake spun her around and clasped her again in both his arms. "I missed you," he told her, needlessly.

"I missed you," Tami said.

They also missed dinner later that evening.

. . .

The next morning they went down to the lobby restaurant for a big breakfast.

"The convention's deadlocked," Tami said cheerfully, between bites of her butter-and-syrup-slathered waffle. "Sebastian's ahead, but he doesn't have enough votes for a first-ballot victory."

Jake nodded. "Pat Lovett's out trying to rustle up every vote that he can find. The uncommitted delegates are lining up to see what we're offering them."

"Same with Sebastian," Tami said, reaching for her coffee.

And Jake thought, The trouble is that we can't say a word about the deal with Medvedev. A public revelation would kill the deal. And maybe kill Medvedev too.

"I've got to go check in at the news media center," Tami said, "before the opening ceremony. Don't know when we'll be finished."

Tapping his jacket pocket, Jake said, "I've got my cell phone. Just give me a buzz."

Her smile lit the restaurant. "Every hour on the hour," she said. Then she added, "If I can."

"Pat wants me to circulate among the delegates on the floor, talk to them about the space plan, how it'll boost employment and all."

"I thought that kind of talk went on in smoke-filled back rooms."

With a smile and a shake of his head, Jake countered, "Most of the rooms around here are non-smoking."

"But you still use them for twisting arms."

Pretending shock, Jake said, "We don't twist arms! We tell people the truth and let them see the sense of what we're saying."

"So does Sebastian."

Going serious, Jake said, "No. His people are the ones twisting arms. He's calling in every favor he's given since he first arrived in the Senate."

Tami looked decidedly unconvinced. Then, switching topics, she looked out across the crowded restaurant. "Have you noticed how many call girls are working the hotel?"

"Call girls? No."

"Come on, Jake. You're not a corpse. The place is swarming with hookers."

"I only have eyes for you."

Tami's expression went from dubious to appreciative. "Me too," she said, so low that Jake barely caught it.

But the spell lasted only a moment. Their waitress hurried by and dropped their check on the table.

Jake grabbed it. "This one's on the Tomlinson campaign."

"I've got an expense account too," Tami complained. Mildly.

Jake couldn't suppress his grin. "We'll talk about that tonight."

After a day of settling procedural details, the conventioneers went out on the town. Philadelphia was not known for its nightlife, but a couple of thousand convention delegates went seeking entertainment and found it. Easily.

The next morning, despite hangovers and grossly exaggerated tales of romantic encounters, the delegates got down to the serious business of nominating candidates for the presidency.

Several dark horses were named, more to put them in a position to bargain with the eventual winner than as serious contenders.

Senator Tomlinson was nominated by aged warhorse Senator Zucco, who stressed the new beginnings that the Tomlinson space plan offered the nation, and the world. (And New Mexico, of course.)

As soon as Zucco finally mentioned Tomlinson's name, Lovett's people exploded in a frenzy of marching bands and high-stepping cheerleaders. Watching from Tomlinson's suite in the Loews Hotel, Jake half expected to see Amy out there strutting with them. The auditorium rocked with noise as carloads of glittering confetti descended from the ceiling.

Jake was impressed with Lovett's choreography. Across the room the senator grinned at the display, then turned to his wife and wisecracked, "Somebody down there likes me."

Senator Sebastian was the final nominee, and the celebration for him was even bigger, with drone aircraft flitting through the auditorium dropping SEBASTIAN FOR PRESIDENT souvenirs onto the yelling, laughing, celebrating delegates.

Standing next to Tomlinson, Pat Lovett watched the festivities with unalloyed admiration. "Drones," he muttered. "We should've thought of that."

. . .

With a handful of campaign insiders, Jake watched Tomlinson's evening speech on the Brandeis campus from the campaign headquarters suite in Philadelphia's Loews Hotel.

The senator spoke in a large tent that had been erected on the school's grassy campus. The tent was packed with university bigwigs and parents of the graduates, all listening to Tomlinson's vision of what the future could hold. Despite the evening's muggy heat, he soon had his audience spellbound.

The senator started by delineating the difference between the rule of law and mob law. "In our ongoing struggle against terrorism," he said, "we mustn't descend into the same tactics that the terrorists use: if we drag people out onto the street and kill them because of their names or their beards or the color of their skins, we're no better than they are.

"America has been built on the fundamental freedoms that are based on the bedrock of the rule of law. We assume that you have to *prove* that a man is guilty before you punish him. We assume that the rule of law is what stands between us and the terror of the mob."

Then the senator's speech shifted to the space plan, with its bright promise of developing the frontier overhead.

Stretching his right arm in the general direction of the nearby Atlantic Ocean, Tomlinson said, "The sea was once a barrier to the Europeans, a wall that fenced in their hopes to expand civilization, to grow and prosper. Their dreams ended at the water's edge. But they learned to build ships that traversed the sea, and transformed the ocean from a barrier into a highway. Civilization grew and expanded. People built new worlds, governed by freedom and the prosperity that only free men and women can create.

"Today we look up and see the barrier of outer space, a vast and seemingly unpassable wall that prevents us from expanding civilization anew. But we have learned to build craft that can traverse that barrier and turn it into a highway that leads to new wealth, new opportunity, new civilizations.

"A new age awaits us out in space. This generation of Americans can lead the world to a new era of peace and prosperity for all the peoples of Earth."

As one person, the crowd rose to its feet and mightily applauded the new vision.

Sitting in the Loews Hotel suite, Jake felt his eyes misting at the dream Senator Tomlinson was promising.

• • •

As expected, the first ballot failed to produce a winner in Philadelphia. Sebastian was a mere twenty-eight votes short, but Tomlinson's strong showing forced a second ballot.

And maybe a third, Jake thought as he watched the proceedings from Tomlinson's suite. And a fourth.

It's going to be a long convention, he realized.

Oratory flowed from the speaker's platform like lava pouring from a volcano. Down on the convention floor deals were proposed, discussed, made and unmade. The delegates voted again, and again Sebastian came close to victory, but could not clinch it.

Despite Lovett's wishes, Jake avoided the convention center as much as he could. Too crowded, too noisy, too steamy with politicians great and small eagerly pushing their own agendas, their own state's favorite programs, their own egos.

Sitting wearily in an armchair in Senator Tomlinson's suite, Jake watched the televised proceedings in a growing funk of worn-out numbness.

This is how we select our leaders, he told himself, while a delegate from North Dakota waxed almost lyrical about farm subsidies. Neither Tomlinson nor Sebastian had shown themselves at the convention. It was a long-standing tradition that the candidates did not appear among the delegates until one of them had won the nomination.

By the time Jake got back to the Downtown Courtyard and crawled into bed, dawn was beginning to lighten the sky. Tami was already in bed, sound asleep, with a quizzical little smile on her lips.

. . .

"How do we break this goddamn deadlock?" Lovett wondered, after the fourth ballot came out exactly like the third.

Jake saw the frustration on the campaign manager's face, heard it in his increasingly abrasive tone. At this rate, he thought, we could be here 'til Christmas.

Jake was sunk into an armchair in the second bedroom of the senator's suite, a place of relative calm for the inner elite. Lovett and O'Donnell were standing near the wall-screen TV with Tomlinson. Amy hadn't put in an appearance yet; she was catching up on her sleep after spending the night and early morning watching the TV coverage.

Even the normally unruffled senator was beginning to look frayed. "So what can we do, Pat?" he asked.

Lovett shook his head. "We're holding our own, but we're not making any progress. If we don't think of something, and soon, we're going to start losing delegates."

Tomlinson laughed derisively. "We won't have to lose very many of them to hand Sebastian the prize."

"There must be *something* we can do," Lovett insisted.

Kevin O'Donnell, looking more pinched and cantankerous than ever, shook his head. "Sebastian's people are sticking to him like they've been cemented in place."

"How the hell does he do that?" Tomlinson wondered.

"More than a dozen years in the Senate," O'Donnell answered. "He's got a helluva lot of favors to pull in."

"Well, we've got to do *something*," Tomlinson insisted. "We can't go on like this much longer."

The bedroom door swung open just enough to allow one of the aides—a pretty young blonde—to stick her head in and announce, "A Mr. Patrone is on the phone, Senator. Says he has to talk to you. It's urgent."

Tomlinson looked baffled. "Patrone? Who the hell is Patrone?"

Lovett answered, "Sebastian's campaign manager."

Bargaining

Senator Tomlinson, Pat Lovett, and Jake sat squeezed together on the rear seat of an ordinary taxicab as they rode to a meeting with Umberto Patrone, Senator Sebastian's campaign manager.

Jake had been surprised when Tomlinson told him to come along with Lovett and himself.

"Me? Are you sure, Frank? I'm not—"

"You've been with me since the beginning, back in Montana," Tomlinson answered firmly. "I want you with me now."

"And you know the space plan inside out," Lovett added. "If it comes to bargaining, you'll be in the middle of everything."

Jake nodded and tried not to look smug. Especially when the senator told Kevin O'Donnell to stay at the hotel.

"I need you to look after things here, Kev," Tomlinson said. "Keep everything in order."

O'Donnell nodded. "I'll handle any incoming calls. If they ask for you I'll say you're tied up in conference."

"That's the ticket," the senator said, with a pat on O'Donnell's shoulder.

Now the three men were riding through Philadelphia's darkened streets, downtown, away from the hotels and the crowds and the convention center, toward a rendezvous with Sebastian's campaign manager somewhere near the Delaware River.

They passed block after block of row houses, an occasional restaurant or bar on a street corner. Quiet streets, working people's homes. Hardly anyone on the streets this close to midnight; the area looked almost deserted, although lights shone in the windows of just about every house.

"This is where the voters live," Lovett murmured. "These are the people who decide who the next president will be, Frank."

In the darkness of the rear seat, Jake saw Tomlinson bob his head up and down. With a sigh, he said, "Democracy is the worst form of government you can imagine—except for all the others."

Winston Churchill, Jake knew. Good quote.

At last the cab glided to a stop next to a sports stadium of some sort, dark and empty, looming across the night sky like a slumbering beast. A long black stretch limousine was already parked along the curbside ahead of them, beneath a tall streetlight.

Mafia staff car, Jake said to himself.

"Is this where the Phillies play?" he asked the driver.

Looking up into his rearview mirror, the black cabbie shook his head. "The Eagles. Phillies play across the way." Then he added, "Not that either one of 'em is any damned good."

Jake couldn't suppress a grin. Philadelphia fans had a reputation for being unforgiving.

They got out of the cab. The night was warm, but with a breeze blowing in from the river. Jake smelled something unpleasant. Oil refineries? he wondered. Lovett paid the driver as a tall lean man ducked out of the stretch limo parked ahead of them. Wearing a dark suit, he was even an inch or so taller than Tomlinson.

As the cab pulled away Jake suddenly thought, This would be a good place for a Mafia hit. Then he shook his head. Too melodramatic. I hope.

"Senator Tomlinson?" the tall man called.

"That's me."

Opening the limo's rear door, he made a sweeping gesture with one hand. "Right in here, sir."

Jake followed Tomlinson into the limousine's ample interior. In the illumination from the overhead light, Jake saw a pair of strangers—and Senator Bradley Sebastian.

Hunched over halfway into the limo, Tomlinson hesitated, obviously surprised.

"Hello, Brad," he said, reflexively putting out his hand.

"Hello, Frank." Sebastian barely touched Tomlinson's extended hand.

Sebastian introduced Patrone and another aide as the tall man closed the limo door and went up front to sit behind the steering wheel. Jake noticed that the partition between the driver and the riders was firmly closed.

Tomlinson sat on the side bench, closest to Sebastian, while Jake and Lovett arranged themselves next to the senator. Jake slid over far enough for Lovett to sit next to Tomlinson.

Opposite the three of them was a minibar, crystal decanters, and heavy-looking glasses. Untouched, from the looks of it.

"Sorry for the cloak-and-dagger atmosphere," Sebastian said, his voice sounding slightly scratchy. He's been doing a lot of talking, Jake realized.

Tomlinson nodded. "I understand." Looking through the limo's side window, the senator smiled. "I guess nobody's going to snoop on us out here."

"I hope not," Sebastian said, smiling back wearily.

Patrone was a smallish man, with a round face and a receding hairline. His jaw looked stubbled. Probably has to shave twice a day, Jake thought.

"We want to talk to you," Patrone said, in a low, almost growling voice, "to work out a way to get past this deadlock that's developed."

"Oh, that," Tomlinson said, almost carelessly. "That's easy."

Looking squarely at Sebastian, he went on, "You withdraw your candidacy and pledge your voters to me."

Sebastian did not even smile. He looked drawn, older than the campaign portraits Jake had seen, even older than he appeared on television. No makeup, Jake decided.

Straight-faced, Sebastian replied, "I was thinking that *you* withdraw and pledge *your* people to *me*."

Tomlinson shook his head the barest centimeter.

"We can't go on like this," Patrone said. "Another deadlocked vote and Hackman's people are going to start talking him up as a compromise candidate. Then you'll both be out in the cold."

"We can't have that," Sebastian said. "We've got to bring the party together, instead of splitting it like this."

"Hackman can't beat the Democrats," Patrone grumbled, "no matter who they nominate. If he gets the nomination we'll lose in November."

Lovett asked, "So what do you propose?"

Patrone said, "For the good of the party, we've got to break this deadlock. Otherwise we're giving the White House to the Democrats."

In the wan glow from the streetlight outside, Jake saw that Sebastian's face was set in a rigid mask. He'd seen that expression before, many years ago. It was the same look his own father would wear when he was tired of listening to Jake's pleading.

Why can't I go to college, Dad?

We can't afford it.

But Mr. Caldwell says he can get a partial scholarship for me.

Then let him pay the fucking bills! I'm not going to.

And that was that. Jake worked summers and nights and weekends while his father drank with his pals.

Sebastian's set in stone, Jake realized. Just like my dad.

Patrone was saying, "Senator Sebastian only needs a couple dozen more votes—"

"Goddamn it!" Sebastian exploded. "I *deserve* the nomination! I've put in damned near twenty years in the Senate. You're just a newcomer, an upstart. What have you done to deserve the nomination?"

"The energy plan," Lovett replied mildly.

"And the space plan," Jake added.

"Public relations twaddle," Sebastian countered. "Big fancy programs that sound great. But it's the day-to-day work that counts. Not how many times you can get your picture on the cover of the newsmagazines."

Tomlinson's face went taut with anger. Lovett gripped the senator's arm and repeated to Sebastian, "All right. We agree that for the good of the party we have to find a compromise. So what do you propose?"

For a long moment there was absolute silence in the limousine. Then Sebastian replied, sullenly, grudgingly, "The vice presidency."

Tomlinson actually gasped. "Vice president? That's like a retirement home."

Focusing on Lovett, Patrone said, "The two of you together on the ticket would be unbeatable. You would clobber the Democrats in November."

"You might be right," Tomlinson said to Patrone, unsmiling. "How about I handle the top spot and Brad runs for veep?"

"Unacceptable!" Sebastian snapped.

"Same here," said Tomlinson.

"Now wait a minute," Lovett said to Patrone. "You're saying our two guys should work together to take the White House in November."

"That's right," Patrone replied before anyone else could respond. "For the good of the party. Together, they'd be unbeatable."

"For the good of the party," Lovett echoed.

"The delegates would love it. The two of you would be nominated by acclamation. Wouldn't even need to count votes."

"There's only one problem," Tomlinson said, his face grave. "I'm running for president, not second place."

"So am I," Sebastian snapped.

Jake asked, "What about the space plan?"

"What about party loyalty?" Sebastian countered. "This isn't all about you, you know."

"No," Tomlinson replied, with a cold smile. "It's all about you."

Before the two senators could work themselves into a real fight, Jake reminded them, "We're talking about the space plan."

Sebastian's expression turned sour. "We won't need a public relations gimmick like that, not if we pool our voting blocs."

"But it's important!" Jake insisted.

Patrone shrugged. "Maybe."

"Not maybe," Jake countered. "It's attracted voters all over the country. Especially the younger voters, the people you'll need to win in November. It's given people hope, it's even bringing other nations together. It could be an international breakthrough!"

"Pie in the sky," Sebastian grumbled.

Jake was on the verge of telling them about the undeclared war with Russia. Instead, he said, "No, Senator. Space is important. It means jobs. It means the future. The United States could lead the way to a new world."

Patrone turned to Sebastian. "It's a vote-getter, true enough."

Lovett added, "You can't expect Frank to just drop the idea after he's worked so hard for it."

"Is it really that important?" Sebastian demanded.

"Yes!" Jake and Lovett—and Senator Tomlinson—answered in unison.

"Look," Sebastian said, suddenly sounding reasonable. "I'm not against your plan. I just don't see that it's so damned important."

"Not important?" Jake yelped. "A program that could generate hundreds of thousands of new jobs? Whole new industries? A program that could bring cheap, clean electrical energy to people all around the globe? Create new lightweight metals? Ultrapure medicines?"

"When?" Sebastian challenged. "How long will it take to achieve these lofty goals of yours?"

Tomlinson jumped in. "If we don't start now we'll never achieve them. The future starts now, Brad, it starts right here and now. We can change the world, make it brighter, healthier, safer. And the time and place to start making the change is right here and now."

Sebastian shook his head. "I just don't see it that way."

Jabbing a finger at the senator from Florida, Tomlinson said, "Remember Ted Turner? Remember what he often said? 'Lead, follow, or get out of the way.' Which is it going to be for you, Brad? Are you going to lead or follow, or get rolled over by the future?"

Before Sebastian could do more than glower, Patrone asked, "Are you willing to accept the vice president's spot on the ticket?"

Lovett responded, "Are you willing to adopt the space plan?"

With all eyes focused on him, Sebastian pursed his lips, then answered, "If I have to."

Jake said, "That means you'll end your opposition to the loan guarantee bill?"

Looking as if he'd rather be boiling in oil, Sebastian said, "I suppose Zucco could get it out of committee and put it on the floor of the Senate for a straight up-or-down vote."

A crooked little smile breaking out across his stubbled jaw, Patrone said questioningly to Lovett, "Pat, do we have a deal here?"

"If the senator wants it," Lovett replied.

Jake had never seen Tomlinson look so unsure of himself. His usual brilliant smile was gone. His face was set in a guarded, worried expression. Frank's uncertain! Jake realized. For once in his life he doesn't know which way to jump.

"Let me get this straight," he said, stalling for time to think. "If I drop out of the race, you'll nominate me for vice president."

Sebastian nodded, just once.

He doesn't like this any more than Frank does, Jake saw. But he wants the White House badly enough to do the deal.

"And you'll drop your opposition to the space plan," Tomlinson continued.

Before anyone could reply, Jake added, "And you'll let the loan guarantee bill come up for a vote on the Senate floor."

"Yes," said Sebastian. The single word sounded to Jake like a desperate man's cry for help.

Patrone asked, "So we have a deal?"

For a breathless instant the limo's interior was absolutely silent. At last Tomlinson nodded tightly. "We have a deal."

As they rode back to the midtown area of hotels and conventioneers, the limousine was strangely quiet. Neither Sebastian nor Tomlinson had anything more to say, and their aides looked as if they were afraid that a single spoken word might shatter the fragile agreement they had just reached.

As they glided through the nearly empty streets, Patrone spotted a taxi stand with three yellow cabs parked beside an all-night diner.

"Is it okay if we let you off here?" Patrone asked, almost imploringly. "We don't want to let the delegates see the two of you together. Not just yet."

"Or the news media people," Lovett added.

So Jake, Lovett, and Tomlinson got out of the limo, which immediately drove off, as if in a hurry to get away before anyone could recognize its riders. Jake saw that the cabs parked along the curb were empty.

"Probably in the diner," Lovett said. "I'll get one of them."

Within a few minutes the three of them were jammed together in the taxi's rear seat, on their way back to Tomlinson's hotel headquarters.

Tomlinson shook his head tiredly and muttered, "The vice presidency isn't worth a bucket of warm piss."

Lovett almost smiled. "Cactus Jack Garner, FDR's first vice president, back in nineteen thirty-two."

"It's not going to be like that," Jake said to Tomlinson.

"You're going to be more like Lyndon Johnson when he was vice president. He ran NASA's space program. Kennedy got the credit but LBJ ran the show."

"That's what I'll be doing," Tomlinson said. "It's the best I can look forward to."

"LBJ became president," Lovett noted.

Wryly, Tomlinson asked, "You want me to have Sebastian gunned down, Pat?"

"Lord no!"

The senator hung his head, as if ashamed. "My father wanted me to be president, not number two."

"That can still happen."

"In eight years," Tomlinson said quietly. "Maybe."

Jake pointed out, "Frank, in eight years you'll only be a little past fifty. In eight years you'll be getting credit for getting us back to the Moon and making private space companies into a new center of growth and opportunity. They'll be comparing you to Henry Ford and Jimmy Doolittle: founder of a whole new industry."

Tomlinson managed a feeble smile. "That would be nice."

Lovett jumped in, "Then the White House will be yours, Frank. No problem." Grinning encouragingly, he added, "You won't even need me to manage your campaign."

With a sigh, the senator quoted, "Yes, isn't it pretty to think so."

. . .

By the time Jake got back to his suite at the Courtyard hotel it was well past one a.m.

Tami was wide awake, sitting on the living room sofa in velvety pink pajamas, watching a pair of network news analysts—one male, one female—rehashing the convention's votes and speeches.

She jumped to her bare feet as Jake came through the door.

"So how did it go?"

"How did what go?" Jake asked.

"Your meeting with Sebastian's people."

Jake stared at his wife. He hadn't mentioned a word to her about the meeting.

"How'd you know—"

Tami smiled knowingly. "I'm a newswoman, remember? I find out what's going on."

"It's supposed to be a secret."

She shrugged. "I can keep my mouth shut . . . for a while."

Suddenly feeling tired of the whole business, Jake plopped down on the sofa. Tami sat beside him.

"Come on, give," she urged.

Puffing out a sigh, Jake said, "Frank's taking the number two slot, telling his supporters to back Sebastian for president."

Tami's eyes went wide. "He'll accept the vice presidency?"

"He's not happy about it, but he'll do it. Sebastian's promised to support the space plan."

"What a story!"

Leveling a finger at her, Jake warned, "Not a peep about this. Sebastian's people will announce it to the delegates at tomorrow morning's session."

"Can I interview Frank?"

"Tomorrow."

"No! Tonight! Right now!"

"In your pajamas?"

"Come on, Jake. This is *news*!"

Jake shook his head. "No. Frank's very upset about this. He thinks he's let his father down."

"I guess he does."

"The important thing is that Sebastian will back the space plan," Jake repeated.

Tami went silent for a moment. Then, "So you'll be staying in Washington."

Jake nodded and heard himself say, "And I want you to stay in Washington with me."

Her eyes widened.

"I've spent enough time without you. I hate it. I want us to be together."

Very softly, Tami replied, "So do I, Jake."

"I want you to leave KSEE and come back to me," he said. It was the hardest sentence he had ever uttered.

Tami nodded. "I've spent a couple of months without you. I don't want to live that way."

Jake stared at her. "You'll come back to Washington?"

"Yes."

All the air gushed out of Jake's lungs.

"I love you, Tami."

"And I love you, Jake."

He wrapped his arms around his wife and they clung to each other for long, long moments.

Jake whistled in the shower and hummed to himself as he shaved. Tami's coming back to me! He marveled at his stupendously good fortune. For her part, his wife remained in bed, snoring lightly. Jake grinned at her as he dressed.

It wasn't quite seven a.m. but Jake figured that Tomlinson would be up and around, so he left a note telling Tami where he'd gone, then hustled out into the empty, quiet hallway and up the elevator to the senator's suite.

As he expected, Tomlinson was awake, shaved, and dressed in a dark pinstripe suit: Washington working uniform, Jake said to himself.

The senator opened the door himself, looking a little bleary-eyed.

"Oh, Jake," he said, sounding surprised. "I thought it was breakfast."

"Am I too early?" Jake asked.

"No . . . no," said the senator. "Come on in. Keep it quiet, though: Amy's still sleeping."

The suite's living room looked perfectly in order, but quiet, empty. Even the TV was silent, dead.

As he stepped across the sitting room to the big sofa across the handsomely patterned carpeting, Jake began, "Frank, I've never asked you for a favor before—"

The doorbell buzzed softly.

"Must be breakfast," Tomlinson said. "Can you let the guy in, please?"

Jake realized that the senator was depressed. Or maybe he just hasn't had enough sleep. It's still kind of early.

Sure enough, a waiter was standing out in the hall with a rolling cart bearing breakfast for two. Jake let him in while Tomlinson sank onto the sofa in silence.

"Just leave it here," the senator told the waiter, before he could start uncovering the dishes.

Jake signed for the meal, adding a decent tip, and the waiter left.

"You had breakfast yet?" Tomlinson asked.

"No, I came up here. I need to ask—"

"Help yourself," the senator said, with a nod to the breakfast cart. "I'm not hungry."

Jake sat himself next to Tomlinson. "What's the matter, Frank?" he asked, knowing what the answer would be.

Tomlinson buried his face in his hands. "Vice president," he mumbled.

Trying to lighten things, Jake said, "It's better than a sharp stick in the eye."

"Not much."

"Come on, Frank. You'll be running the space plan, turning our dreams into reality."

"My father's dream was for me to be president."

"So you won't make it this time around. You'll have plenty of opportunities—"

"I failed him," Tomlinson said, mournfully. "I let my father down."

Jake had expected the reaction. After all these years, after all Frank's achieved, Alexander Tomlinson was still pulling his son's strings.

As gently as he could, Jake replied, "Frank, your father would be proud of you. Vice president of the United States! You'll be the next president, after Sebastian."

"No," Tomlinson muttered. "This is the end of my road."

"It's only the beginning," Jake insisted. "For god's sake, you came out of Montana a total unknown here in Washington. You've made a name for yourself, you're a nationally recognized political leader."

"Who's settled for vice president. That's not what he expected."

Getting close to exasperation, Jake snapped, "Frank, your father is dead. You've got to stop letting him run your life. You've got to cut the umbilical cord."

Tomlinson smiled wanly. "The umbilical cord connects to the mother."

Ignoring that, Jake went on, "You can outshine Sebastian any day of the week. You'll be directing the space plan! You'll be guiding our return to the Moon. A whole new era will begin, under *your* direction."

With a meager shake of his head, Tomlinson said, "No, Jake, it'll be under *your* direction. I'll be just a figurehead."

"If that's what you want to be."

"I want to be president."

"Then do a good job as vice president and you'll get to the White House. You can't miss!"

"I missed this time."

"Then try again!"

"In eight years."

"In a hundred years, if necessary. In a good cause there are no failures, Frank. Only delays."

Tomlinson stared at him. "My father—"

"Your father's dead and gone. It's time for you to decide what you want to be when you grow up."

Tomlinson blinked several times. Then, "Christ, you sound just like him."

Oh god, Jake moaned inwardly. Am I going to become a father figure to him?

"Jake, what I want to be is president."

"Then start along that road now, right now, today. Join forces with Sebastian. Help him win the White House in November and start us on the road to the stars. So you don't make it to the presidency this time, you'll be the next president, after Sebastian."

"You think so?"

"Yes!"

"Eight years is a long time."

"Not if you're busy. Not if you're directing our return to the Moon."

"I'll need your help for that, Jake. I'll need a lot of help."

"You'll get it."

The beginnings of a real smile stole across Tomlinson's handsome face.

"With my looks and your brains," he muttered, "we can do it."

"Damned right."

For several moments the senator was silent. Then he nodded at the breakfast cart. "Let's dig in. Pat's going to be here at eight sharp."

Jake held up a hand. "First, I've got to ask you for a favor."

"A favor? For you?"

"For Tami. She needs a job at one of the local TV outlets. Anchorwoman."

"Earl ought to be able to work that out."

"For you. When I asked him he put me off."

"I'll talk to him about it. And I'll put in a word here and there. We'll get her situated, one way or the other."

"Thanks, Frank."

Grinning, Tomlinson said, "Give and take, that's what politics is all about."

"I'm taking," Jake said, "but I haven't given you anything."

"The hell you haven't," Tomlinson said, reaching for the breakfast cart. "Give and take. We'll make a politician of you yet, Jake."

"God forbid!"

Facing the Future

The convention center literally rocked from the thunderous applause of the delegates. All of them, from all fifty states and the various territories, women and men, whites, blacks, browns, were on their feet pounding their hands together and yelling, whistling, cheering as Tomlinson and Sebastian stood on the podium, clasped hands raised high in the air, beaming smiles at the roaring auditorium.

The noise hurt Jake's ears, even though he was on his feet, too, yelling as loud as he could.

The ovation seemed to go on for an hour. At last the convention chairman, his bald head beaded with perspiration, started rapping his gavel, calling for order. It took a while, but ultimately the delegates quieted down and retook their seats.

The chairman bellowed into the microphones arrayed on the lectern in front of him, "I move that we nominate the Sebastian-Tomlinson ticket by acclamation!"

The crowd exploded again into cheers and applause.

It's done, Jake said to himself. Sebastian for president, Tomlinson for vice president.

The crowd settled down again and Sebastian stepped forward to give his acceptance speech. It was dignified, optimistic, and ended with, "And we *will* win in November, never doubt it!"

Turning from the microphones, Sebastian reached out

smilingly to shake Tomlinson's hand, then stepped back to allow him to accept his nomination.

His brilliant smile back in place, Tomlinson looked over the rows and rows of expectant delegates. The huge auditorium fell absolutely silent.

Then he began, "This is the beginning of a new era. The American dream—alive, vital, glowing with promise—is expanding beyond the confines of Earth. We will lead the way into space, to the Moon and beyond. The dream will become reality, and a new generation of Americans will lead the way for all the peoples of Earth to reach new heights of freedom, and prosperity."

And Jake realized that B. Franklin Tomlinson had at last broken free of his father's hold on him. He's going beyond anything the old man could envision. He's his own man at last.

. . .

The next few days were a blur to Jake. He hardly saw Tami, except when the two of them tumbled exhausted into bed. Everybody wanted to interview Sebastian and Tomlinson. And Jake, as well. He talked until his throat felt raw, explaining the space plan, how it will generate new jobs, whole new industries.

Jake followed Tomlinson across the country, filling in eager news reporters and self-important commentators about the space plan. Tami—once again a member of Earl Reynolds's public relations team—set up interviews and background discussions.

Jake was surprised that so many politicians' aides wanted to learn the details of the space plan. But then he realized that the aides would feed their politicians as much information as they could handle, and carry the load from there. The politicians were the people who faced the public; the aides were the ones who did the work.

It was at the launch of another Astra Super rocket, at New Mexico's Spaceport USA, that Jake bumped into Billy Trueblood again. In the middle of the pre-launch party, in the Spaceport's capacious headquarters building, the young Zuni came up to Jake.

"Hello, Dr. Ross." He was wearing a faded denim jacket over a checkered shirt and blue jeans, with a band of rough turquoise stones around his neck.

"Billy, how are you?" Jake had to practically yell to be heard over the noise of the buzzing, chattering crowd.

A rare smile split the young Zuni's normally somber face. "I'm okay, sir," Trueblood answered. "I'm fine."

"Good."

"For the first time in my life I'm doing what *I* want to do. I'm my own man now."

Jake didn't know what to say. Trueblood's come a long way in a couple of weeks, he thought.

"I've been appointed the Zuni representative of the Young Astronauts program," Billy said proudly.

Honestly delighted, Jake said, "That's great! Did Nick set that up for you?"

"Mr. Piazza had nothing to do with it!" Trueblood snapped. "I worked through the tribal council. By myself, and for myself. I'll be working with Isaiah Knowles, the ex-astronaut."

"That's wonderful, Billy. I'm proud of you."

"I'll be traveling to DC a lot, especially in the beginning. There's a lot I have to learn."

Draping an arm across the young man's broad shoulders, Jake promised, "Tami and I will show you around. There's lots of very good restaurants in Washington."

With a laugh, Trueblood said, "You'll be my friendly native guides, huh?"

"Damned right," said Jake.

. . .

Still chuckling, Trueblood disappeared into the crowd. Jake turned around and saw Tami coming down the stairs from the balcony where the news media people had been stationed. He pushed his way toward her.

She rushed into his arms. "Jake! I just got a call from Earl Reynolds, back in DC. He's got me an interview with Margarita Viera at WETA!"

"The Washington PBS station," Jake said. "I worked there myself for a few weeks."

"She's offering the weekend anchor slot, Earl told me," Tami bubbled. "And I'll do specials, interviews . . . it's a dream!"

Overjoyed, Jake said, "You've earned it, Tami."

"This is your doing, isn't it?"

Still clinging to her, Jake replied, "I asked Frank to help, yes."

Tami kissed him. And Jake kissed her back, there in the middle of the crowd who had come to witness the launch.

"FIVE MINUTES AND COUNTING," the overhead speakers announced. "COUNTDOWN PROCEEDING ON SCHEDULE."

Arm in arm, Jake and Tami headed for the grandstand outside the Spaceport America building.

The grandstand was filling up with people streaming out of the headquarters building. The sun was just touching the western hills, turning the sky red and violet. The wind was calm, but Jake felt tremendously keyed up.

"WETA-TV," Tami kept repeating. "I'll host on national broadcasts, specials, and whatnot."

"Can't keep a good woman down," Jake said, with an ear-to-ear grin.

"ONE MINUTE AND COUNTING," the loudspeakers blared. "COUNTDOWN PROCEEDING ON SCHEDULE."

Two miles away, the Astra Super rocket stood straight and tall on its launchpad. This was an unmanned launch, designed to land construction equipment safely on the lunar surface; later crewed missions would use the equipment to start building a permanent base on the Moon.

Jake saw roostertails of dust scurrying away from the launch-pad as the last of the technicians hurried to safety.

"THIRTY SECONDS AND COUNTING."

Jake felt his guts clenching inside him. The crowd climbing up into the grandstand started counting down in synchrony with the loudspeakers: "TWENTY . . . NINETEEN . . . EIGHTEEN . . ."

Jake saw the umbilical cords drop away from the Astra Super. Now the rocket stood alone against the red-streaked twilight sky.

". . . TEN . . . NINE . . . EIGHT . . ."

At T minus five seconds a cloud of steam billowed around the rocket's base. Then flame lit the cloud from within and the rocket booster began to rise, slowly, majestically, leaving the Earth.

Higher it rose, higher and faster. The sound reached across the distance to the grandstand, wave after wave of roaring thunder, shaking every nerve in Jake's body. He clung to Tami, their faces uplifted as the Astra Super climbed across the sky, free of the bounds of Earth, heading toward the Moon.

Heading into the future.

ABOUT THE AUTHOR

BEN BOVA is a six-time winner of the Hugo Award, a former editor of *Analog,* former editorial director of *Omni,* and a past president of both the National Space Society and the Science Fiction Writers of America. Bova is the author of more than a hundred works of science fact and fiction. He lives in Florida.